PENGUIN BOOKS

Death or Glory: 2
The Flaming Sword

Michael Asher has served in the Parachute Regiment and the SAS. With his wife, Arabist and photographer Mariantonietta Peru, he made the first west–east crossing of the Sahara on foot – a distance of 4,500 miles – with camels but without technology or back-up of any kind.

He is a Fellow of the Royal Society of Literature, and has won both the Ness Award of the Royal Geographical Society and the Mungo Park Medal of the Royal Scottish Geographical Society for Exploration.

He has written many books, including *The Regiment: The Real Story of the SAS* (Penguin, 2007). The bestselling first Tom Caine novel, *The Last Commando*, was published in 2009.

Death or Glory

PART 2

The Flaming Sword

MICHAEL ASHER

PENGUIN BOOKS

PENGUIN BOOKS

Published by the Penguin Group
Penguin Books Ltd, 80 Strand, London WC2R 0RL, England
Penguin Group (USA) Inc., 375 Hudson Street, New York, New York 10014, USA
Penguin Group (Canada), 90 Eglinton Avenue East, Suite 700, Toronto, Ontario, Canada M4P 2Y3
(a division of Pearson Penguin Canada Inc.)
Penguin Ireland, 25 St Stephen's Green, Dublin 2, Ireland (a division of Penguin Books Ltd)
Penguin Group (Australia), 250 Camberwell Road, Camberwell, Victoria 3124, Australia
(a division of Pearson Australia Group Pty Ltd)
Penguin Books India Pvt Ltd, 11 Community Centre, Panchsheel Park, New Delhi – 110 017, India
Penguin Group (NZ), 67 Apollo Drive, Rosedale, North Shore 0632, New Zealand
(a division of Pearson New Zealand Ltd)
Penguin Books (South Africa) (Pty) Ltd, 24 Sturdee Avenue, Rosebank, Johannesburg 2196, South Africa

Penguin Books Ltd, Registered Offices: 80 Strand, London WC2R 0RL, England

www.penguin.com

First published 2010
2

Set in 13.5/16 pt Garamond MT Std
Typeset by TexTech International
Printed in Great Britain by Clays Ltd, St Ives plc

A CIP catalogue record for this book is available from the British Library

ISBN: 978-0-718-15503-2

www.greenpenguin.co.uk

To Mariantonietta, Burton and Jade,
with thanks

I

Lieutenant Thomas Caine lay with his elbows dug into cold sand, scanning the el-Gala landing ground through his binos. His sandgoggles were pushed back over his cap comforter: he wore a khaki overall on top of shorts and KD shirt, rubbersoled commando boots, full battlekit. He had a .45-calibre Colt in a holster on his belt, and the weapon slung over his shoulder was a Thompson sub-machine-gun, with a nonstandard bayonet lug and a one-hundred-round drum magazine. It was 0310 hours on a moonless night. There was just enough ambient light for Caine to make out the grasshopper shapes of the Axis aircraft drawn up on the sides of the runway, two hundred yards distant: Caproni Ca.309 bombers, Ju-87 Stukas, Messerschmitt Me-109Fs. Beyond the aircraft, unseen in darkness, a knot of airfield buildings, anti-aircraft posts, and machine-gun nests crouched on the edge of a tar-black sea.

The Itie gun crews would probably be dozing at this hour, but in any case Caine wasn't worried about them. Their big ackack guns had too high an elevation to engage ground targets, and their 12.7mm Bredas would be set to fire on fixed lines only, to prevent collateral damage to the aircraft. Caine spotted no fence, no minefield, no tank-traps, no searchlights, no prowler guards. If he and his SAS boys got the job done as efficiently as they'd managed it in rehearsal, they would be in like Flynn, and out again before any lookout eyeballed them. The 'drome was wide open: the planes were fat and sitting birds.

The RAF recce had suggested no more than thirty kites on the field. It was too dark for Caine to be sure, but if it was right, his team was carrying just enough Lewes bombs to deal with them all. It was crucial not only to wreck the planes completely to prevent cannibalizing but also to bag the lot: any crate they missed would be airborne come first light and on their trail as quick as axle grease.

Caine put down the glasses and basked in silence, letting his raw senses probe the surroundings. This was the first time he'd commanded an SAS airfield raid, but he'd been up the Blue too long to neglect the virtues of stillness and patience. Nothing stirred on the aerodrome. A windsock jellyfished languidly on its pole; a seabreeze brought whiffs of salty, sunleached decay, scorched oil, aviation fuel. When he felt that he'd missed nothing, he sashayed down the slipface of the dune to where his squad was crouched in a huddle. The whites of their eyes stood out on bearded faces blackened with grime and burnt cork.

Caine gave terse instructions, letting his hands talk. The SAS team didn't need detailed orders: they'd rehearsed this raid so often they were perfect. Caine designated the present location as their emergency RV, then made signs to Lieutenant Bertram Audley, a cleancut ex-Guards officer, the next most senior rank after himself, to take up a position on the dunes with a covering group. Audley nodded and signed to his pair of Bren-gunners: the three of them crawled up to the place just vacated by Caine.

Caine gave them time to set up, then formed the

remaining nine men into Indian file, with himself in the lead. Once among the planes, they would divide into three groups of three, each taking a section of five aircraft at a time and leapfrogging each other until all the charges were wadded in. Their timepencils would be set at diminishing delays from forty-five minutes to ten. Immediately behind Caine were the other two men of his group: the lean, blond, storklegged Sergeant Harry Copeland and the massive, six-foot-seven shaghaired giant Trooper Fred Wallace. Like Caine, all the SAS men were clad in combat overalls and full battle webbing, including haversacks stuffed with primed Lewes sticky bombs and timepencils. They carried pistols and an assortment of grenades; some had Lee-Enfield rifles. Every third man hefted a Thompson sub-machine-gun.

The demolitions squad spaced themselves out five yards apart and began the advance to target, working through a gap in the dunes and mooching in on the planes at an oblique angle. They moved over the sandy, stony ground with almost unbearable slowness, in the manner drilled into them in SAS night training: lifting their feet, feeling for any small obstacle – a pot hole, a boulder, a dry twig. Every man covered his own arc, and the tail-end Charlie – a gorillashaped French Canadian lancejack named Gaston Larousse – took three backward paces to every seven forwards. Caine halted the file at intervals: the men froze, scanned their arcs, listened to the night.

The blind hammerbill snouts of the first Capronis loomed above them, larger than life in the starlight. Caine continued moving forward until the other two groups had peeled off left and right. Then he led Wallace and Cope towards a section of 109Fs: the Messerschmitts were the key targets because they outclassed anything the RAF could muster. Caine halted, cradled the stock of his overweight Thompson at his shoulder: the others stole forward to lay the bombs. Caine listened, his polished stonegrey eyes working left and right. The night remained perfectly tranquil, yet he felt a twinge of uneasiness that he couldn't explain.

He was distracted by a low thump and a scarcely audible hiss from Wallace: he was at the big man's side in three paces. Wallace nodded to a fistshaped cavity in the 109's fuselage where he had just punched his horny knuckles right through: it was soft threeply wood. 'She's a bloody *dummy*,' the giant growled. Caine's jaw dropped.

As Caine reeled in shock, Copeland stalked up behind them on his camelline legs and examined the cavity. He jogged along the line of Messerschmitts rapping the fuselage of each, like a surveyor testing walls for dry rot. He was back with the others in a moment, his corkblack face taut. 'Plywood and canvas on pipeframes,' he whispered. 'Mockups, the whole bleeding lot.'

Caine worked his signal hand frantically. 'Get the boys out, *now*.'

It was a redundant order: the other squads had had the same epiphany and were flitting back through the avenues of planes like bat shadows. Moving fast and silent, Caine's group followed close behind.

They cleared the aircraft, fanned out across the open ground. They were only a hundred yards from cover when an eery voice shrilled out of the darkness. Caine never did find out what it said: at the same instant the night was shattered by the *chunkachunk* of Bredas, the stiff staccato snap of rifles, the sewingmachine burp of SMGs, the pop of grenade slingers and Very lights. The air whiplashed, the earth crumped, the darkness was quartered by yellow flare.

Caine felt rounds whip past him like giant bugs: the air flapped and tremored. In the flarelight he saw an explosive round pop Penfold's skull like a beachball, saw Ashdown crash squealing in agony, his kneecap blown out. Some of the SAS men were still running, others were prone, pumping rounds back at the hidden enemy with their Colts and Tommies. Big Wallace was roaring and whaling grenades, his spadesize hands working like a trebuchet; Copeland bowled a primed No. 76 Hawkins: it blatted apart, warped air with a brilliant starfish of white. Caine shoulderbraced his Tommy-gun, sank to a crouch, pulled steel, sutured an arc of .45-calibre ball and tracer in the direction of the ambush. '*Get out of it, lads,*' he screamed. '*Take cover.*'

Grenades busted; bombs rumped. The air rippled, the ground jerked, grit and dust and shrapnel barbs mushed: cottonwool whoffs of smoke groped the field like lady's fingers. Enemy fire faltered. Ashdown was limp but still breathing: Caine grabbed him by the collar and started to drag him, his eyes desperately questing the dunes ahead for the flashbang of Audley's support. '*Covering fire,*' he bellowed towards the hidden officer. 'Come on, man, for Christ's sake, *open up.*'

No answering fire. Smoke wafted: enemy rounds whacked and bumped. Caine kept dragging the deadweight body, saw black blood soaking blond earth; he clocked

Wallace blamming off two shots in quick succession from his sawnoff Purdey shotgun as he scrambled through the gap in the dunes. He saw Copeland and a trooper carrying another casualty. Enemy rounds cooked air, lufted pecks of dust around their feet. Caine jogged after them, panting, spearing long rips of fire onehanded from his Thompson. No comforting Bren fire jagged out from the dunes. '*Covering group*, *open fire*,' Caine yelled again in Audley's direction. Still no answer.

An Axis grenade hit the ground near him and crunched: Caine ducked, needle shards of steel pinwheeled over his head. He looked round for the grenade thrower, clocked an Italian soldier – a mask of bared white teeth and bulging white eyesockets, 22-inch sword bayonet carrying dull starlight. Caine snapshotted him pointblank, heard the *tunk* of rounds stoving flesh, saw the body slump. A bulky, redhaired figure scurried past: Caine saw a shambling simian shape silhouetted in a flash as the man hurled a smoke grenade with one hand, blemmed off a Tommy-gun burst with the other. It was the surly lancejack, Gaston Larousse, who threw himself flat on Caine's right, growling, 'Beat it, skipper. I'll cover.'

Caine resumed dragging Ashdown, hearing the low lump as Larousse potted suppressive fire at the hidden ambushers. Within seconds Caine had covered the remaining yards to the dunes and ducked in through the gap, laying Ashdown gently against the base of the slipslope. Apart from Larousse, he was the last man in. Vaguely aware of others milling around, he slipped the shell-dressing from Ashdown's pouch and began to rip it open with his teeth. 'Don't bother, skipper,' a voice murmured in his ear. He glanced up to see the prematurely wizened face of his old comrade, medical orderly Corporal Maurice Pickney, frowning at him. 'He's had it,' Pickney said. 'Bled to death – must've hit an artery.'

Caine stuffed away the dressing numbly, noticing the body of Lennox laid out in the sand like a butcher's package: the side of his skull had been sheared off, grey matter bulged from shattered white fragments of skull. 'Dead,' Pickney said.

Caine felt anger surging through him. Lennox, and Ashdown; Penfold left on the field. He switched magazines and jerked back the top handle savagely. 'Where's Audley?' he raged.

Pickney was about to answer when Copeland slithered down the duneslope next to him. 'Bugger's lit out,' he said.

Enemy rounds wheezed over the top of the dunes: Caine could see tracer scouring the darkness above him like wild shooting stars. He heard the *thump-thump* of a Thompson firing back. 'Wallace covering Larousse,' Cope commented. 'The Canuck is coming in.'

Almost before the words were out, Gaston Larousse staggered around the side of the dune, the muzzle of his Tommy-gun still smoking. He leaned against the duneside, battling for breath, let out a long sigh, stuck a cigarette in his mouth. 'The Ities are coming,' he rasped.

Big Wallace crashed down through the loose sand, landing on all fours like a huge, dark jaguar. Caine leapt to his feet. 'Back to the jeeps,' he gasped. 'Leave the dead. Let's go.' The jeeps lay at the other end of a long gully of sand, gravel and camelthorn. The five SAS men pelted along it with the speed of Olympian sprinters: just as they made the end of the gully, Caine spotted torches behind them on the dunetops. The lads ripped the camnets off the hidden vehicles: Caine realized that only three of their four wagons remained. '*Audley*,' he cursed.

Caine, Copeland and Larousse pivoted into driving seats, toed starters. As Caine's motor soared, he clocked the outlines of enemy troops on the dune crests above him. Sub-machine-guns chattered and popped in the darkness. The other jeeps were already screaming, spinning rubber, gouging up nebulae of sand. Caine rammed the gearstick into first, heard the clunk behind him as Wallace cocked down the twin Vickers 'K' machine-guns pintlemounted on the back. 'Hold on to your hat, mate,' Caine bawled. He braced the throttle. The jeep lurched, belched fumes, accelerated into a long curve, stalled suddenly, creaked to a standstill.

Caine swore, dimly registered Itie troops surfing down the slipslopes only fifty yards away. He tipped the starter, heard the engine splutter, heard rimfire, sensed enemy rounds crumple air around him. He pressed the starter once more, felt something tug at the sleeve of his overall: there was no pain but warm blood started trickling down his bicep. 'Dammit,' he swore. He hit the starter a third time: the engine ramped. At the same instant the twin Vickers behind him shrieked out a deafening metallic squall that drowned the sound of the engine, blunderbussed ball, fire-breaker, high explosive, in long sequences of crimson flame. The salvo scattered the first rank of Ities with what seemed like the swing of a massive invisible wrecking ball. Caine socketed the gearstick with a hand already glued with blood, hit the throttle hard. Knobbed tyres spun, punted sand-dust. The jeep shot off into the darkness after the others, with big Wallace, gripping frantically on to his guns for balance, still blitzing fire.

2

When Lieutenant Colonel David Stirling pulled back the tarpaulin flap and stepped out of the cave, the skyline was streaked with slim javelins of fire. He stood sucking quietly at his pipe, his peaked service cap with the SAS flaming sword badge skewed on his head. His 'A' Squadron boys were making use of the last moments of daylight to prep the wagons, to lay out a landing ground for the Bristol Bombay due in later. Stirling would be returning to Cairo by air with the wounded: the rest of the lads would go back to the 'A' Squadron position in the Great Sand Sea, to keep up the pressure on the coastal railway, ahead of *Lightfoot* – Monty's Alamein push.

The el-Hatiya forward base was sited in a wadi near the sunbleached ruins of an Arab village: low chalk cliffs riddled with caves and overhangs, shrouded with meagre palms, brakes of tamarix and flat-topped acacia. To the east, a track wound down through a corkscrew pass, a thousand feet to the floor of the Qattara depression, the great basin of quicksand and saltmarsh that stretched a hundred and fifty miles north-east towards the Alamein line. To the west lay a flat playa, its surface sparkling with mineral salts, where tiny black frogspawn figures were clearing away boulders and laying out tins filled with petrol-soaked sand. The petrol would be ignited after dark to form a flarepath for the incoming plane.

Beyond that lay open desert – earthenware plains, dogsfang hills, shattered ridges, lavascree talus – petrified country the Ancient Greeks had believed to be the lair of serpent-haired Medusa, the gorgon whose look turned everything to stone. At midday, with the colours leached out of it, the desert was a stark, featureless glare. At this late-afternoon hour, though, brushed with wild sunset shades, swellfished out in three dimensions by muscular shadows that transformed the hills and ridges into galleon prows, the panorama took on epic proportions: a fitting background against which great and noble deeds might be wrought.

Not that anything great and noble had been wrought this time round, Stirling reflected. It had been ten long hours since Audley's party had arrived back from el-Gala reporting Caine's demolition squad missing in action. Stirling hadn't believed it at first, but with a whole day now gone by and no sign of Caine, he was reluctantly obliged to accept that the party might not be coming back. That meant nine trained SAS men – including one of the best officers he'd ever recruited – lost, for no return. It put the seal of doom on current SAS operations: his own parallel raid to Fuja, the previous night, had been aborted without result.

Stirling walked slowly down the wadi watching the lads ready the transport for the move: stripping jeeps and 3-tonners of their scrim nets, backing out wagons from overhangs and tamarix groves, revving motors, unscrewing wheels, removing metal rims, checking tyre pressures, glugging petrol, peering under engine covers. Further down the wadi, Stirling made out the musclebound form of the squadron commander, Major Paddy Mayne, standing at the tailboard of the wireless jeep. Mayne's broad hand, bandaged against desert sores, lay on the shoulder of the W/T operator, who was tuning in a No. 11 set, a fag in his mouth, big rubber earphones clamped to his head. In the gilded aura of sundown, the figures looked unreal – like images in a peepshow, Stirling thought.

Three long whistleblasts from a sentry high on the cliffs made him jump. It meant ground troops approaching: all along the wadi, SAS men grabbed weapons. Stirling saw Mayne draw his .45-calibre Colt and move towards the bend in the wadi with the speed and grace of a panther. Not to be outdone, Stirling dashed after him on bigboned, stiltlike legs. Before he'd covered half the distance, though, a single battered jeep clanked into view. Tom Caine was at the wheel, and five other SAS men were clinging on for grim life.

The vehicle was a sorry sight, running on naked wheelrims, tyres gone, radiator leaking, enginecover and bodywork gouged with bullet holes big enough to put your thumb through. As she spluttered to a halt, the boys crowded around her: tanned, ragged, bearded, filthy figures in shorts and chapplies. They shouted, gabbled questions, demanded news of mates who'd been on Caine's op.

Caine slid wearily from the driving seat, held up a blood-smeared hand for quiet. His eyes were redrimmed, haunted, his head lapped in a squalid field-dressing soaked in blood. Gore trickled from a bandage on his left arm. 'See to Preston first,' he coughed. His lips were brittle and black with thirst, his tongue swollen and pastecoated. His voice was so thick with fatigue that his words seemed hewn out of granite. In the back, Copeland, Pickney and Larousse were already passing the pasty-white, half-comatose Trooper Billy Preston into willing hands. A stretcher materialized: Preston was whisked off towards the MO's truck.

Big Fred Wallace eased himself down next to Caine, and Stirling saw that a dirty dressing had been applied to the giant's left leg: the bandage was covered in blotches of dried blood. 'You going somewhere, boss?' Wallace demanded bluntly.

Stirling eyed him, torn between guilt and irritation at the man's impertinence. He was about to answer when Paddy Mayne appeared behind him, pressed full canteens of water into the hands of Caine and Wallace. 'Go easy on that stuff, mind,' he told them. 'Your guts will be like potato crisps after a jaunt like that. Drink too much at once and the shock'll kill you.'

Stirling frowned. Whatever he did, Mayne always seemed to be there before him, quicker with words and actions, ready to help without intruding, knowing instinctively how to relate to the men, how to gain their trust. In return, they worshipped him. Stirling couldn't help being jealous: hailing from an old, landed family as he did, the one thing he should have excelled in was handling men. It didn't seem fair that this middle-class upstart, a law student on Civvie Street, should be so much better at it than he was.

He fumbled in his pocket for cigarettes, found none, saw that Mayne had once again beaten him to it. The big Ulsterman was handing round Wills Gold Flake, lighting them with his own bandaged paws. Stirling watched enviously. Wallace took a long, grateful drag, his tiny black eyes fixed on the CO.

'Well, Corporal . . .' Stirling began.

'*Trooper*,' Mayne corrected him. 'This is Trooper Fred Wallace, late of Sphinx Battery, RHA, one of Caine's boys on the *Runefish* run . . .'

Stirling's eyes flickered with irritation: Paddy would know everything, from the names of their wives to their birthdays. 'Yes, of course,' he said. 'Lieutenant Audley came in not long after first light and reported your group missing-in-action. I waited ten hours, but I have to confess I'd rather given you up.'

'*Audley?*' Caine hissed. Staring about him, he clocked the blackhaired, squarejawed subaltern's face grinning at him among the crowd. As they locked eyes, Audley bared dazzling white teeth, gave him the thumbs up. Caine looked away, reminding himself that he and the ex-Guards officer had a bone to pick. He pulled the fag from his mouth, breathed smoke from his nostrils. 'We'd have been here a lot earlier, sir,' he told Stirling, 'if it hadn't been for the Stukas. We got jumped on the way back . . .'

He paused, recalling how dawn had come on them as they broached the hinterland's high soda plains, bringing with it a sea mist as dense as cream. They had enjoyed its cover for an hour but, almost the moment it had faded, they'd been made by a Ghibli shuftikite which had evidently been looking for them. The Stukas had jumped them within twenty minutes.

Caine's team had just had time to scramble out of the vehicles before the bombs and straffing-rounds struck. Two of the jeeps had taken direct hits and gone up like rockets, showering them with shrapnel shards. Caine had copped a three-inch laceration on the scalp, Wallace a peppering in the right leg. A redhot fragment had ripped a ligament in Larousse's thigh, and both Copeland and Pickney had been sprayed with minute splinters that reduced their hands and faces to red pulp. Preston had been hit in the arm by a spiralling steel splinter that had opened up the elbow joint and exposed the bone.

The third jeep had been holed but was still serviceable. Caine had plugged her radiator with bits of PE from the Lewes bombs: they had no water, but the lads had kept the radiator topped up by taking turns to urinate into it – a hallowed SAS tradition. It had worked, but it had been a painful journey across sharp hammadas which had shredded the tyres, across sandsheets so soft they'd spent more time out of the jeep than in.

The Stukas hadn't reappeared. They'd made use of the heat gauze to mask their progress from the air but still it had remained agonizingly slow. The jeep's suncompass had been shot off in the attack and Caine had been obliged to revert to navigation by prismatic, which meant halting the vehicle regularly to get a fix. The lack of tyres meant keeping to a snail's pace, anyway, and they might have gone round in circles all night had Wallace's hawk eyes not picked out the tiny figure of the 'A' Squadron sentry, a cardboard cutout silhouetted high on a ridge, from five miles away.

Pickney took charge of Cope and Wallace, leading them off to the sawbones' wagon. Stirling glanced at Caine's wounds. 'You'd better go to the quack and get your dressings changed,' he said.

'I'm all right, sir,' Caine said. 'I'd rather get debriefed while it's still fresh in my head.'

Seeing that Caine was unsteady, Mayne put a massive arm around his shoulders and guided him into the main cave, where he sat him down on a petrol case. 'All right, Tom?' he said. 'Sure, I don't want you going down with delayed shock.'

'Yep,' Caine said. 'I'm fine, thank you, sir.'

'Don't give us that balls. Hurts like hell, so it does.'

'It doesn't. I can't feel a thing.'

Mayne brewed tea on a spirit stove. Stirling came in, sat down beside Caine, shook hands with him. 'Whatever the case,' he said, 'I'm delighted you made it.'

For a moment none of them spoke, and the word 'debacle' flickered ominously in Caine's mind. He watched Mayne at work. All his movements – the way he coaxed a flame from the cooker, poured water into the kettle, or set out the mugs – were assured, economical, precise. From the surface, you would have taken him for a hardnosed bruiser, he thought. In fact, he was kind and solicitous, as graceful as a ballet dancer, though Caine would never have made that particular comparison to his face. Sixteen stone of solid muscle, Mayne was both a champion boxer and a rugby international who'd been capped for the British Lions.

For all that, though, 'Paddy' remained a paradox. The vets had warned Caine not to rub him up the wrong way: after he'd had a few, he could switch from Jekyll to Hyde in the blink of an eye, and when that happened neither friend nor foe was safe. Stirling was as different from Mayne as chalk from Cheddar: diffident, understated, a dreamer whose head often seemed to be in the clouds. Caine had no doubt that he was brilliant, but in battle he'd rather have had Mayne at his back: the Ulsterman had a sureness about him, an air of cool confidence that made you feel you'd follow him through the jaws of hell.

When the kettle had boiled, Mayne poured tea in enamel mugs, mixed in Carnation milk and sugar, added fingers of one hundred degree proof Woods rum from a stone jar stashed in his haversack. They drank the tea in silence, savouring it. Caine felt the legendary Woods 'rocketfuel' bite. 'By God, that's damn' *good*,' he coughed. Mayne handed him another gasper, took one himself. Stirling relit his pipe, raised his eyebrow at Caine.

'The Ities ambushed us on the landing ground, sir,' Caine said. 'They were in company strength – very good discipline, too. I took a long shufti before we went in, didn't hear so much as a burp out of place. We found out the planes were all dummies: we'd almost got back in cover when they banjoed us.'

'There's no doubt they were expecting you, then?'

'No doubt all all, sir. It was too well planned to be random chance. We lost three men dead, Ashdown, Penfold and Lennox . . .'

He heard the catch in his own voice as he called the honour roll. He'd lost men before, but he never got used to it. As always, he held himself personally responsible for the deaths of his comrades: he should have spotted the enemy, should have sensed something amiss. He wondered if he'd been too hasty, if he'd been lured from caution by vanity, by his greediness to knock out thirty Axis kites on his first airfield op.

Caine remembered that he wasn't the only one who'd returned from a raid. 'How'd it go at Fuja, sir?' he enquired.

Stirling bit his lip: a shadow crossed his face. Mayne scowled, stamped hard on his fag-butt as if crushing a cockroach. Stirling's single long eyebrow puckered: his brown eyes gleamed. 'I'm afraid Fuja was equally catastrophic,' he said. 'We also ran into a company of Ities lying in ambush. Fortunately, I sent Paddy ahead with a recce party. If he hadn't spotted them before we went in, we might not be here to tell the tale.'

'Hah.' Mayne grinned. 'How many times is that I've saved your bacon now, sir?'

Stirling scowled. 'All right, Paddy,' he said. 'Yes, you've pulled our fat out of the fire on numerous occasions, but really, who's counting?'

'No one,' said Mayne, suddenly embarrassed. If there was one thing Stirling detested, it was lineshooting, and Mayne agreed with him. 'I'm sorry, sir. I just want to make sure I'll not be reassigned to a desk at Kabrit.'

Stirling guffawed. His 'bag' of aircraft had never been in the same league as Mayne's, and it was rumoured that, earlier in the year, he'd had the Ulsterman assigned to admin duties, simply in order to outdo his 'score'. SAS operations had suffered in consequence: while Stirling was brimful of original ideas for the regiment, he was notoriously unlucky when it came to carrying them out.

Stirling returned his gaze to Caine. 'We managed to withdraw without casualties,' he went on, 'but that isn't much compensation for failing to knock out a single Axis crate.'

'Och, 'twas the same story at Benghazi last month,' Mayne said bitterly. Caine noted that his reedy voice sounded incongruous in such a hefty man. 'Same at Tobruk. Seven *hundred* casualties: a cruiser and two destroyers scuppered.

Now el-Gala and Fuja. Last couple o' months has been one ballsup after another for special service ops: Axis saw us coming every time. They say walls have ears, and loose lips sink ships, but I don't believe it. I reckon we've got a rat in GHQ –'

He was interrupted by the sound of a scuffle from beyond the hanging tarpaulin: a string of roared obscenities, the distinctive snap of a fist hitting flesh. 'What the devil was that?' Stirling demanded.

He lifted the flap and the three of them peered out.

3

Lieutenant the Honourable Bertram Audley lay sprawled in a heap in the sand, clutching bloated lips, staring wide-eyed at Fred Wallace. The gunner towered over him, his Neanderthal countenance transformed with rage. Mayne asked no questions but reacted with characteristic speed. Skipping out through the cave door, he whacked Wallace on the jaw with a clout that smashed into the big man with the impact of a charging baby rhino. There was a crack like a snapped sapling: Wallace sat down hard on the ground next to Audley, his eyes blank and distant.

'What the hell is this about?' Stirling demanded. Audley and Wallace picked themselves up, dusted sand off their drill shorts. Wallace, rubbing his jaw with a hint of surprise in his eyes, jabbed a sausage-sized forefinger at Audley. 'Can you *believe* this, sir?' he spat. 'He asked me to be his *servant.* He deserts his post, leaves us in the lurch, gets three of our mates whacked, then he has the nerve to ask me to *skivvy* for him. I'd rather skivvy for Benito Mussolini.'

'What are you on about?' Mayne snapped.

'Lieutenant Audley 'ere was detailed to give us covering fire, sir, but when we got bumped, where was he? Buggered off and left us, that's where. I heard Mr Caine call for him three times. If it weren't for Corporal Larousse's bravery, the whole lot of us wudda got scragged. He run out on us, loses us three good lads, then he only has the cheek to ask me to be his bloody *servant*.'

Audley, trying to stem the trickle of blood from his nose with a wad of handkerchief, drew himself up. He was nowhere near Wallace's height, but he had the poise and good looks of a filmstar: liquid blue eyes, curly dark hair, and teeth so white they might have been painted. 'I did *not* desert my post, Colonel,' he said, appealing to Stirling. 'Just after Lieutenant Caine's group went in, I spotted Axis troops advancing from the rear. They hadn't seen us, so I decided to go after them and bump them before they could do any damage. We followed them, but they vanished into the night. It was at that point that we heard all hell break loose from the landing ground, and it was every man for himself.'

He spoke in the cutglass drawl that befitted his status as the son of a marquis, ex-Coldstream Guards officer, winner of the Military Cross. His words had the weight of utter conviction, as if the authority of the landed nobility that had lain behind him for centuries couldn't possibly be challenged. He glared at Wallace. 'Desert my post? Never. How dare you impugn the name of the Audleys? Ask Buxton and Creasy – they were with me.'

Wallace's ogre face cracked a grin. 'I already talked to them, sir. They said you *told* 'em the enemy was there, but they didn't see sweet FA. Said you *ordered* 'em to leave the post.'

Audley sent another appealing look at Stirling. 'After all, sir, I *was* in charge, and I don't doubt my eyesight is better than theirs.'

Stirling nodded, apparently satisfied; Caine and Mayne

looked dubious. Audley dabbed at his nose. 'I want this man charged with assaulting an officer,' he sniffed.

Stirling regarded him gravely. 'That's a serious charge,' he said.

He glanced at Mayne: both of them suddenly burst out laughing. Audley stared at them in astonishment. Caine was puzzled for a moment, then he remembered that, when Stirling and Mayne had first met, Mayne had just been expelled from 11 Commando for beating up his adjutant: in the SAS, the occasional thumping of a superior was frowned upon but not considered a particularly heinous crime.

Stirling's chocolate-coloured eyes twinkled at Wallace. 'It'd better not happen again,' he said. 'but I think you can consider yourself duly punished.'

After dark, waiting on the landing ground for the Bombay to arrive, Caine helped Mayne ignite the petrol-tin flares that would guide in the aircraft. The regimental quack, Captain Malcolm Pleydell, had washed his wounds, changed his dressings, administered sulphenamide. Caine still felt shaky but had turned down the chance of flying back with the wounded. They stood at the end of the line, watching the petrol tins gush orange flame, like rows of Chinese lanterns. 'Don't worry about Audley, Tom,' Mayne told him. 'I don't believe in his phantom Axis troops, but even if they did exist, dumping his post like that put the whole squad in jeopardy.' He sighed. 'Between you and me, it's not the first time he's screwed up.'

'Why does the CO put up with him?' Caine enquired. 'I thought the idea of the SAS was to take only the best.'

'It is.' Mayne grinned. 'At least, in theory. It's like the all-ranks comradeship bollocks they used to talk about in the commandos: it's one thing to gob off about it, another to put it into practice. Everyone's got his Achilles' heel, Tom: Stirling'll recognize a man's merit, all right, but he still has a slight yen for the old school tie. The Honourable Bertie gets excused because he's son of a marquis, and all that rot . . .'

He was interrupted by the drone of aeroengines. 'Here she is,' he grunted. 'Right on time.'

The Ulsterman picked up an Aldis lamp, began to flash signals to the aircraft. Caine went to see off his wounded comrade, Billy Preston: he was lying on a stretcher ready to be slotted into the plane, attended by Pickney and by Medical Officer Pleydell, a humorous-looking man with a high forehead and a ragged beard. Caine saw that Preston was bleachfaced. 'Is he going to be all right, Doc?' he enquired.

Pleydell looked worried. 'It was a bad one, Tom: hit the joint, splintered the bone. In a case like that, there's always a chance of ulnar nerve palsy. He's still in shock: touch wood he'll pull through by morning.' He glanced at Caine. 'Sure you're all right, Tom? You don't look too hot, either.'

Caine mumbled something, but his words were drowned as the Bombay swept in, a giant black griffin skimming fifteen feet above the line of blazing torches. Her undercarriage hit the surface with a warp of air and an ominous creak of wheels. The drone of her engines was deafening as she taxied to a standstill. The pilot cut engines and the humming died: Pleydell leaned down to grasp the handles at one end of the stretcher; Pickney shuffled round to the other side. Caine beat him to it. 'Hey, let me do that, Maurice,' he said.

As he bent to grasp the wooden handles, there was a peehashing in his ears that had nothing to do with the Bombay's engines. A squadron of heavy bombers was taking off inside his head: a mob of savages was playing his skull with a thumping, kettledrum percussion. Caine missed the stretcher's handles and staggered forward. He was aware of something collapsing like a dead weight on the playa's surface but was out cold long before he knew it was himself.

4

The RAF Lysander was a minute from the dropzone when the dispatcher yelled, 'Prepare to jump.' With his left hand, Caine clung tightly to the strop clipped to the runningbar near his head and tried to get a purchase on the quivering steel deck. The floor was slick with vomit, the air putrid with the stink of aviation fuel, vibrating with the racket of the Bombay's twin engines. Caine's head was spindling, his pulse racing, sweat ribbing his face as he fought to stay focused. There were eleven SAS trainees in the stick, and he was No. 2 – second man out. Only Lieutenant Trevor Sutherland, Black Watch, stood between him and the open door.

The dispatcher bawled, 'Red on.' Every muscle in Caine's body went rigid. Nothing existed but that oblong of light in the plane's side, the mystic entrance to the slipstream, to the raw yellow surface of the Sinai peninsula a thousand feet below.

The green light twinked: the dispatcher squealed, 'Go.'

Sutherland was gone. Caine heaved his own body towards the door. This was his first jump – first of the half-dozen he had to complete to get his wings and to qualify for his 2 shillings per day parachute pay. He knew he wasn't going to be a jibber: nothing on earth would stop him now. He teetered in the doorway gasping at the wind on his face, and in that instant he glimpsed Sutherland's body plummeting helplessly through the sky: his parachute had failed to open and he was tumbling to his death.

Caine awoke bellowing: he was in a hospital room that stank of disinfectant and vomit. Sunlight flooded in slats through a barred window. For a few moments he swished down the tail end of the dream, remembering how it had seemed to him afterwards, swaying at the door, that he'd heard Sutherland scream. The RAF parachute-jump instructors had told him later that this wasn't possible: the jumper's voice would have been whipped away by the slip-stream. They even doubted that Caine could have reached the door fast enough to see Sutherland's body plunge into the abyss. He was no longer certain about that himself, but Sutherland's death had been real enough. Caine had been among the detail sent to retrieve the corpse from the DZ later the same day. Sutherland's body had been curled up intact in a shallow crater, and Caine knew he'd never forget the expression of sheer terror frozen on the dead man's face.

Later, the RAF dispatcher had shown him Sutherland's ringclip – an attachment like a dog's leash clip – by which the static line was attached to the runningbar in the aircraft. The clip had broken under pressure and had failed to jerk Sutherland's canopy open. It had been deliberately sawn through: the small ridge of metal left intact was certain to snap under the weight of the parachutist. The dispatcher, who blamed himself for not having spotted the defective clip, had reminded Caine of something his own memory had been trying to deny: that only minutes before takeoff, Caine and Sutherland had swapped parachutes. The sawn-through ringclip had been intended for Caine: Sutherland had died in his place.

The Special Investigation Department – the Redcaps' plainclothes branch – had interviewed every trainee in the stick, including Copeland, Wallace, Pickney, Trubman,

Larousse, Audley and the others, finding no reason why any of them should want to murder Caine. Suspecting political sabotage, they'd handed the case over to Field Security, a division of the Intelligence Corps. Major John Stocker, the Defence Security Officer who'd headed up the investigation, thought the crime pointed to fifth columnists among Egyptian maintenance crews but had never proved anything. The only real result of the case was the banning of Gyppos from work on special service flights.

Caine's involvement with the SAS had kicked off a few weeks before the incident, when, one night at Shepheard's Hotel, he'd been accused of impersonating an officer. David Stirling had been there, and had seen off the MP who'd confronted Caine – his old nemesis from the commandos, Major Robin Sears-Beach. At his flat the following morning, Stirling had offered Caine a field commission in the SAS.

This wasn't pure chance. Stirling admired Caine's achievement on *Runefish*, a decoy operation designed to persuade Rommel to invade Egypt instead of going for Malta. The ruse had been effective: Rommel had advanced, believing he'd reach Cairo in a week, only to be thrown back decisively by Claude Auchinleck at Alamein. Although the aftermath hadn't gone quite as planned – instead of retreating, Rommel had dug in opposite the Eighth Army on the Alamein line – it was a major turning point in the campaign.

Runefish was also a nodal point in Caine's career: not only had it brought him the DCM and a reputation as one of the best desert warriors in the business, it had also brought him Betty Nolan, a former actress recruited by special ops division G(R) to play the role of 'Wren First Officer Maddy Rose' – a GHQ courier bearing the bogus *Runefish* material. Since then, Nolan had filled up Caine's life.

Surprisingly, though, he'd hesitated before accepting Stirling's offer. When Caine joined the army, he'd realized that he had it in him to be a leader – that if he towed the line, the sky was the limit. Even though the gentry still ruled the roost, it wasn't unheard of for talented privates to end up even as generals.

At the same time, though, Caine wanted promotion on his own terms. It was a kind of squinted vanity, maybe, but he had a reputation for 'treating orders as a basis for discussion'. He'd already held a commission once in the Royal Engineers, and had lost it because he didn't see eye to eye with his commanders. He did want his commission back: he thought he deserved it, but he didn't want to be put in that position again.

He was ready to sacrifice his life for his country, but he didn't feel that it ought to be squandered. Personally, he reckoned *Runefish*, at most, a qualified success. Of the twenty-two men he'd led up the Blue, only five had come back – all of them wounded. Most people would have said that it was worth forfeiting a small number of men for the good of the majority, but Caine never saw things that way. He carried a private cross for every man killed in action under his command.

Stirling had told Caine that the SAS was a unit without a rigid chain of command: a unit in which there was comradeship between officers and enlisted men. The idea, he said, was to operate in small groups of maybe five men apiece, each man so highly trained that the group could swing a hammer out of all proportion to its size. The SAS way was economy of force. Though parachute trained, they weren't conventional airborne troops: they operated behind enemy lines using stealth if possible, force if necessary. They would never fight a dingdong scrap with big battalions, never be used as 'cannon fodder'.

Caine didn't buy any of this. He'd heard the 'rank doesn't matter' guff jawed about in the commandos by officers who privately despised the enlisted men and had no intention of giving up their privileged status. The 'no cannon fodder' idea wasn't original either. The brass had made the same claim about the commandos but had wasted their training on badly planned raids, delaying actions, massed advances-to-contact with bayonets fixed. Still, whatever pie-in-the-sky Stirling was peddling, Caine had eventually let himself be persuaded. He didn't want an RTU to the Sappers, and with the old Middle East Commando disbanded, there really didn't seem to be any other place to go.

He'd agreed to join the SAS on one condition, though: that his mates Copeland and Wallace would be taken on, too. Stirling had signed them up, had even offered them promotion: the reversal of his normal practice of reducing NCOs to troopers on recruitment. Copeland had been made up to sergeant. Wallace had scoffed at promotion and remained a trooper – the best rank ever invented, he maintained. Two more of Caine's mates from the *Runefish* op had volunteered for the SAS: medical orderly Maurice Pickney and signaller Taffy Trubman. The overweight Trubman had dropped out of the course but, not wishing to let a first-class W/T operator slip through his fingers, Stirling had kept him on anyway.

Caine hadn't been awake long when a FANY nurse bustled into the room and informed him he was in the 15th Scottish Military Hospital. He'd been shipped in on a stretcher the previous day, she said, together with an SAS trooper named Preston. Caine had been out cold for twenty-four hours, suffering from delayed shock and concussion. When he asked about the trooper, though, the nurse's face went tight: he knew at once that Preston hadn't made it.

She changed the dressings on Caine's head and arm and left him brooding on the inequality of war – why Preston, not him? Caine had been in harm's way more times than he'd had cold breakfasts, yet here he was, still alive, while Preston was dead. The worst thing was that the longer you survived, the closer your death sentence seemed to hang over you – it was like getting near the end of the pack in a game of Snap when no one had snapped yet. The spring was always winding up.

He dozed off: he dreamed of Betty Nolan, and the three Huns he'd had to kill with his bare hands to liberate her. When he awoke, he found himself gazing into her sea-green eyes. He blinked, thinking that he was still dreaming, but when she picked up one of his scarred, calloused hands between her two smaller ones, he could feel her flesh and bloodwarmth flowing into him. She was real, and her presence in the room was magical – the drab monochrome sterility of the place seemed to explode into brilliant colour. There could never be anything common about Nolan, Caine thought. She was perched elegantly on the side of his bed, her well-turned legs folded, looking like a model for a recruiting poster: khaki drill bushshirt and highwaisted trousers, triple pips on the shoulderstraps denoting the honorary rank of captain that went with her job in G(RF), the new raiding-forces planning cell. Above her left breast pocket she wore the ribbon of the George Cross she'd won on the *Runefish* op.

Nolan's corngold hair was rich and heavy. She had let it grow out since they'd first met, and now wore it combed back on one side and swinging forward on the other, Rita Hayworth-style, allowing a single kiss curl to caress her cheek. The eyes were soft, filmy with what might have been suppressed tears, her lips slightly parted, displaying the charming slight overlap of her front teeth. Caine felt her breath on his forehead as she bent down to brush his lips with her own. 'Oh, heck,' she whispered, sitting back, pointing to a half-bottle of Haig's whisky and a packet of Player's Navy Cut cigarettes on the bedside locker. 'Now I'm going to have to *give* you those.'

Caine put his arm around her slim waist, feeling the curves beneath the starched uniform. When he looked into her eyes, it was like gazing at a miniature lightshow inside crystals, depths within depths. He saw the hint of challenge there, coupled with the melting submission he'd noticed the first time they'd ever kissed – that dreamy, far-away look that drove him crazy, that made him want to undress her then and there. He kissed her open mouth. 'I've missed you,' he said. 'I can't wait to be with you.'

Nolan kissed him back. 'I suppose catching a Blighty one – or two – wasn't all bad,' she said.

'Now you're here, it was worth every twinge.'

Caine's eyes sought out the scar on the side of Nolan's

neck, where, four months previously, a Hun bullet had punched through her flesh, just missing her collar bone. It reminded him of the last action they'd fought on the *Runefish* mission, an action which, at the time, had seemed without the slightest chance of survival. They had survived against all the odds, though, and every day since then had seemed an unexpected bonus.

Nolan extricated herself from his grip, rocked back, fished in her bag. She came out with a new, brass-coloured Yale key on a keyring. She gave it to Caine. 'What's this?' he asked.

'It's the key to my new flat. I've been moved.'

Caine opened his mouth to ask why, and she placed a finger on his lips. 'There's no problem,' she said. 'The old place was compromised by Eisner, and . . . with his threat and everything . . . you know . . .'

Caine frowned. Before the Nazi spy Johann Eisner had escaped from custody three months earlier, he'd told one of his interrogators, '*I'll see that Nolan bitch in hell, if it's the last thing I do.*' Not only was Nolan the one witness to his rape and murder of a woman in a Cairo nightspot, but she had also indirectly brought about his arrest during Op *Runefish*.

'Just a precaution,' Nolan said. 'I'm sharing the place with a Wren – Pat Rigby.'

'Pity,' Caine grinned, taking the key. He was about to kiss her again when the FANY nurse appeared and announced that visiting time was over. Nolan got up hastily and gave him a peck on the forehead. 'Don't leave it too long,' she said.

5

On the stage of the Kit-Kat Cabaret, Hekmeth Fahmi gazed back at the sea of smoky faces, barely visible to her in the subdued light. She soaked up the applause, tilted her golden body in the spotlights' flush, swung her cape, blew kisses, flung back wild chestnut hair. Men in the audience wolfwhistled, shouted encores, tossed flowers. She caught a red rose and held the stem between her teeth: the cheering reached a crescendo.

Tonight, Hekmeth had certainly lived up to her reputation as 'Cairo's most rousing exotic dancer'. She had capped her famous bellydance routine with the cloakdance, an act that was both aesthetically beautiful and stunningly erotic. Wielded with skill, the heavy cloak could produce perfect helixes, vortices, swirls and veronicas that seemed to cast a silver shimmer around Hekmeth's equally perfect body in a continuous diaphanous flux. The act was a difficult one and needed constant practice but, once again, the crowd had loved it.

With a last shower of blown kisses, she draped the cloak around her bare shoulders and hurried offstage. One of her assistants, Hayek, a beady-eyed, cask-chested Turk with a soft paunch and legs like palm-planks, had positioned himself in the tunnel. 'Excuse me, miss,' he said. 'The major is waiting for you in your dressing room.'

Hekmeth's musselshell eyes flickered like green switchblades in the lamplight. 'What the hell is he doing there?' she demanded. 'Why did you let him in?'

Hayek shifted his bulk from one treetrunk leg to the other, blinking: Hekmeth was probably half his weight: her head scarcely reached his shoulder, yet she was like a paperwasp when aroused. 'He insisted, miss. Said he had something for you. Something important.'

Hekmeth didn't take her eyes off Hayek for a long minute. Then she inhaled sharply, flounced off down the tunnel. She pushed open her dressing-room door, saw Major Clive Beeston standing stock still by the divan, his back to the full-length mirror. He was only a little taller than Hekmeth, and perhaps forty-five years old, with a narrow cleanshaven face lined with deep furrows, a yellow moustache, grey eyes under goldwire spectacles. He wore smart battledress and carried a service cap with the Intelligence Corps badge tucked neatly under his arm in the prescribed manner.

Hekmeth strode up to him, dropping her cloak, exhibiting her body clad in its tiny black bikini decorated with sequins and tassels: she wore concentric necklaces of rare beads, hoop earrings, bracelets and anklets that chinked as she moved: her small hands and feet were stained brown with henna. Beeston watched her weak-kneed, breathless, taking in her small but flawlessly proportioned body: erect breasts, strong hips, the ripe belly with the jewel in the navel that automatically drew a man's gaze. Her face was mobile and expressive rather than beautiful. Her lips weren't unusually full, yet there was something she did with them, some soft puckering of lips over teeth, that was irresistibly seductive. Her skin was smooth and tawny, her green eyes – inherited from her Circassian grandmother – were of an almost feline intensity, her hair was an exotic, floating wilderness of bushy brown. Beeston knew that he would do anything to have her: lie, betray his comrades, give away secrets – perhaps even kill.

She halted in front of him, touched his lips with a finger, picked caressingly at his breast pocket, pressed her mouth close to his ear. 'What are *you* doing here, Clive?' she whispered.

Beeston tried to slip his arms round her waist, but she giggled teasingly, angled away from the groping hands. The major gasped, aching to take her, to press her down on the divan with her legs around him, to explore her, to possess her completely. Despite her seductive manner, though, he sensed that she was angry with him. 'I got the address,' he stammered. 'I thought I'd surprise you.' His voice was husky with lust.

'I told you never to come here, darling.'

Beeston clenched his fists as if to stop his hands seizing her. 'I know,' he said, 'but I had to see you. I couldn't wait.' He paused and looked at her with beseeching eyes. 'You don't know what a risk I took getting it. I had to approach the special allocations officer and feed him a cock-and-bull story about security measures. If I hadn't been with the DMI, I shouldn't have got away with it at all and, in any case, if anyone asks who enquired he'll remember it was me.'

Hekmeth's eyes were crescent moons. She hooked a slender arm around his head, parted her lips, slanted his face towards her, kissed him first softly on the neck, then harder on the mouth. Beeston was breathing hard: he tasted her perfume, felt strands of hair tingling his face, saw the breathtaking gleam of compliance in her eyes. 'Give it to me,' she breathed.

He sensed his advantage: now it was his turn to be coy. 'I've half a mind not to,' he said, 'after the way you received me – after all the information I've given you. I'm risking everything. I could go to the firing squad for this.'

Hekmeth cupped his face in both hands, removed his spectacles. 'Ah, but it's worth it, isn't it, darling?' she hissed. 'Worth every minute, no?'

She kissed him again, letting her tongue glide gently into his mouth, guided his hand, first down to her brassiere, then, when that was gone, across her jewelled abdomen to the place between her legs. She began to run her hands down his body, unbuttoning his battledress blouse, working at his belt buckle.

A moment later they were on the divan, Beeston thrusting inside her with a fast, powerful rhythm, his hands exploring her shoulders and breasts. Hekmeth's ornaments jingled with his thrusts. She wrapped her thighs up around him, threw back her head so that her hair fell over the edge of the bed in an explosive mass. She clutched him tightly with her arms, brought his head down to kiss her again, abandoned herself, panting, crying, heaving.

When it was over they lay side by side catching their breath. Beeston was reaching for cigarettes when Hekmeth said, 'Where's the address, Clive?'

He froze in the act. 'I told you,' he said. 'I've a mind not to give you it. It could get me into a lot of trouble. Why do you need Nolan's address anyway?'

Hekmeth tilted her elegant head to one side, letting her thornbush mass bristle. 'That's none of your business,' she said. 'It's better that you don't know, anyway.'

Beeston took a cigarette and lit it. 'If anything happens to Nolan,' he said, 'they'll find out it was me.'

'Nothing's going to happen to her,' Hekmeth said. She stroked his hand, her mobile features lighting up: her eyes glittered, her lips flickered, exposing the pearlwhite teeth. 'Give it to me, darling,' she said.

Beeston's sullen look hardened, but his resolve failed to hold out in the headlamp glare of her charm. A moment later he stubbed out his unfinished cigarette, stood up. He picked up his battledress blouse, slipped his hand into the breast pocket, produced a wadded square of paper. He slapped it into her open palm. Hekmeth beamed once in triumph, then her face shut like a trap. She sat up straight. 'I told you not to come here, darling,' she said. 'Your days are Mondays and Thursdays at the houseboat. Now get out, and don't make a fuss or you'll regret it.'

The major looked as if she'd just hit him with a mallet. His mouth worked soundlessly. He hovered, trying to say something cutting: he realized that he no longer had any bargaining chips. 'So now you've got what you want, you're packing me off?' he said petulantly.

Hekmeth did the alluring, seductive thing with her lips. 'Didn't you get what *you* wanted, darling? Coming here was dangerous for both of us. If you get caught, what will happen to me?'

Beeston began to dress hurriedly, wondering why he, a senior officer at GHQ, and a married man with a wife back in Blighty, should humiliate himself, should risk his life, his liberty, his reputation – everything – over a Gyppo hussy, a slut whose pimps, it was rumoured, brought strangers in off the street to fuck her for nothing. 'I ought to slap your face,' he said.

'But you won't, will you, darling? You haven't got it in you to hurt me. We both know you'll soon be back with your tongue hanging out like a dog, desperate to fuck me again. I'm like a drug to you, Clive. Like opium. You don't like me, but you've got to have me. Just get out, now. I'll see you at the houseboat at the usual time, but don't come back here again. Ever.'

Beeston's eyes bulged. He sent a last desperate glance to her, then withdrew, and closed the door.

He left by the stage entrance, walked to the end of the alley, then turned into the stream of humanity flowing along the corniche. There was supposed to be a curfew in Cairo, but no one took it seriously. The street was packed with soldiers, sailors, airmen: British, Commonwealth, Free French, Slavs, Poles, Cretans, Greeks, all meandering along in boisterous groups. Since he'd last been here, new bars seemed to have blossomed on every street corner, each with its bevy of garishly attired sirens outside. The scents of apple-tobacco, hashish and coffee drifted from open shopfronts. The jingle of horsedrawn gharries and the honk of motor taxis blended in with the endless babble of street vendors crying their trivia – trays laden with flywhisks, pens, haircombs, safety razors, toothbrushes, soap, shampoo and dentifrice. There were men offering girls, shoeshine or dirty postcards: there were girls offering themselves. When Rommel's victory had seemed imminent back in June, these same streets had been a wasteland.

Now, after a three-month relative lull in the fighting, the Mother of all Cities was awake once more.

Beeston had been trained in countersurveillance, but he was too preoccupied with thoughts of Hekmeth to notice the couple in mufti lurking in a doorway near the Kit-Kat's main entrance: a small, balding, bespectacled man with eyes like blue Very flares and a younger woman with a pneumatic figure and a cataract of dense red curls. Both were wearing tropical suits with fashionably padded shoulders whose colour was pale but indefinite in the lamplight. They were Major John Stocker and Lieutenant Celia Blaney of Field Security, and they had seen Beeston enter the Kit-Kat stage door an hour earlier. They'd been waiting for him ever since.

'Do you think we ought to follow him, sir?' Blaney asked. She was new to the watching game, and anxious to get it right. Stocker had taken her on as his new assistant because he found her a genuinely nice girl, not cocky like so many became when they found themselves in a society where females were as rare as hensteeth. She had a quiet way of speaking, a tactful way of putting things – kind, without being ingratiating – and she was always on the ball.

Stocker shook his head and stuck his pipe in his mouth. He watched Beeston vanish into the shadows with a feeling of satisfaction. His first hunch that the major might be a traitor had come by chance: from his interrogation of the spy Eisner, who'd let drop that the houseboat he'd taken at Zamalek was moored next to that of a military intelligence officer: '*Who'd suspect the neighbour of a senior British intelligence officer of being a spy?*'

It was only later, after Eisner had escaped, that Stocker remembered this comment. He'd quickly established that the houseboat next to Eisner's was occupied by a Major Clive Beeston, who, to Stocker's great interest, turned out to be liaison between the DMI, Director of Military Intelligence, and G(RF), the cell that controlled special service ops, including those involving the LRDG, the SAS, and G(R) undercover agents. Beeston was thus in a perfect position to supply data to the Hun on secret raiding missions: Stocker was now certain that the failures at Benghazi, Tobruk, Fuja and el-Gala were down to him.

Eisner had been quiet since getting sprung from military custody by a gang of Egyptian cutthroats back in July, but Stocker had been able to keep indirect tabs on him via *Hellfinger*, a new wireless callsign that had appeared on the net at about the same time: he was sure *Hellfinger* was Eisner. The one thing he didn't know, though, was Eisner's whereabouts. He hadn't arrested Beeston yet because he hoped to use the major to flush him out.

Stocker gave Beeston a few minutes, then nodded to Blaney: the two of them struck out into the crowds. They didn't speak until they'd reached their jeep, parked down a sidestreet with the cover up. It was Blaney who took the driver's side. She paused before pressing the starter. 'Do you think he gave Hekmeth Nolan's address, sir?' she enquired.

Stocker began to fill his pipe from a pouch of Dark Empire Shag: he changed his mind and stuck the pouch back in his pocket. 'I'd put money on it,' he said. 'I'd also like to think that Eisner will have it very soon.'

'How did you cotton on to the fact that Hekmeth was working with Eisner?'

'It was a hunch, and it's still no more than that, really: Eisner let drop that Hekmeth was a friend. Then I discovered that she lived in a houseboat on the *same dock* at Zamalek. It seemed too much of a coincidence: Eisner, Beeston and Hekmeth, all close neighbours. I concluded that they must all know each other. Then the trace we put on Beeston revealed him rushing off from Grey Pillars early, twice a week, regular as clockwork, always carrying a briefcase stuffed with documents. He turned out to be visiting Hekmeth on her boat, and it was obvious that he was having a regular fling with her: it didn't take Sherlock Holmes to deduce that she was peddling her charms for secrets.'

'Excuse me, Major, but how do we know that Hekmeth isn't dealing with the Hun directly?'

Stocker shook his head. 'It's unlikely. She's an Egyptian, don't forget, not a German. She's not a trained spy, either, and she doesn't know how to operate a wireless. No, she's got to be passing Beeston's intelligence on to someone else: I can't prove it, but I'd bet it's our friend Johann.'

'Pity you never caught *him* paying her a visit.'

Stocker chuckled. 'I did think at first they might be lovers. When I talked to Eisner, though, I got the impression that he doesn't like women. I don't mean he's queer or anything but that he's got some deep-seated fear of the female sex, one that stops him having a proper relationship with a woman. And hence his obsession with Betty Nolan: *I'll see that Nolan bitch in hell if it's the last thing I do.*'

Blaney winced. She felt for the starter with a delicate toe, hesitated again. 'Why don't we just put a trace on Hekmeth?' she asked. 'Surely she'll lead us to Eisner sooner or later.'

'We've tried that already and it didn't work. Either she's too wily, or she's making contact with him in a way we haven't discovered.'

'So you believe that, once Eisner knows where Nolan is, he'll try to snatch her?'

'Yes, and we'll be waiting for him when he does.'

6

Caine got himself discharged from hospital in the afternoon, took a horsecab to the railway station, checked his weapon into the lockup. The storeman squinted at his sandcoloured beret with its flaming sword badge, at the SAS wings and DCM ribbon on his chest. 'You a pilot, sir?' he enquired.

He arrived at Nolan's place in Garden City an hour after sundown, wild with anticipation. Since he'd seen her at the hospital the previous morning, he hadn't been able to get her off his mind. He could imagine that liquid look in her eyes, the acquiescent, waif-like expression that drove him mad with desire, mad to hold her, to feel her lips on his, feel her body moving in his arms. When he rapped on the door, no one answered. He knocked a second time: still no response. He felt in his pocket for the key. He had hardly inserted it in the lock when the door snapped open. His smile faded: instead of Nolan's melting eyes he found himself staring down the barrel of a .38-calibre Enfield revolver in the hand of a hefty Military Police sergeant with a peachred face. 'Who are you?' the sergeant demanded.

'Who are you, *sir*,' Caine growled. He didn't normally pull rank, but the Redcap's impertinence annoyed him. 'I'm Lieutenant Tom Caine, 1st SAS Regiment.' He put out a hand, suppressed the pistol's barrel gently. 'Never point a weapon at anyone, Sarn't,' he said. 'Not unless you intend to kill them, that is.'

The sergeant lowered the pistol. 'SAS Regiment?' he repeated. 'Isn't that some kind of dummy outfit . . . *sir*?'

'Yep,' Caine nodded, 'and I'm one of the dummies. Now, where's Captain Nolan?'

'Gone, sir.'

For a split second Caine wondered if he'd missed the joke. Then it hit him that a Redcap hadn't been posted at Nolan's door with a weapon at the ready just for window dressing. He sucked breath through his teeth, felt scalp-hairs prickle, felt his skin go cold. 'I want to speak to the officer in charge,' he said.

The sergeant holstered the revolver, threw up an insolent salute, pointed to the sitting room. Caine hustled past him with a hard glare. In the room, scouring the remains of overturned and shattered furniture, was a team of Field Security staff. Caine recognized Major John Stocker, the DSO who'd investigated the sabotage incident on his parachute course. With him were a shapely female lieutenant with a mass of ginger curls and a tall Redcap major with postbox slits for eyes and a coypu's front teeth. Caine didn't know the woman, but he recognized Rodent Teeth instantly: his old enemy from the commandos, Major Robin Sears-Beach, now Deputy Provost Marshal of the Military Police. The three officers turned to gawk at him as he came in.

'Lieutenant Caine,' Stocker said absentmindedly. 'I was wondering if you'd turn up.'

The woman's syrup-coloured eyes were interested; Sears-Beach scowled.

Caine noticed a corporal crouching on the floor, taking blood samples: his heart bumped. He stared at Stocker. 'What's going on, sir?' he demanded. 'Where's Captain Nolan?'

Stocker's eyes glinted darkly. 'It's not *her* blood,' he said. 'At least I don't think it is. Her flatmate, Second Officer Rigby, was shot in the chest by intruders. She's alive but unconscious.'

'*Intruders?*' Caine licked sandpaper lips. 'What about Nolan?'

'Gone,' Stocker said. 'Abducted, I'm afraid.'

The room reeled. Caine gripped the back of an upright chair to steady himself as a pattern of lightsquares diapered about him like a carousel. For a second he couldn't get any words out. He forced himself to take deep breaths, shrugged off the mobile display, found himself gazing into Stocker's face. 'It's a mistake,' he grunted. 'She can't be gone. You haven't searched the place properly.'

There was the faintest pink glow on Stocker's cheeks, as if Caine had caught him doing something scurrilous. 'We've gone over the flat with a fine toothcomb,' he said. 'They got in via the bathroom window.' He nodded towards sticks of smashed chairs, scattered ornaments, upended tables. 'As you can see, she put up quite a fight.'

Caine shifted his gaze to Sears-Beach, saw a gleam of satisfaction in the Redcap's gimlet eyes: he seemed pleased to observe Caine's discomfort. Caine turned back to Stocker. 'Nolan only changed address recently,' he said. 'No one knew she was here . . .'

'*You* knew,' Sears-Beach cut in. 'God only knows how many *other* men she told.'

Caine grasped the hint: his eyes burned acid. He took another breath, found Stocker regarding him uneasily. He had a feeling that there was something going on here, something Stocker wasn't telling him.

The DSO whipped off his glasses and started cleaning them with a piece of four by two. 'It's my fault,' he said. 'I thought she'd be safe . . .'

Caine gasped. 'Don't tell me it's Eisner? I thought he was out of the picture.'

The DSO sighed, placed his glasses carefully back on his nose, stuffed away the four by two. 'Unfortunately,' he said, 'he's back.'

'So you're saying this is his work? He shot Rigby, kidnapped Nolan . . . ?'

Stocker shook his head. 'No, I'm not saying that. There were at least three of them. Eisner may well be behind it, but this isn't his style. He wouldn't have left Rigby alive, for a start – not to recover and identify her attackers. Since he has sworn to kill Nolan, why kidnap her at all: why not just do her in on the spot?'

He was about to say something else when Sears-Beach cut in again. 'As far as I'm concerned, Nolan could be in cahoots with Eisner. I never trusted that tart, anyway.'

'*Tart?*' Caine's vision blurred as if the MP had just spat in his eye: hot lava squirted in his chest, a silent shriek of rage shrilled in his eardrums. Before he even realized what he was doing, he'd swung round on Sears-Beach, whalloped him twice in the face: his fists moved so fast that the major's expression didn't have time to change before his eyes went dim. He hit the floor with a clump, out like a light.

For an instant no one budged. The security detail in the room ogled Caine, unable to believe they'd just seen him knock down a deputy provost marshal. Then the surly MP sergeant who'd met Caine at the door moved in on him, a baton raised in his hand. Caine ripped the stick from his grip, tossed it aside, gave him a sharp head-butt that sent him crashing into the wall.

'Stop it,' a contralto voice sang.

Caine wheeled round to see Celia Blaney drawing a bead on him with a .38. She cupped the sixshooter double-handed in a professional manner: her golden-syrup eyes held conviction. Her hands were steady.

Caine watched her, wondering whether to call her bluff. Out of the corner of his eye, he noticed Stocker backing away, shaking his head. Caine reckoned he could flatten the redhead before she pulled the trigger, but he knew he wasn't going to. He could never attack a woman, not even in this foul mood.

He raised his hands. The MP sergeant was up almost at once, swearing at him, restraining his arms, handcuffing him with rough jerks. Stocker hung back; Caine watched Sears-Beach clamber to his feet, probe his jaw, touch the dribble of blood from his nose. He gaped at Caine through wide, incredulous eyes; his battered face lit up suddenly with delight, as if it had just dawned on him that Christmas had come early. 'I *knew* it,' he gloated triumphantly. 'I knew I'd have you sooner or later, Caine. Funny how everything comes to those who wait.'

7

When the LRDG patrol carrying Captain Eric Hooker of G(R) arrived at Eighth Army TacHQ, Burg el-Arab, the sun was coming up over the Mediterranean, a blood-orange globe strangled by fingers of cloud, bathing the sea with cool copper light. Hooker had a 9mm round lodged in his neck: he'd lost some blood but was feeling like the luckiest man on earth. Riding high from the morphia the LRDG orderly had given him, he refused to report to the forward surgical unit before he'd talked to the GOC. He hunched in a camp-chair in the HQ tent, gulped hot tea, puffed a cigarette, grinned at Eighth Army's top brass, who clamoured around him in anticipation: Chief of Staff Maj.-General Freddie de Guingand; Chief Intelligence Officer Brigadier Edgar 'Bill' Williams, Desert Air Force Commander Air Vice-Marshal 'Mary' Coningham; Lieutenant Colonel John Airey, Commanding G(R); a bevy of staff specialists and ADCs – and the GOC, Lieutenant General Bernard Law Montgomery himself.

Hooker, the half-British, half-Belgian son of a Nile Delta cotton manager, found it hard to believe that the skinny type with the jerky movements, the capybara features and the eggshell skull was really the legendary Monty. His eccentric dress – shapeless woollypully, buttondown shirt, civvie corduroy pants, and tankie beret festooned with unit badges – gave such an odd impression that for one dizzy moment Hooker wondered if he'd happened on a Mad Hatter's tea party.

Hooker coughed smoke, drooled tea. For the past fortnight he'd been tramping around the Green Mountains of Cyrenaica dressed as a Senussi, speaking Arabic like a native, gathering intelligence on the possible deployment of chemical weapons by the Axis. His mission had been cut short when he'd walked obliquely into an ambush being set up by a platoon of the 999 Afrika Division. Caught off guard, both sides had fired blind. It had been Hooker's lucky day – the round in his neck was hell on fire but hadn't done any vital damage. He'd still managed to tramp thirty miles off the mountains to the emergency RV.

He felt Monty's gaze fixed on him. 'I don't want to press you, Eric,' he coaxed, 'but the presence of chemical weapons in the Green Mountains could be a serious threat to *Lightfoot*.'

Hooker shovelled a breath, felt all eyes upon him. 'I understand, sir,' he said, his voice strained but even. 'There's no doubt about it. The Senussi are being used as guineapigs for testing some kind of poison gas.'

A tremor ran through the audience: Hooker's expression had become distant, as if he were witnessing some horrific scene visible only to himself. 'Ghastly stuff is going on there,' he said, shivering. 'The centre of all the activity is a crater they call *Il-Citadello* – the Citadel.'

'The Citadel,' de Guingand echoed. 'That name rings a bell.'

'It's occupied by special troops,' Hooker went on. 'A company of 999 Afrika Division'

'*Those* bastards,' whooped DMI Bill Williams, a bearlike officer who bawled rather than spoke and whose lenses were so thick that his eyes could not be seen for their reflections. His enormous frame and stentorian voice were misleading. The bluff and hearty manner concealed a sharp intellect that had pitched him from subaltern to general's rank in little more than a year. 'Triple Nine is a penal unit recruited from convicted felons,' he said. 'Thieves, murderers, thugs, rapists, scum of the Nazi prison system.'

'I thought they were the ones *running* the country,' de Guingand chuckled. A splutter of laughter spread round the table.

Hooker nodded, his eyes blank with pain. The GOC's features reminded him less of a capybara now, more of a Jack Russell terrier. 'The Senussi kept on about a fellow they called al-Malaikat al-Mowt. It means "the Angel of Death" in Arabic. They gabbed on about this chap as if he were the grey eminence behind everything. When I pushed it, though, no one knew a darn thing about him, not his nationality, nothing. Some reckoned he was Vichy French, some Jerry, others Italian – I even heard Greek mooted. Seemed to think he was some sort of demon incarnate . . . some of them swore they'd seen this fellow at the site of massacres, swooping out of the sky like a giant bat.'

Monty raised his eyebrows. 'All right, Eric, but let's leave Senussi superstition aside. What about this chemical agent?'

'From what I gathered, sir, hundreds of Senussi have been forcibly moved to the Citadel over the past few months. If anyone resists, the Huns torch their camp, shoot the men, rape the women, abduct the kids. The

Senussi reckon they've never seen it so bad, not even when the Ities stuck them in concentration camps in the twenties.'

He rasped another breath. 'In the Citadel they're put in a holding compound. There are other prisoners there, I was told – mostly Ities who occupied the place before the Hun came: ex-colony farmers, Italian forces, AWOLs, political exiles – Bolshies mostly. Every morning, the Jerries choose a group of men, women and children as that day's test subjects. They're marched to an observation area. That's where they're exposed to the gas: the tests are observed by boffins in white coats.'

'And what are the effects?' Williams boomed.

'Fear,' Hooker said. 'A fear that makes you think everyone is out to kill you, that gives you the urge to lash out at any stranger who gets near. At least, that's what I was told by the few Senussi I met who'd been exposed to it and recovered. Apparently some go bonkers and get over it quickly, others never recover. One fellow I heard of cut the throats of his own children, wife and two brothers, then topped himself. Two parties of men tore each other apart with their bare hands. A woman who'd been in the Citadel invited three Senussi to roll her in the hay, then cut their balls off with a rusty knife. Bled to death, the lot of 'em . . .'

'Good God,' Monty grunted.

Hooker closed his eyes, his senses beginning to drift. The wound in his neck was throbbing savagely.

'Sir,' Airey appealed to the GOC, 'I really think he should have that wound looked at . . .'

'It's not a problem,' Hooker wheezed. 'I'm all right, sir.'

'Did you see any of this with your own eyes?' Monty enquired.

Hooker gulped, put a hand to his throat. 'I did see some things I've never seen before. Men and women running round their camps stark naked, tearing out their hair, howling like animals. Citadel returnees throwing themselves over cliffs. One morning they took me to see this chap hiding in a cave. They reckoned he'd cut his father's block off with an axe then butchered his mother and sister. From what I could tell, he was blubbering on about demons, and the Angel of Death.' Hooker halted for another brief introspection. 'I was about to leave, when this chap peers at me from the shadows of the cave. My God, his *face*: the sheer *horror* on it – you'd think he'd glimpsed Old Nick himself . . .'

The officers stared back at him, transfixed. Most were war veterans who'd got their knees brown long ago, but Hooker's tale had induced an atmosphere of dark foreboding, as if evil spirits were lurking there in the gloom. '*My God*,' the GOC said again.

He was about to add something when the tentflap was thrown back, letting in a gush of warm sunlight, wafting with it the dapper figure of Major Paul Stanton, the TacHQ medical officer. 'That's quite enough, sir,' he announced fearlessly. 'This man's got a bullet in his throat and it needs to be surgically removed *pronto*. Could you let me have my patient now, please?'

Monty spent the breakfast break strutting along the seashore, hands clasped behind his back, like an exotic wading bird. He was worried and, as if to prove it, the old battle scar on his chest was acting up. It brought back Ypres, 1916, where, as a subaltern in the Warwicks, he'd headed a bayonet charge. There he was, waving his sword about like a cretin, until a Hun round had smacked into his chest and blasted out the other side. If it hadn't been for the sheer luck of one of his men falling dead on top of him, shielding him from further harm, he might not have come through it at all. He'd survived by chance and willpower, got promoted captain, got awarded the DSO. It was only by a whisker that he'd missed the Victoria Cross.

A different war, a different world. The subaltern of Ypres was now General Officer Commanding Eighth Army. Taking over from Auchinleck that August, he'd been shocked to discover that the rank-and-file had acquired a loathing for the general staff. Enlisted men would turn their backs on his car rather than salute him. In his entire career, he'd never encountered such low morale.

Careful PR had changed all that. He'd spent weeks visiting units in the field, shaking hands, doling out endless rounds of 'V' cigarettes, making certain his face was known to the men. Speaking in the down-to-earth language they understood, he'd dismissed everything the Eighth Army had done previously as 'wrong' and made it clear that the only general capable of defeating Rommel was Monty himself.

The *Lightfoot* breakout was due to kick off on 23 October, and Montgomery had poured vast resources into its secret complement, *Bertram*, a brilliant and complex deception strategy. *Bertram* actually hinged on two simple factors – the date of the offensive, and its direction. Here, in the midst of stark and coverless desert, where a man could spot enemy movement miles away, the GOC had to make the Axis believe that his forces would use a route different from the one planned, on a date other than the one intended. To convince them, he and his planners had to devise one of the greatest illusions in history.

Even the threat of chemical weapons had to be judged in the light of this illusion. Poison gas deployed during *Lightfoot*'s early hours might be disastrous: the same substance delivered two days later could be a damp squib. The questions that concerned GOC most were how to use his intelligence sources and how to manipulate his actions to *Bertram*'s best advantage.

Monty joined the rest of the crew around the table in his mobile command vehicle, a giant pantechnicon the size of a mobile library, festooned with maps. As he entered, John Airey called his attention to a stereoscope set up astride a pair of aerial photos lying on the tabletop. As chief of G(R), Airey was Hooker's boss, a foxylooking needle of a man in wireframed spectacles, with torpedo shoulders and a narrow waist. Monty peered through the lenses at the aerial shots. 'This is the Citadel,' Airey told him. 'The only direct Int. we have on it was gathered by a commando party that happened on the place during the *Runefish* mission, last June . . .'

Monty looked up at him. '*Runefish*? I read that report. Amazing feat. Pulled off by that ex-Sapper commando sergeant . . . Abel no . . . Caine, wasn't it? And the young woman . . . what was her name?'

'Nolan.' Airey nodded. 'Elizabeth Nolan. They gave her the George Cross . . .'

'That's right, I remember. That slip of a girl could teach

us all a thing or two about guts, eh? Magnificent. What happened to them by the way?'

'I'm proud to say that Nolan is one of mine,' said Airey. 'She's with the new G(RF) raiding forces planning cell at GHQ. Caine and what was left of his boys mostly got mopped up by Stirling's SAS.'

Monty pulled a face. 'I've met Stirling,' he said. 'Spoilt brat, absolutely potty. His SAS mob have made a pig's ear of every op.'

Airey made a sound in his throat that might or might not have been agreement. 'Getting back to the photos, sir,' he went on, 'you can see clearly that there are signs of Axis activity in the crater . . . tented camps, what look like a prisoner compound and admin block, MT park . . . no sign of a production area or storage tanks, but . . .' He pointed to a curving dark line. 'There *is* a small-gauge spur line, which disappears under the rock overhang. Leaves the crater by way of a narrow defile. If you look a bit further down here, sir, you'll see that there's an airfield under construction nearby. That's where the railway terminates . . . looks as if they're building a warehouse there too.'

Monty put the stereoscope aside, squeezed his narrow chin between finger and thumb. 'So the storage tanks and production area are underground?' he asked. 'The railway shifts gas cylinders to the airfield, where they're loaded on to planes?'

Airey stood up straight, stretched cramped limbs, removed his glasses. 'That's about the size of it, sir – or will be, when the airfield's complete.'

'Good. Well done, John. Now let's study this, gentlemen. Take your seats, please.' There was a scuffing of chairs as the officers took their places around the table. Montgomery steepled slender hands. 'Have we any idea *what* this agent is? I mean, what exactly are we up against?'

The massive Williams nodded to a thin waif of a major in ill-fitting KDs sitting quietly at the end of the table. He had a hairless pink face and was bald except for tufts of hair sprouting above each ear. 'This is Major Cyril Beacham,' he announced in foghorn tones, 'one of the top Ordnance Corps boffins on chemical warfare.'

Beacham turned pinker, his eyes glued to a dossier open in front of him. 'Er . . . Well, sir,' he stuttered, eyes still downcast, 'I . . . er . . . have several reports here from MI6, dating back as early as 1938, about what we call a . . . a DA . . . a "disorienting agent" named *Lysergsäure Diethylamid* – commercial name, Olzon-13. It's been under research by the Sandoz pharmaceutical company in Zurich for years. Now, the effects of Olzon-13 seem to match those described by Captain Hooker. Basically, it induces the symptoms of paranoid schizophrenia in healthy subjects. That means intense suspicion of others and a tendency to act aggressively towards them. In a war situation, that could mean armed men turning their weapons on each other. A standard respirator would give some protection, but this agent requires only microscopic amounts to be effective. As far as we know, there's no antidote, but we might find one given time.'

There was silence while the staff took this in. Once again the hiatus was broken by Monty. 'Thank you, Cyril,' he beamed. 'So, we know where it's coming from, and what it is. The big question is, how to make absolutely certain it's out of the picture.'

De Guingand chewed a pencil thoughtfully. 'Two options, sir,' he said. 'Air or land. Air would be preferable – quick and clean . . .'

'Not effective, though,' Bill Williams lunged in. 'Bombing raids are hit or miss affairs at the best of times.'

Monty's beady gaze shifted to Air Vice-Marshal Coningham, who gestured towards a dishevelled RAF squadron leader at the end of the table – a squat man wearing a flying jacket over his khakis: blue chin, bushy eyebrows, carroty hair. 'Squadron Leader Mark Bentham,' Coningham said. 'He's had personal experience of the Citadel.'

'Certainly have, sir,' Bentham said in a smoky voice. 'Very nearly lived to regret it, too. I flew recce over that crater when the first reports came in. They've got the approach sewn up tight as a duck's proverbial – whole show is protected by ranks of radar detectors and scores of 40mm ackack guns. I took a fortymil shell in the tailplane. Only got out by the skin of my teeth . . . Thing is, sir, the fact that all the key plant is underground, in rock bunkers, would rule out an approach from that *particular* angle, but it wouldn't mean –'

'It's obvious to me,' the GOC cut him off rudely, 'that if all the key installations are below ground, an airstrike isn't even an option.'

The squadron leader stared at Monty flabbergasted, the wind taken out of his sails. He opened his mouth, shut it again, glanced expectantly at Coningham.

The air vice-marshal frowned, shifted uncomfortably in his seat, took a long breath. 'I think that might be a rather hasty conclusion, sir,' he said in a clipped, pedantic tone. 'I believe the squadron leader was going on to say, that, since the enemy will have to bring the gas out of the bunker sooner or later, and will presumably shift it by train, the best approach would be to wait until that point in time and send in our strike while it is vulnerable, that is, while it is being moved. We could set up an OP in the area – a G(R) team with a wireless, say – who would keep a twenty-four-hour watch on the railway, and vector us in . . .'

The GOC was already shaking his head. 'No, no, Mary. Our air resources are too precious to be squandered in that way. The losses would be far too high to contemplate . . .'

'Excuse me, sir,' Coningham insisted, evidently irritated by the GOC's refusal to listen. 'Our assessment is that, using this approach, our losses would be no more than 10 per cent.'

Montgomery still wasn't listening. 'Nonsense,' he scoffed. 'No, my mind's made up, Mary. Our only option is a sabotage raid: we need to get men inside those caves.'

There was an awkward silence as the officers mulled over this statement. To most, Coningham's proposal seemed sound: they had never heard Monty so apparently inimical to air power. And if the GOC had already decided on strategy, why bother consulting the experts in the first place?

At last, Williams said, 'It would have to be a special service unit, sir. What about the LRDG? They're the only decent raiding outfit we have.'

'They aren't trained in sabotage,' de Guingand said curtly. 'Their role is forward reconnaissance. No, with the commandos gone, the only group capable of doing this job is the SAS.'

Monty made a noise that sounded suspiciously like a

raspberry. 'That bunch of misfits? By God, we're *really* scraping the barrel.'

There was an uncomfortable shifting of feet and elbows: it subsided only when Airey brought out two sheets of pink foolscap from his folder and passed them to Montgomery. 'This letter was handed in at our Cairo office yesterday by SAS sergeant Harold Copeland,' he said. 'It was addressed to him, smuggled out of the Green Mountains by a G(R) agent. Perhaps you should take a shufti, sir.'

With a mystified glance, Monty spread the pink sheets out on the table in front of him. The text was handwritten in ink in an italic script whose neatness was marred by smudges and crossings out. Although perfectly intelligible, the content was so full of clangers it had obviously been written by a foreigner. Monty read it through with mounting interest: it was a catalogue of horrors and atrocities committed by German forces in the Green Mountains – murder, rape, arson, abduction, massacre and the use of human prisoners for testing chemicals. Monty saw that it closely corroborated what Hooker had told them earlier, but what surprised him was the conclusion: '*You, my dear Harry, and your good friends, Thomas and Fred, and the other boys. You must help us as we helped you when you were here. You are our only hope. For the love of Jesus Christ, I beg you to come and set us free.*' It was signed 'Angela Brunetto'.

Monty looked up. 'Who *is* this woman?' he demanded. 'What's this about?'

'Brunetto is the wife of an Italian deserter,' Airey explained. 'She helped Caine and his crew escape during the *Runefish* operation. In fact, she probably saved their lives. Sergeant Harry Copeland was Caine's 2 i/c on that mission: he and the woman obviously had some sort of thing going. The "Thomas" mentioned is Tom Caine.'

The GOC sat back, scratched his head. 'So we have a personal plea for help addressed to this . . . Copeland . . . a debt of honour to one of the victims of the atrocities, who asks him directly to set them free. You're saying that we should send Caine to do the job – blow up the chemical stocks, take out this "Angel of Death" fellow, liberate the prisoners?'

Airey's eyes lit up: he leaned forward eagerly. 'It could work, sir. Caine is the only officer who has actually *been* in the Citadel. He and his crew owe this Brunetto woman, so they'll have a private incentive for going in there. The clincher, though, is that Caine has already proved he's mustard at this kind of stunt. If anyone can pull it off, it's him.'

Monty's expression remained sceptical. He fidgeted. He pursed his lips. He scratched his chin. 'I don't know,' he drawled. 'Didn't you say Caine's SAS now? I don't want to get into bed with Stirling's bunglers.'

De Guingand cleared his throat nervously. 'Why not request Caine for the mission,' he said, 'but give Stirling the planning and support role? Whatever you may think of him, he's actually not bad at organizing this kind of scheme. Let David provide the backup.'

Monty frowned at him. 'You *know* Stirling, do you, Freddie?'

De Guingand decided to declare his interest. 'Actually, I do, sir,' he said, smiling a big, beaming, good-natured smile. 'I've known him since we were at Ampleforth together. With all due respect, sir, I feel you've misjudged him. It's true that he's over the top sometimes. He's used to getting his own way. He gasconades, thinking he can charm people into doing anything he likes. At the end of the day, though, he's got some damned bright ideas.'

'Yes,' the GOC sneered. 'I've seen them. He walked right into a trap at Benghazi – Luftwaffe made mincemeat of him.'

He paused, examined de Guingand's broad, good-humoured face intently: he came to a decision. 'Very well then, Freddie,' he growled. 'I'll give Stirling a bash at it, but you will make it clear to your *chum* that the operation will be commanded in the field by Caine, and Caine alone. I do *not* want it hijacked by some twit whose only qualification is that he was born with a silver spoon. Stirling's role is *purely* organizational. And I'll tell you one thing, Freddie: if he cocks this one up like he did the Benghazi scheme, he'll be out on his shell-like ear.'

8

In a holding cell at Military Police barracks, Bab el-Hadid, Caine stalked from wall to wall cursing himself for having assaulted Sears-Beach and his sergeant. Not that he didn't believe the MPs had had it coming: it was only that his reckless act had got him stuck in the pokey, when he should have been scouring the city for Betty Nolan.

He'd known Nolan a few short months but couldn't contemplate life without her now. Neither of them had expected to survive *Runefish*: up the Blue, facing death, they'd bonded with the unstickable glue of the condemned. During the past few weeks, the thought that he had her to come back to was all that had kept him going. Now she was gone, it felt as if the whole world had crashed and burned. He beat his fists against stark brick walls as though he could break them down. If he could only get out of there, he would find her: no one and nothing would stand in his way.

The lock snapped, the iron door cranked open: Sears-Beach came in. Caine noted with a passing trace of pleasure that his jaw was swollen, his nose dressed with sticking plaster. The major had doffed his battledress and donned khaki drill – boots, knee-high socks, shorts, bush shirt, peaked service cap, scarlet cover. He carried his favourite plaything, a silver-topped swaggerstick, wedged tightly under his right elbow.

The MP bared wirethin lips, displaying his hare's teeth as if they were trophies. 'Your war is over, *my friend*,' he told Caine. 'Assault on a senior officer? You aren't going to wriggle out of this one. Any luck and the court-martial will hit you with ten years' hard labour. You are about to become the only man in the annals of the British Army to be reduced from lieutenant to private *twice*.'

Sears-Beach looked so smug that Caine had to fight to stop himself punching him again. He clenched his fists. 'They can do what they like to me,' he said, 'but you're not getting away with calling Betty Nolan a tart *or* a stool-pigeon. If it wasn't for her, Mussolini would be king of Egypt now. And let me tell you this, *my friend*: she's twice the man you'll ever be.'

Sears-Beach's wire lips quivered: the hand gripping the swaggerstick shook with suppressed rage. 'All right, Caine,' he said. 'I'll tell you what I'll do – there's an empty cell at the end of this block. Meet me there in five minutes, and we'll have it out. You and me – no spectators. A fair fight, no rank, no privilege: face to face, man to man. Strictly between us, and no comebacks whichever way it goes. It's high time you learned the correct way to address a superior officer.'

Caine bristled, raising his chin. 'You're on.'

A wolverine smile played across Sears-Beach's face. 'Good,' he said. 'I'll leave your cell door open.'

After he'd gone, it crossed Caine's mind that this might be a trick. At a court-martial, his leaving the cell could certainly be made to look like an escape attempt, could aggravate the case against him. He didn't trust Sears-Beach: on the other hand, if he failed to show up, it would seem as if he were afraid to face him: the sneer that was sure to decorate the idiot's features in that case was something he couldn't bear to think about.

The moment he stepped into the empty cell, though, knew he'd made the wrong move. Sears-Beach stood with his back to the far wall, stripped down to his shorts and a white PT vest. His rodent features, rendered slightly ridiculous by the sticking plaster, twisted into a triumphant leer. He was trying to conceal something behind his back. Too late, Caine saw that it was a heavy rubber baton.

The cell door slammed shut: Caine half turned to glimpse two gigantic Redcaps behind him. '*Hold him*,' Sears-Beach yelped. The MPs grabbed his arms in a steel grip: Sears-Beach whacked him hard in the belly. He doubled over, gasping with pain and shock. A hand snaked around his chin, yanked his head up. 'I *warned* you,' Sears-Beach crooned. 'I *told* you.' He leaned so near that Caine could smell his sweat. 'You think I don't know about the trick you and Stirling pulled on me? That night at Shepheard's, eh? You were still only a sergeant then. You lied to me, and that high-and-mighty Stirling lied, too. Thought you'd made a fool of me, Caine, didn't you? You and that Nolan bitch . . . you hear me, Caine? I hope they find the *bitch*'s body in a drain, with her guts hanging out and a broken bottle up her cunt. No one makes a fool of me, Caine. There's only one fool here, and that's you.'

Caine roared, flexed his great chest muscles, stamped down savagely on the feet of his captors. He felt their grip on his arms loosen: before he could take advantage of it, though, Sears-Beach sprang at him, whacked him again in the stomach. He whunked Caine's shoulders and arms, thrashed his knees, his thighs, his shins, in lightning succession, his face manic with pleasure. Pain coursed through Caine's body: he struggled for breath, found himself unable to hold back the screams. He tried to kick out at Sears-Beach, to dodge out of the baton's trajectory, to roll with the hits. The big MPs twisted his arms high behind his back, holding him rigid: the major whacked him with practised precision, hard enough to raise angry weals, not quite hard enough to fracture bone.

Caine's head sparked electric, blitzed red and yellow. A glancing clout on the skull cut him loose: his senses fuzzed, faded out. When he came round he was on his hands and knees, vomiting on the floor. He was aware that his arms were no longer pinioned: he saw Sears-Beach's rat face in front of him, saw bloodless, stringy lips working over the wedgelike teeth. The major was panting with exertion, reptile eyes glittering. 'Had enough, Caine?' he sneered.

Caine fought to speak, found his mouth choked with vomit. He coughed up paste, snorted blood.

'I want to hear you say it, Caine,' Sears-Beach grated. 'I want to hear you beg me to stop. Go on. *Beg.*'

He touched Caine's neck with the end of the club, lifted his chin. Caine's stonewashed eyes bored into him. 'Not so tough now, are we, Caine?' Sears-Beach scoffed. 'Not such a hard man now? Come on, I want to hear you beg.'

Caine remembered Moshe Naiman, the Jewish interpreter mutilated by the Germans on the *Runefish* mission. This was nothing compared to what Naiman had suffered, yet his friend had remained defiant till the end. Caine retched, hoiked spats of gore, lunged suddenly forward with all his strength. The hard bone of his temple connected with the major's nose in precisely the same place where he'd landed a punch earlier that day. Caine heard the septum crunch, saw flesh squidge, saw blood gush from gunbore nostrils. Sears-Beach shrieked, reeled, gabbled. Bellowing, the big MPs heaved Caine up: one of them kneed him in the groin, the other stomped his legs from under him, sent him lurching to the floor. Sears-Beach squeaked with fury. All restraint gone, he put the boot into Caine's belly, chopped at his testicles with the baton. Caine felt red agony surge, felt his head swim, felt his senses slip. He tried to curl up: another kick landed in his ribs. Sears-Beach jumped on his stomach, stamped on his hands. Caine attempted to crawl away, fought to stay conscious: hands yanked him up again. They beat him until his universe was alight with exploding moons and bursting stars, and then darkness absorbed him completely.

9

The warden unlocked the cell door: the clank roused Caine from his doze. David Stirling stalked in stoop-shouldered, spruce in KD slacks, battledress blouse and service cap, his unlit pipe stuck upside down in his mouth. Caine tried to stand up, felt a bell clapper in his skull, felt his pulse ramp like a steamshovel. 'Don't bother, Tom,' Stirling said.

Caine sat down heavily on the bunk. Stirling stood peering down at him, his continuous ridge of dark eyebrow knitted. He looked at the mess of bloodstains on Caine's blouse, inspected the purple weals on his arms and face: Caine saw fury in the coffee-coloured eyes. Stirling drew the pipe from his mouth. 'What did that bastard do to you?' he demanded.

'Nothing,' Caine said: his tongue was swollen, his lips felt like lorry innertubes.

Stirling shook his head, sucked his teeth, made a tutting sound. 'Sears-Beach is a bastard,' he said. 'It was about time he got his head punched . . .' He broke off, and Caine saw sympathy in his expression. 'Problem is, you assaulted him in front of witnesses. You played right into his grubby paws.'

Caine touched the shrapnel wound on his scalp. The dressing was gone and the stitches were broken: it gaped like a crater under his groping hand.

'He called Nolan a tart. He suggested she was a Nazi stoolpigeon, sir. I wasn't going to stand for that.'

Stirling shook his head in disbelief. 'You put your commission on the line for sticks and stones? You're a bloody fool, boy.'

His eyes didn't leave Caine. He knocked his pipe against an open palm. 'I took a gamble in getting you your pips back, Tom. The fossilized shit at GHQ don't like field commissions, especially for a bloke who's already proved himself a loose cannon. You brought off a coup on *Runefish*, though, and I was able to push it through. Now you've gone and thumped a superior officer. I thought Paddy Mayne was bad, but you . . .'

Caine blinked giddily, wiped mucus off bloated lips with the back of a hand. His head felt as if it had been scoured inside by steel wire. Stirling stuck his pipe in his mouth, started pacing up and down the cell as if he himself were the prisoner. He stopped at the wall, pivoted abruptly back to face Caine. 'All right,' he said. 'I can get you out of here, but on one condition. You're needed to lead a special operation in the Green Mountains: it's going to be as tight as *Runefish* or even tighter. Monty asked for you personally . . .'

Caine's soapfilled eyes widened: before he could comment, though, Stirling went on. 'I'm going to cut the bullshit, Tom. The SAS is in the GOC's bad books, thanks to the setbacks we've had lately. Monty isn't big on special service ops, and this might be our last chance of staying on the orbat. More than that, though: this op could be vital to his next push . . .'

Caine tried to smirk, found his mouth wouldn't work

properly. 'Surely, sir,' he mumbled, 'there're plenty of good men who could . . .'

'I said he's asked for you *personally*,' Stirling snapped. 'He was impressed with your record on *Runefish*: he doesn't *want* anyone else. Now, am I supposed to tell him that my best man is in the chokey for belting an MP officer?'

Stirling looked excited and angry, as if he'd been fought into a corner. Caine watched him struggle to control his indignation. 'Here's what's going to happen,' Stirling said. '*You* are going to accept the mission. *I* am going to get you out of here: *we* are going to drive to Kabrit, where you will be briefed. Is that clear?'

Caine eyed him, his body rigid. 'I'm sorry, sir, but I can't do it. Betty Nolan has been abducted. Eisner may be behind it. If I get out of here, the first thing I'm going to do is track her down and scrag that Nazi swine . . .'

Stirling's eyes blazed darkly. 'Sears-Beach must have addled your brain,' he said, shaking his head. 'Haven't you got it? You either take the mission, or you stay on jankers for the rest of the war. That's you finished: dishonourable discharge, DCM retracted, branded for life. For all we know, Nolan might be dead by now, but even if she isn't, even if she miraculously comes through, you'll only ever see her through the bars of the chokeyhole. Is that what you want?' He paused for breath. 'They've put DSO Stocker on her case. If anyone can get her back, he can. I said I could get you out on one condition, but actually there are two: the second is that, if I do, you'll give me your word that you won't even *think* about chasing after Nolan.'

Caine put a hand to his forehead: the bellclapper in

there was clanging against his skull like a wrecking ball. Nothing was free in this man's army, he thought. He'd laid his life on the line over and over again, and yet here he was, in jail. He'd heard all the gab before: the way he felt now, they could stuff their mission; damn the SAS, damn Monty, damn his next push – all that mattered was getting Nolan back. For a moment he considered hedging: he could agree to take the stunt then do a bunk at the earliest convenience. Didn't they say that all was fair in love and war? Yet he knew he wasn't capable of such a deception: belting a man who'd insulted Nolan was one thing, lying was another.

He considered it for a long, hard moment. 'Sorry, sir,' he said at last. 'I can't do it. I've been in the army since I was sixteen: it's my family and my home. I've always been willing to do whatever was asked of me. I'm a professional soldier, and I don't expect gratitude . . .' He paused and stood up. 'Look, sir, I *am* ready to accept the mission, but I have a condition of my own: that I'm allowed to look for Nolan first.'

Stirling's eyes popped in disbelief. 'The bloody *impudence*,' he gasped. 'You think you can set *conditions*? In *your* position? You must be raving bonkers.'

Caine swallowed dryly. 'I probably am, sir. But I owe it to Nolan to get her back: if I can't do it with the army's sanction, I'll do it without. I'm afraid you'll have to tell the GOC it's no dice.'

For a moment it looked as if Stirling might explode: his sharp face was grey with frustration. Instead, he stabbed the empty pipe back in his mouth, marched towards the door with a look of utter disgust on his face. He banged on the door with his fist: Caine heard the warden unlock it from the other side. Before he went out, Stirling turned on his heel.

'Caine,' he said, 'you have just made the biggest mistake of your bloody life.'

10

The warden brought lukewarm tea, bully beef, hardtack biscuits. The medical officer, a nervous captain with glasses like whirlpools, treated his wounds with sulfapowder, raised an eyebrow when he saw how many old battlescars Caine's body carried. 'It's a wonder you're still on your feet,' he said.

When Caine woke next morning the soreness and the swelling had eased. He got up and splashed cold water on his face from the bucket. The door rattled: he wheeled round ready to meet Sears-Beach's rabbit teeth, found instead the snowblue eyes of Sergeant Harry Copeland. Caine was amazed to see him: they didn't allow social visits in the holding cells. Cope wore battledress: SAS wings and MM ribbon on his chest, sergeant's chevrons up, sandhued beret perched on bogbrush hair.

They stared at each other, stuck for words: Cope handed him a packet of army-issue 'V' cigarettes. Caine shook out two, gave one to Cope. 'Let's see who gets the maggot,' he said, tamping his. Copeland snickered: army lore had it that you would always find at least one dead maggot in a packet of 'V's.

Cope lit the smokes with a Swan Vesta. There was nowhere to sit but the bunk, so they took an end each.

Caine let smoke trickle through his nostrils, eyes fixed on Copeland: his mate was on edge and obviously had a disagreeable message to deliver. 'You didn't come here just to give me fags, did you?' he said lightly. 'You must have got special permission. Anyway, I thought "A" Squadron was with Paddy up the Blue.'

Copeland's eyes were steel opals in the cell-light. He blustered smoke, stared down at the redlead floor. 'We were,' he said, 'but Stirling pulled us back to Kabrit. There's going to be a new stunt in Tripolitania ahead of Monty's push. "A" and "B" Squadrons both.'

Caine cocked an eyebrow. 'Tripolitania? That far? I thought "B" Squadron hadn't even finished training yet.'

'They haven't. Talk about getting your knees brown: a lot of those "B" Squadron boys wouldn't know the desert from a seaside jaunt.'

There was a pause. Copeland shifted, stood up, stamped out his cigarette. He took off his beret and ran long fingers through his goatgrass hair. 'I want to show you something, Tom,' he said.

'All right.'

He brought sheets of pink writing paper from his breast pocket, unfolded them, passed them over. Caine took them. 'What's this?' he asked, smirking. 'Not another dear John?'

Copeland gave him an anaemic grin. 'Just read the damn thing,' he said.

Caine read the letter: it was a catalogue of abduction, torture, murder and massacres in the Green Mountains of Cyrenaica, ending in a harrowing account of the death of a girl named Lina: a band of Jerries had gang-raped her, cut her throat, hurled her body over a cliff.

Caine stared at Copeland. '*Lina?*' he said. 'What the . . . ?'

'Finish it,' Cope snapped.

'You, my dear Harry, and your good friends, Thomas and Fred, and the other boys. You must help us as we helped you when you were here. You are our only hope. For the love of Jesus Christ, I beg you to come and set us free.'

It was signed Angela Brunetto.

Caine read the name, darted an uncertain shufti at Cope. 'What the heck is this about?' he asked.

Cope shook his head, drew a breath. 'Since we were in the Green Mountains in June, the whole place has gone ratshit,' he said. 'It's all in the letter – Huns carrying out massacres, abductions, suicide, crazy Senussi butchering women and children. You remember that girl Lina?'

'Of course I do. The one I almost . . .' He bit back his words, choked by a memory of deep brown eyes, high oriental cheekbones. 'Fucking *animals*,' he whispered.

He handed back the letter, eyes still glued to Copeland's face. 'So what's behind this?' he asked.

Cope held his long, stringy arms akimbo. 'Jerry's brewing up some kind of chemical weapon in the *Citadello* – you remember, Angela's place? Fact is, Tom, they're using the Senussi *and* the Italian deserters as guineapigs, testing this stuff out on them. According to the DMI, all the ructions are spinoffs from that. There's at least one company of a special Hun mob called 999 Leichte stationed there . . .'

Caine sniffed. 'All right,' he said slowly, 'but who briefed *you*? The DMI?'

Cope's shoulders drooped. 'It was Stirling. Stirling briefed me.'

'I see,' Caine said stiffly. 'So Stirling sent you here?'

Cope's face reddened. 'Not exactly, no. I mean, yes, sort of . . . I wanted to come.' Sweat popped his brow, but Caine didn't make it any easier for him. Cope's eyes flared suddenly. 'Look,' he said. 'All crap aside, you know how I felt . . . how I *feel* . . . about Angela. She's in deep shit, dammit. Not only her, everyone – Itie deserters, the Senussi – the lot. You've read the letter. Angela begged for my help – for *our* help. Remember how she got us away from the Boche on *Runefish*? Even though it meant putting her life on the line, even though it meant endangering her people's safety? Do you reckon it's a coincidence that the Axis moved in there just after we left? No way. It was our fault. *We* drew Jerry's attention to the deserters, to the Citadel. We owe Angela, you *know* we do.'

Caine clicked his tongue, sucked his teeth. 'So you showed the letter to Stirling?'

'Not just Stirling. It's done the rounds: DMO, DMI – even Monty's seen it. It isn't only the letter, skipper. The Brylcreem Boys have recced the place: we've got reports from G(R) agents, even aerial shots. There's no doubt about it: a chemical weapon *is* being produced there. Stirling reckons Monty's worried as hell. This stuff could put the kibosh on his advance. It could shift the whole balance: wreck the whole campaign.'

'So *this* is the mission,' Caine said, almost to himself, 'the mission Stirling tried to foist on me yesterday. He briefed you on it, didn't he? He told you, *Go in there, use the old pals act, badger him to take it*? Didn't he?'

Cope's brow puckered. He wiped away sweat with a bare palm. 'All *right*,' he said, almost shouting, eyelids blinking like shutters. 'Yes, it *is* the mission. Of *course* it's the bloody mission. Of *course* Stirling sent me, Tom. How else would I have got here? You're facing ten years in the pokeyhole. Who's that good for? You? Betty? Stirling? Me? His Britannic Majesty? You should be doing what you're good at, not rotting away in clink.'

Caine looked furious. 'So you and Stirling cooked this up between you?'

'Don't talk soft, mate: this is a serious stunt. You'll take a small crew: me, Wallace, Pickney, Trubman, Larousse, a few other blokes. We go in by wagon, penetrate the Citadel on foot. We take out the chemical weapon. We liberate the prisoners. We bump off the commander, and we run for it.'

'Just like that, eh?' Caine sniggered. 'Stirling's got you on his team now, eh? Convinced you it's all going to be easy?'

'Who's talking *easy*? When did we ever do *easy*? Like when we stormed that Senussi village on *Runefish*. When you saved that girl . . . Layla. It wasn't our business, but you said, *I won't be able to live with myself if we don't go in*. Well, that's how I feel right now, Tom. All right, yes, Stirling *did* set me up. All right, I *did* agree to do it. But only because I know he's right. You can't blame Stirling, Tom – he's stuck: Monty asked for you by name. If you don't do it, the GOC could easily bin the regiment the way they binned the commandos. But I'm not asking you to do this for Stirling: forget Stirling, forget Monty, forget the DMO. Call it *the old pals act* if you want. Call it what you bloody well like: I'm asking you to do it for Angela, for Lina, for the folks at the mercy of the Hun out there, but most of all for me.'

He broke off, and Caine saw that he was desperate. He knew Stirling liked to get his way: he'd used Cope all right, but that didn't mean his mate wasn't sincere. Copeland wouldn't have done it unless he felt it was right: he was as straight as a die.

Caine stood up, squared his wide shoulders, his face grim behind the purpled eyes, the mask of scars. 'I can't, Harry,' he said. 'Betty's been taken: Eisner's probably behind it. I can't let it slide.'

Cope screwed up his face. 'I heard about Betty,' he said. 'It's bad. I'm sorry, and I know exactly how you feel.' He stopped, groping for words. 'But there's nothing you can do about that now, Tom. This stunt is your only way out. If you jib, they'll dump you in nick and throw away the key. Stirling won't be able to do anything – he's pushed the boat out too far already. Your getting stuck in the detention camp won't save Betty, and Angela's people will be up the spout, not to mention Monty's push. It all depends on you.'

Caine sighed. Copeland had a knack for seeing the big picture, for expressing it clearly: it probably came from his schoolmaster years, Caine thought. Taking the mission might scupper his chances of finding Betty Nolan, but Cope was right: staying behind bars wouldn't do much for her either. And Cope was right about another thing: a lot of people's lives might depend on him. He shrugged, knowing that Copeland would have done the same for him: he couldn't let his friend down. 'All right,' he said. 'Tell Stirling I'm in.'

Copeland had himself let out: he was back with Stirling inside ten minutes. The warden accompanied them to the office, handed over Caine's kit. Then the three SAS men marched across the square together, Caine limping slightly. They'd almost made the main entrance when a lean, buck-toothed figure barred their way: it was Sears-Beach. Caine saw to his satisfaction that the major now wore a field dressing on his nose. He peered squinteyed at Caine, then at Stirling. 'What the devil are you doing?' he demanded. 'You've got no authority to remove my prisoner.' His voice sounded so comically nasal that Caine had to snigger.

Sears-Beach sent him a murderous glare, scratched his nose under the dressing, forced himself to look back at Stirling. The colonel gave him a disdainful smile of the type he reserved for duffers and imbeciles. 'Now, *that's* just where you're wrong, Major,' he said, removing a snuff-coloured field envelope from his pocket. 'And unless a major now outranks a half-colonel, I *would* appreciate it if you'd address me as either *Colonel* or *sir*.'

He handed over the letter. Sears-Beach stared at it as if it were infectious. 'What's this – *sir*.'

'It's a letter,' Stirling sighed. 'It states that Lieutenant Thomas Caine DCM, 1st SAS Regiment, is considered too valuable a military asset to go before a court-martial. It further states that this officer is to be released forthwith.'

Sears-Beach looked as if he were too stunned to open it. He gazed from the envelope back to Stirling, his breath coming in snorts. 'Where . . . where did you get this, sir?' he stammered.

Stirling's eyes crinkled. 'As you will see, if you would be so good as to read it, the letter is signed by the General Officer Commanding, Eighth Army, Lieutenant General Bernard Montgomery. It is also endorsed by the Commander-in-Chief, General Alexander, and your immediate superior, Colonel Edward Bagfellow, *Chief* Provost Marshal of the Military Police.'

Sears-Beach's eyes bulged: he poked fretfully at the field dressing. He tore open the letter, scoped the text as if scouring it for loopholes. His shoulders sagged. He shifted his feet. He cast cobralike glances at Caine through hooded eyes.

'*Do* move aside, Major,' Stirling told him wearily. 'You rear-echelon deskwallahs *may* have all day, but *we* do not.'

Sears-Beach slouched out of the way, his eyes on fire. Stirling put out a hand as if to take the letter: instead, he seized the major's shirtcollar with steelhard fingers. He yanked Sears-Beach's head down savagely, hissed in his ear. 'I promise you this, you cocksucking bastard. You lay so much as a *finger* on one of my boys again, I'll send Paddy Mayne to cut off your prick and ram it so far down your gullet you'll choke to death on the soggy bellend. Paddy loves coppers, preferably dead or maimed for life.'

11

The No. 12 targets popped up left, right and centre. Tom Caine snapshotted slugs blindfold towards the sound of bells, clicks, drills, with no idea whether his rounds had struck home. It was his first time on the simulated night-shooting range, and his introduction to the .30-calibre Garand semiautomatic. It had already made one thing very clear to him: how damned hard it was to hit a target you couldn't see.

He'd fired four clips, eight rounds a clip. The Garand wasn't magazine fed like the Lee-Enfield: fresh clips had to be inserted from the top. But there was no cocking handle, either – recycled gases from the detonation process cocked the mechanism, facilitating an incredibly rapid rate of fire. Caine heard the *ping* as the last clip selfejected, laid the rifle on the mat. He whipped off his balaclava blindfold, blinked in raw ochre light, breathed in odours of brimstone, salt and dust. Stirling and Mayne emerged from the concrete bunker fifty paces to the rear.

They were at Kabrit, an old commando camp in the Canal Zone, now SAS homebase – a few acres of saltcrust desert with a board at the gate bearing the legend '1st Special Air Service Regiment': jerrybuilt huts, parachute-training gantries like relics of some antique fairground, ragged rows of tents set in depressions sandbagged against air attack. The camp backed on to the Suez Canal, a razorslash of supernatural blue sliced through the leopard-hued promontory of the desert. From the opposite bank, Sinai's blasted wilderness rolled on and on till it melted into the spectral fata morgana of the eastern sky.

Caine paddled air, flexed outsized biceps and pectorals, stretched his shoulders. In the two days since Stirling had sprung him from Bab el-Hadid, the stiffness in his joints had faded. His blunt, freckled face still bore the livid mauve tracks of Sears-Beach's treachery but he'd tucked the attack into the lumber room of his mind. Sears-Beach would get his just desserts in time: for now, only Nolan mattered. At night, he lay in his camp bed staring at the canvas roof, tortured by images of her broken body. At times he was seized by an almost overwhelming impulse to break out of camp, rampage through Cairo leaving no stone unturned till he had her back in his arms. He'd given Stirling his word, but still it took a huge effort of will to restrain himself.

Caine went forward to the butts with Mayne and Stirling to examine the Figure 12s. He was amazed to find he'd hit them all. 'Not bad,' Stirling commented.

Mayne smirked at his CO's understatement, knowing that *not bad* was his highest accolade. He slapped Caine's shoulder. 'Best damn nightshooting I've ever seen,' he growled.

Stirling stuck his unlit pipe in his mouth. 'So how'd you rate the Garand, Tom?'

Caine crinkled his forehead. 'Nice weapon, sir, but I wouldn't swap it for my trenchsweeper. That *ping* when the clip's ejected is a dead giveaway. Can't fault it for speed, of course.'

Mayne looked doubtful. 'Sure, 'tis hard to beat the old SMLE. A good shooter like your Sarn't Copeland there can fire it nearly as fast as a machine-gun. A marksman can bring down a man at two thousand paces.'

Stirling scoffed. 'That's peanuts, Paddy. With M2 ball ammo, a Garand will hit a target at three and a half thousand paces. You can probe reverse slopes of hills at two thousand, using the drop of the shot. How's *that* for a game of soldiers?'

Mayne pursed sulky lips: he didn't look impressed.

They walked back through Caine's firing position. Stirling picked up the discarded rifle. 'Firepower is what it's about, Tom,' he said. 'Half your section will have Garands, half Brens. Of course, I'm not saying you can't take your Thompson.'

'How many men do I get, sir?'

'Eleven – two groups of five, plus yourself as section commander. Doesn't sound a lot, I know, but SAS style is to go in small and carry a very big mallet.'

They marched towards the HQ area through a maze of ranges that swarmed with SAS men. The place was electric with the rattle of smallarms fire, the pancake thump of antitank weapons, airshredding detonations of grenades and Lewes bombs, the bitterlemon scents of cordite and scorched dust. '"B" Squadron going through its paces,' Stirling observed. 'They were supposed to be ready before *Lightfoot*, but there isn't a snowball's chance in hell of it. I asked Monty for three hundred Eighth Army combat vets who wouldn't need training. Blighter laughed in my face. That's another good reason why we have to bring *Sandhog* off.'

Sandhog was the designation of Caine's new mission: Stirling and Mayne had briefed him on it the previous day and, for no logical reason, he'd acquired a bad feeling about it. Maybe it was due to his brooding over Nolan, or maybe it was the fact that he'd survived against the odds so many times he felt his luck was due to run out. Or it might have been the overblown air of cloak-and-dagger that surrounded it: Stirling had instructed him to keep the target under his hat until he was up the Blue. 'I'm not saying there's a leak,' he'd said, 'but you know the saying – three men can keep a secret as long as two of them are dead.'

At the armoury tent Caine exchanged the Garand for his Tommy-gun. They moved on to the admin area: HQ personnel in shorts and chapplie sandals were prepping four wagons in yellow Eighth Army colours – loading compo rations, water tins, ammo boxes; changing wheels, chugging petrol, cleaning guns. Caine knew there was a shortage of everything, including desertworthy vehicles; he was impressed that Stirling had provided what he'd asked for: a pair of longbonnet Bedford 3-tonners and two Willys Bantam jeeps, all with strengthened springs and aeroscreens, equipped with Bagnold-type suncompasses, sandchannels, sandmats, and condensers like oversized compo tins. The jeeps were an SAS speciality – small, mobile, four-wheel-drive gun platforms, each with a pair of Vickers 'K' aircraft-type machine-guns mounted on the back and a big .50-calibre Browning on the front.

On the other side of the wagons a canvas awning had been strung up: half a dozen men were trafficking along trestle tables, stripping, cleaning, assembling Bren-guns,

Garands, pistols; testing mags, loading rounds, priming No. 36 grenades, lapping Lewes bombs in hessian, coiling fuse. 'These are your lads,' Stirling told Caine. 'I've given you your men from *Runefish*, plus one or two extra.'

Caine noted the molelike head of signaller Taffy Trubman: he was leaning against a table piled with wireless spares, connecting batteries to a circuit tester. Maurice Pickney was working through the men, doling out syrettes of morphia and Benzedrine pills in brown envelopes. Caine spotted Gaston Larousse – the surly Canuck whose covering fire had bailed them out at el-Gala. He was hunched roundshouldered over another table, giving all his attention to a two-inch mortar. Caine hadn't seen Larousse since the el-Gala op. 'Grand job you did back there, mate,' he said.

Larousse looked up; his lynxlike eyes flashed. A powerful shank of a man with a blue jaw and an air of smouldering superiority, he'd acquired a reputation as a savage in hand-to-hand combat: the kind of soldier who liked to get up close with a knife or bayonet, who notched up enemy kills on his riflebutt. A Quebeçois by birth, his story went that he'd married a Jewish Frenchwoman, with whom he'd had two boys. His wife and sons had been caught in Paris during the Nazi invasion and had vanished off the face of the earth – murdered by the Gestapo. Cloaked in his own mantle of brooding cynicism, Larousse seemed to regard the war as an affair of honour between himself and the Nazis: other participants were merely incidental. The lads respected him, Caine knew, but he didn't have any close buddies. The exception was big Fred Wallace, who had a penchant for adopting oddballs and outsiders. The

Canadian shrugged his stooped shoulders. 'Who cares who wins,' he growled.

On the next table, two lanky, illmatched men were sorting out climbing gear – ropes, lightlines, pulleywheels, grappling hooks – conversing in whispers as if an invisible wall separated them from their comrades. Caine sensed that they were men who'd depended on each other for so long that they'd become like two arms on the same body. 'Gibson and Rossi,' Stirling told him. 'Your cliff-climbing and demolitions specialists.'

Both were sixfooters: Rossi, closed and silent, beanpole slim, with a downturned gash for a mouth and eyes like black studs, had the long, sallow face of an undertaker. Gibson gave an impression of manic energy: mobile features brown and cracked like sundried tobacco, a tight-lipped mouth, quick to smile, and the slightly reproachful eyes of a goodnatured man to whom the world had not quite lived up to expectations. His hair was a crop of silver prickles, his body lean and hard, his muscles like twisted steel cables. He spoke with a cowboy's drawl. Caine was wondering if he might be another Canadian when Stirling said, 'Gibbo is our token Yank. US born, but he has dual French nationality thanks to service with the Foreign Legion. The original Beau Geste – decorated twice, wounded three times, reached the rank of master sergeant.'

Gibson beamed like a rock splitting open.

'How come you're with us Brits, then?' Caine enquired.

'Refused to serve under the Vichy government, sir,' the cowboy said. 'Cleared out of Tunisia when Pétain took over, hitched a boatride to Egypt. Served with your commandos. When they got the old heaveho, I was twiddling my thumbs in Cairo, ran into Colonel Stirling. He said he was taking French volunteers for the SAS: since I'm technically Frog, the door was open.'

'What about you, Rossi?' Caine asked, turning to Gibson's mate. 'With a name like that, you ought to be an Itie.'

Rossi's glassbutton eyes gleamed. 'I'm *Swiss*,' he said wearily. 'Not all Italian speakers are Ities.'

'Ricardo was a well-known alpinist before the war,' the cowboy cut in, as if he was accustomed to speak up for his mate. 'He's a naturalized Brit, though. He was a climbing instructor in the commando school, then transferred to active duty in the Middle East. We worked together in the commandos.'

Caine noticed that both men were wearing non-regulation knives – the cowboy's a Bowie with a blade as broad as a man's wrist culminating in a fanged point; Rossi's a slimbladed stiletto, almost like a Sykes-Fairbairn fighting knife but with a serrated edge on one side. Then it came to him: 'I've *heard* of you two,' he said. 'When I was in the commandos. You're the pair who used to go in along the Libyan coast by folboat, scale cliffs the enemy thought were inaccessible, lay charges and boobytraps. Yep, I remember now – they used to call you the Reapers. You were notorious for slitting Itie throats and fading into the dark.'

Gibson and Rossi exchanged a look. Rossi drew his dagger and showed it to Caine. 'Swiss Home Guard knife,' he said. 'She is my – how you say – my *good luck* charm.' He kissed the blade in a way Caine didn't quite like.

'Always preferred a bayonet myself,' he commented.

'That's a soldierly weapon. Personal knives are all right, as long as you know how to throw them. If you don't, you might as well carry a penknife.'

Caine picked up an item of kit he didn't recognize, a short tube attached to a coil of line, with a multi-pronged grappling hook sticking out of one end. 'What's this?' he asked.

'One of the new rocket-propelled grapples,' Gibson explained. 'I guess the stunt's gonna entail some cliff-climbing, eh, skipper? If so, that's supposed to be just what the doctor ordered.'

As they moved off, Caine felt Rossi's eyes follow him. 'What are we doing with an Itie in our ranks, sir?' he asked.

Stirling chortled. 'Rossi? A bit of a nutcase maybe, but then, who wouldn't be after all the throat slittings he and the cowboy have done? It's rumoured they used to saw enemy heads off with those knives, just to make sure the chap didn't get up again. Mutilation's not good form, of course, but sometimes it can't be helped. Apart from that, there're no flies on those boys: proved themselves time and time again.'

Caine noticed Fred Wallace at the next table and excused himself from Stirling to share a word. The big gunner was cleaning what looked like a length of stovepipe about a yard long and four inches in diameter, funnel-shaped at both ends, with handgrips underneath. As Caine approached, he saw that Wallace had a wound on the temple, covered with sticky tape. Before he could ask about it, though, the big man shoved the stovepipe reverently into his hands. 'Seen this, skipper? M1 antitank rocket launcher. Yank design – they call it the bazooka. Daft name, innit? Replaces the Boys antitank rifle. Not before time, neither – that piece of dogshit couldn't knock the skin off a banana.'

Caine weighed the tube in his hands – it was surprisingly light. 'Thirteen pounds,' Wallace informed him. 'Fires a 2.37-inch M6 rocket with a high explosive charge. Can penetrate four inches of armour plate at a hundred and fifty yards. Maximum range is about four hundred yards – you can deploy her to whack out tanks or AFVs, or for assault on a fixed position. Needs a two-man team, though.'

Wallace took the launcher out of Caine's hands as if he were jealous of him holding it too long. He hefted a black metal rocket from the table and passed it to Caine. The round seemed top-heavy: its explosive head was a bulge on a slim tube ending in balancing fins. Wallace pointed to a protrusion in the head. 'Safety pin,' he said. 'Remove it and the rocket's armed. Watch yer step, though – when armed, the M6 rocket'll go kerbluey if you drop it even from a couple of feet.'

Caine passed back the rocket with new respect. 'You've fired it then?' he asked.

Wallace nodded proudly. 'Trained on it yesterday, skipper. Only one drawback with the stovepipe – she's got a fifteen-foot backblast. Stand behind her when she's in operation and you get yer balls fried.'

'I'll remember that, mate.'

Caine was on his way back to Stirling when he heard another familiar voice, this time raised in anger. Peering behind one of the 3-tonners, he found Harry Copeland in a dingdong with a stumpy, barrelchested corporal. Cope sported a spectacular black eye that hadn't been there when Caine had last seen him: he connected it mentally with Wallace's wound and guessed they'd been fighting. Copeland's body was braced in the predatory stance that always made Caine think of a big wading bird about to take a fish, his eyes flashing, his blond hair bristling like yellow wire. 'We're not going up the Blue with those tyres,' he was saying. The familiar schoolmasterish ring in his voice reminded Caine that, unlike Wallace, Cope was an ambitious man who was chuffed to have been promoted to sergeant and awarded the MM: he wanted to keep climbing the ranks, perhaps even gain a commission. Copeland hailed from a prosperous family: his father was an architect and his brother, Michael, a successful solicitor in Civvie Street, was now a captain in the Marines. Copeland possessed a sharp mind, had organizing skills as good as any officer's and better than most. Caine knew that his assertive air wasn't arrogance – it derived from the fact that, as one of six children, he'd always had to compete for attention. He had long ago guessed that Harry and his brother Michael were still fighting an undeclared war.

'An' I'm tellin' *you*, Sarn't,' the little corporal raged, 'it's all we've bleedin' got. Yer can take it or leave it.'

Cope loomed over the NCO, a fitlooking bowlegged little man with a globeshaped head and the cheeky, puckish face of a monkey. Caine noticed that two fingers were missing from his left hand.

Stirling came up to investigate. 'What seems to be the trouble, Corporal?' he enquired.

The little NCO turned his football head towards his CO with an expression of indignation, as if he felt that

Copeland, a newcomer in the regiment, had trespassed on his authority. 'Sarn't Copeland 'ere sez these tyres ain't good enough for 'im, sir.'

Stirling eyed Cope curiously. 'What sort of tyres do *you* think we ought to have?' he asked.

'Dunlop or Goodyear, sir,' Copeland replied without hesitation. 'These synthetic things are useless. When the rubber gets hot they crack, and that could be fatal up the Blue.'

Stirling nodded. 'Ever since the Japs took Malaya there's been a shortage of rubber,' he said. He glanced at the corporal. 'Have we got any Dunlop or Goodyear tyres?' he asked.

'We 'ave, sir, but you wanted to save 'em.'

Stirling flushed slightly. 'Have them broken out,' he said. 'Only the best for Op *Sandhog*.'

The corporal waddled off to give instructions. 'By the way, Tom,' Stirling said, nodding after him, 'that's Corporal Sam Dumper, ex-RAOC ordnance mechanical engineer. He's going to be your fitter and quartermaster on *Sandhog*.'

'What happened to his hand?'

Stirling blinked. 'A timepencil attached to a Lewes bomb got activated by accident on the way back from one of our ops. The other lads evacuated the truck sharpish, but Dumper stayed, tried to defuse it. He managed to move the charge to a safe place but got his fingers blown off in the process.'

Dumper was back in a moment, beaming, the altercation forgotten. He and Caine shook hands. Stirling gestured towards a nearby tent. 'Corporal,' he said, 'I'd like you to show Mr Caine some of the special kit we got him.'

'Trezz beans, sir.'

The air inside the tent was hot, tart with odours of gunoil and hessian. The place was stacked with weaponry and ordnance. Dumper bypassed mortars, grenades, mines, explosives, fuse, detonators, primers and timepencils and showed Caine an assortment of oddlooking devices collected on a tabletop. 'Decoy kit,' he announced, tapping his nose. 'Evens the odds when you're outnumbered 'undreds to one. There's a miniature smoke generator, noisemakers, pintail bombs – and some *very* nasty stuff that'll suit them Reaper geezers down to the ground: pressure and pressure-release switches. *I* was all for getting' explodin' rats an' camel turds, but the CO wouldn't 'ave it.'

Chuckling to himself, Dumper moved towards a corner of the tent, picked up a black box fitted with headphones and what looked like a telephone mouthpiece protruding from the front. 'Tactical Ear,' he declared. 'Picks up and magnifies sound – just the job for night stag, when yer straining to 'ear the enemy creepin' up on yer.'

Caine listened to the headphones, amazed. 'I can't believe you managed to get all this kit,' he commented. 'I mean, Q staff are usually the most miserly swine on earth. Wouldn't let you have the skin off their shit unless you gave them three good reasons why you wanted it.'

'No truer word spoken,' Dumper said, winking. 'It's Mister Stirlin', yer see, boss. Such a charmin' gent, no one can refuse 'im.'

Caine examined what seemed to be a large oblong

boxcamera with an eyepiece on the back. 'What's this?' he asked.

'Oooh, careful with that, sir. It's the most valuable fing in the 'ole show. Even *I'm* surprised the brass let us 'ave this one, but the colonel ain't above 'alf-inchin' kit if it takes 'is fancy. That's an RG infrared nightsight, that is. God only knows 'ow it works, but you can see in the dark wiv it . . .'

'Incredible,' Caine said. 'I heard they were working on a nightsight, but I'd no idea they'd perfected it.'

'Yeah, well, it ain't exactly *perfected.* This is a prototype. Do me a faver, and don't bust it or lose it, or let Jerry get 'is 'ands on it, because it's worth a bleedin' mint.'

'Guard it with my life.'

Dumper nodded, his gaze falling on the Tommy-gun on Caine's shoulder. 'Bayonet lug?' he enquired, raising a thick eyebrow. 'You fit that yerself?'

'Yep,' Caine nodded proudly. 'All my own work.'

Dumper whistled, a smile of admiration on his lips. 'That always *was* the problem with them big mags. Guaranteed to fall off just at the wrong moment. Good work, though – you an ex-Ordnance Corps man, sir?'

'Get out of it. Blacksmith by birth, mechanic by profession, Sapper down to the maker's nameplate.'

'Shame, a good officer like you wasted on a crap mob like that. I'll tell yer what, boss, I'll swop yer a Garand for that trenchsweeper.'

'No way. I'll stick to my old faithful.'

There was a moment's silence: Dumper eyed the Tommy-gun wistfully. 'You ain't much like most officers we get 'ere, sir,' he observed. 'Where you from, anyway.'

'East Anglia. Fen country. You know it?'

Dumper nodded. He drew out an ancient calfskin wallet, opened it, showed Caine photos of a startlingly beautiful blond woman and two attractive strawhaired girls. For a second Caine wondered if the woman really belonged to this little gnome of a corporal – he'd known men to flash around snaps of filmstars as bogus 'girlfriends' just to impress. It couldn't be the case here, though, because the two little girls, while very pretty, had an unmistakably Dumperish cast.

'Katie and Leslie, my little princesses,' Dumper said proudly. 'And that's Queenie, my wife. Me, I'm from the East End of London, see. Cockney born an' bred. Usta be on the buses in Civvie Street. The girls got evacuated up your way durin' the Blitz. Fens – back end o' nowhere. First time they'd ever seen a cow. Usta think milk came out of a tap.'

He put away his wallet, tittering, and Caine dekkoed his watch. 'Well, if that's all, Corporal, we've both got a briefing to attend.'

'Half a mo, boss,' Dumper protested. 'There's a barrerload of paperwork to be got through yet. You know the drill. Everything 'ere's got to be signed for in triplicate. Every single round's got to be accounted for. Just make sure you bring it all back in one piece, used cartridge cases an' all, else you'll be payin' it off at a shillin' a week for the rest of yer bleedin' life.'

Caine's face dropped. He was about to stammer an objection when the tent flap was thrown back. Stirling entered, grinning from ear to ear. 'I heard that,' he said, hiccupping with laughter. 'Loves to have his little joke does

Dumper. He's tickling your zonker, Tom. In the SAS we have no documents, no written plans, no records. Everything that counts is in my head.'

'I just 'ope yer 'ead stays where it is, then, sir,' Dumper commented, winking at Caine. 'Otherwise we're up Queer Street, an' no mistake.'

12

Caine found his crew drinking tea and smoking in the briefing tent. No one called them to attention when he and Stirling entered. Caine bumped into Wallace and Copeland. 'I see you two have been scrapping again,' he said. 'I can't leave you alone for two minutes before you're at each other's throats.'

'We wasn't fightin' each *other*,' Wallace roared indignantly. 'I had to pull Sergeant Cleverclogs here out of a very nasty corner. His own fault, mind. If he hadn't insulted them ENSA girls, we'd have been in clover. That little darlin' Sadie Jameson was all over me, till Turniphead opens his big trap.'

'All *over* you?' Copeland snorted. 'She couldn't get away from you quick enough, only you were too pissed to notice.'

'All right,' Caine said, nodding. 'What happened?'

'We was in Cairo on a forty-eight pass, and we goes to an ENSA show,' Wallace explained, 'starring Sadie Jameson and Gloria Fielding. Couple of little crackers. After the show, we goes into their dressin' room . . .'

'You mean you *barged* into their dressing room,' Cope said, 'which was out of bounds to enlisted men.'

'So what? Who dares wins, innit? I wanted to give Sadie some flowers. She was tickled pink, and we was getting on like a house on fire, when Gloria asks Sergeant Cleverdick 'ere 'ow he likes the show. Know what he says? "I've heard

ENSA stands for 'Every Night Something Awful'," he says, "but I never really believed it. I mean, do you actually get *paid* for that?"'

Despite himself, Caine guffawed. 'Not very gentlemanly of you, Harry.'

'Fred only went for the tits and bums,' Copeland protested. 'They weren't short of those all right, but *singing*? It was a cats' chorus – I mean, I could have done a better show myself.'

Wallace glared at him, knotting camelthorn eyebrows. 'Oh yeah, if people wanted to hear a bullfrog with a bellyache, you'd of done marvellous.'

He turned back to Caine. 'It weren't funny, skipper, I can tell you. Next thing you know, the girls is screeching for their bodyguards to sort us out. Four or five bruisers turns up . . . and o' course, there's a bit of a shindig. If Harry hadn't of been my mate, I'd a dumped the bugger for what he said. As it was, we downed the lot of 'em and scarpered quick before the rozzers arrived.'

Caine fingered his own bruises unconsciously, and Wallace caught the movement. His indignant expression turned into one of concern. 'Look who's talkin' about gettin' in scraps,' he said. 'Pot callin' the kettle black, that is.'

'In my case it wasn't exactly a scrap – more of a massacre. I did get *one* good one in, though.'

'That gutless bastard Sears-*Bitch*. I swear I'll kick his arse into next year if I get 'old of him.'

Caine smiled, knowing that Wallace meant every word of it. If the big man believed he was avenging someone he cared about, consequences didn't worry him. Caine could look after himself better than most, but he was always touched by the gunner's loyalty. Wallace wasn't a thinker like Copeland, neither did he have Cope's ambition. He would volunteer for any dangerous job going just for the hell of it: even as a gunner in the RHA he'd opted to crew porteed Bofors guns for the Long Range Desert Group, despite the high casualty rate. When the Middle East Commando had asked for recruits, he'd been first in line.

Wallace didn't talk much about his background, but Caine knew that as a youth he'd done time in prison for thrashing two older boys in revenge for his pet mongrel, whom they'd kicked to death for amusement. He'd beaten them up so badly they'd both ended up with splinted limbs and wired jaws. His two years behind bars had been a devastating blow to the Wallace family: his father, Wilf, was a semi-invalid whose legs had been shattered in the Great War and who found it hard to get work. His mother, a quick-tempered battleaxe of a woman, had simply vanished one day, leaving Wilf with four young children, of whom Fred was the eldest.

In prison, Wallace had acquired a loathing for confined spaces and a determination to escape from the restricted atmosphere of his home town. The army seemed the only available path, but his enlistment in the Horse Gunners after his release from jail had been the prelude to a family tragedy. His brother, Frank, had followed him into the Gunners and had been killed at Dunkirk. His two sisters had found employment making shells in an armaments factory and had died when the place was bombed in the Blitz. His father had died of grief shortly afterwards and, deprived of his entire family, alone in the world, Wallace had sworn that the Germans would pay.

'I appreciate the sentiment, Fred,' Caine said. 'But you won't get away with downing an MP officer. Not like when you belted Audley.'

Wallace waggled his jaw, remembering Paddy Mayne's punch. 'Audley had it comin'. I don't care *what* Stirling says.'

'Forget it, mate. Keep focused on the stunt.'

'Yeah, well, it'd help a whole lot if you told us what the stunt *is*.'

'All in good time.'

Stirling touched Caine's elbow. 'I think there's one chap you don't know,' he said, beckoning over an oliveskinned, blackhaired soldier who was standing alone – a man with limbs as long as those of Copeland but so thin he looked emaciated. Caine took in fiery dark eyes set deep in a cadaverous face, a nose like a kedge, sunken cheeks and an elegant, pointed chin. Close up, he was astonished to see that the man's features bore a striking resemblance to those of his late comrade Moshe Naiman, killed on *Runefish*.

'I'm guessing you're our Jewish Palestinian polyglot,' Caine commented as they shook hands. 'You're a dead ringer for Moshe Naiman.'

'I ought to be,' the man said dryly. 'I'm Emanuel Netanya. Moshe Naiman was my younger brother – well, half-brother: same mother, different father.'

Caine raised his eyebrows in astonishment. 'Moshe was a brave man,' he said. 'A hero.'

Netanya didn't smile. 'I've heard that you were with him when he died. Is that so, sir?'

Caine had made no secret of the fact that he'd assisted the maimed and dying Naiman to kill himself, but he hadn't expected to be confronted by a family member like this.

'Not exactly,' he said. 'I was with him just before the end.' He swallowed. 'He was in a terrible state – foot blown off, shot in the leg. I wish I could have got him out, but I couldn't.'

Netanya's eyes were cold. 'I'd be obliged if you would give me a full account some time, sir,' he said.

'Certainly. How come *you're* here?'

'I'm attached from SIG.'

Caine nodded. SIG – the Special Information Group – was a unit recruited mostly from German-born Jews resident in Palestine. They spoke fluent German – most of them spoke Arabic and Italian too – and were trained to impersonate Afrika Korps personnel on missions behind enemy lines. The Nazis considered them traitors as well as subhumans: if bagged, the best a SIG man could hope for was a quick death. Caine had been deeply moved by Naiman's courage on the *Runefish* op but found the presence of his half-brother disturbing. He had a feeling that Netanya had volunteered for the op purely out of revenge. No one could blame him for that: half the men in the section had a personal grudge against the Krauts. A soldier motivated *only* by revenge, though, could be a liability to the mission.

'My father was murdered in a Nazi deathcamp,' Netanya said, as if an explanation were required. 'I was sent to Palestine for safety in '37 but, one way or another, Hitler has robbed me of most of my family.'

'Join the club,' Wallace murmured gravely. 'That's you, me and Larousse, all three.'

Stirling clapped his hands for attention. 'That's it, gentlemen,' he said. 'I think we're all here. Take your seats. Lieutenant Caine, over to you.'

13

Caine stood in front of a covered wall map, pausing for a moment as the men scuffled with chairs. He suckered a breath, surveyed the keen, hard, expectant faces. 'I'll tell you straight, boys,' he began, 'the stunt you've volunteered for is a bitch. For security reasons, I can't reveal what the target is until we're up the desert. All I can say now is that *Sandhog* comes straight from the GOC himself: its success is vital to the outcome of the next offensive, and so to the entire campaign. That means there's absolutely no pressure on us at all.'

There were whoops and murmurs of excitement from the men, most of whom had been expecting a standard SAS raid. 'We'll be operating in Libya,' Caine went on, 'in the Green Mountains area. I've divided the op into three phases: the march in, the hit and the march out. For now, I can only give you details of the march in. We'll be using two jeeps and two 3-tonners, heading west through the Alamein line. We're going to keep off the barreltracks to avoid enemy spotters. We'll be RV-ing with an LRDG patrol this side of our lines.'

Gasps of indignation broke out from the audience. 'Not them tossers,' Wallace chuntered. 'Who needs *them*?'

Caine had expected this. He was acutely aware of the rivalry between the two special units. The LRDG had been around longer and considered themselves the 'real' desert experts: in the recent shake-up, though, they'd been forced to concede the major raiding role to the SAS and had to be content with reconnaissance and transport roles. If they resented this, Caine's crew also resented having to share their exclusive stunt with the LRDG, especially in a manner that made it look as though they couldn't even find the way to the target without outside help.

'Don't worry about them,' Caine said. 'Believe me, *Sandhog* is pure SAS – something the LRDG couldn't bring off in a month of Sundays. Their role is strictly to get us to first base. After that we're on our own. Now . . .' He picked up a pointer and moved over to the wall map. 'The LRDG patrol will meet us here, at a lone pinnacle called the Ship's Bell.' He broke off to give the RV's map reference, instructing the lads to commit it to memory rather than write it down. 'The LRDG, under the command of Captain Oliver Roland, will escort us as far as the Jebel, which we'll be approaching from the south. We make landfall here . . .' he poked the map again with the pointer '. . . at the Shakir cliffs.'

He gave the coordinates, then put the pointer down and surveyed the attentive faces. 'Shakir is a four-hundred-foot cliffwall rising out of the desert piedmont, stretching on for miles. If there's a single place in the Green Mountains the Axis *won't* be expecting an approach, it's there . . .'

'Four 'undred foot?' exclaimed Dumper. 'It's goin' to be damn' 'ard work gettin' them wagons up, then, boss.'

There were cackles of laughter: Caine ended them by rapping hard on the table with his fist. 'This isn't a joke, ladies,' he said. 'No, Corporal Dumper, we can't get our vehicles up there, and we're not going to try. We're going to leave them on the piedmont for the LRDG to pick up later, load the kit into manpacks – you should all have been issued with one of the new hundred-litre manpacks – and climb the cliff, hauling the kit up after us. We're going to cover the rest of the way to the target on foot. That's why I said this stunt is one hundred per cent SAS. It's what we've been trained for. The Axis won't be expecting a march-in like this in a million years . . .'

A rumble ran round the group. Caine could tell that the men were impressed, especially Gibson and Rossi, whose eyes were sparkling with anticipation. Caine focused on them. 'Corporal Gibson and Trooper Rossi – you will head the climb. Everyone on the crew has been trained in cliff-climbing . . .' He shuftied Taffy Trubman guiltily, remembering that, alone of the group, the bulky signaller hadn't done commando training. Trubman clocked the look and turned pink. '*Almost* all of us have been trained in cliff-climbing,' Caine corrected himself, 'but we're not experts. Your task is to get the section safely to the top with the kit intact. Is that clear?'

Rossi stared back at Caine with his eyes, giving no indication that he even spoke the same language. The cowboy's thin lips cracked a grin. 'We got it, skipper.'

'Hey, hold on a sec,' a voice cut in. Caine looked around, knowing who had spoken. Copeland was running a hand through his hair, a sure sign that he thought he'd detected a flaw. 'I've seen the gear we've got,' he said. 'It'll amount to about two hundred pounds apiece. That's like each one of us lugging an extra man on his back. To move tactically through the hills packing that lot we'll need a covering group, which means we're going to have to work relays. It's only a quick calculation, mind, but I'd say it'll cut our progress down by fifty per cent. That means it'll take us twice as long to reach the target.'

Caine waited patiently for him to finish, a halfsmile playing on his lips. 'You're quite correct, Sarn't Copeland,' he agreed, 'but you kicked in early. I was going to say that, once in the hills, we RV with a donkey caravan led by friendly Senussi. The donkeys will carry the heavy stuff for us: that should speed up our progress.'

Copeland didn't look as impressed as Caine had hoped. 'You sure you can trust those Arabs?' he enquired doubtfully. 'You know as well as I do there's big trouble in the Jebel right now. Who *are* these Senussi anyway?'

Caine smiled. 'They're a band led by a certain Sheikh Adud . . .'

'Adud? Our old mate from *Runefish*? Father of the beautiful Layla?'

'The very same. It's true that the Senussi clans on the Jebel are more disturbed than they've been in years, thanks to Axis atrocities and a local commander they call the Angel of Death . . . but more about that later. The crucial point is that we *can* trust Adud. The RV with the Senussi has been set up by our G(R) agents operating undercover in the hills.'

Copeland fell silent and Caine dekkoed the other listeners. There were no more objections. 'Good,' he said. 'That's about all I can tell you for now. On the march in, it's desert rules, as usual. I want strict discipline. Vehicle crews check petrol, oil, water and tyre pressure at every halt. We'll be motoring like the clappers on this one, so co-drivers can expect to stag. We'll be going at night, but we'll also be using the heat haze to motor during the day. It won't make us invisible, but it'll give us a fighting chance. Keep petrol tanks topped up. If any wagon runs out of juice and holds us up, I'll flay the culprit alive. Observers, I want all mounted guns buffed every chance we get, and the quilts kept on until action stations. When we halt in daylight, scrimming up takes precedence over anything else. Corporal Dumper . . . you double as i/c MT maintenance and quartermaster.'

'Very good, skipper.'

'Corporal Trubman, you're i/c signals. You've got a No. 19 set inbuilt on one of the lorries and a separate No. 11 to take into the hills. I want comms with HQ established at my discretion, but I don't want you to use standard W/T procedure. Is there any alternative?'

Trubman squinched a chubby cheek between finger and thumb. 'The LRDG use French commercial procedure to baffle the Jerry "Y" Service,' he pouted. 'I can do the same.'

'Excellent,' Caine beamed. 'Corporal Pickney, I want at least one stretcher and a first-aid kit in every wagon, and the main stock in one of the jeeps for quick access.'

'Right you are, skipper,' Pickney said, squinting, his face like a cracked clay plate. 'We're going to need Mepacrine. That's a malarial area, and we don't want to risk going down with fever.'

'Good point. I'll leave it to you to draw enough Mepacrine for the section from RAMC stores.'

'What's the drill regardin' badly wounded, skipper?' Wallace asked.

'The *drill* is to abandon the wounded,' Caine said. He

paused for a moment, reviewing the faces. 'I can tell you now, though, that while I'm still standing, anyone who's hit, no matter how badly, will be brought back if it's humanly possible.'

He glanced at Stirling hastily, as if expecting a reprimand, but the CO stared back at him pokerfaced. 'All right,' he continued. 'Now, if your wagon hits a stick, only the immediate crew gets involved in the extraction, unless otherwise ordered. Action on being spotted by a shufti-wallah: freeze till the bugger's gone, then run like hell.'

'What about action on strafing or bomb attack?' the cowboy enquired.

'We've got our usual four choices: freeze, run for cover, disperse or shoot back. This op is covert, but still, nine times out of ten, our best response will be to let them have it. If we get jumped on the move, gunners open up immediately. Don't aim at the kite: put up a field of fire in her line of dive . . .'

'But skipper,' Copeland objected, scratching at his stubble of hair again. 'Some kites – like Macchis or Messerschmitt 109Fs – fly too fast for a field of fire to be effective . . .'

'Granted, it doesn't always work. It does work sometimes, though. It's the best chance we've got.'

'What about enemy forces, sir?' Netanya asked, his mild but distinct German accent sounding strangely incongruous in a meeting of Allied special service troops. 'Apart from the aircraft, I mean.'

'All right, good question. Off the beaten track, the desert's likely to be quiet. If we do run into an Axis patrol, we'll play it by ear. If we decide to play hard, we wipe them out, no prisoners. In the Jebel, our main threat is from Leichte 999 Afrika Division, a mob of criminals scraped up from Kraut jails commanded by regular officers and NCOs. This is a tough outfit. Don't be under any illusions, lads, we're up against it. We're a single section against the whole weight of the Panzer Group, the Luftwaffe, and the Regia Aeronautica. We're superbly trained and we pack a big punch, but once we've done the job, getting back home is going to be dicey . . .'

He paused and gazed around. 'All right. As I said, you'll be briefed on the target on the way. If there are no more questions, Colonel Stirling wants a word.'

Stirling stood up stiffly, removing his unlit pipe from his mouth. 'Thanks, Lieutenant Caine,' he said. 'To say there's a lot riding on *Sandhog* is an understatement, lads. Some deskwallahs at GHQ are saying the SAS regiment isn't worth its salt. True, we've had a few setbacks in recent months, but we know we're the best, and this time we're going to prove it. The whole future of the war could rest on what you eleven lads do in the next few days. You aren't *allowed* to fail this one. The time has come for death or glory, gentlemen: I want you to go in there and show the world, once and for all, that who dares wins.'

There were cheers, wolfwhistles, handclaps from the crew, broken only by the dulcet tones of Sam Dumper. 'There ain't eleven of us, though, Colonel,' he piped up. 'Whichever way yer slice it, I still make only ten.'

'He's right, sir,' Copeland said. 'We're a man short.'

Stirling eyed Caine in consternation. 'Sorry, Tom,' he said. 'He should have been here. I completely forgot.'

'Who, sir?'

'Your eleventh man. Just hold on a moment, would you?'

The colonel marched briskly out of the tent: he was back within two minutes, accompanied by another officer. With a sinking heart, Caine recognized the dazzling Hollywood smile of Lieutenant the Honorable Bertram Audley.

'This is your missing man,' Stirling announced. 'Lieutenant Audley has been busy on other matters, but he's now free. Tom, he's going to be your second-in-command on this operation.'

Caine felt himself flush. *Sandhog* might well be the most dangerous, difficult and important mission of his career, and Audley was the last man he wanted to share it with. The greenest 'B' Squadron recruit would have been better.

'With all due respect, sir,' he said, 'I generally appoint my own 2 i/c. Sergeant Copeland and I have worked together on previous missions, and we know each other's ways. I had assumed that Copeland would be . . .'

'Not at all,' Stirling insisted. 'Lieutenant Audley won the MC for bravery . . .'

'Sergeant Copeland won the MM, sir –'

'Yes, yes, I know, but we can hardly place the son of a marquis, a former Guards officer, winner of the MC, under a *sergeant*, can we? No matter how good an NCO he may be. No, Lieutenant Audley will be very handy, you'll see.'

Caine hesitated. He was tempted to say that if Audley was so 'handy', why not let him run the whole damn shebang? He, Caine, had more important things to do than kamikaze stunts: like finding Betty Nolan, for example. He was about to dig his heels in when he caught an almost imperceptible headshake from Copeland. He knew what it meant. He could walk out, but he'd already seen where that path ended – in jankers, at the mercy of shitheads like Sears-Beach. Caine fought back acid words and exhaled slowly. So much, he thought, for the 'equality between officers and men' that Stirling had spouted: another fine SAS principle bit the dust.

'Rightoh, sir,' he said.

Stirling beamed. Audley treated Caine to his best Gibbs dentifrice smile.

As the men dispersed, heading for the tent flap, big Wallace caught up with Caine. 'I'm warnin' you now, skipper,' he growled. 'If Audley and me goes up the Blue together, only one of us is comin' back alive.'

14

On the third morning out of Kabrit, Caine's column traversed a sandsheet as smooth as bleached bone where dust devils whirled in macabre dance and eyes blinked at them out of the nothingness like polished stones. The four wagons formed and broke, etching pale tramlines across the surface, layering the air behind them with long sequences of powdered dust. The men fell into a holy silence, as if they were in a vast, bluedomed cathedral, scanning the way ahead through their goggles, searching for some blemish on the landscape, some flaw in the desert's mindnumbing spell. The soundless vacancy of these great reaches awed them. Fred Wallace tried to challenge the silence by belting out popular songs, but even his strong voice soon faltered, crushed by the ponderous weight of the void. In all of that great emptiness, they were the only things moving, yet Caine often had the sensation that they too were standing still.

Time seemed frozen. He would glance at his watch, note the hour, then look at it again five hours later to find that only ten minutes had gone by. He knew that if he let himself turn inwards, he could soar off on a beam of light for aeons, coming back to earth with a bump to find that five hours really *had* passed in what seemed like ten minutes. He could not allow himself such absences, though, first because, when he let his mind drift, it always spun towards images of Betty Nolan, like a magnetic needle seeking north; second because, as navigator, he had to keep his eyes fixed on the sun compass, logging every small deviation with meticulous care.

Late in the morning, the sandsheet petered out, giving way to windgraded serir – long beaches of fine volcanic gravel with pools of sand – and gypsum flats that glistened like ice. Here, at least, were features for the eye's focus – notched ridges like the backs of halfburied dragons, interlocking rubblestone escarpments with slopes of ivory sand lying against them like skirts. Far away to his left, Caine could see gauze rippling along the wall of a low inselberg and, beyond that, the edge of a dunefield that seemed to run along the entire length of the southern horizon. At first sight the dunes stood out like the sails of golden galleons riding the sea winds, but they deflated as the sun rose higher, until they were no more than gentle swellings along the edge of the world. At last Caine saw what he'd been looking for – a single crooked finger of rock that seemed to beckon to him from a skyline where haze billowed like shreds of tattered cloth. It was the RV point: the Ship's Bell. At the base of this chimney, they were to meet the LRDG.

He pointed it out to Harry Copeland, who had been guiding the jeep *Doris* moodily, a cigarette stuck to his heatsplit lips, the throttle open, one hand on the steering wheel, his ostrich legs draped across the folded aeroscreen. Cope sucked in smoke, tossed away the butt, lowered his legs and gripped the wheel with both hands. The tone of the tyres beneath them had changed from the soothing mesmeric hiss of rubber on sand to the new, more businesslike crunch of windbrushed stone. Caine roused himself for a shufti at the other wagons. The 3-tonner they'd christened *Veronica* lay on his left. She was being driven by the grizzle-faced Gibson, with his oppo, Rossi, in the co-driver's seat and Dumper at the Bren-gun on the observation hatch. To Caine's right lay the other lorry, *Glenda*, with Netanya at the wheel, Pickney co-driver, Taff Trubman on the gun. To her right, slightly to the rear, came the second jeep, *Dorothy*, carrying Audley and Larousse. The men, even those inside the covered cabs, were grey with dust, looking like strange, pale, upright insects in their huge dust-goggles. The wagons' shadows were tight, directly beneath their bodies, and the leached-out sun stood high, like a hole in glass. Caine didn't need a watch to tell him noon was approaching. When the sun reached its zenith, the suncompass would become temporarily useless to them. If they were to make the RV before the halt, he reckoned they had fifty minutes tops.

Caine watched the gilded stylus of the Ship's Bell dip above the ridges and instructed Copeland to adjust his course. Cope was just easing down on the throttle when Wallace laid a skillet-like hand on Caine's shoulder. '*There*, skipper,' he said softly. 'Dustcloud – left, two o'clock.'

Caine sat up, pushed back his goggles, strained his naked eyes at the place Wallace pointed. A pall of dust was rising between them and the hogsback ridge and the faroff edge of the dunefield, standing out above the sparkling mirage like distant shipsmoke. Caine had Copeland give the three-honk signal for general halt. When *Doris* scorched to a stop, he stood up, trained his glasses on the dustcloud. 'It's a column,' he said. 'Not large, but moving fast.'

'Could be the LRDG,' Cope suggested.

That was always the big question, Caine thought: friend or foe? He'd been caught on the hop more than once by Boche masquerading as friendlies. He'd even been shot up by RAF aircraft who'd mistaken his convoy for Jerry. When in doubt, all actions had to be regarded as hostile.

'It's the Hun,' Wallace rasped, probing the distance with his own binos. 'I'd stake my arse on it. See the way the wagons are bunched? That's not LRDG, it's Jerry. Huns huddle tight.' Caine heard the conviction in his gruff voice.

There was a pregnant pause while the big gunner continued to dekko the approaching convoy. 'Those ain't stripped-down LRDG Chevvies, neither,' he commented at last. 'Axis wagons. Five of 'em, all soft skins – two Merc 3-tonners and three Breda sixwheelers. The leading wagon's a Breda, and she's porteeing an ackack gun on the back, ready to fire from the wheels. Probably twenty mil.'

Marvelling that anyone's eyesight could be that acute, Caine took another squint through his glasses. He could distinguish the five vehicles now, and Wallace was right – everything about their disposition screamed aggressive action. There was no doubt that the enemy had spotted them, but there was more: Caine had the inexplicable intuition that the Boche hadn't come across them by accident – they'd been waiting to banjo them. It was just a feeling, but the nagging question that kept on popping up in his mind like a No. 12 target was: *What happened to the LRDG?* LRDG patrols had vedettes out constantly: they would never have missed enemy movement from a leaguer just a few miles off.

The other vehicles had skewed to a standstill behind Caine's jeep, *Doris.* Caine lowered his glasses, spat out dry saliva, took deep breaths to steady his bumping heart. He'd broached the possibility of meeting enemy patrols in the briefing but he hadn't really expected it to happen this far behind their own lines. He'd chosen this course and this RV because it was far off the barrel-routes, where even friendly forces rarely trod.

He had Wallace pass him the bullhorn he kept in his kitbag behind. 'We've got a Hun column at two o'clock,' he bawled through the mouthpiece, keeping his voice casual. 'Moving up fast on a collision course. I'd say we've got ten minutes max. No time to scratch your arses, ladies. *Action stations.*'

There was a scramble of activity on the wagons as gunners and co-drivers swapped places or divested weapons of dustproof quilts, loaded, locked and readied them in an industrial symphony of metallic snaps, scrapes, cracks and rattles. Caine spied Dumper behind the Bren on *Veronica*'s cab, taking a last-minute glug from his waterbottle. He lifted the bullhorn. 'Sam,' he bellowed. 'Get that stovepipe jacked up, *now.*' He dropped his gaze to the open window on the driver's side, where the cowboy sat placidly at the wheel, his dark goggles giving him the look of a hoar-headed old spider. 'Gibbo,' he roared. 'Get three or four antitank rockets, arm them, join Sam on the cab. Rossi's to take your place as driver. There's a mounted ackack gun on the way – the first wagon in the column. As soon as you get in range, whack it out.'

The cowboy flashed grityellowed teeth and gave him thumbs up. Dumper had already vanished from the hatch.

A moment later both their heads bobbed up again. Dumper held the rocket launcher clamped to his shoulder while Gibson rammed home a rocket, wrapped his arms round Dumper to steady him. Caine sat down, stripped the dust-cover off the big halfinch Browning mounted on the dash, braced it, cocked it, peered through the sights. The enemy column was still there and getting closer by the second.

There was a scrunch of gravel as *Dorothy* drew up alongside him in a nimbus of dust, Audley in the driver's seat, Larousse manning the twin Vickers in the back. The bow-shouldered Canuck was standing very still, braced over his machine-guns like a big cat poised to pounce, his fingers steady on the triggerguards, his eyes soldered to the encroaching column. Audley's fingers twitched on the steering wheel. His face had a greyish tinge: his blue eyes glittered like tarnished jewels against his dustcaked face but the gleaming Hollywood grin was nowhere to be seen. 'You aren't *really* going through with this, are you, old boy?' he demanded unhappily. 'Only you know what David drummed into us about avoiding dingdongs. Wouldn't it be better just to run for it?'

'It would,' Caine sighed, 'but it's too late. They're here.'

For a second, his stoneglazed eyes focused on the dark torpedoes breaking the light, gliding towards them on the mercury tide. They were closer now, and the distortions of light, distance and speed gave the illusion that they were several times larger than he knew they really were. 'All right,' he said, glancing back at Audley, 'here's what we do. We move in fast, hit the column with everything we've got. While they're reeling, we head for that ridge.' He pointed left towards the single hogsback lying to the south, between them and the faraway dunes. 'From there we make for the sandsea. If we give them enough of a drubbing, we can easily outrun them that far. Once we get into the dune-field, they won't follow.'

'The *dunefield*?' Audley repeated. 'Hold your horses, old boy. I mean, how the devil do *we* get through it ourselves?'

'Got a better idea?' Caine enquired, his eyes rippling. 'Maybe you think we ought to run back to Cairo, and to hell with *Lightfoot*. Let the blighters sort it out themselves, what?'

Audley's face went taut. 'Now look here, old chap, er . . . I didn't mean . . .'

'Then just follow my lead, and stick together. We'll get through it all right.'

The sky was azulene blue without a blemish, the white sun oozing heat like dripping fat. Moving fast in the wagons, they hadn't felt it, but sitting still was like being barbecued. Gasping, Caine drew his Tommy-gun from the seatbrace, finding the stock almost too hot to touch. He yanked back the tophandle, shunted a round up the spout. In the driver's seat, Copeland was working the chamber of his Lee-Enfield sniper's rifle, a last cigarette dangling from the corner of his mouth. He replaced the weapon in the brace and checked his Browning .45. Behind them, Wallace peeled the quilts off the twin Vickers 'K's, eyeballed belts and feedpans, hefted iron, fed rounds into twin breeches with a double chunk. He swivelled the guns left and right to make sure they traversed smoothly on their pintlemounts. Caine replaced his Thompson in the seatbrace and measured the enemy's distance with his eyes. He took one last dekko at his column to make sure everyone was ready.

'*Go!*' he roared.

Motors snarled, wheels ground gravel. As the wagons rocketed forward, spumesurfing dust, Caine experienced a surge of dazzling clarity. The light seemed to double in intensity, objects in his purview became inexplicably vivid, as if a world he'd been seeing from behind a veil had suddenly flipped into brilliant focus: the Jerry wagons reaming towards them, the first Breda with the 20mm gun on her back, the four-man crew at the ready, the gun manoeuvring, the caravan of trucks behind, the Mercs swaying stiffly, the Bredas' independently sprung wheels rumpling with the desert surface. He could see men in the cabs – keen, bright eyes, desert-scoured faces, mirror images of his own boys. He could see machine-gunners at the observation hatches on the Breda trucks – men with bare torsos and peaked caps, traversing Schmeisser MG30s.

Caine's wagons were closing on the enemy, scraping up dirt at forty miles an hour. The SAS men went dead quiet, their eyes fixed on the Axis wagons, dashing nearer and nearer. Suddenly, the German ackack detonated. Caine clocked the cottonwool wreath of smoke hanging from its muzzle, heard the *whooomph* of exploding gas, *saw* the two-pound tracer shrilling air, tacking straight at him. He ducked, felt the air twang, heard the ripping paper roar as the round slavered overhead, felt the rockwave as it ramped the desert skin behind *Doris* raising a ten-yard-high totem pole of burning dust.

The Jerry gunners were just shoving another round in the breach when the bazooka belched fire from *Veronica*'s cab. Caine heard the rocket's belly-sickening creak like a broken saw on metal, heard it grate air, spunk the Breda with a sound like a gigantic handslap. He saw the truck volcano apart in a scarlet-and-brown supernova, arraying the air in chains of fire-ripples, showering blood, bone, nerve fibre, mangled iron, jangled steel. He just had time to register the shock on the faces of the two Huns in the cab when the fuel tank went up with a secondary *baroooomfh*. What was left of the Breda rose raggedly, four feet in the air, burst apart in a heartstomping fireflash as bright as the sun.

The SAS men ducked the flying debris; their wagons nosed on through cloying wraps of smoke and dust. '*Fire*,' Caine bawled. He pulled metal, felt the Browning buck on its mount, saw linesqualls of tracer curve into the smog. From behind him, two sets of twin Vickers shuddered and bullroared, gunnysacked cartridge cases, snickered out snaketongues of flame, snagged at the half-invisible Jerry trucks like electric whips. Wallace and Larousse bent their backs into the work, swivelled barrels, tugged steel. From the cabs of *Veronica* and *Glenda*, Trubman and Dumper *tackatacked* supporting fire.

The second Breda cannoned at *Doris* head-on through the spall, the machine-gunner on her cab lickettyspitting fire. Schmeisser MG30 rounds slingshotted, peeshashed past Caine's ear, corked *Doris*'s radiator. Caine sighted up, cranked iron, yoiked a delta of halfinch slugs that ripped up the truck's windscreen, blinded the driver and his mate, minced the cab roof, sent the gunner toppling backwards with ruby notches in his shoulder and thigh.

Straddling the bucking *Doris*, Wallace rattled bright-yellow javelins of incendiary, ball and tracer at the oncoming truck, thundered, '*Choke on this, you bastards.*' His rounds chunked the Breda's fuel tank, diced up her front tyres. Caine saw her list to one side, blubbing oilsmoke from the tank on the other. The Breda limped to a halt. The lefthand cab door cracked, two Huns dropped out, bronzed chests and faces glass-lacerated, clad in shorts, one hefting a 9mm Schmeisser SMG, the other a Gewehr 41 semiauto. They crouched down, they sighted up, they broadsided fire.

Hun rounds *whooffed*, skewbladed air, grazed *Doris*'s bodywork, chewed a tyre. Cope felt her heave and sag under him like a dying horse, felt a bat's wing tickle his scalp, felt warm blood seeping, fought to right the reeling, swerving wagon. Caine fingered iron, felt the Browning's mechanism chomp, heard it misfire. In the split instant it took him to click that she'd jammed, he was out of the wagon with his pregnant Tommy-gun blockshouldered, juggernauting straight at the Jerry drivers, mouth set in an 'O'-shaped scream.

He snaredrummed slugs at the first driver, cratered a line of red furuncles across his bare chest. A bullet took the second in the eye socket, squidged fluid, blowfished out from the back of his skull in a splotch of brains and bone chips. The Jerries slumped against the truck, leaving squigs of gore dripping off her chassis. Traileyed, Caine saw Cope shooting Grant Taylor-style, his .45 pistol in his hand, his face powdersmeared, goreblack from the graze on his head. 'No, no,' yelled Caine. 'Get back to the wagon, mate.'

Wallace was still on the jeep, raking the second Jerry truck with long sweeps of fire. Then the Vickers jammed. Wallace tore at the working parts furiously as if determined to rip the iron apart with his bare hands. He shoved the guns away in disgust, yanked his Bren from her brace, leapt out of the jeep. He hurtled up the field behind Caine, boosting tracer from the hip.

Germans hurdled out of the back of the third lorry – four-five-six of them cradling Gewehr 41s and SMGs. The last two trucks were grinding up in support, the MG 30s on their cabs burping and clattering through smog and dust. Caine heard ricochets, felt lead saw air, clocked a squat Jerry bracing a rifle. He boned shots, saw the man's hip detonate, clocked jagwhite bone sticking out, saw black blood spritz. A skittleheaded Jerry beaded him with a 9mm Luger, hefted steel. Caine felt the parabellum round zizz past, squeezed metal, felt his breech block clump on a vacant chamber. He heard a deafening *whomp*, snorted carbon residue, saw the Jerry's head raddled like a sieve, the body flicked back five yards by an invisible force.

He wheeled, clocked towering Fred Wallace, Bren shoulderslung, sawnoff twelvebore smouldering in his big mitt. They heard Copeland throatwarble, saw him gripped in a headlock by a blond Hercules who was forcing a razor-sharp sword bayonet into his face. Cope's right hand was closed round the Jerry's thick wrist as he struggled madly to deflect the blade. '*Shoot the cunt*,' Copeland shrieked. Caine fumbled for his pistol, had just snapped the weapon into his hand when buckshot snaffled meat with a smack like a shovel flatsiding mud. He saw the pelt of the Jerry's chest peeled back like butcherpaper, glimpsed white ribs and red organs pumping. Hercules' body rumpled and collapsed. Caine snatched a No. 36 grenade from his front pouch, pinned it with his teeth, tossed it among the enemy group, yorped, '*Four seconds*,' hit the deck. From under his elbow, he had time to see a bald, thickset German sergeant shrieking and dancing a rumba from a Garand M2 round that had just drilled through his arse when the No. 36 bomb krummhorned, burnished air, swatted the Jerries down like bluebottles.

Caine peered up at jerking, maimed bodies, saw a Jerry with his leg dangling off, another with tassels of red meat where his arm should have been. At that moment the cab of the third Breda burst apart with an earsplitting *wha-ummff*, forming a multipointed star of white light that sucked in the surrounding air in one gigantic intake, spewed it out in a fifty-foot geyser of dirtgrey smoke, ochre flame, roiling iron shards. Caine was knocked off his feet again by the blast.

He dragged himself up. Through the whorls of smoke dust he saw Jerries jumping out of the intact trucks. He eyeswept the area for Copeland and Wallace but couldn't see them in the billowing smoke. Instead, he clocked Larousse, Pickney, Gibson and Rossi flitting in through the fog like spectres, snapshooting Garands, putting up an impenetrable wall of fire, holding back the debussing Huns. Caine heard the *ping* of ejected clips and smiled grimly – the Garand might be noisy, but its firepower had certainly paid off. Pickney's driedprune face loomed out of the miasma of sandmist and smoke. 'Skipper,' he hissed urgently, 'there's another Axis convoy coming up behind us. We'll never take them on too.'

Caine's pulse flipped. He already knew he'd made a tactical mistake – the plan had been to hit and run, not to debus and get drawn into close-quarter combat. They'd been outnumbered to start with, and now the Boche had reinforcements on the way. 'Pull out,' he croaked. 'Back to the wagons.'

They made a tactical withdrawal in pairs, working the buddy-buddy system, one covering, the other moving, making use of the dense smoke and the superior shooting of the Garands. *Doris* was almost hidden by dustcloud, and when Caine got back to her he found Dumper proned out by the front leftside wheel. The fitter had just managed to change the punctured tyre singlehanded under enemy fire, breaking off every few minutes to blaze off full clips, keeping Hun heads down. Caine threw himself next to him just as he pulled out the jack.

'Was that you and Gibbo bazookaing that lorry just now?' he asked.

'Yep. Stroke o' luck, I reckon.'

'Not luck. Bloody good shooting, mate.'

The landscape to their rear was clear of smoke, and Dumper pointed out a string of black beads on the skyline – the second Jerry column. It was still some miles away but it was closing in fast. 'We've gotta get out of here, skipper,' Dumper huffed, 'or we'll get fried.'

At that moment, three figures emerged from the sand-mist. It was Wallace and Cope, dragging with them a Jerry prisoner. 'Hey, skipper,' Wallace rumbled, 'look what the cat dragged in.'

The Jerry looked aggrieved and irritated rather than afraid. His long face was dark with scabs and burns, his eyes redburred, his hair matted blood. 'I know you said no prisoners,' Copeland cut in, 'but I reckon we need to know why this column's here.'

Caine weighed it up – as usual Copeland had grasped the situation with remarkable clarity. He did have questions to ask, but what they would do with the prisoner after that, he didn't know.

'Tie him in the other jeep,' he said. 'We'll take him with us. Are all the boys clear of the fire zone?'

'Yep,' Cope said, as Wallace hurried the German off towards *Dorothy*. 'I didn't see Audley, though.'

'He's still in his jeep,' Dumper chortled, gesturing his maimed hand behind them. 'The bugger must like it there.'

There was a sputter of rifle and sub-machine-gun fire from the direction of the blazing German trucks. The SAS men ducked as rounds huzzed, snatched air. Caine peered into smoke, made out dark figures skirmishing forward. 'Here they come,' he spat. 'Start her up, Harry.'

Cope pivoted into the drivingseat as Wallace ran back and jumped in behind. The big man braced the Vickers and made a second attempt to clear them. Caine popped Tommy-gun taps; Dumper blebbed rifle rounds; Copeland toed the starter. The engine stuttered, faltered, died. Caine's heart twisted: he remembered a round clunking through the radiator. He potshotted Jerries racing out of the sandmist, getting closer now. He saw a German topple. Cope tried again, still no luck. 'The motor's hit,' Caine gasped.

'It ain't,' Dumper soussed. 'I bleedin' checked it, *di'n' I*?'

The engine engaged. Copeland revved, jabbed the horn, sounded the three short, three long blast signal for *Move out, follow me*. As he racked up first gear, there was a delighted howl from Wallace: he'd finally managed to get the guns cleared. He ratcheted rounds into chambers. Caine just had time to hear the engines of the other wagons firing up before the sound was drowned out by the thunder of twinned Vickers 'K's.

15

The four vehicles streaked away from the battlesite, each enveloped in a bolus of fine dust, leaving neat sets of double rail tracks, white on the dark serir. Caine guided the column towards the hogsback ridge he had pointed out to Audley earlier. It was less than a hundred feet high, he reckoned – a single spine of shattered putty-coloured shale stretching across the plain – but it would give temporary cover while they made for the dunes. They'd had a good headstart. Of the first Axis column, only two wagons were serviceable: with the dead and wounded, it would take the Hun time to get their act together. As far as that went, Caine's ploy had worked. The other column was too far away to catch up easily, as long as the SAS didn't hit a stick. Caine closed his eyes and said a silent prayer to a Providence he didn't really believe in that the going would stay solid.

'Skipper,' Wallace rasped from behind, 'there's a smoke cloud over that ridge. Not dust, know what I mean? Smoke.'

Caine shoved back his goggles, observed the ridge through his binos – with the jeep rattling along at top speed, it was hard to keep the lenses trained. For a second or two, though, he managed to zero in: Big Fred's 'Mark 1 SAS eyeball' had again hit the spot. Tatters of dirty grey smoke were straggling over the outcrop, too dark and static to be dust. There was no doubt about it – something behind the hogsback was burning, or had been until recently. Caine kicked himself mentally for not having clocked the smoke in the rush to get away. The Hun column had come from this direction. Had they left behind a damaged wagon? Was there a nasty surprise waiting for the SAS there? Or was it something else? Subconsciously, Caine hedged around the obvious explanation, the answer to the riddle that had been tugging at him since they'd first sighted the enemy: *What happened to the LRDG?*

If they hadn't just come out of a ferocious contact, the sight that met their eyes as the column swung round the butt end of the ridge ten minutes later would have made them spew. The gutted frames of the five LRDG Chevvies lay in a rough semicircle, each in her own patch of scorched and bloodspattered ground strewn with blackened bits of motor, twisted weapon shards, reeking tarpiles that had once been tyres, shapeless ammoboxes, bloated jerrycans, melted-down dashboards with wiring spilling out like flayed intestines. Bodies were everywhere – smouldering, lying humped in the sand, appallingly burnt or disfigured, maimed, disembowelled, surrounded by torn, blistered and bloody body parts. Caine saw one corpse that was black from head to foot, limbs brittle as charcoal, eyes eggpoached in their sockets. Not far away he saw an enormous black Nubian vulture perched like an incubus on a man's chest, pecking out his tongue. The pall of putrid smoke that lay over the scene smelled like the stench from a burnt-out abattoir.

Cope stopped the column twenty yards from the wrecks, and they studied the scene in silence. The battle here had been short, sharp and extremely violent. 'That ground patrol didn't do all this on their own,' Dumper mouthed. 'There was aircraft in it, I'll be bound.'

'Yep,' Wallace agreed. 'Must have been early morning. We never heard nothing, know what I mean? Them wrecks is very near burnt out.'

'An ambush,' Caine concluded. 'The Krauts lured them here, away from the RV maybe. Banjoed them from behind the ridge.'

He snatched his Tommy-gun from the seatbrace and made a move to jump out, but Dumper gripped his arm. 'Take it easy, skipper,' he growled. 'The Hun has a nasty habit of boobytrappin' wrecks like this. Could of sown Thermos bombs, AP mines, any shit.'

With a sudden burst of fury, Caine raised his Tommy-gun, cocked it, stitched half a mag of .45-calibre bullets across a broad arc. The others winced at the racket: the rounds punted up puffs of sand and gravel but set off no explosions. The vulture spread ragged wings and lurched clumsily into the air, a long ribbon of black and red flesh hanging from its beak. Caine fired his last round at it, but missed. As he made his weapon safe he noticed Copeland giving him a tightlipped frown. 'Skipper,' he said, a hint of exasperation in his voice, 'there's nothing we can do here. If we delay, we're just handing ourselves to Jerry on a plate.'

'Them aircraft could come back, too,' Dumper added, and Caine could hear the apprehension in his voice.

'*Listen*,' Wallace grated.

Caine cocked his ear, thinking that the big man was referring to Axis motors. Instead, from somewhere nearby, there came a faint but distinctly human moan. It came again, louder this time. 'Someone's alive,' Caine said, looking incredulous. 'There's a survivor here.'

A second later, all four of them were out of the jeep with their weapons at the ready, spreading out ten yards apart, sticking to the ground Caine had cleared with his Thompson. The corpses were clad in tattered, ripped and scorched British Army battledress with greatcoats and cap comforters, confirming that the engagement must have been fought in the early morning, before they'd stripped down to their shorts. That was more than six hours ago, and Caine wondered what the Jerries had been up to since. The surface was chopped up by superimposed tyretracks, showing that there'd been a lot of manoeuvring of wagons, but that didn't tell him much.

Caine crouched to examine a cadaver lying chest up: a bearded face, blue with death. The trooper's stomach was gouged out, a crimson pit full of black blood and greyish-white guts. The lower part of his left leg had been ripped off; the notched white bone of a kneejoint protruded. Caine stood up and clocked Harry Copeland leaning over another body – a headless man slumped chestdown over a Bren-gun. Cope looked as if he was wondering whether to salvage the weapon. '*Don't touch it*, *Sarn't*,' Dumper yelled from behind him.

The little Cockney waddled up and asked Copeland to stand back. He lay down full length behind the corpse, extended a stubby arm around its chest and yanked it over on top of him. There was a flash, a deafening spattercake thud, a gout of gravel and sandsmoke. Caine and the others hit the deck. The Bren flew into the air, zeezed over

Copeland's head, smacked earth five yards away, a bent and broken gunmetal spider. Dumper, protected from the blast by the headless corpse, jumped up with a scowl on his face. 'Grenade,' he spat.

'How the hell did they know we were coming?' Caine heard Cope demand.

'They didn't,' Dumper growled. 'They're just a bunch of shicers.'

Caine heard a motor purr behind him and turned to see Audley approaching at the wheel of *Dorothy*. There was a hint of querulousness behind the fading patent smile. Larousse was poised over the guns behind him, perusing the scene with watchful black eyes: the German POW lurched uncomfortably in the co-driver's seat, his hands lashed to the pintlemount of the forward gun. He looked scared now, as if anticipating punishment for the carnage in front of them.

Caine waved Audley back. 'There might be someone alive here,' he bawled. 'Go and keep an eye on the enemy.'

'We haven't got time for this, Caine,' Audley said, his voice cracking. 'They're right on our tails.'

'We're not ditching any wounded.'

Audley tried to switch on his engaging smile but couldn't quite manage it. He had just turned the jeep when Dumper yelled, 'Over here, boss.'

The surviving LRDG man was lying in a shallow depression behind a nest of boulders, where he'd been invisible from a distance. As the four of them closed in on his position, a distinctly cultured English voice groaned weakly, 'Don't come . . . any closer. I'm booby . . . trapped.'

Caine scoured the area with hooded eyes. Once again,

though, it was Wallace who clocked the obstacle. 'Tripwire, skipper,' he said. 'Over there, in the rocks.'

It took Caine a moment to spot the wire. He knelt down on one knee, slinging his Tommy-gun across his back. 'Fred,' he said, 'I want you to go and get Pickney. The rest of you keep back. I'll see if I can disarm whatever's on the end of that wire.'

Cope was starting to fidget. 'Tom,' he said, 'the Jerries'll be here any minute.'

'I know,' Caine replied, ironfaced. 'Audley already said that.'

He fell on his belly and started to crawl towards the nest of stones, keeping his eyes fixed on the tripwire. One end was tied to a peg stuck in the ground, the other disappeared behind the rocks. It took him only a minute to find the 'spudmasher' grenade attached to the end – the wire had been tied to a ring on the bomb's arming pin. Caine's fingers, deft from years of tuning engines, quickly secured the pin and detached the ring from it. 'All clear,' he murmured.

He looked down into the depression and saw lying there on his back in a patch of goredyed sand an officer he recognized. It was Captain Olly Roland of the LRDG, the man who was to have commanded their escort. Caine shuffled quickly down to him and saw that the skin of his scalp had been peeled back, hair and all, like a flap of thick parchment, exposing a mass of oily blood vessels and grey matter. Roland didn't try to look at Caine: his face was a sootblack mask: there were two vacant dark caverns where the eyes had once been. Both his hands had been sheared off, probably by a bomb, Caine thought, because his arms now ended in cooked black stumps, which he held crossed over his chest like a dead Egyptian pharoah. He had an ugly gunshot wound in the shoulder with an exit hole so big Caine thought it must have been made with a round as thick as a man's thumb. One of his legs lay at a crooked angle, reduced to streamers of roasted flesh and saw-toothed bone. Roland's bearded face was covered in dried blood that had cracked like old leather, the blackened skin taut from pain and loss of blood. That he was still alive, Caine couldn't credit.

'You're all right, sir,' he said, his voice hollow. 'The orderly's on his way.'

Roland's empty eyesockets stared up at the cloudless sky. 'Caine? That you?' he croaked, his voice a wispy trickle.

Caine slid out his waterbottle, uncorked it, held it to Roland's broken lips.

'Just a sip, sir,' he said. 'Don't worry, we'll get you out of here.'

Roland drank a little. When Caine lowered the water-bottle, the officer's scabbed lips were moving as if he were making an effort to speak. Caine put an ear close to his mouth.

'Don't be . . . a stupid . . . bugger,' Roland hissed, so faintly that Caine had to strain to make out what he was saying. 'I'm not going anywhere. I just needed . . . to tell you. The Boche. Knew we were here. They knew. Some-one. Told them.'

'That's impossible, sir,' Caine said softly.

Roland panted, licking the bleeding, suppurating lips with a bloated tongue, rocking his shoulders from side to side as if attempting vainly to get up.

'They knew. I tell you,' he gasped. 'They were looking. For us. For you.'

The frail sound of his voice trailed off: his eyes glazed, the rocking ceased. Maurice Pickney pushed through the onlookers and squatted next to Caine, plumping down his medical chest. He made a quick, careful inspection of Roland's body, his old maid's face grave, his cured leather brow creased. He felt for a pulse, put his ear to the captain's mouth. He shook his head. 'He's gone, skipper,' he said.

Caine stood, picked up a drone of motors and a grating of gears from beyond the ridge. It was the enemy convoy. He could tell from the sound distortion that it was further away than it seemed, but there was no doubt it would be here soon. The others were staring at him, faces tense.

'Skipper,' Copeland said, making an obvious effort to skim the tension from his voice. 'We have to get out of here. Think of *Sandhog*. We can't afford to get bagged.'

Caine stepped away from the dead man. 'All right,' he said. 'Let's go.'

16

As Caine's jeep passed the 3-tonner *Veronica*, the cowboy stuck his buckskin face out of the open window. 'Boche are about a mile back, skipper,' he said. 'They're huggin' our tracks, but me and Rossi just left them a little present – a baker's dozen of No. 2 mines.'

Caine gave him thumbs up. 'Nice work, Gibbo,' he said.

Before *Doris* moved into position at the head of the column, Caine eyewalked the desert to the north: he spotted the Axis wagons approaching, a file of silver limpets riddled with heatgauze. They were advancing slowly, yet it seemed to Caine that they exuded a sense of purpose, the tenacity of bloodhounds on a sleuth. He knew it was only too easy to imagine such things up the Blue, but Roland's phrase, *They knew we were here*, kept tapping at his head like a woodpecker.

He snapped back his goggles, trained his glasses on the edge of the dunefield ahead, trying to gauge how far off it lay. The sun was past its apogee, and the dunes appeared to be inflating steadily, as if some giant were filling them from immense bellows. Caine put the distance at fifteen miles. 'Full throttle,' he told Cope.

The desert here was scattered with nodules of sandstone, windcarved into statues like giant chalices – wide heads on lean stalks. The surface was ribbed with shoulders of snuff-toned earth, peppered with spike-brush, esparto grass, little explosions of desert sedge. Between the fertile gashes, long spits of sand lay in low drifts, slumping into shallow sandtroughs where the heat haze rose in trembling swirls, like smoke. The wagons had been going for no more than ten minutes when Caine heard a series of dull thumps from far behind: the cow-boy's mines had been tripped. 'That'll give the buggers something to think about,' Wallace crooned.

A few moments later, Audley's jeep pulled alongside *Doris*. 'Just had a gander at the Huns,' Audley shouted. 'Gibbo's calling cards bagged at least a couple of them. The convoy's stopped.'

'Not for long, though,' Caine bawled back. 'They'll be on our tracks again soon enough.'

'Hold it, skipper,' Wallace skirled in his ear. '*Glenda*'s hit a stick.'

Caine swore. This was just what he'd been afraid of. As Cope turned the jeep round, he saw that *Glenda* had hit mishmish so deep that her wheels were submerged. Her driver, Netanya, was trying to extricate her by revving her fast, only succeeding in digging her further in. *Veronica* had already halted some distance away. The cowboy was still at her wheel, but Rossi had taken Dumper's place on the observation hatch. The stumpy fitter was at the stick, testing the sand around *Glenda* with a steel rod.

The two jeeps pulled up near *Veronica* simultaneously. Caine jumped out and leaned across *Dorothy*'s bonnet. 'Backtrack five hundred yards,' he told Audley. He pointed to a low terrace of scalloped sandstone. 'Take up a defensive position at the end of that ridge, where you've got a good view. If the enemy gets within half a mile, give 'em a burst to keep their heads down, and beat it back here quick.'

Audley nodded at the German prisoner tied to the Browning's pintlemount.

'What about *him*?'

The Jerry looked barely conscious, and Caine felt a pang of sympathy for him. 'Gaston,' he said, looking at Larousse. 'Move him to *Veronica* and cuff him in the back. Make sure he's secure, mind. I need to talk to this bloke.'

As Larousse led the prisoner towards the other truck, Dumper hurried over to Caine, still hefting his steel rod. He looked hot and bothered. 'It's a crashdive job, skipper,' he reported, wiping sweat off his oversized head. 'The mishmish goes down for ever. This rod is six foot and it went in all the way, no effort. It's goin' to need some real periscope work.'

Caine's heart sank. A 'crashdive job' meant that the wheels were wedged deep into the sand – a problem made worse by Netanya's revving. 'Periscope work' meant that hi-lift jacks and a lot of hard shovelling would be needed to get her out.

'It's the way Netanya drives 'em, boss,' the little Cockney complained. ''E don't seem to realize the gears an' clutch ain't synchronized on a freetonner. Instead of changin' direct, 'e works down froo the gears. Finks e's drivin' a bleedin' Roller.'

'Get all the boys over,' Caine told him.

He jogged over to *Glenda* to inspect the damage. Netanya dropped out of the cab and came to meet him, looking embarrassed.

'Sorry, sir,' he said. 'The surface all looks the same. Just bad luck.'

Caine squinted at the lorry's tyres and saw at once that the pressure was too high. He'd given specific orders that drivers should adjust tyre-pressure on sand as a matter of course. Netanya had neglected it here, and this small mistake could have put the whole mission in jeopardy.

Caine bit back a mouthful of invective. 'You've got about ninety pounds of pressure there, Manny,' he said acidly. 'Fifteen is plenty.'

Netanya nodded glumly, but Caine didn't press it: they'd been crossing alternate patches of gravel and sand since the morning, and deciding on the correct pressure in such variable terrain was a real headache.

Dumper was already letting air out of the tyres: the rest of the boys were swarming around the truck ready to start shovelling. Caine measured the length of the mishmish pool, pacing it in both directions. He decided that the best course was to reverse out. He joined the rest of the lads, kneeling on the hot sand, sweating like warthogs, digging frantically with shovels and bare hands, sending occasional glances to where *Dorothy* stood sentinel half a klick away.

It was a losing battle. The sand was too soft, and the more they shovelled out, the deeper the wheels sank in. After ten minutes of back-breaking toil, Caine squatted back on his haunches and wiped sweat off his brow with his tankie silk scarf. Copeland stalked over to him on his waderbird legs, clad in shorts and chapplies. He hadn't had a chance to clean the graze on his scalp and his hair was caked with a mixture of sweat, dust and congealed blood. He flashed a glance towards Audley's jeep.

'There's no way we're going to extract her, Tom,' he said. 'If we stay any longer we're going to get caught with our pants down.'

'You mean dump her?'

Copeland's face had assumed the familiar expression of superiority that must have worked well when addressing a class of fourteen-year-olds, Caine thought. 'Let's face it, Tom,' Cope said solemnly. 'We're going to dump all the wagons in the end. It's not worth risking the operation for a truck.'

Caine considered it. 'We can't do it, Harry,' he said. 'She's carrying almost all our water. What we need is something to stop the rear axle sinking – maybe some of those old petrol boxes would do the trick. We're also going to need all the hi-lifts we've got to raise the wheels enough to get the sandchannels under them.'

Dumper and Gibson ran to *Veronica* and came back with shards of broken-up petrol boxes. Caine took the flat plywood pieces: crouching beneath the Bedford's chassis, he placed them under her rear axle, working fast, but being careful not to disturb the fragile sandcrust. Wallace, Copeland, Rossi and Gibson struggled to set up the stiltlike hi-lift jacks by each wheel and worked the handles frenetically until the sweat was pouring off them in rivulets. 'Watch it, skipper,' Cope warned him. 'The hi-lifts are wobbly as hell.'

Dumper and Gibson were ferrying the perforated steel sandchannels from *Veronica*, laying them in the sand by Caine – they were hot to the touch. The hi-lifts creaked, the jacking team huffed, sucked their teeth in the sharp heat; the 3-tonner's wheels rose an inch, an inch and a half, two inches. Caine took the end of the first sandchannel, gasping as the hot iron burned his fingers. He was just about to crawl under the chassis again when Wallace's voice rasped, '*She's goin'*.'

The jacks slithered and shifted: the truck's three-ton weight reeled. Caine had just enough time to throw himself clear before she crashed down in her grooves, with a slam of metal and a clang of springs. The men cursed, collapsed in the hot sand, tried to recover their breath. They were up a second later, though, their eyes flickering wildly in *Dorothy*'s direction. Copeland's eyes bored into Caine like skewblades. '*Skipper*,' he pleaded. 'If they bump us now we've had it: Audley won't keep them back for more than two minutes.'

Caine glanced at his watch, then at the sun, then at *Dorothy*. Audley and Larousse hadn't budged nor given any sign of enemy movement. He dekkoed Cope, watching him, feet apart, hands on hips. 'Let's give it one more go,' he said. 'If we don't get her out this time, we'll leave her.'

The truck was as deeply wedged as she'd been when they'd started. They had to go through the entire process of digging out sand, placing wood under the rearaxle, working the hi-lifts now with a sense of desperation, expecting the Hun to appear any minute, unable to erase from their minds either the savage contact earlier or the sickening abbatoir scene they'd witnessed at the ridge.

This time, though, the jacks held, just long enough for Caine to slide the sandchannels under the wheels. When they were snugly fitted, he bawled at the team to release the hi-lifts. The lorry settled on to her sandchannels with a sigh, Caine took a last shufti at *Dorothy*, then jumped into the cab.

He started her up, threw her into reverse, let in the clutch. The truck lurched backwards, tossing and swaying like a fishfloat in water, the whole crew heaving from the front. Finally, she rolled back, and Rossi and Gibson belted in the spare channels with perfect precision. A moment later her tyres crunched on terra firma. Caine set the rear brake, cranked the transmission into neutral and dropped from the cab, leaving the engine running. 'Come on, lads,' he yelled. 'Let's get packed up and get the hell out of here.'

17

As the boys raced to stash away jacks, shovels, sandmats and sandchannels, readjust tyre pressures, top up fueltanks, Caine made a sign to Audley to come in, then had a dekko at the sky. The sun was tilting over to the west, a fire meridian now suffusing the leached-out pallor of the afternoon. There were smears of purple murex and flamingo pink across the world's edge, like daubs in a child's painting book. A moment later *Dorothy* slalomed to a halt beside him. Audley shoved back his goggles and Caine saw an expression of relief on his face. 'No sign of them, old boy,' he announced. 'Not even a dust-trail. They must have given us up as a bad job. Maybe Gibbo's mines did more damage than we thought.'

Caine nodded but made no comment. He couldn't believe that the Hun had abandoned the chase when they'd been coming on with such apparent resolve. True, Gibbo's mines might have made them wary. They might have been afraid of walking into more traps: rather than turning tail, though, he thought they might be making a circling movement of some kind, staying below the skyline, planning to bump his convoy further on. Whatever the case, he was uneasy: it didn't feel right.

He turned his back on Audley, dimly registered the sound of *Dorothy*'s motor receding, idling, then accelerating. He glanced back to see that she was heading north again and assumed that Audley was taking the initiative – going to see if he could find the Hun. Caine helped the lads stow away the last of the kit and was about to walk back to *Doris* when Fred Wallace gargled, '*Shuftikite.*'

Caine froze in midstep: the stark simplicity of it hit him like a rabbit punch. Of *course* the Axis column had called in air support. That was why they'd hung back beyond the horizon. He was a stupid duffer: in their haste to get moving, not even Copeland had broached this possibility. They should have remembered the signs of aircraft-strafing at the LRDG site.

He heard the aeroengine almost at once, a full thirty seconds before the aircraft hummed into view, a silver gnat plummeting gracefully through the rainbow skeins of dust. He didn't need his binos to tell him that she was a CR42 biplane of the Regia Aeronautica. '*Stop*,' he yelled. 'Stop what you're doing. *Now*.'

He followed the silver insect with his eyes as she trawled across the leaden sky with a maddening slowness – almost a deliberate impudence – that made him want to reach for a weapon at once and blast her down. He traileyed the scene around him – vehicle tracks, people tracks, the untidy configuration of wagons, the raggletaggle clutch of men, the heaps of sandspoil, the plumes of dust still hanging in the air from the unsticking – it wasn't possible that the pilot could miss them.

An instant later the biplane tippled wings, banked and dumped altitude, crooning down in a long arc almost directly towards them. Caine's pulse zipped. With an intuition born of years up the Blue, he knew for certain that she was coming in on a straffing run. The CR42 was outdated and slow, but that was exactly what made her dangerous as a spotter. Macchis and Messerschmitt 109s were much faster, and their pilots were therefore likely to overlook what was going on downstairs. The CR42 wasn't a match for an RAF Spitfire, but she toted a half-inch Breda firing deadly armourpiercing needle bullets, as thick as Wienerschnitzl. A belt of those could easily devastate Caine's little column.

The first time he'd been straffed, years back, he'd been so terrifed he couldn't move. It still scared him, but not as much now, because he knew that the manoeuvre was almost as hazardous for the pilot as for his targets. Unless the flier wanted to risk squandering his shots, he had to get the kite in low – as low as twenty feet from the surface – and that left her wide open to ground-to-air fire.

The CR42 was still well out of her own effective range when Caine came to a decision. 'Wallace, Larousse, man the Vickers,' he roared. 'Trubman, Rossi, the Brens. I want a wall of fire in front of that crate before she gets in straffing range. Anyone with a Garand or a Bren put in his tup-penceworth: fire directly *in front* of the aircraft, not *at* her.'

Caine watched Wallace sprinting bigboned for *Doris* and remembered that Audley and Larousse had gone off for a recce. He swore, knowing that this effectively halved his main firepower. 'Dumper, Gibbo,' he roared. 'Get the bazooka jacked up. If the kite gets through the firewall, blow her out of the sky.'

He'd hardly finished his sentence when he heard Wallace trombone the working parts on the twin Vickers, saw him traverse muzzles, raise elevation. He clocked the aircraft dropping towards the column like a hawk – five hundred feet, two hundred feet, a hundred: he caught the biplane's batshadow racing across the sand. '*Watch my tracer*,' Wallace bullhorned.

The Vickers cymballed thunder, gouted fire, curved steaming orange tracer directly in the CR42's divepath. From the cabs of *Glenda* and *Veronica*, the mounted Brens kicked in, belched, ticktacked, squelched green tracer in long bright rods: the brilliant dotted lines of colour merged, mingled, entwined, wove together in a spectacular rainbow barrier of light. Caine, armed with his shortrange Tommy-gun, could only watch. From all around him came the bass *boomph*, *boomph*, *boomph*, *boomph* of Garands and the staccato *tacktacktack* descant of Brens as the other SAS men opened up. Caine felt the air buck, felt his eardrums flutter, breathed cordite, took in the thrashing torque of aero-engines as the pilot tried desperately to pull out of the dive. Squinting in the lowering sun, Caine could see the Italian tricolore on the double wings, could see the pilot's head, his mouth spread in a mad rictus beneath the flying helmet and goggles.

The biplane yawed and bobbed. Her path started to flatten out. Caine's heart dropkicked: the firewall was always a dicey tactic, and it looked like she'd made it through. Fifteen yards forward and to the right of Caine's position, Dumper and Gibson were crouched at an oblique angle to the aircraft's trajectory, their bodies locked together in a tight clinch. Dumper traversed the muzzle a fraction, lined up the crosshairs a tad in front of the biplane's nose, and gripping the forward pistolgrip with his disfigured left hand, took first tension on the firing mechanism. 'Watch the backblast, mate,' he rumbled.

The bazooka shockwaved fire, backslashed flame and smoke. The air shizzed; the rocket skeetered, greasetrailed, kerblunked into the airplane's frame. For a split second nothing happened. The CR42 careened on in a breathtaking powerglide. Then her body bulged, ballooned, bludgeoned apart, karooned into curds of flame with an earsplitting *krooooompp*. The pilot's squarejawed leer vanished: the fueltanks starflashed in a spectacular many-pointed red dwarf, the wings disintegrated, shrapnel and blazing canvas tatters rained down.

The biplane skewbladed over the heads of the SAS men, a shapeless mass of flaming airborne wreckage, a dying skeleton of blazing aeroskin and crazily tangled sidestruts. She lufted on far past their small leaguer, drooling fire, dribbling smoke, losing height rapidly until what was left of her slapped to earth, dissolved into an octopus-head of tarsmoke and a layer of charred wreckage that spread across the desert for hundreds of yards.

Caine's men clapped and whooped. Dumper and Gibson stood up and made neat little bows to the cheering audience. Dumper held the bazooka high in both hands, as if presenting it for approval to the gods. As they trotted back into the leaguer, Wallace and Pickney danced a samba and blew them mock kisses. For a moment a carnival atmosphere reigned. Caine plumped down. 'Good shooting,' he beamed. 'Now let's get moving before that bloke's mates come alooking.'

For a few moments the men gathered by *Doris*, clearing weapons, lighting cigarettes, glugging water gratefully from feltcovered canteens. 'Shall I get comms with base, boss?' Trubman asked, his bulging face bright red from the strain of the past few minutes. 'Report the contact?'

'Maintain wireless silence for now, Taffy,' Caine said, drawing deep on a Black Cat cigarette. Whatever procedure they were using, W/T chatter could always be dee-effed, and after what they'd been through today, Caine had become wary of exposing his position. Slinging his Garand, Trubman rolled his coalsack body away unhappily to *Veronica* to disconnect his antenna.

Caine walked over to the jeep. Copeland was already back in the driver's seat, and Wallace was cleaning the Vickers with a piece of rag. 'Reminds me of the first time I tried to shoot back at an Axis kite,' the big man said. 'Just before Dunkirk it was. Me and this other chap was mannin' an LMG on the back of a Morris truck. Minute we opens fire, the bleedin' lug snaps off the tripod, dunnit. Had to take turns holdin' the damn thing on our shoulders while the other fired. Bloody hopeless.' He winked at Caine. 'No bazookas in them days, Tom.'

Caine grinned at him, and looked around. 'Where the heck have Audley and Larousse got to?' he demanded.

'Audley said they'd clocked a gazelle,' Wallace snarled. 'Just after we got the wagon unsticked. Must of gone to shoot it.'

Caine nodded, furious that Audley had let him assume he was doing a recce. He was faced with the choice of waiting for *Dorothy* to come back or leaving without them. He had almost decided to let them catch up on their own when the *thumpa thumpa thump* of Vickers 'K's drummed out from somewhere not too distant. Caine and Copeland sat up, scouring the desert for movement. Wallace dropped his cleaning rag, trained his twin weapons in the direction of the shots. 'You don't reckon he's tryin' to snag gazelle with a *machine-gun*? he asked incredulously.

Before anyone could answer, there came the rattle, crack and bump of small arms from the same direction. 'That's the Hun,' Cope hissed.

'Start up,' Caine snapped, waving to the drivers of the other two wagons to do the same. Motors roared. Heads bobbed out of hatches, and Caine heard the plunk of Brens being cocked. He grabbed the big-calibre Browning mounted in front of him, remembered it was jammed and snatched his Thompson instead. *Dorothy* creased suddenly into the leaguer riding a skirl of dust, Audley driving, Larousse stooped over smoking guns in the back. The jeep careened to a halt a yard from *Doris* and Caine saw Audley's eyes bulging in his ghostwhite face. He was trying to blurt out something, but was so worked up he couldn't talk. Larousse cut across him. 'It's the Krauts, sir. Six or seven softskins led by an AFV – looks like an Sdkfz 222 light armoured car. They've worked a flanker round us, and they're moving in – not more than a half-mile away.'

Audley nodded frantically. 'Sorry, old boy,' he warbled. 'I know I shouldn't have gone after game, but if we hadn't, we'd never have spotted them.'

Caine bit his lip. 'Take up position as tail-end Charlie,' he ordered, 'and get ready to go like a bat out of Valhalla. We're going to outrun the Jerries and hit those dunes before last light.'

18

The German patrol was back on their trail: Caine's drivers pushed their vehicles up to top speed but couldn't throw them. 'They're gaining on us,' Wallace croaked at intervals. 'Can't you go any faster, mate?'

The wagons spread out in air formation, spraying dust, bumping over stony ground, searing through hard gravel and sand, zigzagging and crossing over each other's tracks to present harder targets if the Hun got near enough to open up.

Every time Caine looked, the enemy was there – a belt of black links shawled in haze, coming on with that same sharklike doggedness he'd sensed from the beginning. 'Hope to Christ we don't hit another stick,' Copeland commented huskily. 'Then we'll *really* be scuppered.'

'Shut up,' Wallace bawled at him. 'Don't say it. Just keep going.'

Standard tactics would have been to stop and lay ambush, but the Hun were too close for that. Caine considered sowing mines, or just halting to make a stand, but rejected both ideas as hopeless. The only thing they could do was to make sure they kept out of range of the AFV's cannon long enough to reach the dunes.

The sun was lowering, the desert surface turning watered gold. The dunes had grown steadily from barely perceptible bulges to giant, towering sandcliffs, so steep and formidable that the idea of driving across them seemed ludicrous. Caine reckoned some of them were three hundred feet high, but he had no idea how far they extended south – his map was inaccurate and lacking in detail. From a mile away the sandwall came into sharp focus – a continuous defensive rampart of interlocking crescents whose slipslopes of creamy amber sand rose at acute angles to knifeblade crests. Copeland's mouth fell open.

'There's no way,' he muttered. 'Skipper, there's no way up those things. We'll never do it. We're knackered.'

Caine craned his neck to study the dunewall, and his spirits sank. He knew that a sandslope couldn't exceed an angle of about thirty-three degrees before it collapsed, but these slopes appeared to be tilted at the maximum angle – the sun's position made it impossible to discern small differences in gradient. As the jeep hummed nearer, he raked the slipfaces desperately with binos and naked eye, searching for the smallest chink, the slightest hint of a way in. There wasn't any.

A sudden boom of ordnance made them all jump. It was followed by the hoot of a shell slashing air. They ducked instinctively. The shell thumped earth, kicking up a fountain of sand and stones directly behind them.

'Keep going,' Wallace rapped urgently. 'They ain't in range yet.'

The dunes towered above them, phantasmagoric whale-like monsters high and dry on the world's greatest beach. Caine's eyes darted left and right, searching for a way out of the cul-de-sac he'd painted them into. He swore viciously, banging a fist on the dashboard. He couldn't believe it. There *was* no way into the dunes, nor was there any way around them – the sandrange stretched for miles in both directions. They were trapped, with an enemy column behind them, headed by an armoured car. He racked his brains for a ploy, but the only choices that presented themselves were making a kamikaze fight of it, or surrender. He thumped the dashboard again, so hard that his knuckles bled. Whichever way he chose, it meant the end of *Sandhog*, the end of their chances of destroying Axis chemical weapons, of rescuing *Lightfoot* from oblivion. It might lead to the failure of Monty's offensive, and through it . . . Caine didn't even want to ponder the possible ramifications. One thing was certain: it would end his chances of seeing Betty Nolan once and for all.

Caine turned to Copeland, his throat dry and a clawing, nauseous feeling in his stomach. Heading for the dunes had been his idea from beginning to end – even Audley had objected to it. It had been arrogance pure and simple, and now he could kick himself for his stupidity in attempting such a ploy without knowing what he was heading into. 'You'd better stop,' he told Cope, his voice flat and lifeless. 'We can't go any further. That's it.'

Copeland glanced at him, his eyes standing out like quartz crystals against a deathly face. He throttled down, changed gear, slowed and stopped. The wagons behind followed his lead. Caine stood up in his seat and turned to find out where the enemy was. The black caravan was nearer than before. Caine knew there would be no chance of fighting it out – not unless they simply wanted to make a suicidal last stand. There was no cover, and the Jerry Sdkfz 222 armoured car, with her twentymil gun, would blow all four SAS wagons into the sky before she even got into bazooka range. His machine-guns and mortars might take out the other Hun vehicles from a thousand paces, but they'd make no impression on the hardskin. And why should Jerry commit them at close range when he didn't have to?

He saw the faces of his crew staring at him from the aeroscreens and hatches on the other wagons, puzzled but trusting, awaiting his orders. He felt sick to the stomach at the thought that he'd failed them. These were good men, for the most part exceptional men. And now they were all going into the bag, where they'd probably remain for the rest of the war. He, Caine, deserved it for his bad leadership, but the other lads didn't. They'd had faith in him and he'd let them down.

He sat heavily. 'You got that infrared nightsight?' he asked Wallace, his voice hollow.

The giant's eyes widened. 'It's here, in your kitbag, skipper,' he said, puzzled, 'but it ain't much use to us now.'

'Better destroy it,' Caine growled. 'And find something for a white flag.'

'Hold on a sec, Tom,' Copeland said. 'You don't mean you're *giving up*.'

Caine shrugged. 'Unless you know a way of driving up a thirty-three-degree wall of soft sand . . .' He paused, as a last-ditch idea hit him. 'We'll climb the duneface on foot. We'll lose all our kit and the wagons, but some of us might make it to the top.'

'But skipper . . .' Wallace stopped himself in mid-sentence. 'Look,' he said, pointing his shovelsized hand.

Later, Caine didn't know whether the sun had that moment emerged from a cloud haze, or just dropped a fraction of a degree, but its beams had suddenly hit the skirts of the dunes at an oblique angle, passing like a magical hand over what had seemed a perfectly regular surface, revealing veins, gullies and channels that hadn't been visible a second before. Caine saw with a frisson of excitement that, exactly where the crests of two high dunes intersected, a narrow cleft had opened up. It was only three yards wide – it would be tight going – but as long as the sand at the bottom held, he knew there was a good chance that all four wagons would get up.

'See that cleft,' he told Cope. Copeland swallowed hard and nodded. 'I want you to go for it, full throttle. Top speed right to the summit. I guarantee you'll make it.'

The jeep's motor clattered. Cope rammed the gearstick into first, let in the clutch, eased the throttle up as far as it would go. Wallace waved the other wagons on, but Caine didn't look behind. He just prayed that the drivers remembered all he'd told them about driving on sand. 'Whatever happens, don't decrease speed,' he shouted at Cope. 'Go at it as if you're taking a hurdle.'

The bottom of the cleft was a hundred yards away. Copeland whamped the jeep into second then third, changing back down into first as she hit the bottom of the sandramp. 'Hold on, Fred,' Caine yelled, closing his eyes, knowing that this was the acid test. If the lower skirts of sand supported *Doris*, she would get all the way up: the other wagons would only need to follow in her tracks. The jeep lurched sickeningly. Caine felt her tyres slip, and for a second he was sure she was going to stick. Then her wheels found purchase: she tipped backwards, almost throwing Wallace out. She catapulted up the slope as if floating on a cushion of air, gliding like a sleigh on snow, so smoothly that only the flickering needle on the speedo told them she was moving at all. Seconds later they were on top, hundreds of feet above the surface. Instead of facing a steep downhill slope as Caine had expected, though, he was astonished to see that the sand ran on through low ripples for at least half a mile before merging into the sandglare beyond. 'Keep going,' he bawled.

There was another blast from the German armoured car behind them: this time they didn't hear the whistle, only the *crump* as the shell burst harmlessly on the desert floor. '*Missed*,' Wallace declared. 'Still out of range.'

Looking back to see if the other wagons had made it, Caine saw *Veronica* vault over the dunecrest, bounce on her big balloon tyres, her canvas cover flapping madly. Even from where he sat, Caine could make out the glee on the faces of Gibson, Rossi and Pickney, as if they'd just come off a thrilling rollercoaster ride. Before she had even caught up with them, *Glenda* appeared behind her, wobbling slightly as she broke the crest. Caine clocked Trubman on the hatch looking nervous, and Netanya in the cab, his cadaverous features set in an expression of absolute concentration.

Seconds ticked and there was no sign of *Dorothy*. Caine told Copeland to slow down, an apprehensive look on his face. No sooner had Cope eased the throttle, though, than Audley's jeep reeled into view, weaving from side to side so wildly that Caine thought for an instant that she was going over. He saw Larousse grimly hanging on to his gunmountings, Audley fighting the wheel as he swerved, ploughed through sand ripples and finally got her under control only a few yards from *Doris.* Audley blinked at Caine apologetically. 'I don't think the Boche are coming,' he shouted. 'Looked to me like they stopped.'

Caine wiped sweat off his brow with his scarf and shivered suddenly, realizing that the day had turned cool. 'Talk about a close shave,' he said.

19

Just after sunset, they happened on a dustbowl among the dunes with a hard salt floor. As the wagons roared down into it, a small flock of gazelle stampeded in the opposite direction, white tails bobbing in the halflight. Audley let out a whoop and charged after them, trying to run them down, cheered on by lads on the other vehicles – all but Wallace, who cursed savagely and, before Caine could stop him, grabbed his Bren, put a .303-tracer round across Audley's bows, narrowly missing the petrol jerrycans strapped flat on the bonnet. The bullet took the wind out of Audley's sails: he gave up the chase, but drove over to *Doris* looking murderous.

Caine and Wallace were already donning their battledress trousers and coats against the rapidly cooling air when Audley jaunted up to them, scowling. 'I want that man put on a charge for attempted murder,' he announced, pointing a bony finger at Wallace. 'He took a potshot at me.'

Wallace, wrestling a cap comforter over his tangle of bristling black hair, gave an explosive guffaw. 'Don't talk daft, man. I'm a champion marksman with a Bren. If I'd wanted to bump you off, I wouldn't have *missed*.'

'Kindly address me as *sir*. What the hell do you think you're doing, opening fire on an officer?'

'I told you – *sir* – I wasn't shootin' *at* you. I was trying to stop you killin' those gazelles – beautiful animals. No need to run 'em down.'

'Hear that?' Audley said, glaring at Caine. 'He'll have to answer for attempted murder, *and* insubordination.'

Wallace stuck his roughstubbled mandrill face into Audley's, his eyes glinting darkly like tarnished coins. 'Yeah,' he boomed, 'and Ashdown, Penfold and Lennox? Who's answerin' for them?'

'Those men were killed *in action*, you great booby.'

'Yeah, they was. An action where the chap as was ordered to give coverin' fire *deserted his bleedin' post*. If it hadn't been for Larousse, we'd all have been snuffed.'

Audley sucked his teeth, turned his indignant gaze on Caine. 'Are you going to stand by and listen to this gorilla abuse an officer?' he demanded.

'He's right, Fred,' Caine said slowly. 'You're out of line.'

'Out of line?' Wallace repeated. 'Funny, I didn't notice Gary Cooper here in the dingdong today. Of course, he don't approve of dingdongs, do he? Or maybe he was just savin' his energy for knocking down poor little creatures as can't fight back.'

'How dare you?' Audley blazed at him. 'My jeep got stuck in a rut . . .'

'Didn't stop Larousse joinin' in, did it?'

'Shut it, Fred,' Caine broke in. 'You're over the top . . .'

'Damned right he is,' Audley hissed. 'He took a shot at me, and I promise you, I'm having him up before the CO the moment we get back.'

'Fred,' Caine said, sticking his arms into his duffel coat, 'I want you to go to *Veronica* and take charge of the prisoner. Get the cuff key from Larousse. Jerry'll need some attention from Pickney. No rough stuff, eh?'

Wallace grunted and shuffled off, leaving Audley and

Caine confronting each other. Caine finished buttoning up his duffel coat, pulled down his cap comforter and stuck a cigarette in his mouth. He offered one to Audley, who shook his head impatiently. Caine lit his cigarette with his Zippo and replaced the lighter in its protective condom. He blew a cone of smoke that hung in the still air. 'Wallace shouldn't have said that, Bertie,' he said, 'but we've fought two hard actions today and only outran the Hun by the skin of our teeth. We're all dead beat and on edge, and in this state bad things sometimes get said. I wouldn't take it seriously.'

'Take it seriously?' Audley spat, his eyes burning. 'He impugned my honour.'

'Yeah, he did, but you'll survive. And there's no question of him trying to kill you. Like he said, if he wanted to put a round through your brainbox, he wouldn't have missed. He's just got a thing about animals – doesn't like to see them ill treated. This isn't the Guards, Bertie. You can't expect Tommies in a crack unit like the SAS to be in awe of you just because you've got two pips on your shoulder, stand to inherit a fortune and talk la-di-da. You've got to *earn* their respect. In any case, it's not a good idea to threaten men with official charges – not when you've got to go into combat with them on a daily basis. You know what I mean?'

Audley looked flabbergasted. 'Are you trying to –' He was cut short by a single crisp gunshot that slammed out from the other end of the depression.

'What the blazes was that?' Caine snapped. He seized his Tommy-gun from *Doris* and cocked it with a snap. With Audley following, cradling his Garand, and Gibson, Rossi and Dumper in close pursuit, Caine moved cautiously out of the leaguer. The remaining men took up defensive positions. A slice of moon had come out, a curved dagger-blade, and the depression, with its steep sand walls, was washed in silver. In the moonlight, Caine saw a dark figure labouring towards him, a tall, emu-legged shadow with a loping stride. It was Harry Copeland. He had his SMLE sniper's rifle and a haversack slung over one shoulder and was bent forward, lugging something heavy on his back.

When Cope saw the others coming, he stopped and threw down his burden. Caine saw that it was the carcase of a fullygrown gazelle, brown and tan in the moonlight, its sprawling legs elegant even in death. 'One shot, five hundred yards,' Copeland announced proudly. 'I wouldn't have bothered, but I thought the boys deserved a treat.'

The five SAS men gawped at him in amazement. 'Boy, that was hot shootin',' the cowboy gasped. 'How the heck did you spot it?'

Cope shrugged. 'I had this . . .' He swung the haversack off his shoulder and held it out to Caine. 'The RG sight. I thought you wouldn't mind me borrowing it, skipper, and we've never tested it. I can tell you now, it works a treat.'

Before Caine could take the sight, Dumper snatched it out of Copeland's hand. 'Careful with that thing, Sarn't Copeland,' he crowed. 'More than my life's worth if you wrecked it.'

Caine chuckled ruefully, remembering how near they'd come to destroying it earlier on.

When Cope dumped the gazelle carcase in front of Wallace in the leaguer a few minutes later, the big gunner blinked darkcushioned eyes at it and spat. 'What the hell did you go and do that for?' he demanded.

'Boys needed fresh meat.'

'I'm not cookin' it,' Wallace declared, turning his back. 'I'm not touchin' the poor thing.'

'All right then, I'll cook it myself.'

Wallace wheeled round on him, incensed. 'I should of let them thugs bash your head in back in Cairo,' he rumbled. 'And I should of . . .'

'Fred,' Caine cut in, 'where's the Kraut?'

'Over by *Glenda*, with the quack. Maurice said he'd need a few stitches. Larousse is there gettin' his own wound looked at, keepin' an eye on him.'

Caine raised an eyebrow: the Canuck hadn't even reported a wound. 'Larousse got it bad, did he?'

'Nah. Bayonet slash in the calf. Nothin' serious. You want to talk to Jerry now, skipper?'

Caine sighed and looked around. Pickney had set up a makeshift dressing station at the tailboard of *Glenda*, about forty yards away: Caine could see him working on the German prisoner, who was seated on a petrol box, with the sacklike shape of Larousse looming over him. 'Let's leave it a while,' he said. 'I need a brew.'

A brewcan was already rattling on the Benghazi cookbox Wallace had set up – an ingeniously improvised device made of a petrol flimsy with the top sliced off filled with petrolsoaked sand. Caine sat down on the ground with Audley, Copeland, Dumper, Gibson and Rossi. Trubman was working on the wireless, leaning on the signals board that folded down from *Veronica*'s body, trying to get comms with HQ. Netanya had taken first stag as prowlerguard. Caine was pleased to note that the drivers had formed the wagons into a rough defensive square, each vehicle covering one arc, throwing down their bedrolls and kit in the middle.

Gibson handed round Camel cigarettes and listened to the customary jibes about camel dung with a good-humoured smirk. 'Mebbe you prefer those "V" cigs you Brits get issued with,' he chortled. 'A maggot in every pack.'

Wallace served tea in enamel mugs to everyone except Copeland.

'Hey, where's mine?' Cope demanded.

'You, you murderer,' Wallace snarled, 'you can drink it out of your arse. I'm done with you.'

The others laughed as Copeland got up, suppressed rage on his face. 'You're done *with* me, you great baboon,' he scoffed, pouring tea into a mug. 'You nearly did *for* me in that melee today, chum. You waited a whole minute before you snookered that big bastard trying to pigstick me in the eye with a bayonet. What were you waiting for, Christmas?'

'Don't talk soft,' Wallace snorted. 'It weren't more than fifty seconds.'

Cope ignored him, waving his full mug, slopping hot tea. 'I know the skipper's weapon jammed, but there's no excuse for you. Trying to put the wind up me, weren't you? Thought it was a funny joke? Well, your funny joke nearly got me whacked, so don't talk about being done with me, mate, because as far as I'm concerned you've *had* it.'

'Yeah, I *did* mess up,' Wallace shouted at him. 'I should of let the bastard top you. Then we'd all be better off.'

Copeland blinked and stared at Caine. 'You know, skipper,' he said in a loud voice, 'there's a handbag factory in Cairo where they *buy* gazelle skins. I was talkin' to one

LRDG chap who'd collected so many he touched for a hundred and fifty quid. I was thinking of collecting a few myself.'

Wallace dumped his mug with a clatter, slung his Bren across his broad, beefy shoulder. 'I'm going to relieve Manny,' he muttered. With a last smouldering glance at Copeland, he strode off into the dark.

As the boys guffawed, Caine closed his mind to the bickering, sipped his tea gratefully. It could do with a dash of Woods rocketfuel, he thought, but he was too tired to go and get the flagon. He took a drag of his Camel and gazed up at the stars – they were slightly blurred, which told him there were dustclouds in the air, but he could still make out some familiar constellations – the Plough, the Pleiades, Orion. The weariness of the day hit him like a bolt.

Entering the sandsea hadn't been the end of their toil. In fact, they'd penetrated another fifteen miles before sunset, crossing half a dozen sets of dunes. Caine had led the convoy back and forth along the duneskirts, scanning the slipslopes until he found an opening – there was always some way through, no matter how slender, although they'd hit sticks a couple of times, in one of which *Veronica*'s exhaust system had been damaged. As the shadows had lengthened, it had become easier to spot gaps, clefts and channels in the sand, but it wasn't until after the sun had melted into a peach and cream mist over the edges of the sandsea that Caine had finally been satisfied the Hun weren't on their trail.

A cold wind whipped across the depression. A sudden ghostly bang from the body of the jeep *Doris* made them all jump – Rossi spilled his tea and swore in Italian. Dumper howled with laughter. 'Metal contraction,' he announced gleefully. 'Happens when the air cools very fast, like tonight.'

The shock seemed to have reminded everyone that there were jobs to be done. Dumper went off to get his tools to repair *Veronica*'s exhaust, Copeland asked the cowboy to bring a 10lb tin of butter from *Glenda*. 'Gazelle meat's tasty,' he told him, 'but there's no fat on it – not an ounce.'

He looked round for a knife sharp enough to skin the animal. 'Hey, Ricardo,' he said, remembering Rossi's razor-sharp knife, 'can I borrow your blade?'

Rossi groped in his belt, then stood up, looking annoyed. 'It's not here,' he grumbled. 'Has anyone seen it?'

'You probably dropped it in the contact,' Caine suggested.

'No, I've had it since then. What happened to it?'

He stalked off, mumbling to himself, scouring the ground around the leaguer. Gibson went to get the butter. Copeland sorted through the cooking gear and came up with a carving knife and a machete. Caine glanced at his watch and realized it was almost time for the Greenwich time signal: he had to take a starshot to fix their position. 'By the way,' he told Copeland as he got up, 'you need to get that graze looked at.'

Cope shrugged. Caine unwrapped a theodolite and lugged it over to *Veronica*, where Dumper already had his head under the rear end. Trubman was resting his bulk against the W/T stall, tuning into the BBC. 'Ready for Greenwich, mate?' Caine enquired.

Caine spread the legs of the theodolite while the signaller slipped out a Zenith Chronometre stopwatch. They waited. Suddenly, the Greenwich time signal squibbed out across the airwaves, an alien communiqué from a distant world. Trubman counted off the pips, stopped the watch on the sixth. He gave Caine a thumbs up. Caine took the starshot, matched it against RAF astronomical charts for the day's date, then compared it with the estimate of their position he'd calculated from dead reckoning. They were within half a mile of the point he'd figured they were at – not as accurate as it might have been, but not bad considering they were in the middle of a sandsea.

Caine followed the aroma of roasting meat back to *Doris*, found Copeland already basting gazelle joints on a steel sandtray inserted in a pit he'd doused with petrol. Netanya and the German prisoner were standing around drinking tea while Larousse hovered silently in the background with his Garand slung, a mug in his hand and a cigarette in his mouth.

Caine dumped the theodolite back in the jeep. 'Where's everybody else?' he asked.

'Wallace is on stag,' Copeland said. 'Dumper and Trubman are still busy. Gibson and Rossi went to see the quack. Don't know where Audley is – probably went for a crap.'

'What about your wound?'

'I'm going to see Maurice – soon as the meat's done.'

Caine glanced at the German, who was clad in battledress and a greatcoat Pickney had lent him. He was a man in his early twenties: a long face, high cheekbones, wiry blond hair almost like Copeland's, heavylidded eyes that were pools of hard steel in the moonlight. He didn't look at Caine but stared sullenly into the middle distance, as if trying to pretend he wasn't there.

'Have you talked to him?' Caine asked Netanya.

The Palestinian nodded, his face eerily skeletal in the wan light. 'Got his name, rank, number and date of birth. He's Corporal Hans Leiter, 90th Light Division.'

'So the column that attacked us was 90th Light?' Caine said, looking at the German.

'Yes,' Netanya answered for him. 'I already asked that.'

'I want to know *why* they're here,' Caine told him. 'I mean, what's a small patrol like that doing behind our lines?'

The interpreter repeated the question to the prisoner, but it evoked only a shake of the head and downcast eyes.

'All right,' Caine sighed. He took a step towards the corporal, planting himself directly in front of him, fixing him with a stone-eyed stare. 'Tell him this. He can either explain why his unit is here and get handed over as a POW to our MPs on the Alamein line, or . . .' He drew his Browning pistol with breathtaking speed, snapping the slide back with such force that the prisoner jumped. He placed the muzzle of the pistol to the German's forehead. '. . . he can leave his bleached bones here for the vultures to pick . . .'

The corporal squinted sourly at Caine's massive, topheavy torso, hardmetal eyes meeting the lieutenant's unyielding, sandhoned gaze. He began to speak slowly to Netanya, thrusting his hands deep into the pockets of his greatcoat. The Palestinian stopped him after a moment and turned to Caine. 'Seems his column's under special orders to intercept an enemy group headed west . . .'

Caine's eyes widened. He eased the pistol away from the German's head. 'How were they to recognize this column?' he asked Netanya.

The interpreter repeated the question. The corporal listened, nodding, his hands still in his greatcoat. He opened his mouth as if to answer, but in that instant jerked his right hand out of the pocket in a movement so fast Caine was taken by surprise. Bright steel flashed: the Jerry stabbed viciously at Caine's neck. Caine just had time to bring his arm up in a defensive position before the sharp stiletto stuck through the sleeve of his duffel coat, incised flesh, jarred bone. Caine rocked back in shock: a rifle cracked with an earbursting *bumph*, *bumph*, *bumph*, *bumph*. Rounds bit flesh with the sound of splintering wood: Caine leapt aside, his eyes wide with horror. '*No. No. No*,' he shrieked. It was too late. *Bumph*, *bumph*, *bumph*, *bumph*. The corporal shot forwards, blood squirting from slugs that had demolished his temple and stoved in his chest. He pirouetted gracefully with his arms raised, long gouts of gore spritzing from his thighs and neck. He tottered for a moment, his hands describing ineffectual infinity symbols, then his body collapsed heavily into the sand.

He was slumped on the desert floor oozing blood, the knife still in his hand. '*Shit. Shit. Shit*,' Caine howled, nursing his injured right arm with his left hand. The cut was numb, but the sleeve of his coat was soaked in gore. His head and chest were wet with blood that wasn't his own. He wiped his eyes with his good hand and glared hotly at Larousse, whose ungainly frame was still hunched over his smoking Garand, inkwashed eyes fixed on the dead Jerry as if he thought the corpse might come to life. Harry Copeland stood transfixed: he held his Browning pistol in a ready stance, but it was clear that he hadn't fired. All eight shots had come from Larousse, and it hit Caine that the Canuck had fired a full clip. 'What the *hell* . . . ?' he spat.

Larousse's eyes were wet sapphires in the moonlight. His face didn't relax. He lowered the rifle, groped calmly in his ammo pouch, popped a fresh clip, worked the chamber. 'He tried to kill you, skipper,' he growled.

Speechless, Caine turned back and saw Copeland squatting over the Jerry's body, his fingers working rapidly at the bloody neck. Caine knelt down beside him. The salty ground was slick with blood. 'He's dead,' Cope said.

Caine swore venomously. Gravel scrunched: he looked up to see the other lads running in from all directions, weapons at the ready.

'What the devil is going on?' Audley demanded.

Wallace peered at Caine, his dark face like tarpaper. 'You all right, Tom?'

Pickney gave the dead Hun the once-over, then turned to Caine, who was still nursing his wound. The orderly cut away his sleeves with scissors and slapped a field dressing on the bloody incision. 'It's deep but clean,' he told Caine. 'You'll need stitches.'

Copeland, still kneeling by the corpse, prised the knife out of stiff fingers, holding it up in the moonlight. It was a dagger similar to a Sykes-Fairbairn commando knife but with a serrated edge on one side. 'Where did he get this?' he demanded.

'It's *mine*,' Rossi cried suddenly, snatching the dagger out of Cope's hand and examining it. 'It's my Swiss Home Guard knife.'

'Question is,' Copeland said, standing up, 'how did it get into the prisoner's possession?' Caine saw that his mate was eyeing Rossi accusingly, wearing his familiar schoolmaster expression, as if he'd just pulled up a student for some serious breach of the school rules. Cope was still grasping his Browning, and though it wasn't pointing directly at the Swiss, his stance had a certain menace to it. 'You know, Ricardo,' he said, 'I think you've got some explaining to do.'

The men rolled up in their sleeping bags slugeyed that night. Much to Wallace's glee, the gazelle meat had turned out to be inedible. 'You berk,' he howled at Copeland. 'You shot a female in kindle. Tainted meat. Bloody good shootin', *Sergeant*.'

Cope opened his mouth to say something, but Dumper cut him off. 'Reminds me of when I was attached to 7th Armoured,' he drawled, his eyes twinkling in the starlight. 'The food were so stinkin' rotten, someone called the cook a bastard, see. Well, cookie complained to the RSM, didn't 'e, and five minutes later the sarn't major comes stompin' into the mess wiv 'im, lookin' daggers like he's gonna 'av someone 'anged by the neck. "Now what I want to know," 'e sez, "is 'oo called this bastard a *cook*."'

The lads exploded with mirth, but Cope glowered, too tired to rise to the taunt. While the others had been burying Leiter, he and Caine had questioned Rossi on how the prisoner had managed to get his knife. Rossi simply didn't know, unless the Kraut had picked it up somehow. After all, he'd had nothing to do with the prisoner all day – Leiter had been tied up in *Dorothy* with Audley and Larousse;

Larousse was the one who'd cuffed him in *Glenda*; and it was Wallace who'd released him. Rossi hadn't even gone to see Pickney until after he'd finished stitching up the Jerry. In the end, the cowboy had got fed up with them 'picking on his buddy', as he put it, and told them to lay off.

Caine agreed. Pickney had sutured the stabwound in his arm, which hadn't severed any artery but was awkward and painful. In any case, what concerned him as much as *how* the prisoner had got hold of the knife was *why* he'd attacked him when he was so obviously being watched. How could he have imagined he'd get away with it? Maybe he didn't care.

After the rest had retired, Caine lingered on a little longer drinking tea with Wallace and Cope, who were doing their best to ignore each other.

'I thought the lads pulled off two pretty impressive actions today,' Copeland commented. 'I mean, crikey, three Kraut wagons taken out, a CR42 . . . all those casualties.'

'It went our way, yes, but . . .'

Cope caught the doubt in his voice and shot a glance towards him, a dim birdlike outline in the fading moonlight. 'What's up, Tom? You think we should have done a bunk like Audley said?'

Caine shook his head. 'No, it's not that. I mean, it would have been ideal if we could have withdrawn, yep, but given the conditions, bumping them was all we could do. It's just that I had this hunch from the start that they'd been *sent* to look for us. I thought it might be just my imagination until Roland said the same thing, just before he snuffed it: *They knew we were here*, he said.'

'That bloke was out of his mind with pain, Tom,' Wallace

protested. 'Both his hands was blown off, his eyes was like cokeholes in snow, and his leg were raw shishkebab. Not surprisin' he were rambling.'

Caine shook his head again. 'Fred,' he said, 'the prisoner *admitted* his column was under special orders to intercept an enemy unit . . .'

'It could have been *any* unit, though. Didn't have to be us.'

'Yeah, and what other unit happened to be taking this route across the Blue? If it *was* us, they must have known where the RV was, and only a handful of people knew that.'

'You saying there's a traitor in our own mob?' Wallace demanded indignantly.

'No, of course I'm not. It's just that I thought RV locations were supposed to be confined to one or perhaps two people in SAS command, and members of the patrol itself. The idea that it could be any of our boys is ludicrous.'

'I dunno,' Copeland whispered, gazing guardedly around at the sleeping men. 'I mean how much do we know about some of these lads, skipper? Rossi reckons he's Swiss, but he sounds like an Itie to me. What about Netanya? There's something creepy about that bloke. Is the cowboy really a Yank? A lot of Krauts served in the Legion before the war . . .'

Wallace snorted contemptuously. 'Bollocks,' he swore softly. 'Obviously the prisoner weren't talking about *us*.'

'We'll never know now, will we?' Caine said. 'Larousse whacked him out.'

'He was just doin' his best to protect you, Tom,' Wallace hissed, sitting up. 'That bloke hates Krauts: they murdered his wife and kids in France, remember? An' let me tell you, if I'd of been there, I'd of done the same thing.'

'All right, Fred. I know Larousse had my back.'

Wallace gave a leonine yawn and stood up, shouldering his Bren. 'Tell you what, Tom,' he growled. 'I wouldn't sweat it over a dead Jerry. Those buggers took Gaston's wife and kids and my whole family, and the more of 'em we leave for the shite-hawks, the happier I'll be. Only good Kraut's a dead 'un, as my old dad used to say.'

He scooped up his bedroll with a shovel-like hand, and swinging the bundle over his shoulder, stumped up to his sleeping space with ogre's strides.

20

Caine hardly slept. He was haunted by recurrent images of bodies maimed and eyeless, of corpses floating in winecoloured groundswells, of a Jerry stinging his flesh with a blade he'd inexplicably managed to acquire, and being culindered by Gaston Larousse, whose close-set eyes illuminated his memory darkly like the double bores of Wallace's sawn-off. He was turfed out of a doze by Audley's yells and jerked his Thompson free from his sleeping bag to find the cowboy lopping off the head of a snake with his Bowie knife. The snake was small – only a foot long – and its scales glinted pinkly in the starlight. 'Sandviper,' Gibson grunted, probing the severed head with the talonlike knifepoint. 'Venom of that thing'll snuff you in four hours tops. I seen it happen, and it ain't pretty.'

Caine was dozing again, dreaming of Betty Nolan's slender figure floundering in a sinkhole, when someone prodded him. Trubman's lobster eyes augured him in the darkness, his face unnaturally pale and shiny with sweat. 'I've picked up wireless chatter nearby, skipper,' he said, voice quavering.

'Ours or theirs?' Caine asked.

'Ours. Big tank leaguer, about ten miles away I'd reckon. Happen it's a whole division.'

'All right, Taff, thanks. What's up with you, anyhow?'

'I reckon it's sandfly fever. Got bitten a few times at Kabrit.'

'Wake Maurice. He's got dope.'

When Caine opened his eyes again, dawn was stealing blandly over the dunes. An ochre fireglow nuzzled the desert's eastern rim, but there was no warmth in the air. Caine ramped a dune to get the circulation going: the knifewound in his arm throbbed: the sand grains were sharp icicles through his chapplies' open sides. From the top he saw an ocean of dunes in replicated patterns, the exact same shade and shape as the sandviper's scales, like an unimaginably vast serpent with its coils wrapped around the world. There was something voluptuously feminine about it too: the way the sandmounts lay, undulant and gently curved like the recumbent bodies of nude women. That brought him back to Nolan, and a vacant feeling in his guts that made him, even now, want to rush back to Cairo to find her. He pinched his sutured wound until it hurt, driving her image from his head. *Sandhog* was what counted. Fail to knock out the chemical weapons in the Citadel, and *Lightfoot* might founder. Nolan was beyond his help, and there was no turning back now.

Shufti-ing the sandsea with his glasses, he saw that the dunes petered out to the west, giving way to a plain of cool pumice, razored down to the bone by aeons of blown sand. The plain was jumbled with scoria, cut by the bleached ribs of ridges, rock faults like the vertebrae of dinosaurs whose flesh had been flayed off by the lashing of wind and rain. Here and there volcanic plugs and stone chimneys pierced the surface like warped monuments or the squinted minarets of ancient mosques. There was a hint of scalloped mauve hills on the skyline, but Caine couldn't tell if it was an illusion: the horizon in that direction was hazy and indistinct. There was a faint potash smell in the air, and he recalled the occluded stars of the previous night: he was sure a *ghibli* would hit them sometime that day.

The wagons emerged from the sandsea an hour later, following the pointing fingers of their own elongated shadows down to a valley floor that was now hammered cobalt blue, along the steepest slipslope they'd yet encountered. Halfway down, *Glenda* careened into a deep sandtrap that the others had somehow missed: she nosedived forward with an ominous splintering of metal, so hard that Netanya and Pickney were hurled against the aeroscreens and Trubman almost tumbled off the roof. The truck stalled. When Netanya tried to start her up, something deep in her innards whined and clanked like a fractured mangle. Dumper hoved up bowlegged to look. 'I keeps tellin' yer, me old china,' he admonished Netanya, brandishing his maimed hand like a warning signal. 'When you hits mishmish, you gotta change straight from high to low gear in one move. Ain't yer got it yet?'

It took a few minutes for Dumper to scoop enough cold sand from under *Glenda*'s body to discover that her camshaft was broken. 'That's a poser, boss,' he told Caine, 'because we ain't got no spare, and to repair it we'd need weldin' gear, which we ain't got, neiver.'

'We'll have to dump her,' Copeland said.

Caine considered it. He was tempted, but remembered again that *Glenda* was hefting their rations and most of their jerrycans of water: in this desert, water was the one item he didn't want to be without. He remembered Trubman's night-time call about an armoured division in close proximity. Ten miles, Taff had said: they could tow *Glenda* that far. A division was bound to have an ordnance workshop: he weighed up the wasted time against the water, and born of long parched years up the Blue, plumped for the water.

He called Trubman. The signaller's softball face had a green pallor to it, his eyeballs veined with red, but he told Caine the fever had receded. 'Where do you reckon that division is?' Caine asked him.

Trubman blinked and pointed across the plain to the south. Caine looked again across the ribbed brown and grey pumice, acres of slag, tiers of sawtooth escarpments with great buttress skulls looming out of them like polished bone masks, dumps of scree, crooked spires and steeples gristled with a dark patina like cracked rawhide. Dust devils sucked across the flats down there, like constantly meandering drilling spikes, but somewhere, beyond the gleaming alkali lakes and the maze of sculpted stone, Caine thought he saw a wisp of firesmoke snaking above a distant ridge, like the emanation from a single cooking fire; just for an instant, quickly dispersed by the wind. His gaze was drawn towards it: he lifted his glasses, swept the area back and forth – and gasped.

There, stationary on the plain, a good ten miles off, he thought he saw a vast leaguer of vehicles. He lowered the glasses, wiped grit out of his eyes and focused them again. Years up the Blue had taught him that the human mind could produce almost anything in this desert – vast, iridescent cities, gushing rivers, the pure crystal waters of inland seas. He'd grown accustomed to living in the mirage – the sheer dreamlike *strangeness* of the landscape never ceased to give him a frisson. Yet he'd have staked his life that this vision was real.

The leaguer lay on the desert floor without any attempt at camouflage, rank upon rank of vehicles: tanks, armoured cars, Bren-gun carriers, artillery limbers, gun batteries, forward transport echelons, supply wagons, field workshops, field hospitals, signals detachments, mechanized infantry, armoured units in troops, squadrons, regiments, brigades, stretching on and on and on into the gauzy distance, like a vast collection of Dinky toys out of a child's fantasy. He lowered the glasses, and he noticed that Audley, at his elbow, had spotted it too. 'It *is* real, isn't it?' the subaltern asked.

'Yeah, it's real all right.'

'Crikey,' Audley said, his voice low and slightly awed. 'It must be 10th Armoured, Bob Gatehouse's mob. I thought he was up north – what the devil is he doing here?'

Caine took another shufti: the vision oscillated, now seen with clarity, now losing sharpness with the ebb and flux of light. It was difficult to focus for more than a few moments at a time.

On his other side, Copeland was crouching down, peeping through his telescopic sights, as if assessing a snipe. 'It's wide open, though,' he said. 'Why aren't they scrimmed up?'

'May be preparing to move,' Audley suggested.

Caine grunted, but thought it didn't make sense. If the division was about to move, they'd already have armoured car troops out as forward vedettes: engines would be churning, tanks would be manoeuvring, kicking up a nebula of dust. It was hard to be certain from so far away, but there didn't appear to be the slightest movement among the massed ranks.

He took a last look, lowered the glasses. 'It's there, anyway,' he said. 'If they can't help us, no one can.'

Copeland stood up, slinging his rifle. 'I'm not sure about this, skipper,' he said. 'If we make contact with them, *Sandhog*'s going to be compromised. They're bound to report us to HQ, and that signal could be intercepted by the Hun.'

'The sergeant's right,' Audley nodded, also lowering his binos. 'We can't afford to have our presence known.'

Caine weighed it up a second time. 'The Hun already know we're here,' he said. 'They just don't know where we're going, and we're not going to tell anyone, are we?'

They dragged *Glenda* out of the mishmish with hi-lifts and sandchannels. They yoked her to *Veronica* with a tow rope and hauled her down off the dunes on to the gunmetalled valley floor. For two hours they moved across the thirsty plain, the wagons chafing dry on the sunracked surface, rumbling through sloughs of chalkdust so fine it turned the men once more to ghosts and set their teeth on edge. The wagons wound around flat shelves of rimrock, past boulders that had fallen from above and shattered: they wove in and out of canyons where sand had dredged itself into low drifts, where the wind stopped, where the heat hung in heavy wraps in the clints and crevices, emerged again to traverse playas that shimmered like a billion shards of splintered mirrors, to watch the distant ridges rippled in the heat like folds of blown silk. By midmorning the maze was behind them and they were drumming across open serir where the desert surface had warmed and the heat haze melted into mercury lakes and sparkling streams that seemed to encroach nearer and nearer, until the wagons were ploughing ruts along a sandbar, surrounded on every side by a bejewelled and glittering sea.

They breasted a gravel bank, and there it was in front of them: the whole vast divisional leaguer, like a great high-seas fleet at anchor, flotilla after flotilla, echelon after echelon, squadron after squadron, filling miles of desert, as far as the eye could see. The closest vehicles, a squadron of tanks, were only five hundred yards from them. Caine surveyed the massed lines, trying to take in their true extent: hundreds, perhaps thousands, of vehicles of every size and shape, leaguered up in precise logistical order. Except . . . except, Caine thought, as his jeep bumped nearer, that there *was* something fishily unreal about it – the lack of scrim, the fact that it hadn't stirred in two hours, the rigidity of the ranks, the apparent lack of tents, of cookfires, of swearing, sweating Tommies. It felt almost as if it were a ghost division, a wagon graveyard, a mothball fleet dumped in the desert in a precise configuration and then abandoned. Yet not abandoned entirely, because there *were* soldiers about – here and there amongst the serried lines, Caine glimpsed the occasional moving figure in KDs.

'Recognition signal, skipper,' Copeland reminded him.

Caine picked up the big Very pistol, shoved a green flare into the breech and snapped it closed. He was about to fire when he clocked movement in front of him, heard the rumble of motors. The tank detachment nearest to the convoy had suddenly come alive: half a dozen ironclads were already wheeling from a broadside leaguer configuration, pointing their prows directly towards the intruders, kicking up curlicues of dust.

Caine squinted at them, recognizing the hunched, hard-shouldered lines of Mark III Crusaders, six-pounder gunbarrels bristling on their turrets. The tanks lumbered slowly forward trailing dustspouts, their engines, to Caine's desert-tuned ears, sounding feeble and underpowered. It was slightly over the top, anyway, he thought, sending six light tanks to investigate a brace of Willys Bantams and a couple of desert-scarred Bedfords, one of them crippled. These buggers weren't taking any chances, he thought.

He raised the Very pistol, squeezed the trigger, heard the pop, saw the splash of green. He watched the tanks for two seconds, but there was no answering flare. Instead there came a sudden sharp salvo of ordnance, a crisp *bump*, *bump*, *bump*, *BUMP* of shellfire. Caine and his crew ducked, but Caine smelled no burning-glass odour, heard no familiar croak of shells poaching air, no eardrum crease of bursting shrapnel. '*Bastards*,' Wallace roared, shaking a boulder fist at them. 'Didn't you see the bleedin' Very light?'

As if in reply, the Crusaders reamed off a second volley. Caine heard the crack of ordnance, and this time felt the air tremor, sniffed cordite, glimpsed wedges of blue smoke lufting like parachute canopies over the gunbarrels before being whipped apart by the wind. Yet still the shots had a muted sound to them, as though the gunners were using wrong-calibre shells. '*Stop, stop!*' Caine bawled at Copeland. 'They think we're enemy. Hands up, quick.'

The wagons slewed through folds of talc, skewed to a

halt. Caine snapped back his goggles, stood up, raised his hands slowly. He watched the Crusaders trundling towards him like gigantic sheepticks, wondering if *they* could be the enemy. Was this whole thing a setup designed to draw in unsuspecting Allied units, like sirens' singing, and then butcher them when they came in range? He thought of Trubman's night-time message: *a big net of friendly signals traffic Ours. Big tank leaguer, about ten miles away I'd reckon. Happen it's a whole division.* There was surely no way the Axis could fake that.

The tanks were spreading out in ten-pace intervals, smoke and dust clinging to them like dirty cloaks. Again, it struck Caine that something was wrong: he couldn't yet put his finger on it, but he was sure there was an anomaly here. Maybe it was the ungainly way the tanks moved, drawing light, almost slouching, lacking the gravitas you usually felt when you sighted tanks; maybe it was the tinny bleat of their motors, the absence of the rampant clunk of steel tread that always sowed dread in Caine's heart. And what about the ordnance – six-pounders were big shells, after all? Surely they couldn't be firing blanks? He suppressed a sudden urge to snigger.

The Crusaders teetered to a halt in a rough crescent, and Caine saw men scrabbling out – men in khaki drill shorts and black berets carrying Lee-Enfield rifles trimmed with hessian. The Tommies didn't rush them in an untactical clump but advanced steadily in cautious arrowhead, five yards apart, eyes wary, weapons at the shoulder. They looked more like well-drilled footsloggers than tank crews.

Caine slipped out of his seat with his hands still up, his face chalkpowdered and ethereal from the fine dust of the plain, his eyes standing out in the centre of goggle rings like inkblack holes. He watched the Tommies approaching. At point of the arrowhead, there walked a man with captain's pips on his KD epaulettes – a big man with swimmer's shoulders, horsefaced, blubberlipped, clip-moustachioed. His teeth were like shovels; there was a hint of conceit in his eyes and a touch of self-satisfaction in the set of his long jaw. Even going tactical, he had a way of walking, of rolling his shoulders with a slight peacock strut, that Caine thought he would have recognized almost anywhere.

Roger Glenn, ex-King's Royal Rifle Corps, had been a troop officer in the Middle East Commando when Caine had been an NCO there. Caine hadn't really known him well, had heartily disliked what he did know: now, though, he was happy enough to see a familiar face. 'How come you didn't answer my recognition signal, sir?' he demanded, grinning – a red slash on a clown's whiteface. 'Or were those salvoes a salute to old pals?'

Glenn halted a couple of yards from Caine and peered at him. Caine saw that he wore a bush shirt, shorts, suede boots, and a black beret with Royal Tank Regiment badge. He was holding a big Colt automatic attached to a regulation lanyard round his neck, and it was pointing at Caine. He didn't return Caine's banter, nor make any move to shake hands. Neither did he let his weapon drop. He looked over Caine's shoulder at the desert-grimed vehicles and the ragged, dust-blanched crew with an air of supercilious authority, as if he'd spotted some misdemeanour. Caine was unpleasantly reminded of Sears-Beach. The tankies took up positions around the SAS column, and Caine glanced at them: beetred faces and beetle eyes, sandfly-bitten torsos, limbs chapped with desert sores. They had no welcome, no cheery hailfellow for comrades: they still had their weapons trained on the SAS. Caine wondered why, as tank crews, they'd been issued with .303s rather than SMGs or pistols. The Lee-Enfield was notoriously awkward to handle in the confines of a tank.

'Sarn't Caine,' the captain said slowly, in a voice as clipped as his moustache. It was a flat statement rather than a greeting. 'What are you doing here?'

Caine let his arms drop without being told: his men did the same. 'Good to see you, too, sir,' he replied, 'and it's *Lieutenant* Caine now, by the way.'

'Really?' Glenn raised an eyebrow – an action more like a regimental drill movement than an expression of surprise. 'I'm a bit out of touch, old chap.' He squinted frogeyed at Copeland and Wallace but made no effort to greet them. 'Same old crew, I see,' he said.

Caine focused on the RTR badge directly above Glenn's left eye. 'Never had you down as a tankie, sir,' he said. 'Always thought you were a greenjacket through and through.'

Glenn snorted. 'I'm no more a tankie than you are,' he said, curling back dry lips to show the slablike teeth. He peered at the SAS wagons again, and Caine guessed he was looking for insignia. 'Still on special service?'

When Caine didn't reply, Glenn continued. 'Ditto. They *call* us 103rd Royal Tank Regiment, of course.' He let out a hollow horselaugh. 'But it's a special service stunt all the same.'

Caine blinked, confused, then took another shufti at the Crusader tanks parked in formation two hundred paces away. Glenn caught the glance and chuckled. 'Taken in, were you? Good show.'

It fell into place with an almost audible *shuck* – the shaky progress of those Crusaders, the underbred sound of their motors, the eery absence of clank, the flat effect of their guns, the lack of whistle and thump. He stared back at Glenn, his eyes wide inside their circles. 'They're *dummies*,' he said. 'It's a *decoy* unit.'

'*Bingo*,' Glenn guffawed, baring his big teeth at Caine as if he'd just come up with the answer to an immensely hard riddle. '"*C'est un illusion*," as my boss would say. There ain't no such outfit as 103rd Tanks – in fact, there isn't a single real tankie among my boys here. Sleight of hand deceives the eye, what, old chap? Good, though, aren't they? Come and have a gander.'

Now the secret was out, Glenn seemed to relax. He holstered his pistol and waved a wide hand at a beefy soldier nearby. 'All right, Sarn't Ferguson. Let 'em pass.'

He turned to Caine. 'I'll hop in with you,' he said. 'Tell your lot to follow on.'

From a hundred yards, at last, it was easy to see that the 'Crusaders' weren't the real thing. The giveaway was the rims of four rubber tyres protruding from beneath plywood frames cut in the shape of 'tank tracks'. Standing close up, Caine saw that the decoys had been designed with great care. 'Fifteen-hundredweight Morris chassis,' Glenn told him, slapping the wooden body affectionately with a wide hand. 'Tubular frame with plywood and canvas. Gun barrel's industrial piping, of course. Look absolutely authentic to shuftikites at two thousand feet.'

Caine was stunned. 'What about the tracks, though?' he

asked. 'I mean, aren't rubber-tyre marks a bit obvious from the air?'

Glenn led him around to the rear of the dummy, showed him flailchains attached to a wooden arm that could be lifted and lowered by hand. 'We drag these along to make dust and disguise our tracks,' he said. 'Not like having real tank tracks, of course, but if we need something more distinct – a false trail, say – we've got a special wagon for it. If we're lucky, we can borrow a genuine tank.'

Caine thought of the feeble salvo of shellfire. 'You fire blanks?' he asked.

Glenn snorted again. 'Not out of industrial piping, old chap. No, no, no.' He delved into his haversack and came up with an ordinary No. 36 grenade. 'Good old Mr Mills,' he tittered. 'Chuck a few of these and Bob's your auntie.'

'But why . . . ?' Caine was going to ask why an armoured division would deploy fifteen-hundredweight trucks with pipes for guns and grenades for sixpound shells, when the incredible answer hit him like a knuckleduster. 'The entire *division* . . . ?' he whispered, aghast. 'You mean the *whole* leaguer is . . .'

Glenn watched the penny drop with an expression that was a hair's breadth off gloating. 'Dummy? 'Course it is, old chap. Didn't strike you as a bit curious that the wagons weren't scrimmed and never shifted once since you spotted us? Yes, of course, we clocked you up on the dunes. Most of the tanks and AFVs are rubber inflatables, but the lorries are canvas and chickenwire. Welcome to Maskelyne's Travelling Circus.'

'Who's Maskelyne?'

'My boss. Jasper Maskelyne. Don't tell me you've never

heard of the Great Maskelyne, old chap? The world's greatest illusionist? He's one of those music-hall magicians who saw corking bints in half then stick them together again.'

Caine shook his head, mystified. 'And he's here? In the desert?'

'A major in the Sappers, no less. He's the one behind all this.'

There was a short pause while the two men weighed each other up. Caine was awed by the scale of the deception; he was happy to be back in the company of comrades, but the feeling was marred by a memory of Roger Glenn from commando days. The captain had been on the directing staff during Caine's training in the Middle East Commando – one of those sadistic officers who'd taken pleasure in shooting as close as possible to the recruits during live firing attacks. Caine's mate Brian Smith had been shot dead in such an exercise: Glenn was suspected of negligence, but SID had never brought a case.

The hiatus was broken by Audley, sidling up to inspect the dummy. He tried to work his filmstar features on Glenn, who acknowledged the smart Guardee salute with only a nod. 'I say,' Audley commented, 'you had us going for a minute there, sir. Thought we were under fire, what?'

Glenn sized Audley up as if he were something dredged out of a sewer. He didn't deign to reply.

'I don't suppose this Major Maskelyne could magic up a new camshaft, could he?' Caine asked.

Glenn took a long look at him, and Caine thought he saw a momentary slyness in his eyes. 'I don't know,' he said pensively. 'We can't give you a spare, but we might be able to repair the one you've got. Let's go to HQ echelon. I'll have to have a word with the boss.'

The HQ leaguer lay in a depression only half a mile further on, through the ranks of dummy Crusaders. As the SAS convoy wheeled in, Caine saw a command marquee, a fuel dump, water bowsers, a dogsleg of troop tents, a mess awning attached to a cookhouse wagon where a trio of greasy cooks was peeling spuds. Nearby were the blackened remnants of an open fire – perhaps the origin of the smoke he'd spotted that morning. There was an M/T park of vehicular oddments: a Mammoth gunlimber, a tractor, a bulldozer, a small crane, a brace of motorbikes, a clutch of down-at-heel pickups. Further on were a couple of mobile workshops under canvas tops – a carpenters' shop, where squaddies hammered and sawed on benches, and a mechanics' shop, where Caine spotted the blue glimmer of a welding torch. Nearby was a troop of hardtop lorries bristling with signals antennae, dipole Windam aerials strung up between them like washing lines.

Glenn had them halt outside the command marquee, told Caine to wait, and vanished through the flap. Caine slipped out of the jeep, lit a cigarette and gazed round at the camp, taking in the relaxed atmosphere. A few Tommies in shorts, fingers wrapped against desert sores, trawled about carrying clipboards and tools, snuffling and spitting in the heat but taking no notice of the newcomers. Many carried holstered pistols, a few had Lee-Enfields, but some weren't armed at all. There were no sentries, no air defences, no ackack guns – the tents weren't even sandbagged – and no sign of heavy weapons apart from the dummy tanks, AFVs and field artillery scattered across the desert like giant chessmen. Security here was lax and, it seemed, entirely in the hands of Glenn's ersatz tank crews.

A moment later, Glenn called Caine and Audley into the tent, with the stiff admonition that his men were not to wander about. Caine told Copeland to keep his eyes open and pushed through the flap with Audley behind him. Inside, amid a clutter of tables, camp-chairs, books, maps and artist's pads, stood a slouch-shouldered stringbean of a man whose skin seemed stretched taut over a balding, narrow skull. He had a sharp silver non-regulation goatee, a pointed nose and watchful dark eyes under eyebrows like tangles of fusewire. He wore a green civilian shirt with major's crowns stitched on the shoulders and loosefitting trousers of what looked like purple velvet. He carried no weapon, wore no headgear. He was probably the oddest officer Caine had ever seen, and he'd seen some beauties.

'This is Major Jasper Maskelyne,' Glenn announced dryly. 'Our CO.'

The man bowed. 'At your service,' he said, in a voice that was soft yet incisive. He answered Caine's salute with a limp motion of the right hand, opening long, slender fingers to reveal a gold coin. 'Have a sovereign,' he said, holding it out. Caine hesitated. 'Too late,' Maskelyne said. He closed his hand, made a pass and opened it almost at once: the coin was gone. He opened his left hand and Caine clocked the sovereign lying there. Maskelyne shut both hands and presented them as fists. 'Which one is it in?' he demanded, his eyes slitted, comically snakelike. He opened both hands and the sovereign was in neither. 'Or perhaps,' Maskelyne said, reaching out snakelike fingers to tickle Caine's ear, 'it's here.' The major withdrew his open hand and Caine saw the coin revealed.

Maskelyne held it out, his skullhead nodding springlike, as if expecting applause. Caine grinned, Audley clapped uncomfortably. Maskelyne bowed again. 'Currently appearing in the Western Desert,' he intoned, 'by courtesy of His Britannic Majesty's Corps of Royal Engineers.'

He pointed to camp-chairs and the two subalterns sat down: Caine noticed that Glenn had disappeared. '*Illusion*,' Maskelyne declared, sticking a fat, unlit cigar into his mouth and taking it out again, 'is one of the cardinal principles of war. Now the coin is here, now there, now it has vanished entirely. Convince the enemy you are in one place, appear somewhere completely different for a moment, then fade away. A transport column moves south in the dead of night: next morning a whole armoured division has sprouted out of the desert. A few days later, it has vanished without trace. The whole future of Monty's campaign depends on convincing the Axis we are going to strike in one direction when in fact we are going to strike in another. Can you imagine how difficult that is to achieve in the desert, where no concealment is possible?' He waved the cigar, his springloaded head nodding. Caine watched the cigar with fascination, half convinced he was going to magic it away. 'I tell you, lads, what we are pulling off here is no less than the greatest conjuring trick in history.'

He stuck the cigar back in his mouth with a sort of finality, struck a Swan Vesta, inhaled smoke, blew it out. 'Now,' he said, removing the cigar from his mouth, 'I understand you need help with a broken camshaft?'

'Yes, sir,' Caine said. 'I –'

Maskelyne spread his tentacular fingers, cutting him off. 'We can help,' he said, his black eyes fixed on Caine, 'but it will take time. We don't have a welder here, you see, and it will take a couple of hours to get one over. I think you must resign yourselves to bivvying here for the night.'

Caine was about to say that he'd seen a welding torch outside but swallowed his words raw. He didn't quite like Maskelyne, or the way this was panning out.

'So . . . Lieutenant . . . is it?'

'Yes, sir. Lieutenant Caine.'

'What are you doing here, Lieutenant Caine? Apart from breaking camshafts, that is?'

Caine met his eyes. 'That's classified, sir. Special service mission.'

Maskelyne puffed cigar smoke, his skeletal head bobbing gravely on its spring. 'I see, I see. Behind enemy lines, no doubt?'

Caine said nothing. Maskelyne's beetle eyes lingered on the dirty field dressing wrapped round his arm. 'You've already had a contact with the enemy?' he asked. Caine and Audley exchanged a glance. 'Ran into a Kraut patrol,' Audley said before Caine could stop him. 'Shot down a CR42, too.'

Maskelyne swatted cigar smoke with his delicate hand. 'Ah, I see, I see. Nasty. And how did you locate our little circus here?'

'Wireless chatter,' Caine said.

The major smiled, thinlipped. 'Ah,' he said again. 'That's the *real* secret of the illusion. Signallers working round the clock, transmitting bogus messages at every level – tank commanders to troop, troop to squadron, squadron to regiment, regiment to division, division to base. The enemy's "Y" Service monitors the lot – Axis command has a whole armoured div. pictured in its imagination before they've spotted a single tank. The plywood and chicken-wire vehicles are the props that complete the act – the true deception is what goes out over the airwaves. That's the *key*, you see, lads – shuftikites confirm what Axis command already *knows* is there. Only of course, it isn't: like everything else, it is a mirage – it exists only in the mind.'

'Like everything else?' Caine repeated, mystified. 'What do you mean by that?'

'You don't suppose that your mission, whatever it is, is *real*, do you? Of course it isn't. All missions are part of the great shadow-play – a dream, a vision, a hall of mirrors reflecting each other to infinity. The war that you believe is being fought out on the plains of the Sahara is actually being fought out inside your own head.'

Caine nodded, confused. For all he'd understood, the major might as well have been talking Mandarin. He was ready to acknowledge the genius of this decoy plan: what concerned him was his own position. He opened his mouth to speak, but once again Maskelyne cut in over him.

'Did you know,' he demanded, 'that I moved the harbour at Alex?' He nodded, cackling. 'Yes, I did. Pure illusion. Left the real harbour in darkness, gave the impression it was somewhere else by the clever use of light and sound. Enemy bombed empty desert and a few gas lamps and were convinced they'd destroyed it. I'd like to have seen Rommel's mush when he realized it was still there.' He chortled again. 'Ah, sometimes my cleverness astonishes me.'

He shot a probing glance at Caine then grabbed a bottle of Johnny Walker Red Label whisky and slammed it down on the nearest table. 'Have a drink with me,' he said, spearing some tin mugs with his slim fingers. 'Let's celebrate.'

Audley was about to nod when Caine shook his head. 'No thank you, sir.' He stood up suddenly. 'I think we'll need to be pushing off.'

Maskelyne paused in the act of unscrewing the bottle. He put it down carefully, pulled the cigar from his mouth, turned to face Caine. His features looked different – no smiles, no cackles – the magician's mask was gone. 'What about your damaged lorry?' he demanded icily. 'Wasn't that what you came for?'

Caine held the major's insect stare. 'We'll have to leave her with you. No time to wait.' He nodded at Audley. 'Come on. We have to go.'

Audley didn't move: there was a second's cold silence.

'I don't think so, Lieutenant Caine,' Maskelyne said slowly. 'Oh no, I don't think that's going to be possible at all. Now you've seen through my little trick – seen backstage, so to speak – there's no question of your continuing with your mission. What if you were captured, and revealed it to the enemy?'

His eyes were snakelike slits again, but there was nothing remotely comical about his expression now. 'You may already have compromised us merely by coming here. You've fought an engagement: what if a Hun ground patrol followed your tracks? The game would be up, you see.'

He shook his numbskull head, dropped the rest of the cigar, stamped it out in the sand underfoot. Caine dekkoed

Audley: he was still sitting, staring at Maskelyne as if rooted to his chair. He hadn't jumped at Caine's order, and Caine doubted he could trust him when it came to the crunch.

'Look, sir,' he said, making an effort to keep his voice reasonable. 'We're a special service unit on a secret operation vital to the Eighth Army's advance. Our mission comes directly from General Montgomery, and he won't thank you for preventing us carrying it out, I can tell you that.'

The magician sucked his teeth and waggled his head. 'Sorry,' he said dismissively. 'What we're doing takes priority. We've already notified GHQ about you. A squad of Military Police is on its way by plane to take you into custody, even as we speak.'

It was the mention of Military Police and the word 'custody' that pressed Caine's button. Moving like wildfire, he whipped out his Browning, seized the major's spidery arm and twisted it viciously up behind his back. Maskelyne yelled and struggled. Caine felt wiry cable muscles tensing under his grip and realized that the major was stronger than he looked. He flexed his own iron biceps, reinforcing his grip until it was vicelike, and stuck the muzzle of the automatic hard into the cleft beneath the magician's ear. 'You aren't going to make *this* disappear, Major,' he growled. 'This is a genuine Browning .45-calibre automatic. It is *not* an illusion, I can assure you of that.'

Maskelyne stopped fighting, but his thin lips curled into a sneer. 'You'll be court-martialled for this, Caine.'

Caine jagged the pistol's muzzle so hard into the major's flesh that his head was pushed sideways. 'It won't be the first time,' he said. 'And if you think I'm bluffing, I suggest you think again. I intend to carry out my mission even if I have to take out every man in this camp.'

Audley was on his feet, face drained of colour, hands trembling. 'Look here, Caine,' he stammered, eyes popping. 'You can't . . .'

'Go and get Copeland. *Now.*'

'But look here, old boy . . .'

'Go and get Cope. Or I snuff this cocksucker right here, and it'll be on your head.'

Audley shot a hunted look at Maskelyne, who caught it. 'Don't do it,' he croaked. 'You'll both be for the firing squad.'

'Shut up,' Caine swore, yanking the arm up until he sensed it was at breaking point. Maskelyne shrieked. Caine fixed his gaze on Audley, his face livid. 'Get Cope, or I swear he's a dead man.'

Audley dithered, shifting his weight from one foot to the other, his eyes veering from Maskelyne to Caine and back. Caine cocked the Browning's hammer with a click that sounded as loud as a cymbal clash. Audley scuttled out. Caine knew it was on the cards that he'd come back with Glenn, but a moment later Harry Copeland was wading heronlegged through the flap, his SMLE in his hands. His eyes widened when he saw Caine and Maskelyne. 'What the heck . . .'

'Major Maskelyne is coming with us.'

For a split second, Copeland's resolution flickered, and Caine guessed his mate was seeing yet another addition to Caine's long history of impulsive eccentricities, and all future prospects of promotion – even a possible commission – going down the toilet. Then the shadow was gone, and Caine knew Cope was with him a hundred per cent. 'Is anyone else around?' he asked, keeping the pistol lodged in place.

'Nobody. They took *Glenda* to the workshop though – Dumper's there, with Glenn.'

'All right, Harry. Go back out, get the lads into the wagons, start motors, all machine-guns cocked and ready. Find those cuffs we used on the Kraut. I'm going to bring the major out and I want him cuffed in *Doris* while I go and get Dumper.'

'Right you are, skipper.'

'You're going to cuff me?' Maskelyne sneered incredulously. 'I warn you: I've escaped from chained boxes under water, and from half the jails in England.'

'Shut up,' Caine snapped.

He heard motors gunned. He hustled Maskelyne out of the tent in a single headlong rush and a second later was handing him over to Wallace and Copeland in *Doris*. Cope slapped the cuffs on one of his wrists, wrapped them round the mount of the forward Browning and locked them on the other wrist. 'Watch him,' Caine hissed. 'He's tricky.'

He looked around to check that his men were ready, saw Audley at the wheel of *Dorothy*, white as a sheet, and the cowboy leering at him goggle-eyed from the cab of *Veronica*. He wondered if anyone in the camp had clocked the abduction of their CO: the tents and workshops were widely scattered and the few Tommies about seemed too intent on their own business to notice anything amiss. He saw the dark bulk of *Glenda* parked near the workshop where he'd spotted the welding torch earlier, a hundred paces away. 'I'm going to get Sam,' he told Cope. 'If I'm not back in fifteen minutes, go.'

He sprinted towards the workshop, covering the ground in seconds. It was clear that no one was working on the 3-tonner. Three of the sham tankies were mooching in the shade, rifles slung, watching Glenn and Dumper, who seemed to be engaged in a dingdong. The athletic, broad-shouldered officer soared over the little corporal: Dumper was standing his ground, though, hands on hips. Caine shoved his pistol back into its quickdraw holster, strode up to them, catching his breath. Dumper clocked him as he approached, turned towards him, indignation etched on his face. 'Skipper,' he said in an aggrieved tone, 'there's welding gear 'ere, but the captain won't let me use it. Sez we've got to wait for their own welder, and that's gonna take for ever. Seems to fink I'm a cretin. Can yer tell 'im I'm an ordnance mechanical engineer class one?'

Glenn's horse features registered Caine's presence: his eyes narrowed warily. He cracked a false smile. 'We have our rules, old chap,' he said.

Caine stopped about five yards short. 'I've got Maskelyne,' he said.

Dumper looked mystified, Glenn shocked. 'What do you –' he began.

'I'm taking him with me,' Caine cut him off. 'Sam, get back to the wagons. We're going.'

'Hold it,' Glenn barked. 'You're not going anywhere.'

Dumper hovered, looking from Glenn to Caine. 'What about *Glenda*, skipper?' he asked. 'She ain't been fixed yet.'

'She'll never be fixed, and these blokes have no intention of helping us. It was a trap. Leave her. Go back to the wagons.'

'Stay where you are, Corporal,' Glenn spat, looking at

Caine. 'You'll never get away, you know. I'll catch up with you and blast you off the face of the earth.'

Caine made a face, snorted in a passable imitation of Glenn's manner. 'With *industrial piping*, old chap? In those chickenwire jalopies? I don't think so. *No, no, no.*'

Caine saw Glenn grab for the pistol in his holster: his Browning was out before the captain even got the flap open. He saw Glenn's eyes go wide, heard the blubber lips mouthing, 'You're not going to shoot an –', and shot him through the kneecap. The joint shattered with an audible crack of bones and a pop of ligaments, as if it had been bludgeoned with a mace. Caine clocked the splatter of gore, the detonation of ripped tissue and bone shavings, the flaps of skin flayed away from ragged joint ends. Glenn rolled on the ground clutching maniacally at his knee, eyeballs bursting with shock, shrieking like a harpy. 'You *bastard*. You *bastard*. I'll *kill* you. I'll *kill* you.'

Caine was already levelling his weapon at the three enlisted men, none of whom had managed to unsling his rifle. They stared at Glenn's madly jerking, ranting figure, then back into Caine's eyes, steady as paired shotgun bores. None of them made a move. 'I've got your CO,' he told them. 'Anyone takes a potshot at me or mine – just one – the major's dead meat.'

He nodded at Dumper: the little corporal's face was blanchwhite, but Caine was proud to note that he'd drawn his own pistol and was covering the squaddies loyally.

'I'll *get* you,' Glenn screeched, sobbing. 'I'll *have* you, you *bastard*.'

Caine and Dumper backed away, covering their arcs. 'Maybe you will,' Caine said. 'Meanwhile, you can regard that as payback for Brian Smith, who, by the way, had a wife and children. Think yourself lucky. At least I only shot you in the knee.'

The two of them jogged back to the wagons. No one opened up on them, but the gunshot had aroused the camp: Tommies were already milling around the convoy with weapons in their hands, among them the beefy, red-faced Sergeant Ferguson. When they got back to *Doris*, Caine saw that Wallace had the twin Vickers trained on the crowd, keeping them at a distance: Cope had his pistol to Maskelyne's head. Caine swung into the seat next to the magician while Dumper hopped into the back. Caine dug his automatic into Maskelyne's neck, leaving Copeland free to drive. 'We're leaving,' Caine bawled, staring straight at Ferguson. 'Anyone shoots at us, the Great Maskelyne becomes the *late* Great Maskelyne.'

'You won't make it,' the bulky Ferguson bawled back, his face almost scarlet with fury, chubby fingers itching on his rifle stock. 'We'll be after you.'

Caine smiled. 'These Vickers "K"s are effective up to a thousand yards,' he said. 'Get any nearer than that, and it's open season: if you don't believe I'm ready to do you, have a dekko at the state of Captain Glenn.'

Cope hit the throttle: the convoy lurched forward, combing dust. The gunners swung their weapons, covering all angles, threatening anyone who moved. In less than a minute they had scooted out of the dummy tank leaguer and were grinding across the gravel floor, heading north-west.

They'd made a little over a thousand yards before Wallace reported a convoy following them – a handful of the decoy Crusaders and battered pickups from the M/T pool. 'Just keep your guns on them,' Caine told him. 'If they get too close, put down tracer.'

The jeep coursed on: Caine holstered his pistol and grinned apologetically at Maskelyne. 'I'm sorry about this, Major,' he shouted in the magician's ear, 'I really am. I couldn't have you stopping my mission, though. It might be an illusion to you, but to a poor ignorant soul like me, it happens to be important.'

Maskelyne sneered at him sour-faced, his skullhead nodding madly. 'You're a bloody idiot, Caine. You won't even last till sunset. My signallers will already have called up air support: they'll hound you wherever you go, even behind Axis lines. They'll bomb this convoy to a crisp.'

'They'd better hurry up then,' Caine bawled, nodding towards the western skyline. Maskelyne turned and for the first time noticed the darkness gathering there – a writhing fold of grey, red and black creeping across the horizon in a tidal wave, groping tentacles of dust smoke playing across it, diapers of heat haze spangling and flaring in the sunlight, like the scales of monstrous fish. '*Ghibli*,' Caine yelled. 'Big one. Been on the way since last night. It'll be here in half an hour. No one's going to be tracking us through that.'

Maskelyne stared at the encroaching dustwall, looking crestfallen.

'It's all right, Major,' Caine roared. 'I wouldn't dream of depriving the GOC of a man of your calibre.'

Checking that their pursuers were still well behind, he ordered the convoy to stop. He unlocked the magician's cuffs, heaved him out into the desert. Maskelyne stood there, head wagging, a frail, bent figure in his civilian shirt and trousers. 'Your men will get here before the *ghibli*,' Caine told him. 'I'm going to drop a waterbottle and a Very pistol with some flares a hundred feet from here, just in case they don't see you right away. Couldn't let any harm come to you – I'm an old Sapper myself.'

Caine gave him a peremptory salute, and before Maskelyne could answer, Copeland worked the throttle. The jeep skeetered away. Caine dropped the water and flarekit where the major could see them and the small convoy sheered off towards the blackest of sunsets: within thirty minutes the darkout around them was complete.

21

They drove through the storm the whole night, popping Bennies, cowled and goggled against the whiplashing dust. Caine had never been in a storm at sea but guessed that it must be like this – the sense of helplessness, like a straw tossed and ravaged by forces of unfathomable power. The desert had come alive, quivering, explosive, like a giant that had just broken free from the shackles of aeons; the cat-o'nine-tails wind thrashed the raw tissue of their minds, lacerating their thoughts, carrying in its shriek the hysterical voices of banshees, the babbling of demented hellions sniggering and cackling in their ears, mocking them, maddening them with taunts that seemed to cut like razors into their innermost fears. The very earth itself was an anvil that some demon skygod was pounding with a great sledgehammer, clashing iron on iron so hard that sparks seemed to starburst and flare inside their heads and through their veins.

Even before sunset, visibility had been down to a few yards, and after, when the undersea whorls of brown and bloodcrimson had become impenetrable black, it was like driving along the bottom of a churning swamp. They drove on, senses numbed, nose to tail, unable even to hear their own motors, all their focus given to staying with the tail-lights of the wagon in front. It was Caine who guided them: starblind, he was forced to use his prismatic, and that meant stops at frequent intervals, and each time a trek for him of twenty-five paces into the stinging blackness, to get the compass clear of the wagon's magnetic field. The convoy's headlamps were invisible after only a few paces into the dark and, in danger of getting lost for ever, Caine lashed himself to the jeep by parachute cord and was hauled back in like an anchor.

These halts were agonizing, fretful minutes when the drivers couldn't hear their engines idling, when the weight of the storm seemed to press down on them like deep water, crushing their bodies, squeezing the air from their lungs. They coughed and spluttered and spat rackingly through their headscarves, clawed with wild spasms at the dirt in their eyes, as if to rip the very eyeballs from their sockets. In those fraught intervals they would wet their broken mouths with gobs of water sucked from cloth, would top up fuel tanks in pairs, arms entwining each other for fear of being blown away, hands clutching at wagon bodies in case they were ripped out of the wan circle of the headlamps, chugging petrol blindly through filtered funnels, splashing themselves with fuel they couldn't afford to waste. Men would piss into the storm without getting down from the vehicles only to find themselves soaked in their own warm, blowback urine, the wet patches instantly wadded with damp dust, like fur.

They were lost in the trackless dark forest of the soul, a murkwood of whipping demon trees whose branches flailed and clutched at them, tried to jerk them out of their vehicles as they passed. The sand-hail in their faces stung them, forced them to turn their heads aside, yet still they crawled on through the maelstrom, through the sickening, mindfrenzied lunacy of the *ghibli*, which seemed to leach them dry of courage, hope and manhood, to whittle them down to trembling, terrified boys.

Caine tried to concentrate on the object of the *Sandhog* mission, to remember that the *ghibli* was their ally, making them untrackable, yet the wall of noise, the wailing gusts of the storm that seemed to come in crushing waves, wave after wave like a flowtide in a typhoon, rising and falling as if the desert were taking giant breaths, threatening at any moment to tip over the wagons, chased any logical sequence of reflection from his mind. It was hard even to recall who he was or how he'd got there, why he was fighting, what the war was about. He was tormented by spectral images of Betty Nolan's body, flayed and broken, voices of souls he'd maimed and killed, whose lives he'd blighted or cut short, lisping in his ears: *I'll get you, you bastard, I'll get you, I'll get you, I'll get you* – a serpentine hissing through the torrents of the inked-out night.

He tried to keep his senses rigidly set on his compass, checking it every few minutes with his torch, scrabbling sand from his goggles and from its face, instructing the driver to adjust direction left or right, even if the jeep was a fraction of a degree out. Often, in his fatigue, the compass needle swam out of focus and it needed all the strength he could muster to bring his concentration back. He was terrified that the storm had affected the compass readings: he knew that their course was no more than an imaginary line in his own mind, yet he gripped on to it as the only real thing in the madness, the clew of thread that would take them out of the maze.

The headlamps blinked bosseyed and feeble into the

darkness, sometimes picking out rocks and boulders that had to be avoided, obliging Caine to make frantic compensatory calculations in his head. The night was a labyrinth of tunnels without beginning or end: it seemed that they had been trapped there since the dawn of time and would be stuck there for ever. Caine kept his eye on his watch, but the hours passed without meaning – signifying nothing more than the movement of hands on a dial. They had given up hope that dawn would ever come, and yet, after almost ten shattering hours of travel, Caine thought he was beginning to see lighter shades among the swirls of grey and black.

At first it seemed just another hallucination: after twenty minutes, though, he was certain of it. There were spangles of yellow and white in the storm, and he could feel its power waning: the blast waves were hitting them less frequently, and with less force. Visibility extended, first to three yards, then to six. Suddenly, Caine realized that he could hear the noise of *Doris*'s motor over the moan of the wind. It felt as if someone had just switched off the storm's vast generator, as if the giant bellows were pumped out, the raving-mad monster had lain down to sleep, the demons had closed the great blast-furnace doors of hell. Then, suddenly, there was light enough to douse the headlamps. Moments later, unbelievably, the *ghibli* was gone.

The men stared around them lead-lidded and dropping with fatigue, at a new, silent world. It was like a rebirth. Not only had the storm passed, it had passed completely and utterly, as if it had never been. The air was motionless, clear as a bell, the pickled black and tan desert laid out before them like a newly washed skein of cloth. And there, almost near enough to touch, it seemed, the peaks of the Green Mountains stood folded in shadow, jutting out of the desert in tier after tier, crag after jagged crag, like raw, unfinished faces jostling to peer over each other's backs. The men leered at the sight, blowing grit from their nostrils, scratching at their eyes, hardly able to take it in.

Caine ordered a halt, snapped back his goggles for the first time in centuries, and raised his binos. He observed desert piedmont, dry meadows of saltbush and swordgrass, jumbles of boulders, deep dumps of scoria giving way to steep wadis and re-entrants and, beneath the peaks, a smooth brown wall of cliff. He lowered the glasses, got out his map, studied it with dustpasted eyes. There could be no doubt, he thought. Unless he'd gone quietly insane in the night, that was the Shakir cliff ahead of them. He felt a surge of gratitude that almost overwhelmed him: ten hours' slog across the darkest gallery of hell, and yet they'd come out within five or six miles of the landfall he'd been heading for. It was a miracle they'd made it through the *ghibli* at all.

He knew he couldn't ask the men to go any further at this moment. Audley, Gibson, Rossi, Trubman and Netanya had already thrown themselves bellydown on the clean desert surface, as if kissing a long-awaited shore. Larousse, Pickney, Dumper and Copeland sank into the sand dazed and shaky, staring into midspace like aircrash victims, unable to believe they'd survived. Caine clambered out of the jeep with the ponderous actions of a diver. Stretching his big shoulders and pectorals, though, he felt lighter, as if a great weight had lifted off his back. The dark hauntings of the night – Nolan's kidnapping, wounding a fellow officer, abducting a superior, seemed distant memories, events that had occurred in a parallel universe. The silence that had enveloped them since the motors had stopped was uncanny, as though something were missing from the world. 'Get a grip, lads,' he croaked at them. 'Stay switched on. Remember, we're behind Axis lines now.'

Wallace was the only man moving, clanking pannikins, glugging liquor from a flagon, breaking eggs into a king-size pot. The boys watched him, mesmerized. Caine arched duststiff eyebrows, not quite believing what he was seeing. '*Eggs?*' he grated incredulously. 'You got *eggs*?'

'Been savin' 'em for sommat like this, skipper,' Wallace answered hoarsely. 'Desert special, *innit*? Rum, limejuice, crushed dates and raw eggs. We're dead parched, mate. Try an' cram down bullybeef and biscuits now, you'd boke it back up – if yer can get it down at all. This stuff'll have us buzzin' like bluebottles in two ticks, you mark my words.'

Pickney, sitting in a heap a yard away, raised his head and nodded wearily. His eyes were bloodragged and opaque, his face, already prematurely wrinkled, looked like raddled treebark. Like some of the others, he'd spent part of the night riding in the back of *Veronica*, but since her canvas cover had been tied back to prevent the wind splitting it like a taut sail, he'd found no refuge there. No one had slept. Almost everyone had stagged the jeep drivers at some time during the night: Caine, as navigator, had been the only one unable to stand down from point.

'He's right, skipper,' Pickney grunted. 'Liquid is what we need. Add a couple of teaspoons of salt to it, Fred. Stops the body losing water.'

'Right you are, mate.'

Wallace moved through the group, doling out liquor into the tin mugs proffered. When he came to Copeland, he hesitated, bypassed him ostentatiously, and left him till last. Cope made no comment, but Caine snorted softly, realizing that there were some grudges that hadn't simply melted away with the night. He lit a Black Cat, sought out Dumper. The little corporal looked as if he'd aged ten years. He had a cigarette stuck in his mouth and was studying the photo of his wife and daughters as if he'd just been restored to them. 'See what we've got in *Veronica*, Sam,' Caine told him. 'Water, rations, ammo, explosives.' He took a sip of Wallace's concoction and coughed. The liquor burned his mouth and throat, but almost at once he could feel it steaming through his blood like a battlecruiser, standing his sluggish organs to attention with shock. He leaned against *Doris*, exhaling smoke, studying his filthy, bedraggled, bearded crew, seeing sleep possess them, seeing the Benzedrine hangover kick in behind their eyes. He spat in the sand.

'Don't go to sleep, lads,' he said, his voice clearer. 'We're not there yet. Another ten miles before we make landfall, then we've got a spot of cliff-scaling to do while it's still light. As soon as you've had your drink, pack your manpacks, check your escape kits and personal gear. Be back here in five for briefing.'

No one chuntered, not even Audley: Wallace's brew seemed to work on them like magic. Most asked for more and jacked down Bennies with the second helping. In a few minutes they were on their feet with a new fire in their eyes, handing out kit, dusting off weapons, stuffing bandoliers of ammo into webbing. Caine packed his gear from the back of the jeep, but was interrupted by Dumper, who stumped up with a frown on his gnomelike face. 'There's good news and bad news, boss,' he said. 'Bad news is all the bleedin' water flimsies sprung leaks in the night, and the jerrycans was on *Glenda*. I reckon there's only enough water for one bottle apiece.'

Caine swore. 'What's the good news?' he asked.

'We've got fuel, some rations, ammo and grenades, Lewes bombs, mines, spare explosives, bazooka rounds, mortars and mortar rounds. Decoy kit's all right, and so is the climbin' gear.'

He paused and Caine nodded. 'The main thing is that we can do what we came to do.'

'No problem then,' Dumper said, 'but we're a bit exposed here, boss. Don't you fink maybe we ought to scrim up?'

Caine glanced around: most of the lads had finished their packing and were heading back for the briefing. 'Not worth it,' he said. 'We'll be off in a tick.'

As the men were settling down, Caine took another dekko at the landscape. They were well into the piedmont here – undulations of black gravel, wide expanses of heat-cracked clay, glittering saltpans, rock ribs sporting overhangs and suncarved turrets, knots of acacias like broken umbrellas, twisted and bowed by the wind, copses of old tamarix with coiled trunks as thick as ships' hawsers. A flight of sandgrouse took off from the shade of an overhang not a hundred paces away, a flurry of wings, a piping of plaintive birdcalls, a glimmer of light as they banked into a rough arrowhead and slewed off towards the hills.

Caine turned to see that the lads were assembled, eyeing him expectantly. 'All right, boys,' he said. 'Here it is – what we've come for: Op *Sandhog*.' He paused and took a breath. 'There's a big crater in the Green Mountains known as the Citadel: a few of you saw it on the *Runefish* mission back in June. It was then used by Itie deserters and ex-colons, now it's a Hun base where they've been testing a chemical weapon, a disorienting agent called Olzon-13. I can't go into its effects now, but basically it sends folk berserk: soldiers exposed to it are likely to end up bumping off their mates. You can imagine what would happen if it was let loose on gunners or tank crews – or *pilots*, Jesus Christ. Our Int. boys think the Jerries are planning to use this stuff to slow down the Eighth Army during Monty's *Lightfoot* advance, due on 25 October. If they do, the whole push is likely to turn into a shambles. *Sandhog* is therefore vital to *Lightfoot*'s success – which is why, if you are wondering, I was prepared to shoot a fellow officer yesterday, and to abduct another. Major Maskelyne was planning to have us arrested by the Redcaps for compromising his decoy plans, thereby stuffing *Sandhog*. I regret what I had to do, but we are under direct orders from the GOC, and that couldn't be allowed at any cost. *Sandhog* is crucial to the whole outcome of the campaign. Our task is to get into the Citadel by stealth, locate the underground bunkers where the Olzon-13 is being stored and destroy it. Our secondary tasks are, one, to take out the local commander: all we know about him is that he's nicknamed the Angel of Death – and, two, to liberate any prisoners – Itie deserters, Senussi or anyone else – we find . . .'

'*No*,' Wallace's voice boomed.

Caine gawked at him, thinking that, for some reason, the big gunner was making an objection. He saw at once that Wallace's blackglassed eyes weren't focused on him at all but on something over his shoulder. '*No*, *no*, *no*,' the giant repeated, a look of horror on his craggy face. He sprang to his feet, grabbing at his Bren-gun with his shovel-blade hand, still gaping like a man in a trance. 'Never in a million years, you says. I don't fucking *believe* it.'

A frisson of alarm ran round the crew like a bushfire: they were up on their feet in an instant with their weapons and kit in their hands, staring wildeyed at the western sky. Caine whipped round to see what they were looking at, and his heart kettledrummed. Not far away, three Stukas were already falling into a bombing configuration, humming directly in on them out of the gunmetal sky.

22

Wallace took a couple of sevenleague strides towards *Doris*, and Caine knew he was aiming to brace the twin Vickers. The two jeeps were parked cheek by jowl, but none of the guns was loaded or cocked, nor had they been cleaned after the sandstorm. Chances were they'd jam, and Wallace would be dogmeat. Caine gripped the giant's trunk-thick arm. 'Leave it, mate,' he bellowed. 'It's too late.' He pivoted towards the others. 'Take cover – under the overhang – *there*.' He gestured to the spot from which he'd just seen the sandgrouse taking off – the only place, he reckoned, where they had a ghost of a chance. Wallace yanked his arm back furiously, but Caine was distracted by the sight of Sam Dumper racing for *Veronica*, bowlegs stumping, feet kicking dust. '*Sam!*' he screamed. 'For Christ's sake . . .'

The rest of the boys were sprinting for the overhang humping weapons and manpacks. Wallace lifted the half-inch Browning off *Doris* and lumped after them in league-boot paces, hefting the big weapon onehanded as if it were a toy. He and Caine were the last into the shade of the overhang, throwing themselves down just in time to see sunlight flashing like rapiers on gullwings and gondolas as Stukas stripped air in their final jump, engines snarling, sirens bansheeing, jumplights blinking like bloodswilled eyes, twentymil needleguns shuddering rimfire *blat blat blat*

blat. Caine watched helplessly: the aircraft were so close he could see the pimpleheads of pilots rocking in their seats in the teeth of G-force blackout, the sunspot pulse of their cannon. Fifty-pound bombs dripped off gondolas like giant oildrops, the kites swallowtailing out of the jump, engines rasping with the strain, churning air with a dreadbolt thunder as violent as the storm.

Caine saw *Doris*'s bonnet splinched in a radiant octagon of fire, her rear wheels, kicking up off the ground, almost vertical before vanishing into smoke. The air quivered, scraped breath from his lungs, the ground paddled madly, a tsunami of choking grit and dust spliffed over him. Caine portcullised eyelids against it, snapshotted the second jeep, *Dorothy*, coming apart at the seams on his retina, quills of light from the bombbursts pinsticking his blind senses like stilettos, a spiral galaxy of glittering shards, of warped shrapnel flying, wheels revolving like melting tops in four different directions, in multiple vortices of flaring red and black.

Caine opened his eyes, blinked, heard the Jericho trumpets die, the aeroengines level into a purr as the planes went into a long orbit, out of sight. He knew it wasn't over, knew how it would be – how it always was. The Stukas worked like a wolfpack, picking off one element of the convoy at a time, destroying it, then coming back for another bite. They'd taken out both jeeps – they would circle and come in for the 3-tonner. He crawled a few feet forward, clocked a single pyre of black smoke where *Doris* and *Dorothy* had been, burning debris splattered across the ground. He heard a motor hiccup and fire, made out *Veronica*, a topheavy turtle lumbering through the dust and smoke towards the overhang. Caine could see Dumper's oversized head in the cab. He felt his eyes smart – the little NCO was making a magnificent attempt to salvage the stores and kit and so rescue *Sandhog*: the Lewes bombs, the demolitions gear, without which they couldn't pull off the stunt, were all in the 3-tonner. Caine bit stormchapped lips till blood ran, hearing the Stukas' engines shifting frequency above, knowing the Kraut pilots had already spotted *Veronica* moving, knowing Dumper wasn't going to make it.

For a moment it seemed he was wrong. For a long minute it looked almost possible that the little fitter might bring it off. Caine's eyes were riveted on the storm-mauled hull of the lorry as she growled towards them, wobbling slightly, her canvas cover flapping, balloon tyres smoking dust. He could see Dumper's face through the aeroscreen, eyes glazed with concentration as he battled the gears, jaw set, grim with resolve. Caine suckered a disbelieving breath. Seventy yards, sixty yards. *He was going to do it. He was going to make it.* Then the screech of aeroengines and the wail of jump sirens flogged Caine's ears like hunting cries of sadistic triumph: he clocked the Stukas coming in directly behind the truck, waggling their gullwings in anticipation, their fuselages now burnished silver, now dull, like sharks turning slowly from dark to shade in undersea light. Caine ducked, heard the *blump-blump-blump* of cannon, heard the toot of bombs, the low *barooooomffff* as they struck. He heard the clank of mangled iron, sniffed scorched air and burnt petrol, felt the earth rock, glimpsed the Stukas still reaming towards him with their guns sprattling. He felt Fred Wallace yank him backwards into cover as the big rounds whomped up dirt and gravel all along the overhang where the SAS men were hidden.

When he opened his eyes he saw that *Veronica* lay on her side, blue smoke billowing from her bonnet and her cab on fire. There was a three-foot smouldering crater in the desert surface in front of her where the nearest bomb had plumped home, but Caine could see that the 3-tonner hadn't taken a direct hit – she'd been blown off her wheels by the blast and hit by cannon rounds but otherwise she was still intact. He could see a figure in the cab haloed in fire but struggling. It was Dumper. He was still alive, in danger of being roasted to death.

'We've got to get him out of there,' Copeland yelled. 'If that fire reaches the detonators, he's had it.'

Caine jumped to his feet, listening for aeroengines, realizing that they'd already faded into the distance. It struck him as strange that the hawks hadn't come in for the kill, but perhaps the sight of the truck on her side, bleeding smoke, had been enough for them. Copeland was already dashing for the lorry on marathon runner's legs, and Caine struggled to keep up with him, with Larousse, Pickney, Gibson and Rossi panting behind. Caine reached the overturned cab just as Cope was smashing the aeroscreen with his riflebutt. Hands pulled Dumper clear: Rossi and Gibson worked on the flames with fire extinguishers grabbed from inside the cab, already so hot the handles singed their fingers. Dumper was still talking, but was worse than Caine had expected: rounds as big as candles had chunked his thigh and groin and he was losing blood rapidly: the fire in the cab had charred both feet down to the bone, burning off most of his toes.

'Damn it,' Dumper swore. 'I could of made it. I was nearly there.'

His voice sounded even, but his face was feverish, his eyes white with shock. 'You did brilliant,' Caine said. 'You saved the kit.'

Pickney crouched down next to Dumper with his medical pack. He brought out two shell dressings, handed one to Caine, slit the other open. He cut away Dumper's BD trousers from the crutch, saw a pulsing red curry in place of his testicles. Caine saw it and swallowed hard, exchanging a silent glance with the orderly. Behind them, the lads turned away.

Dumper's thigh was spritzing arterial blood. Caine staunched the bleeding and covered the hole, then, while Pickney worked on the more difficult wounds, stood up. 'Let's start unloading,' he told the others. 'Larousse, Gibson, set up OPs in case those buggers come back. The rest of you, get all the gear out, starting with the demo kit. Get everything under the overhang.'

When Caine turned back to Dumper, Pickney was administering a shot of morphia: the little corporal seemed perfectly clearheaded, despite his horrific wounds.

'I s'pose this is as far as I go, boss,' he said. 'Better leave me 'ere for the crows.' He sobbed suddenly. 'What'll Queenie say?'

'Leave you here?' Caine said. 'After what you did? Never. You're going with us, mate, if I have to carry you myself.'

Pickney had just loaded Dumper on to a stretcher when there was a shout: Caine saw the cowboy running towards him, holding his Garand across his body, his face wild. 'Axis column,' he panted when he reached Caine, crouching down on one knee, using his riflebutt as a crutch. 'Half a dozen wagons, skipper. One AFV. Coming straight for us – must be homing in on the smoke.'

'How far away?'

'The AFV is leading, about five hundred –'

He was cut off by a crack like the earth's gut being wrenched open: a shell sawed air over their heads, crumped into the desert three hundred yards away with a tympanic boom that set a forked tongue of dust and debris licking up fifty feet. Caine and Gibson both fell flat: Caine felt the shockwave, squinted around. The enemy column was shielded from view by a low rise: *Veronica* was only part unloaded – the lads had dropped their burdens and thrown themselves prone. Pickney was lying next to Dumper's stretcher with an arm over the wounded corporal. Caine was about to get up when another round peeled back air with a blastfurnace haw, skittling into a brake of flat-topped acacias with a *whuumffff*, setting them ablaze. The shell was still overranged, but they were getting warmer. Caine rolled over and came up in a crouch, his Tommy-gun in his hands. 'Gibbo,' he ordered. 'You and Rossi get the bazooka and knock out that bloody AFV. Fred, Cope, look for a defensive position along the ridge. The rest of you, take whatever's nearest and get back to the overhang. Maurice – you and I'll hump the stretcher. Somebody call Larousse back in.'

The men hefted their loads back towards the overhang as more shells creased over their heads, scooped air, shook earth, lumped up dirt, spread red fire in the bush. Then, just as Caine and Pickney set the stretcher down in the shade, the enemy got the range and *Veronica* took a direct hit, boosting four feet into the air as if jerked up by concealed strings, her body distending and disintegrating in a swastika of black smoke and crossed white limbs. The detonation was followed almost immediately by the thunk of the bazooka, flat and hollow in the distance. Caine waited tensely for more shooting: none came, and he reasoned that the cowboy and Rossi had nailed the AFV and the rest of the Kraut column was hanging back.

He scrambled to Copeland and Wallace, fifty yards down the ridge in a place where the stone had crumbled away to a low, fractured wall between high shoulders. It was an ideal defensive position: they wouldn't be skylined here. Caine arrived just in time to see the enemy armoured car smoking three hundred yards distant, a sixwheeler with her turret bent and crippled. He saw two smouldering Huns clamber out of the turret and roll in the sand. He saw them stand and raise their hands, clocked the cowboy and Rossi and Larousse approach them: Gibbo still had the bazooka in his hands. Caine saw blades flash like forked lightning in Larousse's and Rossi's hands, again and again and again, as the two SAS men plunged their daggers into shoulder, neck and chest. Caine saw blood gush, saw the Jerries drop, heard enemy rounds slash and pizzle around his men. '*Here they come*,' Copeland warned.

Caine peered to his right, saw Afrika Korps infantry skirmishing in precise formation across the dun and toasted desert towards the SAS trio, four hundred yards away and closing. The SAS boys bunked. Caine lifted his Tommy-gun, fired a burst at the advancing Germans – *whomp*, *whomp*, *whomp*, *whomp*. To his far right, big Wallace rattattatted .303 ball and tracer, his Bren pulled in tight to a giant armpit: Caine saw the tracer flare, saw Krauts skittle. Cope had his sniperscope to his eye: Caine heard the breath intake, clocked the gentle stroke of the trigger, heard the crack, saw a Hun head explode in a furry raft of red tissue. Audley, Pickney, Trubman and Netanya ramped up beside them, slouched against the rock wall: Audley and Netanya cranked up Brens, blabbered fire. Pickney shoved a Garand and a bandolier of .30 ammo into Caine's hands: Pickney and Trubman eyehunted Jerries, rattled rapid fire, squeezed iron so fast that in seconds Caine heard the plink of ejected clips. He lamped off aimed rounds to fill the hiatus: the three Brens crackled. Cope worked his bolt: his Lee-Enfield plumped.

The Huns had halted their advance, gone to ground behind low ridges, nests of boulders, swordgrass reefs: muzzlesmoke spliffed, rounds blimped and crickled around the SAS men, severed rock chips droned. A stone fragment clipped Caine's ear, drew blood. He pulled iron ferociously, swearing, *blam-blam-blamm*ing .30 slugs. He saw a goth helmet pop up behind a tuft of swordgrass, put an aimed round straight through it at four hundred paces, saw the helmet jerk and tumble. He heard his empty clip *ping*, scrabbled in the bandolier for another. Three Brens, three Garands and an SMLE were jacking out an irresistible wave of fire: Huns were crawling back, pepperpotting out in pairs, withdrawing out of range. The cowboy, Rossi and Larousse wafted along the rock overhang, yelling in relief, but by the time they reached Caine's position the shooting had stopped. They'd won the first firefight, but Caine knew it wouldn't be the last. He roved the desert with his glasses, looking for the enemy column: he saw dustcloud, but now the AFV outrider was down, the wagons were staying out of sight.

'They'll try and encircle us, skipper,' Copeland said. 'If we stay here we've shot our bolt. We've got to get out.'

Caine nodded, knowing it was true. 'Bren-gunners keep stag,' he said. 'Keep your eyes skinned. Rest of you get back to the overhang. Pack as many Lewes bombs, dets, primers, fuse and timepencils as you can carry. Take as much ammo as possible, even if you have to make room for it by dumping personal kit. Pack water and spare rations . . .'

'There *are* no spare rations, skipper,' Pickney growled. 'We never got them out. And we've only got the water we're carrying.'

Caine spat. 'That's easy then: more space for the demolitions gear.'

Caine made his way back to the overhang with the others: Dumper was still on his stretcher, his eyes wide, flaring at the flawless sky. 'Hey boss,' he croaked as Caine appeared. 'Don't leave me out. All right, I'm hit, but I don't feel a damn' fing: I can still shoot.'

Caine, Copeland and Pickney crouched down next to him. Pickney gave him water from his canteen. Dumper took a swallow, pushed the canteen away, his blood-drilled eyes on Caine. 'Listen, boss,' he grated. 'I got an idea. You bug out, the Huns'll be on you like flies on a turd. They got wagons and you ain't. Leave me 'ere, boss. I'll 'old the fort, *won' I*? Gimme the bazooka – you won't be needin' it. Set up a grenade daisychain, rigged up with No. 2 mines. Gimme the Browning .50 and a spare Bren. I'll keep the fire so 'ot they'll fink the lot of us is still 'oled up. By the time they click, you'll be well away. When they moves in on my position, I'll pull the bleedin' ripcord.'

Caine stared at him, a lump in his throat preventing speech. The knifewound in his arm burned: the blood from his clipped ear dripped down his neck, soaked his shirt. The little NCO, who'd already shown so much bravery, the husband of an impossibly beautiful wife and father of two children, was soberly offering his life for theirs. Offering to save the operation he'd already rescued once. Caine sniffed, felt liquid prick his eyes, caustic with salt. He hadn't had time to think about it during the contact, but what had happened to Dumper was entirely down to his, Caine's, own incompetence. *His* decision to go to the leaguer to get the camshaft fixed: *his* negligence in failing to scrim up as soon as they'd halted, as per his own SOP. Dumper had even suggested it, but Caine had waved the idea away, shattered after the drive through the storm. If anyone should stay to hold off the enemy, it ought to be Caine.

'No way, Sam,' he said, his voice thick. 'You're coming with us.'

Dumper cackled hoarsely. 'Oh yeah, right you are, boss. An' I'm just gonna flit up that four-hundred-foot cliff like a fairy, *ain' I*?'

'We'll get you up. Gibbo knows ways.'

Dumper's smooth white face collapsed. He looked angry now. 'You're talkin' daft, skipper. You're talkin' out yer arse. If you take me you might as well wave the white flag now, 'cos you ain't gonna make it. I don't wanna debate about it. There ain't no time: Krauts'll be back any minute. I ain't goin' wiv yer. I'm stayin' 'ere wevver you likes it or not: stop actin' the amatooer and start bein' a pro for Chrissake.'

Caine wiped moisture from his eyes. He opened his mouth to speak, but words wouldn't come. He thought of Dumper's Queenie: of the two pretty girls fatherless. Why the hell did it have to be *him*?

'Skipper,' Copeland said softly, 'Sam's right. Time's getting on.'

Caine looked up at Cope, saw his blueblade eyes gleaming like brilliants. 'What do you reckon?' he asked.

Copeland took a deep breath. 'I was thinking about Maskelyne – you know, the decoy leaguer. *Illusions*. We salvaged our decoy kit from the truck before she was hit. The pintail bombs give off flashes, and the noisemakers sound like smallarms fire. There's a mobile smoke generator. Like Sam said, we could . . . we *could* leave him . . . with a daisy-chain of grenades and mines. Leave the spare Brens and the bazooka – set 'em up in a rank, you know, so he could reach them all. With Sam shooting for real and the dummy stuff going off, it'd look like there's a whole section waiting for them – and they've already had a taste of our firepower. If we just withdraw, they'll know it and be on our tails like greased lightning. We'll never make the landfall. But if we set Sam up with the decoy gear, they'll be convinced we're still here, all of us. It could hold them back for hours – maybe even till dark.'

'*There*, Lieutenant,' Dumper cut in. 'There's a man as talks sense.'

Caine looked at Pickney, who shook his head. 'It's your decision, skipper,' he said. 'It's down to you.'

He glanced at Dumper, saw his eyes, two fathomless pits, willing him to decide. He sensed that the rest of the lads had stopped packing their manpacks to watch him.

He was aware of the clock ticking. He thought again of Queenie and the girls, of that anonymous telegram dropping like a bombshell into their lives: *I regret to inform you that your husband, Corporal Samuel Brian Dumper, Royal Army Ordnance Corps, has been killed in action . . . I am charged to express His Majesty's high appreciation* . . . He thought of Moshe Naiman, whom he'd helped to die, and of Giancarlo Cavazzi, the mortally wounded man he'd once shot dead. He shivered. He'd sworn that he would never do it again, yet here he was. *It's your decision, skipper. It's down to you.* For a moment, he felt desperately alone.

'*Tom*,' Copeland said: Caine could hear the urgency in his voice.

He took a sharp inhalation of breath and caught Dumper's eye once more, hating himself but knowing it was the right decision, knowing that Dumper knew it, knowing that there was really no other way. 'Just promise me one thing, Sam,' he said, hewing his words out of stone. 'When you go, you'll blow the bloody lot of them sky high.'

23

Betty Nolan was woken up an hour before dawn: the cellar door thumped open, the electric light buzzed. She hadn't been asleep – the handcuffs were too uncomfortable to allow more than a doze – and she was up in an instant, poised on the edge of the bed. The unshaded lightbulb swung on its flex, sending a basket of light rocking across the room. She blinked towards the door, where the Turk, Hayek, stood, feet apart, gold teeth glinting, a gleam in his hard black eyes, a hand rubbing at the bulge in his crotch. Hayek was a powerful man: his shoulders were as wide as Tom Caine's, she thought, but while Caine's body tapered gracefully to a trim waist, the Turk was the same width all the way down, his muscles layered in fat – pot belly, flabby buttocks, chubby legs. In his faded chocolate suit he looked like a cartoon caricature of a sawnoff treetrunk with a grim blue head sticking out.

Hayek shut the door and waddled towards her panting, licking rubbery lips, sweat beading his forehead, still massaging his crotch. Nolan watched him motionless. She'd been expecting this ever since she'd been abducted: the way he'd gobbled her up with his eyes when he brought the lentils and flat bread they fed her twice a day; the way he'd taken every opportunity to brush her breasts or touch her bum. She already knew he was vicious and cowardly: it was the Turk who'd shot Pat Rigby and who'd punched

Nolan herself in the eye before hustling her out of the house and bundling her into the carboot. Hekmeth had been beside herself with fury at these actions: Nolan had seen the bellydancer, who scarcely came up to the Turk's shoulder, slapping him in the face, raking him with her nails till he cowered like a beaten cur.

Now, Hayek arched over her in the rocking light. 'Hussain, he come this afternoon,' he said in lisping, broken English. 'I think we see you no more.' He pouted as if offering a kiss, and drew a bloated finger across his throat with a look of apparent pleasure. His sow's eyes fixed on her, thick lips curdling into a grin. 'I come say goodbye.'

As he reached for her, Nolan found that she was shaking: her breath came in shallow stabs. She'd always told herself that the best way to deal with rape was passivity – don't struggle, let it happen. When the Brandenburgers had been about to gang-rape her back in June, she'd simply lain there, waited for it, expecting to be violated, expecting to die, not caring, because the Nazis had taken away the only man she'd ever loved, and she'd had nothing to live for anyway. Tom Caine had saved her, and now she had Caine. Now it was different: now, every instinct screamed at her to fight.

She thrust herself forward and up, hit him a glancing blow on the side of his bull head with the handcuffs. He yelled, gritted gold teeth, retreated a foot, felt the shallow laceration on his cheek where the iron had cut into his flesh. As Nolan rolled away, though, he attacked again with surprising speed. Panting, drooling spit, he seized her arm, shook her like a rag doll, slapped her with his big open hand, knocked her facedown on the bed. He grabbed her legs, dragged her backwards so that the upper part of her body remained on the bed, knees touching the bare stone floor. Forced on to her crooked elbows, Nolan yelled and screamed, kicked out at him. She squirmed as his coarse hands slipped under her shirt, groped clumsily at her breasts, pawed her belly. He withdrew them and stood back: he kept one hand pressed on her spine and with the other stroked her buttocks through her KD trousers, probed between her legs. She could hear him moaning softly, sucking breath, could feel his sex straining through his trousers against her. The big hands were working on her belt: he had it undone. He jerked her trousers down to her ankles, groaned with anticipation. He had just begun to pull down her underpants when Nolan heard the door crash open a second time, heard Hekmeth's contralto voice shrieking out a stream of Arabic obscenities. The hands left her abruptly: Nolan snatched back her legs, half turning to see Hekmeth striding into the room, black skirts and jewellery flying, her float of tousled chestnut hair wild, eyes burning yellow, brandishing a brutal-looking short whip of the type the Egyptians called a *kurbag*. She waded in on the Turk like a whirlwind, never pausing in her torrent of abuse, laying into him so ferociously that the big man whimpered, ducked, backed away, lifted his arms to fend off the blows, begged for mercy. He deflected most of the lashes with his treetrunk arms, but Hekmeth landed a direct hit on his backside, with a resonant *craaack*. Hayek jumped, screeched, sobbed with pain. '*Get out*,' the belly-dancer bawled at him, pushing him towards the door. 'You disgusting animal. Get out of my sight.'

The Turk retreated through the door yelping, covering

his bottom with his hands. The door slammed shut. For a moment, Hekmeth stood there doing the pouting thing she did with her lips, fighting to control her breath, watching Nolan struggle ineffectively to fasten her trousers with cuffed hands. The bellydancer was a striking sight, Nolan thought, bedecked in rings, bracelets, earrings, anklets and necklaces: mobile red lips, heavily kohled eyes, intricately hennaed feet and hands – not beautiful, perhaps, but alluringly feminine: to a man she would appear to ooze sensuousness. With a final curse, Hekmeth flung the whip on the floor, stamped her highheeled foot in fury. 'Disgusting beast,' she raged. 'Imbecile. He shoots your friend for no reason; hits you in the eye for no reason. Now he tries to assault you against my orders. Bloody, bastard, shit, Turks.'

She brushed back a wayward strand of hair, produced a key from the pocket of her dress, bent over and unlocked Nolan's handcuffs. Nolan thanked her. She finished pulling up and securing her trousers with hands that were still shaking, her breath coming in pants. It wasn't the first time Hekmeth had allowed her to remove the cuffs: she'd had a few minutes' respite every morning, when the bellydancer had helped bathe the sores on her wrists. Nolan knew she could have made use of her free hands before now: the cellar was large, with its own WC, and had evidently not been built as a jail cell. There were plenty of objects she could have used as weapons – shards of the small mirror in the toilet, for instance. Hekmeth had the body of a gymnast: she would be strong from constant exercise, but Nolan had a good eight inches on her and had been trained in unarmed combat. If it came to a scrap they'd be well matched, she thought. For the moment, though, she knew better than to attempt anything. She couldn't say exactly what Stocker was up to, but she was confident that this house was even now under surveillance by his watchers. She couldn't risk taking action until she was certain that Eisner was around.

Nolan's kidnapping had been a Field Security cockup. By feeding her new address to the traitor Clive Beeston, Stocker had hoped to flush Eisner out. FS had had Nolan's flat staked out the day she'd been kidnapped: they'd watched the whole show. She hoped fervently that Stocker's bloodhounds hadn't lost her abductors' trail on the way here, because if so, she was up the creek without a paddle and the whole sacrifice had been a monumental waste.

It was never meant to happen like this. Stocker had anticipated that Eisner himself would make the snatch: the plan had been for Field Security to arrest him or take him out. Instead, Hekmeth Fahmi had arrived at her flat with two bruisers, one of whom – the Turk – had shot Pat Rigby. The FS watchers could have captured Hekmeth and her men, of course: Nolan supposed they'd held off, hoping the bellydancer would lead them to bigger fish.

That hadn't happened either, at least, not yet. Nolan had been locked in the cellar for eight days, waiting for Eisner to appear. Since FS hadn't moved to pull her out, she assumed they believed he would turn up sooner or later: perhaps they had intelligence on his movements from other sources. She wished he would get a move on, though, and prayed that Stocker's men would act promptly when he did come: she'd seen Eisner in the act of sodomizing and murdering Mary Goddard and – as the Turk had suggested in his own crude way – she doubted that she'd survive long once he arrived.

Nolan had spent much of her confinement dreaming about Tom Caine: she'd drawn comfort from imagining herself in his strong embrace. On the other hand, the assignment had been made more difficult by the knowledge that she now had someone to live for. She wondered how he'd reacted when he'd discovered she was missing: Stocker certainly wouldn't have told him the truth: that she was being used as live bait in a failed Field Security plan. She was sure that, given the opportunity, Caine would stop at nothing to find her, even if he had to rampage through Cairo scouring every house.

That was the reason she'd failed to give him any inkling of the plan when she'd seen him in hospital: she'd been tempted, but she knew that, should he learn of it, he would try to stop her at any cost. Caine would surely be away on the *Sandhog* mission by now. She wondered how they'd compelled him to take that assignment while she was still missing: she was sure they'd have had to do it by force.

Nolan crawled into a sitting position and asked Hekmeth if she could use the bathroom. 'Leave the door open,' the bellydancer said.

The lavatory was an Arab-style drophole in the floor. After using it, she peered into the cracked little mirror on the wall, gasping at the sight of her face. Her cheek was an angry crimson where the Turk had slapped her, her left eye still a purpleblack pit where he'd punched her over a week before: her lush blond hair was as mussed and knotted as esparto grass – almost as wild as the dancer's. Her full lips were cracked, her teeth the colour of nicotine: only her seagreen eyes remained bright, as if she'd polished them daily. They were almost exactly the same colour as Hekmeth's, Nolan thought.

She dabbed her cheek with a damp cloth and emerged to find the bellydancer sitting elegantly on a camp-chair near the bed, her small hands playing with a silver cigarette case embossed with her initials. Hekmeth opened the case, handed a cigarette to Nolan and took one herself. Nolan accepted the cigarette with a hand that was still quivering slightly: she sat down on the bed and watched her fingers, trying to control her breathing, trying to will her heart to stop its thump. Hekmeth fitted her cigarette into an ivory holder and lit it with a gold Ronson: when Nolan's hand had stopped shaking, she lit hers too.

Hekmeth blew smoke at the ceiling in a long gust. 'I'm sick of those Turk imbeciles,' she said. 'I should never have taken them with me –' She broke off abruptly. 'Your friend – the one in hospital – I had news of her yesterday. She's not going to die, but she's still unconscious.'

Nolan shivered. 'I hope Pat will be all right,' she said. 'She didn't deserve that.'

'*Deserve?*' Hekmeth scoffed. 'Who deserves anything? It's the bloody war, that's all. Just the bloody war.'

Hekmeth's voice was harsh, but Nolan perceived that her manner was phony: a way of covering up guilt. The bellydancer didn't add anything and Nolan saw an opportunity opening itself up. 'Tell me,' she said timidly, 'how *did* you get my new address? It was supposed to be secure.'

Nolan thought Hekmeth might resent the question, get angry, clam up. Instead, she seemed proud of the fact that she had access to inside information. Her eyes sparkled and her mouth twitched with a hint of smugness. 'I have a friend in GHQ,' she smirked. 'A very good friend.'

'You mean Major Clive Beeston?' Nolan said bluntly, watching the dancer's face fall in astonishment. 'Field Security knows all about him, Hekmeth. They know he's the source of the leaks on raiding forces: they're watching him, and when he goes down he'll take you with him. Why accept that? After all, you aren't a German, you're an Egyptian: your loyalty is surely to this country, not to theirs?'

Hekmeth blinked: for a moment she looked shaken, but she recovered her equanimity with remarkable speed. Nolan guessed what she was thinking: the mention of Beeston's name could have been a shot in the dark – maybe Field Security weren't sure about him at all, maybe Nolan was just testing the ground. Hekmeth took a deep drag of her cigarette, her green Circassian eyes fixed on Nolan's. 'It's just the war,' she repeated. 'It pulls everybody in, even if you don't want it. *You* should know that: you were a cabaret dancer, weren't you? I saw your act at Madame Badia's once . . .' She broke off, sniffing slightly. 'You dance very well, even if your voice is nothing special.'

'Thank you,' Nolan said, grinning at the left-handed compliment. 'I've seen your act, too: you are every bit as good as they say you are.'

Hekmeth bowed. 'It's a pity we both didn't stick to cabaret. You got dragged into the war. We both did . . . and we both have our reasons. I've no idea what yours is . . .'

Nolan let a last small puff of smoke pass between her full lips and crushed out the cigarette butt under her shoe. 'My fiancé was murdered by the Nazis,' she said softly. 'I wanted to get revenge – I didn't care if I was killed . . . but then I met this other man . . . anyway, I *do* care now.'

Hekmeth snorted, stabbing out her own cigarette underfoot. 'You really *do* pick them, don't you, darling?'

Nolan gazed at her, bemused. 'What do you mean?' she demanded.

'Nothing.' Hekmeth sighed, standing up. She took Nolan's wrists, jammed the cuffs back on, locked them. Nolan knew she could have resisted, but this wasn't the time. Not yet. 'Anyway,' Hekmeth said, standing back. 'Hussain will be here this afternoon. I won't have responsibility for you after that.'

Nolan remembered that the Turk had mentioned Hussain's arrival: it was the promised event that had prompted his attack. 'Hussain . . . ?' she said. 'You mean Johann Eisner?'

'We always called him Hussain. Even when he was a kid we called him that.'

Nolan kept her face deadpan, taking care not to betray her interest. The fact that Hekmeth and Eisner had known each other as kids was a vital clue to Eisner's background: the first they'd ever had. She stored the remark away, refrained carefully from asking more. 'You know what he's going to do to me, don't you?' she said, exaggerating the dread on her face, even managing to squeeze tears into the corner of her eyes. 'He's going to kill me.'

Hekmeth guffawed. 'Nonsense. He only wants information. If you give him what he needs, he won't harm you. It's not personal. It's just the war.'

'It's not, and you know it,' Nolan rasped, her voice rising, deliberately hysterical, challenging for the first time.

'He wants to kill me because I witnessed a rape and murder he committed. The Mary Goddard case, you remember? I saw him in the act at Madame Badia's, and he's never forgiven me. It's nothing to do with the war.'

Almost before the words were out she knew she'd gone too far. Hekmeth's face was distorted with rage. '*You bitch*,' she shrieked. 'They tried to frame Hussain with that case, but it was all lies. He'd never do that to a woman. What do you know, you *whore*? When we were kids he looked after me like a sister – never, ever touched me. It's the damned lies of you British, trying to smear his name. You *strumpet* . . . I should have let that animal have you. I wish I had . . .' She picked up the discarded whip, and for a moment Nolan thought she meant to strike her. Instead, she dug the leather thong into Nolan's chin, pressing her head back. 'You think you're clever, don't you, *bitch*? ' she spat. 'Well, let me tell you something. That man you care about will soon be as dead as a doornail. He's not coming back from his mission.'

Nolan's eyes went wide with shock: this time the dread on her face was genuine. Her pulse raced, her face drained of colour. 'How do you *know* that?' she asked, her voice quavering. 'You're bluffing. How *could* you know?'

Hekmeth's features were almost satanic, her normally attractive mouth twisted into a rictus of cruel satisfaction. 'See,' she sniggered bitterly. 'You don't like it – not when it's someone *you* care about. I *know* because Hussain has an agent with your man – what's his name . . . Keen? Kaynes? Hussain has infiltrated his group – that snooty Stirling's ridiculous parashooters. Your handsome prince is walking straight into a trap.'

Her eyes lingered on Nolan's face for a moment, as if she were savouring the effect of her words. Then she turned in a swirl of trinkets and dark skirts and made for the door. A second later she closed it with a bang.

24

Nolan barely noticed her departure. She sat motionless, hands gripping the bed's steel frame, knuckles bleached ivory. The word 'trap' had hit her like a bullet, crushing the air from her lungs. She closed her eyes, fought to regain composure. It couldn't be true, surely? Hekmeth was just getting her own back for what she'd said about Eisner. But she'd known Caine's name: that couldn't be a coincidence, and if it *was* true, he was in mortal danger. Whatever happened now, she had to get out of there, to warn GHQ, to warn Caine. She gasped as it struck her that Caine might already be dead. Tears like tiny jewels popped out in the corners of her eyes, and she wiped them away with trembling, cuffed hands.

She sat frozen for a long while, steadily forcing herself back into operating mode. By a huge effort of willpower, she deleted any speculation about Caine from her mind. She would give the problem all her attention when she was in a position to do so: to be in that position, she had to get out of here alive.

If it was true that Eisner was arriving that afternoon, things would be coming to a head. She had to be prepared. Had it been a mistake to goad Hekmeth by mentioning Eisner's crime? No, it had been the right course: if she hadn't she might never have discovered that *Sandhog* was compromised. As for Eisner, the bellydancer didn't know about his dark side . . . no, that wasn't right. She knew, had probably known for years, but had lied to herself about it because she cared for him. That was why she'd exploded: Nolan had touched a nerve as raw as a tooth abscess. Hekmeth and Eisner weren't lovers: *He never touched me*, she'd said, *He looked after me like a sister* – not *as* a sister, but *like* a sister. They'd been close as kids, not related by blood, but possibly brought up in the same house.

What about Beeston? She'd dropped his name in deliberately to push Hekmeth into a corner. She would no doubt be warning the major, even now, that Field Security was on his tail. Or would she? Beeston would wonder how she'd acquired the information, and the answer might compromise *her*. Even if Beeston had provided Nolan's address, the bellydancer wouldn't want to reveal details of the operation to her informant, especially as Hekmeth was probably aware, in her heart, that Eisner intended to kill her. From Stocker's point of view, warning Beeston wouldn't change anything: it would just give the traitor more rope to hang himself by.

Hekmeth hadn't argued when Nolan had made that remark about her not being German. Eisner was German or maybe half German, but Hekmeth was all Egyptian, so if she was helping the Nazis it wasn't because she felt any loyalty to them but because it was convenient. Nolan would have bet that the bellydancer wouldn't risk her life and liberty for what, in the end, amounted to just another bunch of European bosses.

For all her bluster, too, Hekmeth had a conscience. She felt guilty over the shooting of Pat Rigby: Hayek's attempt to rape Nolan had sent her berserk in a way that suggested she might once have been subjected to the same indignity herself. If so, then the knowledge that Eisner was both a rapist and a murderer of women would not sit well with her: Nolan thought the dancer's explosive reaction bore that out. Setting aside the threat to Caine, which she couldn't deal with at present, Nolan was satisfied that she'd thrown out all she could into the world. She could do nothing now but wait and see what came back.

Nolan waited. The sun came up, pewter sunbeams speared galaxies of dust motes through the two tiny skylights high on the cellar wall. She dragged the bed nearer, placed the camp-chair on it and, balancing precariously, took a long shufti through each of the slits in turn. She had already examined them minutely on several previous occasions: there could be no escape through them, but they did have a view, a view that had told her almost all she knew about the place where she was being held. It was a Nileside villa, and a big one. The skylights revealed an extensive slice of well-tended garden sloping down to the river. Although she couldn't see the water itself, the sails of feluccas drifted past above the hedgerows like the wings of giant cabbage whites. In the garden, she could see a mosaic footpath curving through beds of roses, a patio with a fountain and the edge of what might have been a swimming pool. Previously, she'd seen a man working in the garden – a tall Nubian in a gallabiya – though today there was no one in view. It had occurred to her that a riverside villa like this would probably have a jetty, and that Eisner might arrive by boat. She hoped that Stocker had considered this possibility, and that he also remembered Eisner was a master of disguise, capable of passing himself off as a tradesman or a simple fellah.

She clambered down from her perch, restored the furniture to its rightful places. She had only just finished when the door went *click*. Her heart skipped a beat at the prospect of facing Hayek again, or even Eisner himself. It was Hekmeth, though, still dressed in black, carrying a tray with a cup of water, a bowl of lentils and some flat loaves of bread. The bellydancer shuffled into the room dejectedly without looking at Nolan, laid the tray down on the bedside table. 'Eat,' was all she said.

She didn't unlock the handcuffs this time – Nolan could feed herself quite adequately using her cuffed hands. The bellydancer watched her in brooding silence. When she'd finished, Hekmeth leaned forward: Nolan saw that her eyes were red from crying. 'You said you saw Hussain . . . Johann . . . doing . . . what you claim he did . . . at Madame Badia's,' she began, her voice faltering. 'I want to know . . . I mean, how could you be certain it was him? You'd never seen him before, had you? How do you know it wasn't somebody else?'

Nolan smothered a triumphant smile. Hekmeth had taken the bait, as Nolan had been almost certain she would. She was hooked, and now at least there was a chance. Nolan masked her momentary surge of elation, relaxing her facial muscles as she'd learned to do as an actress, making her features open and patently honest. After all, she had nothing to say that wasn't the truth. 'I didn't know him at the time, of course,' she said. 'I saw him later, in the Detention Centre, before he escaped, and recognized him as the man who'd murdered and raped Lady Goddard. I'd have known him anywhere.'

Hekmeth studied her with hooded, sad eyes. She said nothing.

'I should tell you,' Nolan went on in a subdued tone, almost a whisper, 'that he raped and butchered two other girls that I'm aware of. One was a Field Security NCO, Susan Arquette, chosen because she looked like me. The other was a friend of mine, a cabaret girl at Madame Badia's called Sim-Sim.'

Hekmeth started. '*Sim-Sim?*' she said. 'I knew her. Her real name was Rachel – a lovely girl. Beautiful. Smart. A good dancer.'

'Eisner raped her – sodomized her, actually, like all the others – and cut her throat after trying to force her to reveal my whereabouts. He tortured her: cut off part of her ear. She didn't know anything, but still he violated her and slaughtered her like a pig.'

Hekmeth remained rooted to the chair: Nolan guessed she was holding herself rigidly in check. Suddenly, silent tears began to flow down her cheeks. She sniffed, brushed the tears away with a heavily ornamented hand. She made a visible effort to compose herself, waited quietly for a few moments, then took a long breath. 'My mother was a Ghawazi, you know,' she began softly. 'A professional dancer, singer and musician. I never knew my father. When I was little, my mother was taken on in the house of Hussain's stepfather, Idriss. *This* house: Idriss spends some of the year at another place in Alexandria, and Hussain uses this when he's not here. Hussain was a boy of about twelve when we first came – a few years older than me – and we were friends. He was the son of a German couple who'd owned a hotel at Giza: when his father died, his mother married Idriss, who brought him up as a Muslim with an Arab name. We didn't know what kind of man Idriss was when we first came. My mother thought he was just a businessman: he was, but he was also a trafficker . . . in girls.'

Nolan's eyes widened. 'You mean prostitutes?'

Hekmeth shook her head. 'Not exactly. Not the street-walker kind, anyway. Idriss supplies . . .' she looked sheepish, but forced herself to continue ' . . . supplies girls to the royal palace . . . the king mainly. It's all organized by the royal secretary, Antonio Pulli Bey – an Italian. The king goes through a lot of girls – sometimes four or five a day. Anyway, I don't know where the girls come from: some used to be kept here – in this very room. If they were young, Idriss liked to . . . he called it "breaking them in". When Hussain was older, Idriss tried to force him to do it too, but Hussain didn't want to. Idriss used to humiliate him in front of the girls, make them laugh at him. Once or twice it happened that girls . . . disappeared. It was all hushed up, but there were whispers among the servants that Hussain had punished girls who'd laughed at him. It was just a rumour, you understand. Nothing was ever proved.'

'And you didn't believe it?'

'Why should I? Hussain was always good to me – treated me like a sister. When I was thirteen, Idriss called me into his room and raped me. He's a pig. A real pig. When Hussain found out he was furious. He told his stepfather to leave me alone. He said that I could become a famous bellydancer. That was the first and last time Idriss called me to his room.

'I owed so much to Hussain that I refused to believe the stories about him. Then, Idriss packed him off to boarding school in Germany. When he came back he was different – still good to me, but he'd changed. He'd become a Nazi supporter, for a start – I think he'd already been recruited by the Abwehr. I was a well-known bellydancer by then, and of course, a lot of men wanted me. I thought he'd be protective of me like in the past, but he wasn't. When the war started, he even encouraged me to have affairs – with British officers mostly – so that he could manipulate them, obtain information.

'I started to see another side of him. He was still affectionate to me, but I sensed more and more that he was starting to see me as a tool for getting what he wanted. He behaved callously with other people, too. He would have secret affairs with older, married women – the wives of diplomats who might have access to their husband's papers. Once he'd got what he wanted, he'd just drop them cruelly – even insult them. If they objected he'd laugh and threaten to tell their husbands.'

Hekmeth paused, eyeing Nolan closely, as if wondering whether to continue. Nolan sensed that she was approaching some sort of climax, and nodded encouragingly. 'Mary Goddard was raped and murdered at Madame Badia's,' Hekmeth said heavily. 'You say you were there, and I have no reason to doubt you. After it happened, there were a lot of stories floating about hinting that Hussain was responsible. Of course, I didn't believe them, but I did ask him once if he had anything to do with it. He told me that he didn't even know Lady Goddard . . .'

'But that was . . .'

Hekmeth held up her henna-patterned hand to show that she hadn't quite got there. 'I knew it was a lie,' she went on, 'because I once *saw* him making love to Mary Goddard. Here, in this house.'

'You saw them? How?'

'There's a bedroom here that has a hidden spyhole: Idriss uses it to watch guests – women, naturally. I knew Hussain had a woman in that room, and I was curious to know who it was. I used the spyhole and saw him in bed with Mary Goddard – I recognized her from newspaper photos: she was at least fifteen years older than Hussain. So when he told me he didn't know her, I knew at once that it was a lie, although I couldn't tell him so. Even then, I didn't want to believe it: after all, the fact that he knew Mary didn't *prove* he'd murdered her. I told myself that he'd denied knowing her in case people wrongly suspected him of the murder, but underneath, in my heart, I knew, I had known all the time what he was. I managed to keep on deluding myself, though. But this morning, when you confirmed that you'd actually *seen* him violating her, killing her, with your own eyes. I . . . I attacked you like that because I knew I couldn't deny it to myself any more.'

She took a shaky breath. 'Hussain has betrayed me, betrayed my trust. I'd always thought of him as a protector of women, but he's a destroyer of them. Whatever happens, I can't let him do it again.'

She locked Nolan's eyes for a moment, and Nolan felt she was expecting her to make some comment.

'Let me go,' she said at last, her voice soft, reasonable. 'You know what he'll do to me: the same thing he did to *them*. At least unlock the cuffs – give me a chance.'

Hekmeth got up suddenly and started pacing the room, hands clasped over her chest, as if trying to resolve some terrible internal conflict. 'I know,' she muttered. 'Yes of course I know what he'll do. If I let you go, though, he'll be aware I've helped you, and God knows what will happen to me. Even if I take off the handcuffs, he will know. Yet I can't let him murder and rape any more girls, not even you.'

Abruptly, without explanation, Hekmeth entered the small bathroom and slammed the door. She was gone for about five minutes, then reappeared. She shook her head at Nolan. 'When I've gone, look inside the drophole,' she said. 'I'm sorry, but that's the best I can do. I'm sorry about your man too. I can't tell you anything more that might help him, but at least he's a soldier, not a helpless girl.'

She bowed as if on stage, then flung back her plume of wiry brown hair, swept from the room. Nolan heard her lock the door, hurried into the bathroom, groped in the drophole with cuffed hands. She'd been half expecting to find a key: instead, fixed to the ceramic head with sticking plaster, was a curved Arab knife in an ornate silver scabbard. She unstuck it, clasped it between her hands: she studied the knife, dismayed at what it promised but knowing that Hekmeth had given her a fighting chance.

25

It took forty minutes to set up Dumper at the gap in the rock wall: they arranged him like a crippled spider in the centre of a web of weapons and decoy kit, encircled him in a chain of concealed grenades, mines, mortar bombs. Pickney pumped him as full of morphia and Benzedrine as he dared, until the little Cockney felt he was drifting downstream on a tender pink aircushion, no longer assailed by the dreadful pain in his groin, the agony of his fire-maimed feet. Caine checked that he had the loaded bazooka and his Garand in front of him, the Browning on his left and the spare Bren on his right, that he could reach the operating strings of the daisychain, pintail bombs, noise-makers, smoke generator, and that he had water, matches and cigarettes.

The boys helped each other saddle up their enormous rucksacks: Caine crouched down by Dumper, put a cigarette into his mouth, lit it for him. The fitter puffed smoke with relish, groped in his breast pocket for the precious photo of his wife and daughters, laid it in front of him. Caine had been wondering what parting words he'd have for the brave corporal: how did you say goodbye to the man who'd saved the op? In the event, the only words that came were 'Good luck, mate.' He clapped Dumper's shoulder and stood up, ashamed of his inadequacy, then noticed to his astonishment that Copeland had brought the whole section to unsteady attention, manpacks and all. '*General salute*,' Cope barked. '*Preseeeent arms*.' Caine brought his feet together and snapped up a salute in Dumper's direction: Audley followed suit, and the rest of the troop presented weapons in three clipped drill movements: not precisely Guardee drillpig standard, but it was the gesture that counted, and Caine knew instinctively that it was right. This was the only way to bid a doomed warrior farewell.

Dumper beamed and waved his maimed hand at them, speechless: even as he did so, he clocked blue ghostfigures popping up out of the trembling quicksilver gauze that cloaked the clints and folds of the desert, skirmishing towards the position in slow, tentative probes. He spat sideways into the sand. 'They're here,' he grated. 'Bugger off now, lads: let me do my stuff.' Caine knew these words would be his epitaph: the last he would speak to anyone but himself.

Wallace helped Caine shoulder his manpack, and without another word, the SAS crew faded away into the rippling desert heat-tremors like heavyweight jinns. A few minutes later Caine heard the whizzbang of musketry, the grinding ruckle of machine-gun fire, followed by the flat battercake whallop of the bazooka. He looked back and saw smoke spinnaker up from Dumper's position, adding yet another to the set of dark question marks hanging in the air over their last location: the jeeps, the 3-tonner, the Jerry armoured car, and now Dumper's smoke generator. He wondered grimly whether the Hun would bring the Stukas back if they found Dumper a tough nut to crack, and if not, how long the little corporal would last.

The SAS section spread out in file, five yards apart,

with Caine navigating at number-two position, Larousse tail-end Charlie, and Copeland scouting in the lead. Working his long legs like a pair of compasses, huffing from the weight of his manpack, Cope set up a cracking pace: they had to distance themselves from the enemy while they could, to get off the open plain and into the labyrinths of the foothills before airsupport was once more whipped up.

They had been dreading the heat of midday, but they were saved by splines of murky cloud that slung themselves across the heavens in a ragged alphabet, throttling the sun, skimming off heat, permitting sunlight through only in shafts. As the rattles and crumps of the firefight faded into the background, they panted on, humping their great burdens like a troop of tortoises, pumping amphetamine-fired limbs, hustling gratefully through the river of shadows towards the mountains' beckoning haven.

The weight on their backs was murderous: the creaking straps cut into flesh, and within an hour it felt as if they were carrying the whole world on their shoulders; they moved more slowly now, bent over, wheezing and sweating. Caine had them halt for a five-minute rest every half-hour, warning them to take only sparing gulps from their waterbottles. While they rested, Gibson and Rossi set up ingenious little boobytraps along their trail: packets of PE or armed grenades attached to detonators fired by pressure-release switches, buried under bits of kit; discarded webbing pouches or items of clothing trapped under medium-sized boulders. Any tracker who lifted the boulder to examine the kit would get his face blasted off. Caine hoped no inquisitive Senussi would happen along.

By early afternoon they were climbing up through a sprawl of warped sandstone, along defiles where thin grey sand lay underfoot like a frayed carpet, where lizards drowsing on hot basalt boulders stared at them with unblinking golden eyes, where dead fingers of thornbush clawed out of crevices, where the bones of mules, goats and camels lay in the dust like polished teeth. They started to come across the half-buried remnants of saddles, fragments of rope, fractured hobbles, bits of tattered muslin, ancient waterskins twisted and hardened by the sun, cairns of boulders piled up on wadi sides, tiny stone corrals where newborn kids had been kept, beds of animal droppings like hard black pebbles.

High on the shoulder of the drywash, they found ruins of a Senussi hamlet – mud huts with caved-in straw roofs, walls gouged with gaps like shellholes, doorways like bent and shapeless mouths. Caine told the patrol to rest in the wadi while he and Copeland climbed up the bank to investigate. There were three dead Senussi in the first hut, their bodies bags of bone and leather, half mummified in the heat. The man had been hanged – his body, clothed in tattered strips, was strung by rope from a rafter: his eyes were vacant sockets where carrion birds had pecked them out; the remnants of his parchment-yellow flesh were full of maggots and peppered with angry red gulfs and atolls where his cadaver had been gnawed. The two women lay face up on the floor below in worm-infested heaps, naked, eyeless, straddled in obscene postures, the ends of wooden clubs protruding from between their legs. Their throats had been cut, and their corpses lay on a wine-coloured carpet of blood long ago congealed, tracked through with the signs of rats, birds, insects, foxes and the other small scavengers that had feasted on them.

'*Jesus wept*,' Cope said.

They lurched out retching, forcing themselves not to throw up. 'Looks like the Angel of Death came to call,' Caine croaked. Some of the other huts had been burned to the ground, but they didn't look any further. They turned their backs on the village, scrambled back down into the wadi, putting up a pair of pied crows from an acacia tree: the birds fluttered away cawing, then followed the patrol for a while in fits and starts.

They crested a rise and saw the Shakir cliffs before them, a sheer rock wall jutting out of black talus, winding away on both sides as far as the eye could see. From back at the leaguer the rock had looked smooth as a planed board, but now they were closer Caine saw that the surface was pitted and scored, whittled into butts and chimneys, flying pedestals, soaring buttresses like watchtowers, fluted columns like great lopsided organpipes.

They halted on the edge of the scree at the base of the cliffs, lowering their manpacks into the sand, reaching for cigarettes and waterbottles. They took only enough liquid to wet blistered lips and sandblasted tongues: few had as much as a third of a bottle left, and the prospect of a resupply that day looked grim. They'd been resting only a minute when they heard a low thump from the direction of their final leaguer, a barely audible hammerblow heard from far off. They exchanged glances, knowing that Dumper had just played his last card. 'Poor bugger,' Wallace said. Caine felt a terrible nausea welling up in his stomach: he had wondered how long the corporal would hold out. It was three and a half hours since they'd left their last position, so now he knew. Now he was wondering how quickly the enemy would be on their trail.

Caine fought back the sick, heavy feeling. He smoked, watched the cigarette burn between his fingers, telling himself that when it had burned down to the butt, he must be on his feet again. He gave himself up to a few moments' reflection. The night and the storm had seemed eternal, but since they'd come out of it, events had moved at lightning pace. The enemy had been waiting for them, there could be no doubt of that. The Stukas had fallen on them only minutes after their halt. When they'd bumped the Axis patrol two days back, his intuition told him they'd been expected. The dying Roland had suspected it, too; the German prisoner had confirmed that his unit had been looking for someone. This second attack, though, scotched all claims of coincidence. The Axis knew they were coming, knew about their landfall. There could be a leak at GHQ, of course, but as far as Caine knew, the details of his march in had been confined to Stirling, Mayne and his own team. If there *was* a stoolie, it could only be within the SAS.

Gibson and Rossi were already on the scree, laying out the grappling gun, coils of rope, hammer and pitons for the climb. Caine ground out his cigarette, collected the butt, stood up. He posted Larousse and Wallace out, with Brens, as pickets, to watch for anyone coming up the trail behind them, and told the boys to make a dump of their manpacks: the gear would be hoisted up the cliff on a separate rope. Caine watched the cowboy tie the end of a ropecoil round Rossi's waist, while the Swiss jammed a hammer into his belt and crammed an ammo pouch with pitons: he was wearing KD shirt and shorts, fingerless woollen gloves, and had wound strips of scrim-hessian around his knees. He had removed his sandals and wore only socks on his feet. 'Rock's gonna be damn' hot,' the cowboy told Caine. 'It'd be better to wait till after dark. In any case, they'll see us from miles away climbin' the face.'

Caine shook his head. 'Can't be helped,' he said. 'Time is the essence.' He paused, watching Rossi sullenly slinging his Garand rifle across his back. 'How do you rate it, anyway?'

The Swiss shrugged, narrowed his eyes, not looking at Caine but at the cliffs. 'I've seen worse,' he said.

'We'll have you up,' the cowboy said. 'No problem.'

Caine's gaze lingered on Rossi's feet with their thin covering of army-issue socks. 'You going to be all right without boots?' he enquired.

Rossi's gunblack eyes flickered. 'Boots ain't much good for cliff-scalin',' the cowboy said. 'Not if you're leadin', that is. You need your toes to work into cracks, mebbe get a hold.'

Caine nodded, watched the cowboy fit the grappling gun into a bony shoulder, watched the bleached-out old-man's eyes narrow as they fixed on a rock claw extending from the top of the cliff. The cowboy aimed the rocketgun up almost vertically and squeezed the firing mechanism. The gun cracked: the grapple sleared upwards across the rockface with the rope snaking behind it. It struck the rock with a metallic *bong* and dropped back like a windless kite, hitting the earth near Gibson's feet. 'Shit,' the cowboy said.

He reloaded the grapple, picked out a different target: two overlapping fingers of rock standing out along the clifftop in a 'V' shape, like an obscene gesture. He aimed. He fired. The grapple skittered, the rope undulated: the grapple struck the fingers a glancing blow and fell back again. The cowboy picked up the grapple and swore: 'Bloody useless piece o' crap.'

He fired a third time, and the lads watched with bated breath as the grapple whooshed up the face, tinkled against stone. It stuck: the cowboy jerked the rope hard, but it didn't budge. He swung on the rope: it stayed put. He and Rossi swung on it together: it remained in place. The cowboy beamed, crinkle-eyed. 'That should do it,' he said.

Rossi slank lowshouldered to the place where the rope dangled: he stood at the base for a long moment, contemplating the stone: almost, Caine thought, as if he were talking to it. Then he grasped the rope a full arm's length above his head, pulled himself up until it was tucked under his elbows and trapped the trailing rope between his sockclad feet. He began to climb, steadily, methodically, using the rope at his feet for purchase, with the second rope hanging from his body like a tail. He reached up, pulled down, hoisted his legs, grasped the rope between his feet, extended his arms, his body undulating wormlike, moving with such precision, grace and poise that he might have had sticky pads on his limbs. The lads watched him, openmouthed – all but Trubman were climbers of some standard, but Rossi seemed to work up the rockface without effort, like a human lizard.

Within minutes, his lean body was hanging on the rope two hundred feet above them: he was still going, but slower now, pausing between spasms of movement, taking short rests between every three or four pulls: Caine could imagine the backbreaking strain, the pressure on his arms and legs, increasing slowly as he ascended, the agony of his cracking, exhausted muscles. It took him fifteen minutes to cover the next hundred feet, and by the time he'd done it he was slowing visibly, resting between each pull. The final stretch must have been excruciating, Caine thought: Rossi did it by sheer willpower, moving more and more slowly until he came to a halt below the overhanging fingers, four hundred feet above Caine's head.

Caine watched as, clinging to the rope onehanded, Rossi took a piton from his pouch and worked it carefully into a crack that Caine couldn't see: he eased the hammer from his belt and gave the piton a few judicious taps then, using it as a foothold, balancing like a cat, he hammered a second piton in at arm's length. He unfastened the rope at his waist, tied a slipknot with one hand and looped it over the spike. Still balancing on the first piton, he began to hoist his body up, and at that instant the spike at his feet gave way: Caine gasped as Rossi lost purchase and dropped like a stone.

Caine was just thinking that the Swiss would plummet to his death when Rossi grabbed the grapplerope and swung free, all his weight on his arms, his legs kicking. The cowboy watched stonefaced. The piton bounced down the cliff-face, striking the rock with a clang, falling to earth only yards away. By that time, Rossi had raised himself up to the second spike and, using it as a toehold, hauled his slim body in among the jagged rocks. Caine saw the dark head peering down at them, saw Rossi give thumbs up.

The lads cheered, clapped, muttered words of awe. A moment later, Rossi had fixed the grappling rope more securely and belayed the second line. The cowboy strapped the end of a third coil of rope to his back, tied the securing line around his waist and started to climb. He made fast progress, safe in the knowledge that if he slipped he would be saved by the secure line. Once he'd joined Rossi on the clifftop, he let the third line down for the rucksacks, in a place about ten yards along the cliff. While Caine took his turn on the face, Copeland, Netanya, Trubman and Pickney humped the heavy rucksacks over to the cliff base, where Audley took charge of tying them to the hoisting rope.

By the time Caine reached the top he was shattered, his muscles screaming, his knifewound itching, his throat on fire with thirst: even wearing the securing rope, the climb had been a nightmare. He sat down for a few moments' rest, uncorked his waterbottle: the water was almost gone. He took a gulp, swilled it round his mouth, spat it back. That was the way he'd been trained in the SAS, but he didn't think it achieved much: you couldn't train the body to do without water, any more than you could train it to do without air. If you didn't have it, you were dead.

He watched Rossi gripping the secure rope, helping to ease up the next climber, Copeland, while the cowboy hauled in the manpacks one by one. The day was already beginning to cool, the sun drooping down into the west through galleries of dustflocced cloud. They were on a table of cobbled talus sown with goatgrass like thinning hair, tilting down to a drywash invisible behind a screen of Aleppo pine, flat-topped acacia, waxleafed Sodom's Apple, cactus spatulas of prickly pear. Beyond the wadi, a ragglestone escarpment swelled steeply, dressed in panic grass and stunted thorn.

Glassing the desert to the south with his binos, Caine could still see feathers of smoke rising beyond the sandstone warren they'd tramped through that morning: the last souvenirs of Dumper's stand. A little nearer, within the maze, he made out a plume of ashcoloured dust. He bit his lip, focused in on the dustcloud: it was impossible to be certain, but he'd have bet money it was the Boche, following their tracks. He stood up and pointed it out to Gibson and Rossi. 'Looks like we've got company,' he said.

The Reapers glanced sliteyed in that direction without pausing from their work. 'They won't get far in their wagons,' the cowboy grunted. 'They'll have to do it on foot. That'll take them at least a couple of hours.'

'. . . And if we're lucky,' growled Rossi, blackbore eyes sparking up, 'they'll find a few of our little surprises on the way.'

Caine put away his binos and went to help Gibson dredging up the manpacks. A few moments later Harry Copeland wormed his lanky body over the lip of the rock. With more hands helping, the work shifted pace. Netanya followed Copeland, then Pickney. Four men together heaved the sacklike lump of Trubman up the rockface: the signaller was sweating, panting and trembling when they finally dragged him over the edge. He collapsed in a sweaty heap, blinking at them blindly like a mole, his lips and tongue mucus-smeared from thirst. 'Tell Gibbo to be careful with the next manpack,' he croaked. 'It's got the No. 11 set in it.'

At almost the same moment, Gibson bawled, '*Oh* s*hit.*' Caine ramped over to him, found him peering over the cliff-face with a limp rope in his hands. Caine took a shufti over the gorge: far below him, the figures of Audley, Larousse and Wallace were gathered round the pancaked rucksack that had just come loose and tumbled down two hundred feet. Big Wallace squinted skyward, saw Caine looking, gave him thumbs down. '*Christ*,' Caine swore, 'we've lost the wireless. That means no comms.'

Trubman tromped up behind them, wheezing, his moleface contorted with uncharacteristic rage. 'That turd Audley,' he grated, his voice quaking. 'I *told* him to be careful tying up that manpack. The bloody idiot's gone and lost it. Now what the heck am I going to do?'

'Use signal flags?' the cowboy suggested with a bloodless smile. 'Or we can find us some pigeons, mebbe –'

He was cut short by a distant thud from somewhere to the south. Caine roved the area with his glasses but couldn't see anything. 'Sounds like the Hun came across one of our offerings,' the cowboy said.

'Yeah,' said Caine. 'That means they're on the way. Let's get the last three lads up pronto: we'll set up a bivvy down there in the trees.'

When Audley came up he was nearly pushed back over by a fuming Trubman, who had already examined the smashed wireless and found it beyond repair. Caine had never seen the signaller so mad. 'It was just bad luck,' Audley protested, whitefaced. 'I tied your manpack with what I thought was extreme care. I tugged on the rope, went for a slash: next thing I knew it came crashing down.'

'Yeah, well, the result of your *extreme care* is that we're out of comms with base,' Caine retorted. 'In other words, we're on our own.'

Audley dabbed sweat off his face with his silk scarf, his eyes indignant. 'That caveman Wallace tried to assault me,' he said. 'It's a good thing Corporal Larousse was there.'

Caine made no comment. He turned his back on Audley to help haul up Larousse and Wallace: they came up at the same time, Wallace on the manpack line. By then, half the section under Copeland had already moved their kit down to the wadi to set up a perimeter in the cover of the bush.

When Caine led the rest of the men towards the drywash thirty minutes later, the sun was ditching into a long red sunset, framing irongrey dustclouds with rims of fire. The stony surface turned to beaten pewter: shadows were draped in funereal curtains from the darkling trees. Caine felt drained: his mouth and throat lyeburned, his lips festering with thirst. They'd had nothing to eat and little to drink since Wallace's desert special had pepped them up that morning. The Benzedrine down was kicking in again: they'd been up for most of thirty-six hours without a break. Yet Caine's senses hadn't deserted him. Just before breaking into the trees, he picked up low voices speaking a foreign tongue. He made a signal: the others froze, cocked their ears. Caine identified the voice of Manny Netanya, speaking to someone else in Arabic. He crouched in shadow: Wallace pressed close to him. 'Must be the Senussi,' he guttered.

'This isn't the RV, though.'

Caine motioned the others to stay put: he and Wallace crept silently forward. They had moved ten yards through the trees when a host of spectral white figures slid out of the shadows without a whisper. They wore flowing shirts, cloaks and headcloths and carried ancient rifles: their faces were hooded masks of inkwashed black. There were at least twenty of them, and they had Caine and Wallace covered.

26

The standoff was broken by Netanya, who slipped in among the white spectres crowing, '*Don't shoot*,' snapping out orders in Arabic. Caine saw the interpreter's skeletal face banded in shadow, his eyes deepsocketed in the dying light. 'These are our Senussi,' Netanya told him. 'They've been sent to meet us.'

He spoke more words in Arabic, and the tribesmen relaxed, put up their weapons. Caine called Gibson, Rossi and Larousse, who squirmed warily in through the scrub. Netanya introduced Caine to a short, squat, powerful Arab with a face like scored granite, eaglebeak nose, foxy eyes and bramblebush beard carrying an antique rifle half as tall as himself in hands as broad and hard as gauntlets. The Arab's name was Sheikh Sidi Mohammad, Netanya said.

They dumped their manpacks on the edge of the drywash, squatted down beyond the span of the tangled acacia woods: the light faded out, leaving them in blue-lamped night. The Senussi settled two hundred yards down the wadi bed, sitting very straight and dignified – small, neatbodied, ageless men in threadbare robes and tight-bound turbans, smelling of goat-grease and woodsmoke. Their rifles were tricked out with strips of goatskin and plaited woollen tassels: they carried curveheaded throwing clubs carved from acacia wood and wore daggers on raw-hide belts, and bandoliers of bullets across their chests.

They sat very close together in a half-circle, watchful and silent, their weapons across their knees, smoking powdered tobacco from brass cartridge cases. Sidi Mohammad knelt among the SAS men, passed round a sweating goatskin: Caine tasted mud and tar and goatpiss in the water when he drank.

He gave Sidi Mohammad a cigarette: the Arab smoked holding it upturned between finger and thumb with a curiously incongruous elegance. Caine watched him. 'Where's Sheikh Adud?' he enquired.

Sidi Mohammad spoke in bursts, waving the cigarette. 'He sends his greetings,' Netanya translated. 'Sidi Mohammad has come to guide us to his camp.'

Caine considered the words. 'The plan was to meet Adud at the RV,' he said. 'That must be six miles further on. Why has there been a change of plan?'

Sidi Mohammad launched into what sounded like a long explanation, jackal eyes riveted on Caine's face. 'They thought you might have trouble from the Boche,' Netanya said. 'He reckons it's not safe here: he says we should get moving right away. They'll escort us to Adud tonight.'

Caine shook his head. 'We're not going any further: we're tired and we need rest. Even if those Huns make the cliff, which I doubt, they won't be able to climb it. Unless they're trained mountain troops and have specialist gear with them, they won't even manage it in daylight. I reckon we're pretty safe here for a while.' He paused. 'Of course, he may be aware of other Axis forces in the area: I'd like to know about that Angel of Death chap and what's been happening here lately.'

Netanya's translation evoked a taut shake of the head.

'He says there aren't any other enemy around,' the interpreter said. 'Adud will fill you in on anything you need to know. The important thing is to get moving now.'

Caine was staring around in the darkness. 'I don't see any sign of the donkeys we asked for,' he said. 'And if they thought we might have trouble, why didn't they show themselves before?'

Netanya repeated Caine's words. Sidi Mohammed shifted and poked at his beard with stumpled fingers. He watched Caine as he spoke. 'They weren't sure who we were at first,' Netanya said. 'As for the donkeys, we'll find them when we reach Adud . . .' The Arab rose abruptly, gabbling, waving a calloused hand, standing over Caine on hard bare feet and bandy legs. His face in the moonlight was angry. 'He says we must get going,' Netanya translated. 'He wants us to move right now.'

Caine didn't budge. 'Tell him we're not going anywhere. We're bivvying here, and we'll move before first light.'

Netanya put this to the sheikh: he scowled, raved, shook his head furiously. Then he slung his rifle and stomped off to join his band.

Caine shifted to a crouch: he felt weak with hunger. The Senussi lit a woodfire: Caine heard a plaintive bleating and realized they were slaughtering a goat. 'If it's so unsafe here, why have they lit a fire?' Copeland whispered.

'Yeah,' the cowboy growled, 'and if they intended to move pronto, why bring a goat?'

'It's not like the Arabs to be so hasty,' Pickney commented. 'Usually they only have two speeds: slow and very slow.'

Caine scratched his prickly, sunburnt jaw. 'Anybody salvage rations?'

They scoured their manpacks and webbing, came up with hardtack biscuits, tins of oatmeal, tea, sugar, condensed milk, a few bars of chocolate. They had no water and no firebox: Netanya had to beg a waterskin from the Senussi while the others collected deadfall along the wadi bank. They lit a fire with handfuls of dry grass, boiled water in mess tins, broke up the chocolate, oatmeal and biscuits to make porridge; the aroma of barbecued meat drifted over to them tantalizingly from the Senussi camp. Wallace distributed all the tea leaves they had into mess tins, sniffed savoury meatfumes, huffed to himself. 'It just ain't like them,' he exploded suddenly. 'I mean, the Senussi have a thing about guests – they're well known for it.'

'I thought you didn't hold with eating poor, defenceless creatures anyway,' Copeland jibed.

Wallace licked chapped lips, pinhole eyes lost in the dark furrows of his crumpled face. 'Goats is *domestic* animals, you duffer,' he barked, swirling tea furiously with a twig. 'That's different, innit.'

'No, it isn't. Meat is meat, after all . . .'

'Yeah, and a meathead's a meathead, after all, too.'

'Fred's right, though,' Pickney cut in quickly. 'I mean, we prevented most of Adud's tribe from getting their necks stretched by Brandenburgers only four months ago. Tom saved the life of Adud's daughter *twice*, for Christ's sake. They reckon an Arab never forgets a favour or a wrong, not in forty years, but you notice the sheikh never said a word about it . . .'

'Mebbe a different crew?' the cowboy suggested.

'Maybe,' Pickney said. 'But the Senussi are clannish as hell. I can't see Adud trusting anyone outside his own.'

'Yes,' Audley said, yawning. 'There's something in that. If he wanted to change plan, the right thing to do would be to come in person.'

Caine took a mug of sweet, milky tea from Wallace. 'Maybe they're just mean Senussi,' he said, sipping. 'Whatever the case, though, I want two men on hour stags through the night. Even when you're not on stag, keep your footwear on, your weapons on you and your manpack close: *Sandhog* is finished if those Lewes bombs go walkies. Mr Audley, I'd like you and Corporal Larousse to take first watch. Wake me if anything happens.'

Audley's face dropped. 'Excuse me, Mr Caine,' he protested, 'I'm an officer. I shouldn't even have to *do* sentry duty, let alone take first stag.'

The men went quiet: Caine's teeth glowed, luminous in the moonblue dark.

'You shouldn't have lost us the wireless, either,' Taff Trubman cut in suddenly, his voice unfamiliar in its harshness. 'But you did. Thanks to you, there's now no way we can call for an aircraft or an LRDG patrol to pull us out.'

The men didn't snigger or comment: Audley sat up, fuming. 'It wasn't my fault. I told you I took extra care with your manpack.'

'Whatever the case,' Caine said, waving the argument away. 'As far as routine duties go, we make no distinction between officers and enlisted men. In this unit, everyone does their bit.'

The cold had already fallen by the time they hit the sack: from far to the south there came rumbles of dry thunder and occasional lightning flares like the flicker of damaged neontubes. Some of the lads had ditched their sleeping bags back at the leaguer and had to share, huddling close together with a fleabag between two, held lengthways across their upper bodies. Audley and Larousse took an arc each, lay down in the bushes fifty paces on either side of the circle.

Caine dozed off and woke with a start an hour later. He sat up: an owl hoohooed in the trees nearby and he wondered if it could have been this that woke him. The night was cold and very still, the moon still out, stars spangling the blueness, and there was the momentary scorpion sting of dry lightning far away. His fingers touched the bore of his Tommy-gun in the fleabag: he checked that he had the infrared nightsight near at hand but didn't touch it. Instead, he peered raweyed into the night. The lads were asleep, breathing rhythmically: they were arranged around him like the spokes of a wheel, with their feet to the hub, touching each other, to ensure that everyone was alerted if they had to stand to.

He didn't see Larousse or Audley among them: his watch told him it was past relief time, and he hoped they hadn't succumbed to exhaustion: if Audley was asleep after losing them the wireless set, he'd roast him alive, he thought. He strained his eyes towards the Senussi camp: the fire had burned down and he saw no movement, nothing at all in the darkness but the dying embers.

He suppressed a yawn, debated whether to check that the pickets had been relieved. He had almost fallen asleep again when someone shook his shoulder: a cowled shadow leaned across him. He was fully awake instantly, sitting up, grabbing his pistol with one hand and the arm that had shaken him with the other. He felt stringy muscles yield to his grip, brought his weapon to bear. '*Don't move,*' he growled, but the shadow was not struggling. Instead, it squatted softly beside him in a rustle of black draperies, a hint of sandalwood, a head masked and hooded. '*Get up, Caine,*' a female voice sussurated. '*Quick.*' The hood was abruptly pushed back, and in the ironlight Caine recognized the sloe eyes, high-bridged nose, full lips and gleaming white teeth of Layla, the daughter of Sheikh Adud, the girl whose life he'd saved twice from the Brandenburgers. Her eyes were dark drillbits, her oval face distorted in warning. '*Treachery, Caine,*' she hissed. '*Sta attento . . . beware.*'

For an instant Caine thought he was dreaming. Then he was out of his sleepsack, flat on his stomach grasping his Thompson: he kicked at the others' feet, making a sign for silence as they opened their eyes and lay to. Layla fell prone so near he could feel the warmth of her body. 'Sidi Mohammad is bad Senussi,' she whispered, her mouth almost touching his ear. 'He work with Al-Malaikat al-Mowt. He bring *Tedesci* here.'

Caine sensed the rest of the lads crawling up around him. '*They come,*' Layla hissed in his ear. Caine strained to make out movement then remembered the nightsight, felt for it in his haversack. He brought out the boxcamera-like apparatus, peered through the eyepiece. The night was momentarily peeled back, the wadi seemed bathed in brimstone. At once he clocked a dozen figures creeping along the wadi side towards them, taut bodies whispering along the rim of the trees. They were Senussi, but Senussi transformed: gone the sweeping robes, the headcloths, the stately grace. These Arabs went barefoot, naked but for baggy britches, torsos slick with animal fat, hung with magical charms in hide pouches, heads bristling with greased plaitlocks or shaven down to the bone, faces devilish with antimony. Their almond eyes burned catlike, the black pits of their mouths were set in deadly purpose. In their hands they held rifles, clubs and daggers and they moved with an animal stealth, edging highshouldered through the purlieus with the adroitness of hunting leopards. There could be no doubt about their intentions: they would be on his position in no more than five minutes.

Caine lowered the nightsight, turned his head to the others, nodded towards the nearest bushes, emphasizing the order with a handsign. Leaving their fleabags and manpacks where they were, the SAS men crawled backwards, four or five yards into the thornbush and tamarix. They waited, their weapons ready, their eyes riveted on the sleeping place. Caine scanned the empty sleepsacks and realized with a sudden jolt of horror that not all were unoccupied. Among them, breathing sonorously, was the sacklike mass of Taffy Trubman.

Caine had no time to alert him. Next moment, the Senussi had moved in on the dummy sleepers, throwingsticks held high, wan starlight mirrored on needle teeth and basilisk eyeballs. Caine sighted up on the first Arab to take a step towards the dark mound that was Trubman. He saw the bludgeon raised, the greased iron. The Thompson clappered: gunshots warped the glassbubble stillness. Garands horned out sharp spears of fire. The night heaved and splintered. The bludgeon vanished, the Arab's hand wilted as a bullet severed his wristbones, another tore open his bicep like a paper bag; he seesawed, danced: a dozen rounds pincushioned him. His stalklike neck buckled, his jawbone, malleted off by an M2 dumdum, sailed over Trubman's head in a comet of flesh, toothshards and splintered bone. The Arab coalsacked, fell on top of Trubman, strangled gurgling issuing from his throat, gore hosing from his wounds. Caine saw the signaller sluiced with blood, saw him roll out from under the gouging body, saw him grab his pistol, crawl away. Two more Arabs loomed over him: Caine saw the signaller turn, saw the Browning in his chubby fist, heard the *sprutz* as he belted a round pointblank into an Arab's groin. He saw the smokepuff, heard the screech, saw the Arab boogie in pain. Copeland's rifle shirred like a straplash: a .303 tracer hotwired air, needled Trubman's second assailant in the arse, spearshotted clean through one cheek and into the other, sledded out in a gout of scorched mincemeat, plunged into his jitterbugging comrade's thigh with a wet clap. Blood gouted and sprizzled: the two Senussi went bellydown together, drybreasting sand, bleeding from the ears, spewing gore, bleating and praying. The other Arabs, frozen in the act of clubbing empty bedrolls, roared in confusion, joggling madly, jumping like netted fish, trying to dodge bullets, trying to see where the shots were coming from. A couple fell flat on their faces: Caine couldn't tell if they were hit. Some cursed in Arabic, hurled daggers and throwingsticks blindly, loosed off shots from their ancient rifles: most ran for it, leaping and bounding like spooked antelopes into the lampblack night.

The SAS men fired after them but quickly stopped: their first concern was for the Lewes bombs, and they turned back to survey their sleeping place, now lying under a soapsud warp of smoke and dust. Taffy Trubman stood up shakily, wiping gore out of his eyes, covering the dead and dying Arabs with his pistol.

Caine moved cautiously out of the trees towards him. Of the three Senussi who'd gone for the signaller, one lay still in gorewaxed sand: the two others rolled and thrashed, choking, cursing, trying to get up. Caine drew his bayonet and stepped towards the first: before he could move, Rossi and Gibson stalked in, the knives in their hands going *slick* as they sawed at the necks of the two dying Senussi. Warm blood slathered their faces: the Arabs gargled, went rigid, but the Reapers didn't cease from their butchery until they'd hacked right through the neck vertebrae, cut both heads clean off. They looked, Caine thought, as if they'd done it before. They held up their trophies by the hair, scattering gore droplets as if in benediction, their faces smeared with Rorschach bloodspots like warpaint.

Caine stifled a protest, turned away in disgust, saw Trubman bend over and throw up. 'You all right, mate?' he asked.

'Yep.'

'How come you never pulled out with the rest of us?'

'Just dog-tired I s'pose.'

Caine moved over to Copeland, who was poking at another prone Arab with the muzzle of his rifle. The man was paperpale and appeared unconscious: Caine had seen him go down but didn't know if he'd been shot. He was just saying, 'I'm not sure about . . .' when the Arab's eyes opened wide: he lunged at Cope with a long, curved dagger he'd been concealing in the folds of his baggy trousers. Before Copeland could squeeze iron, a gunshot snare-drummed: buckshot flayed off the naked skin of the Arab's gut in shirttail flaps, exposing raw entrails like handfuls of groping fingers, pitching the shattered body into a five-yard forward flip. Copeland turned his head to see the broad nightracked face of Fred Wallace, eyes like silver pennies, the twineyed bores of his sawnoff smoking in his big hand. Wallace's eyes didn't leave the Arab's corpse. 'That quick enough for you, mate?' he growled.

Caine was so distracted that he didn't notice the other Arab who'd played possum get to his feet panther quiet behind him. '*Sta attento*,' a female voice sopranoed; Caine had half turned when the Senussi struck at him with a throwing stick. Caine ducked, brought up his Tommy gun: in that instant Layla pounced on the Arab's bare shoulders, clinging there like a giant vampire bat. The man jumped, jigged, bellowed, tried to knock her off with backhanded swipes. Caine saw a slimblade knife flash, saw the Senussi girl draw it across the man's throat, saw blood skew from a wound like a gaping fishmouth. The Arab tottered: Layla dropped from his back. Caine blobbed a doubletap into his belly, slapped him into the dust.

There was a moment's silence as the SAS men caught their breath, took in the carnage, the five broken and dismembered Senussi corpses, the slathertrails of blood in the darkness. 'Grab everything and move out,' Caine ordered, pointing at the dense trees on the wadi bank. 'Get in there, all-round defence.'

Moments later they'd humped the heavy kit into the trees and formed a loose perimeter covering every arc. Caine crouched in the centre with Copeland and Layla. 'Thank you,' he told her. 'If you hadn't warned us, we'd have all been captured or killed.'

'The thanks is to Allah,' she said.

Caine looked at her, saw flecks of starlight in her eyes like tiny crescent moons. 'I am so happy see you,' she said, touching his hand lightly with her fingers. It was an extraordinarily forward gesture for a Senussi girl, he thought: but then she was no ordinary girl. Only minutes ago he'd seen her kill a fellow tribesman with a dagger. She stroked the back of his hand, gazing into his eyes so tenderly that he had to look away: he recalled how Nolan had once told him that Layla cared for him.

'What happened to my guards?' he asked.

'Sidi Mohammad and his men, he take them . . . you sleep . . . I see. He leave other men to get you. He take them away.'

'Where?' Caine asked. 'Took them where?'

Layla shrugged, nodding northwards. 'Into hills. To *Tedesci* maybe. Sidi Mohammad is traitor Senussi. He work for Angel of Death.'

'Who *is* the Angel of Death?' Caine said.

The girl shrugged a second time. 'I don't know. Nobody know. He is wicked man, bad jinn, some say.'

Caine called Netanya to speed the exchange: Layla spoke at length, rarely taking her eyes from Caine's face. 'Adud is camped at the RV,' Netanya explained at last, 'with the donkeys. He's been there a couple of days waiting for us. He sent Layla here to look for us while it was still daylight, and she spotted that Sidi Mohammad chap and his band moving towards the Shakir cliffs. She followed them, but she had to stay well hidden. She waited till they settled down and was just going to alert you when she saw them capture Audley and Larousse.'

'She's sure they're not dead?'

'They had orders to capture us,' Copeland cut in. 'They must have done, otherwise they'd have come in shooting, or even picked us off from cover.'

Caine considered it. 'But how did they *know* we were coming?' he demanded. 'Did Layla or Adud or any of their band let it slip?'

Netanya was about to ask Layla when she cut him off, sloe eyes flashing angrily. 'We no tell no one,' she said. 'Hooker – the *Ingleezi* who send us message – he did not say you would come up Shakir. He only told us the meeting place. My father send me to look along all paths: I come here only because I follow Sidi Mohammad's men.'

Caine swallowed dryly, locked eyes with Copeland. Both of them knew this was yet another confirmation that *Sandhog* had been compromised. But how? Only Stirling and Mayne had known they were heading for the Shakir cliffs, but even they hadn't known exactly *when* they'd climb them. Caine hadn't known it himself, couldn't have predicted it with any precision until that morning. Copeland guessed what he was thinking. 'The Axis ground patrol that was tracking us,' he said. 'They must have been in contact with someone up here.'

Caine frowned in the darkness. 'How could they know our plan was to scale the cliff, though? We might have trekked along the base and gone up one of the easier passes miles further on. Our RV with Adud might have been anywhere.'

Copeland was thinking about something else. 'If they're taking Larousse and Audley to the Jerries,' he said, 'they'll torture and interrogate them: they'll find out that our plan is to hit the Olzon-13 stocks in the Citadel.'

Caine sucked his teeth, tasted bile and grit. 'We've got to go after them, get them back. If we go now, maybe we can pull them out before they reach the Jerries.'

'But skipper,' Copeland objected. 'We'd be playing into the enemy's hands. We've only got until midnight on 25/26 October – that's the day after tomorrow. We should move on the Citadel asap, and hope that Larousse and Audley will keep them distracted with red herrings long enough to cover us. And how the heck are we going to catch up with them lugging a two-hundred-pound manpack apiece, anyway? More, because we now have extra manpacks to lug? I'm sorry, Tom, but I think it's crazy.' He paused. 'As for Audley, for all the use he is, we may as well let the Hun have him.'

'He's one of ours,' Caine said. 'We're not leaving anyone to the mercies of this Angel of Death bastard. Remember that Senussi village? We've seen what he's capable of.' Cope went quiet: Caine thought for a moment. 'Here's what we'll do,' he said. 'Me and Fred will go after the prisoners. Harry, you'll take charge of the rest of the boys. Move the kit about a mile up the wadi in case any of Sidi Mohammad's lot come back . . .' He stopped and looked at the girl. 'Layla, you go with Harry: see where they take the equipment. Then run to your father as quick as you can and bring him back with the donkeys to pick it up.'

He sensed her hesitation. 'No, Caine,' she said, her voice low. 'I stay with you. Now I find you I don't leave you again.' There was a tenderness in her voice that Caine couldn't ignore: despite his misgivings, he touched her hand. 'Please, Layla, do as I ask. We have come to kill the Angel of Death: to free your people. This will help.'

She heard the gravity in his voice, nodded reluctantly. Caine got out his map and examined it in veiled torchlight. 'Is your father's camp where it was?' he asked. Layla nodded again. 'Good. When he has picked up our equipment, please tell him to take it back to his camp, not to the meeting place. We will meet him – and you – there.'

Caine turned to Copeland again. 'Right, let's get cracking. You've got Netanya with you for liaison.' As Cope stood up, Caine pulled him aside. 'If we're not back by last light tomorrow, go ahead with the plan as best you can.'

Copeland paused, and though Caine couldn't see his face well in the darkness, he could imagine the frownlines of disapproval. 'Very good, skipper,' he said.

27

Johann Eisner jumped ashore from the felucca, left the boatman to tie up at the jetty. He glanced up- and down-river, took in the ripe and seamy odours, the fantrails of gilded light etched on the water from an afternoon sun lodged like a yellow eye above lawns and whitewashed villas. He saw nothing amiss: anyone watching the boat from a distance would, anyway, see two Nile river rats wearing dirty gallabiyas of striped pyjamacloth and shapeless tarbooshes perched on cropped bullet heads. The only giveaway would be the tips of Eisner's polished black shoes under the long shirt, but he told himself that no one would be looking close enough to notice them, nor the fact that his face lacked the boatman's crusted soapstone features, the vine of furrows from sunblasted years navigating the Delta.

Eisner was mistaken: his arrival had been noted by Field Security watchers sited in the vacant house across the river, one of whom was even now gabbling urgently on a field telephone to John Stocker. Eisner's thoughts were all for Betty Nolan, holed up in the cellar of his stepfather's villa, in the very room where he'd been humiliated as a youth by Idriss's taunting, by the mocking laughter of teenage girls: the room where he'd stifled that laughter with knife and garotte, though not for ever, since it still haunted his dreams. He knew Hekmeth was in the house: his adopted sister had done well in abducting Nolan. Who gave a damn if some other bitch had got herself shot in the process? He regretted the job that had kept him in Jerusalem for more than a week, but what mattered now was finishing Nolan. He intended to get that over with, and talk to Hekmeth later.

He followed the mosaic path through the rosegarden, past the swimming pool and into the cool shade of the covered verandah, where he hastily shucked the soiled gallabiya and tarboosh behind trellis screens. He put on dark glasses, slipped out his stiletto. He passed through the open garden door, went down the stairs towards the cellar.

When the cellar door flew open Nolan was ready: she'd been preparing herself for Eisner's arrival since morning. The fact that he was here meant that either Field Security hadn't staked out the house at all or that they *were* watching but had somehow missed him. Whatever the case, it was down to her: not only her life but Tom Caine's depended on what she did in the next few minutes. Hekmeth's brief account of Eisner's youth had provided her with raw material, out of which she'd fashioned a strategy: she had secreted the knife under her pillow. Whether Eisner would go for her at once, or whether she'd be able to engage him in dialogue, she didn't know: she'd allowed for both options.

Johann Eisner stood in the doorway, watching her with a vulture stare. He was dressed all in black; the wraparound lenses of his shades enhanced his wolfish features – a tall, leanjowled man with a mat of black hair, a thinbridged nose, razor jaws and a slim neck emerging from broad shoulders. He looked almost exactly as he had the last time Nolan had seen him: in the act of sodomizing Mary

Goddard while slitting her throat with a vicious little curved stiletto. She held back a gasp. That very weapon was in his hand now – the knife that had ended the life of Goddard, Sim-Sim, Susan Arquette and God knew how many other women.

'Betty Nolan,' Eisner said gloatingly. He shut and locked the door, and oiled into the room towards her. 'What a pleasure. You don't know how much I have looked forward to this moment.'

Nolan said nothing: she sat handcuffed on the end of the bed nearest the pillow. Eisner moved in on her, took off and pocketed his glasses, touched her chin with cold fingers. Close up, his face was almost nondescript, the kind of face she'd sometimes seen on skilled actors, the kind that had no definite nature of its own but came alive when assuming someone else's character. His eyes, though, were sinister and disturbing: there was a mesmeric quality to them that made Nolan wince. She suppressed the feeling by sheer willpower: not for the first time, her life depended on her acting skill.

Eisner's eyes awled her. 'The *real* Betty Nolan,' he said. 'In the flesh. No more dressing up, no more doppelgangers. I'd know you anywhere – I knew you even when I saw you in the uniform of a naval officer in that staff car . . .'

This wasn't strictly true: he'd recognized her face, but it had taken him some time to remember she was a cabaret girl he'd once seen at Madame Badia's nightclub. Not just any cabaret girl, but *the* girl who'd walked in while he was giving that hag Mary Goddard the business. Nolan was the only eyewitness to that . . . incident. The only one who'd witnessed any of the incidents: the only one able to swear that it was really him who'd done it. That was why he had to get rid of her. 'You caused me a lot of trouble, Betty,' he said. 'All that nonsense about Maddy Rose. You led me a wild-goose chase, in the course of which I had to punish your friend Sim-Sim for her obstinacy. She was quite an animal.' He snickered, licked wet lips. 'I gave it to her till she begged me to stop . . .'

He was panting, his eyes far away, excited by the memory of his brutal rape and murder of a defenceless girl. He let the stiletto blade tickle Nolan's throat: she didn't pull back, neither did she look petrified. This irritated him, and with a savage movement he cut down the front of her blouse, peeling it away from her breasts. He touched her nipples with the point of the knife, one after the other. Nolan sucked air through clenched teeth. She didn't scream.

'That witch I found at your flat . . . Susan, was it? She was quite a beast too, but not the real thoroughbred, not like you. I shall enjoy –'

He didn't complete the sentence, put off by something in her eyes – a hardness he had never encountered before in his victims. Up to now Nolan hadn't shown any of the normal symptoms of fear: it confused and disconcerted him.

He swallowed dryly. 'I am going to do you the way I did Mary Goddard. I'm going to ride you and cut your throat.' His breath was coming in ragged stabs, his tongue snaking out: the very idea of doing it to her aroused him. 'The last thing you will ever feel is me inside you.'

Nolan forced herself to look directly into the smouldering eyes: she kept up the iron stare by pure determination.

'I've faced death before,' she said, almost nonchalantly. 'Why don't you get on with it instead of just mouthing off?'

She knew at once she'd hit the mark: Eisner's razor jaws dropped. His features sagged and he took several steps back. Nolan followed up her advantage with a street-fighter's sureness. 'I know the answer, of course,' she said, cupid lips pouting contempt. 'It's because you're more afraid of me than I am of you . . .' She sniggered, and to her ears it sounded satisfyingly genuine.

Eisner blinked: his eyes had lost their hypnotic sheen. He suddenly looked pale and feeble. 'That's nonsense,' he snapped. 'Who's been . . .'

'Is it? I don't think so. When you were a youth, you murdered and sodomized the young girls your stepfather tried to make you have sex with because they laughed at your impotence, and you couldn't stand it. The truth is you're terrified of women. You can't do it to a girl unless she's turned to jelly with fear and completely in your power.' She paused, spat on the floor without taking her eyes off him. 'You can do what you like to me, but I'm not going to beg you to stop, and I'm never going to be in your power.'

She spat a second time, her eyes wild, she edged imperceptibly nearer the pillow. 'That's the only way you can do it, isn't it, *Hussein*? And even then only if the girl is belly-down so she can't see your face and you can fuck her as if she was a *man*.' The scoffing, jeering laughter Nolan produced was one of her finest ever performances, and it struck home like a .50-calibre needleround. Eisner's face went ghastly white, his knifeblade jaws gobied, his mouth frothed. '*Hekmeth* . . .' he shrieked. '*Hekmeth* told you . . .'

'You're not a man, *Hussein*,' Nolan continued, still snickering. 'You're a pathetic, impotent, little kid . . .'

Eisner ran at her bullroaring, his eyes popping, his mouth a foaming, demonic gash, his stiletto glinting in the lightshafts. It was just what Nolan had been waiting for. She flopped on her back, brought her knees up to her chin as if winding back a crossbow. The instant Eisner came in range she kicked him powerfully in the testicles, both feet together, with every ounce of strength in her body. It was a magnificent kick, and it hit bullseye: Eisner grunted in pain, shivvered backwards across the room, squinched the wall. He was only dazed for a second, but that was all it took for Nolan to grab the knife from under her pillow: she caressed its blade between her cuffed hands, stood up, raised it high above her head.

Nolan had once seen Tom Caine kill a German soldier by throwing the Jerry's own bayonet at him, left-handed, at close quarters. It had been an incredibly skilled act, especially for a right-handed man, and though she'd been horrified at the time, it had saved her life. Caine always said a knife was no good unless you could throw it: since *Runefish*, she'd had him coach her in knifethrowing and had practised day in, day out until she had it mastered.

She hadn't anticipated being handcuffed, but in principle it was no different. Before Eisner had collected himself enough to attack her again, she had flipped the knife with all the power and accuracy she could collect. It wasn't the best throw she'd ever made, but it was good enough. The blade snagged him at the base of the neck, glanced off the clavicle, sliced through muscle, pierced the windpipe. Eisner's eyes trapdoored: he rocked back, gore and froth sudding: to Nolan's disappointment, though, he didn't fall. '*You bitch*,' he gobbled. '*I'll do you. I'll have you.*'

He took a staggering step forward. She backed away, tipping over the bed to form a barrier between them: in that moment sharp yells echoed from the corridor outside. Nolan heard the Turk, Hayek, babbling like a loony, heard the distinct *thrubb-thrubb-thrubb* of a Thompson submachine-gun explosively loud in her ears, heard the *bashowww-bashowww* reverberations of a pistol: birdcaws of pain, staccato curses in Arabic, thumps and wolfhowls. Then a fist or a foot lammed the door as hard as a steel ram and a cultured English voice bawled, '*Field Security. Open up there.*'

Eisner froze in midstride, almost comically nonplussed, Nolan's knife still dangling from his throat, blood bubbling from the wound in crimson dobs, his eyes diamondbright with torment, cleft between rage and fear, between revenge and self-preservation. He ripped his gaze from Nolan to the door. The wood boomed, jumped in its frame as someone hurled their whole weight against it. Eisner ground his teeth, tore Nolan's knife from his flesh, darted for the open bathroom, plinked bloodspots on the floor as he moved. Just as the main door was rent from its hinges and burst open, Eisner slammed the bathroom door shut and shucked the bolt.

Nolan giggled uncontrollably, covered her breasts with cuffed hands, clocked John Stocker's diminutive figure stride in through the fractured entrance, a look of brutal purpose written on his studious, professorial features, cyanic eyes beneath thick lenses glittering, a hot Colt .45 in his hand. She glimpsed other khaki-clad men moving in the corridor, treetrunk legs writhing like pythons on the floor, scented sour gun gas, heard stomps and screams from somewhere else in the house. Stocker looked at the bloodspatters, ranged her face piercingly. 'Where is he?' he rasped.

Nolan nodded at the bathroom. 'In the shithouse,' she giggled. 'Where he belongs.'

28

Nolan walked through the hallway into Stocker's office at 8 Midan Sheikh Yusif, the converted Cairo townhouse that served as a base for Field Security. She wore a freshly laundered khaki drill skirt and blouse, a chipbag cap tilted on her blond curls. Not wanting to go back to the flat in Garden City where Pat Rigby had been shot, she'd checked into the Continental in Ezbekiyya Square. She'd wallowed in a hot tub with an iced beer, confident that Stocker would already have informed Caine that *Sandhog* was compromised. She'd covered the bruises on her face with daubs of makeup: despite the experiences of the past week, her eyes hadn't lost the dreamy, far-off, acquiescent expression that drove most men half out of their minds and Tom Caine to distraction.

Stocker and Stirling were waiting for her, smoking pipes, ensconced in patched and overstuffed armchairs that Nolan guessed had once graced Stocker's study at Cairo University. The whole office was redolent of the classics faculty: a blackboard with names scrawled on it in white chalk, a packed library bookcase, a notched desk piled with dogeared books and files, a battered typewriter, a telephone, dusty tumblers, half-empty bottles of spirits, a pipe rack, tobacco jars, an artist's impression of the Parthenon, a bust of Socrates. The officers stood up to return Nolan's salute – a purely gentlemanly gesture, since both outranked her. They could have remained seated without violating regulations, but Nolan was a valued warrior, and too attractive a woman for that.

Nolan sat down on a rickety sofa, lit a cigarette: a glance at Stocker's face told her all was not well. That Eisner had escaped, she already knew. Who could have guessed that the ceiling of that bathroom held a concealed panel, opening into an escape shaft that led directly down to the Nile? It must have been cleverly hidden, because she'd used that room scores of times, even scoured it for a way out, and had never found it. Stocker's man had crawled along the shaft following the bloodtrail: he'd concluded that Eisner had probably got away by swimming underwater, perhaps to a boat moored midstream.

Hekmeth and Beeston had been arrested: they were currently being held at the Detention and Interrogation Centre at Helwan. Stocker had been debriefing them all evening, but neither could throw any light on *Sandhog*, other than Hekmeth's claim that Caine had a traitor on his crew.

Stocker lodged his pipe against an ashtray, removed his glasses, began cleaning them with a piece of four-by-two: a clear sign that he was agitated.

Nolan noticed, and felt suddenly apprehensive. 'What's wrong?' she enquired. 'Don't tell me it's too late?'

Stocker shook his head. 'Hard to tell,' he said. '*Sandhog* has been out of comms for two days: Caine hasn't checked in, and we can't raise him. That means either his set is U/S or . . .'

'. . . he's been bagged,' Stirling completed the sentence. He, too, looked worried, Nolan thought. That didn't surprise her: both the future of the campaign and of the SAS itself depended on *Sandhog*. Stirling had almost as large an investment in Tom Caine as she had.

Nolan stubbed out her cigarette, halfsmoked. She was about to say something when Stirling continued.

'There's news, though. Yesterday, Caine's group called at the HQ of one of Maskelyne's dummy units in the Western Desert asking for help with vehicle repairs. The visit apparently ended with Caine shooting one of the officers and forcing Maskelyne himself off at gunpoint. They dumped him in the desert: his men picked him up promptly, but he wasn't at all a happy camper. The provost marshal now has a warrant out for Caine's arrest. Major Sears-Beach is reportedly over the moon.'

Nolan looked at him aghast. 'I know Caine,' she said. 'He'd never have done that without a good reason.'

Stirling chortled mirthlessly. 'Damn right,' he said, 'and I know what the reason was. Maskelyne felt Caine had compromised his operation: if any of the SAS got bagged, they might spill the beans. He tried to abort *Sandhog*. Caine's under strict orders to bring off *Sandhog* at any cost: he wouldn't have accepted that for a minute, even if it meant doing something drastic. Caine's that sort of boy. He was right to resist: his mistake was contacting Maskelyne in the first place.'

Stocker nodded and replaced his glasses. 'Is there any news of the missing LRDG unit?' he asked.

Stirling whoffed smoke, shook his head. 'Roland's troop wasn't with Caine when he arrived at Maskelyne's position yesterday. Maskelyne reckoned they'd already fought an engagement: if so, the LRDG might have been so badly mauled they couldn't carry out their escort duties, and Caine went ahead without them. The problem is that we've lost comms with Roland, too. There's a Waco spotter out but they haven't found any trace yet.'

Stocker sighed. 'Looking at the map,' he said, 'I doubt Caine will have reached his objective: he has two days to run before the deadline. In view of what Hekmeth has told us – that there's a stoolpigeon in his section – it *is* possible he's been bagged –'

'How do we know the stoolpigeon story is true?' Stirling cut him off. 'It could be disinformation intended to throw *Sandhog* off track. What easier way to force us to abort the mission than to let drop that it's already compromised? Even if Hekmeth believes it, she might have been set up by Eisner . . .' He lifted a stack of thin personnel dossiers from his knees. 'I've been through the backgrounds of Caine's section, and I can't believe any of them is a Nazi sympathizer. It just isn't on the cards.'

Stocker surveyed Stirling's face gravely. 'Hekmeth said that Caine was *walking into a trap*. Now, it is not, of course, conclusive, but I would suggest that, since only Caine knew *Sandhog*'s target, the trap was the contact Maskelyne mentioned: the one that may have done for the LRDG. If so, Caine evidently survived it, and is thus still on his way.' His eyes gleamed, but neither Stirling nor Nolan looked convinced.

'Sergeant Copeland knew where they were going,' Stirling said bluntly. 'He knew because the letter from the Itie woman that helped sanction the op was addressed to him.'

Nolan raised her chin. 'You're saying Copeland is an Axis spy? There's no way, sir. I know Copeland: he's a good man.'

'I'm not saying anything,' Stirling said. 'I'm not even satisfied there *is* a stoolpigeon. I'm just saying that knowledge of the target wasn't confined to Caine alone, and you know how these things get around.'

Stocker cleared his throat. 'Can I suggest,' he said, 'that, for practical purposes, we make two assumptions? The first is that there *is* a traitor in Caine's section. The second is that *Sandhog* is still operational. If either or both of these assumptions is wrong, we haven't lost much. If they are correct, we need to take action. We need to focus our efforts on discovering who the traitor might be, with a view to informing Caine before it is too late.'

'And how the heck do we do that with no comms?' Nolan asked.

'We'll consider that later.'

Stocker stood up and moved over to the blackboard, picking up a pointer, facing them as if he were addressing a tutorial. He thrust the stick at the scrawled names. 'Eleven men, including two officers,' he said. 'Let us consider them systematically and see if there is anything untoward about any of them.'

'There's some I'd eliminate right off,' Stirling said. 'For a start, the two officers. We know Caine is sound as a bell . . .' he grinned '. . . apart from certain, er . . . *idiosyncrasies* of course; Audley comes from a good family: he's ex-Guards, and has won the MC.'

Stocker looked at him, his eyes bright behind the lenses. 'Very well,' he said. 'But let us not exclude them entirely. Let us just leave them till last.'

'All right,' Stirling said grumpily. 'We'll do it your way.'

Stocker pointed to the third name on the list. 'Corporal

Samuel Brian Dumper,' he said, raising an eyebrow at Stirling.

'Dumper's ex-RAOC,' Stirling said, raising his chin, as if he were being asked to sell out his own men. 'A regular soldier, exemplary record. Won the MM for bravery dismantling a live charge, saving a column and getting his fingers blown off in the process. A London bus driver in Civvie Street. Nothing shady in his background: no Nazi sympathies.'

Stocker crossed out his name with a stub of chalk. 'Corporal Gaston Larousse.'

'Larousse came to us highly recommended from Canadian forces. Ex-combat engineer. Excellent record, currently in for the DCM for his action at el-Gala, where he risked his life to give covering fire while the rest of the section escaped. Larousse was married to a French Jewess and had two children. They were abducted during the invasion of France and were killed by the Nazis. I've seen the report. I think that rules him out.'

Stocker put a line through Larousse's name. 'Sergeant Harold Copeland.'

Stirling sighed. 'Copeland's very bright. He won the MM on *Runefish* with Caine. A hostilities-only soldier, ex-RASC trooper-driver. Middle-class family, a teacher in Civvie Street. There were rumours that he was a communist, but that's nonsense. Actually, he's very ambitious and has his eye on a commission: his brother is a captain in the Marines. The only thing against Copeland is the letter business.'

Stocker considered it. 'But there was independent corroboration, I take it?'

'Oh yes.'

Stocker crossed out Copeland's name. 'Corporal Maurice Pickney.'

'Pickney's ex-RAMC. Superb combat medical orderly, he also won the MM on *Runefish*, during which he was badly wounded. He's from Birmingham, an ex-merchant seaman. He's rumoured to be the other way . . .'

'Really?' Stocker's eyes flashed. 'Now, couldn't that knowledge be used for blackmail purposes?'

'Unlikely. Pickney's got high moral principles, and he's tough as they come in combat. Not the type to give in to that kind of pressure.'

Stocker thought about it for a moment, nodded, scrubbed him out.

For the next thirty minutes they went carefully through all the names: by the end of it, both Nolan and Stocker tended to agree with Stirling that none of the SAS men seemed a likely candidate for Nazi stoolpigeon: Wallace had served a term in prison in Civvie Street for grievous bodily harm, but most of his family had been killed by the Germans, and he'd won the MM on *Runefish*; Netanya was a German Jew who'd also lost his people to the Hun: he'd gone AWOL from his unit in Palestine, but he'd done so to join the SIG: hardly Nazi material; Gibson: an American from a poor Texan family with a first-class combat record who'd quit the French Foreign Legion in disgust at the pro-Nazi Vichy regime. A possible plant? Unlikely: Gibson had personally killed dozens of Axis soldiers, many with his bare hands; Rossi: the same. His mother tongue might be Italian, but he'd accounted for so many Ities that the idea of his being a Mussolini sympathizer or a secret Nazi looked ludicrous; Trubman, a quiet Welsh

Presbyterian who didn't drink and who'd only joined the SAS as a signaller because Stirling pressed him to: another ex-*Runefish* MM winner. Not likely.

At the end of it, they sat back in their chairs, flummoxed. Stocker eyed the crossed-out names again. '*Netanya*,' he said suddenly, staring at Stirling. 'Didn't you have trouble with a traitor in the SIG earlier this year?'

Stirling grimaced. 'You mean Bruckner? Yes, but he was an Afrika Korps POW who helped train the SIG, an ex-Foreign Legion trooper who swore on capture that he was anti-Nazi. We trusted him, and he knifed us in the back. His case isn't the same as Netanya's, though: he wasn't Jewish.'

Stocker went silent. 'Then that just leaves Caine and Audley.'

'I've already said what I think about that, Major,' Stirling said severely.

'Yes, you did.' Stocker paused and removed his glasses, put them back on again, and gazed inquisitively at Stirling. 'How much do you know about Lieutenant Audley, sir?' he asked. Nolan noted that it was the first time he'd addressed the younger man as 'sir'.

Stirling looked annoyed. 'I told you, he's ex-Coldstreams: the eldest son of the Marquis of Leigh . . .'

'Really? Do you know the family personally?'

'No, I've never met them: I grew up in Scotland. My family is Roman Catholic, and I went to Ampleforth. I don't know *all* the English nobility . . . anyway, if I remember rightly, Bertie was brought up in South Africa.'

Stocker held up a dishevelled book in his small hand. 'This is the Army List,' he said. 'I took the liberty of consulting it earlier. A Lieutenant Thomas Caine is listed but, most curiously, there is no Lieutenant Bertram Audley.'

Stirling glared at him as if he'd gone mad. 'It must be a mistake,' he said. 'They sometimes miss people, especially in wartime, when there are so many officers.'

'Indeed,' Stocker said. 'That's what I thought myself. I then examined the list of recent winners of the Military Cross. Again, no Lieutenant Bertram Audley, Coldstream Guards, is recorded as having been awarded that decoration. One mistake, yes: but two seems excessive.'

Stirling had gone grey. 'This is nonsense, Major,' he snapped. 'I know how to settle it. I'll ring the duty officer at 201st Guards Brigade right this minute and ask for Audley's record.'

'An excellent idea.'

Stirling picked up the telephone receiver, consulted a list taped to Stocker's wall and dialled the number. 'Hello,' he said. 'It's Colonel Stirling here, 1st SAS Regiment. I'm enquiring about a Lieutenant Bertram Audley. Yes, he's now serving with my unit. Formerly with 1st Battalion, Coldstreams.'

He relaxed for a few moments as the officer went to check, then said, 'Hello, yes,' and listened, his hand on the receiver tightening visibly. He said thank you and put the phone down. When he turned to Stocker, his face was deathly pale. 'There is no record of a Lieutenant Bertram Audley in the Coldstream Guards,' he said heavily, as if forcing the words out one by one.

Nobody spoke. Stirling got up stiffly and took a step over to Stocker's overloaded bookcase. He found the volume he was looking for, took it out and slapped it on the desk. Nolan saw that it was *Debrett's Peerage.* Stirling scrabbled through the pages with white fingers, then stopped and turned to the index. He traced lists with an almost desperate look on his face. Then he slammed the book closed and thumped it with his fist. 'What a bloody fool I've been,' he swore. 'What a bloody *imbecile.* There *is* no Marquis of Leigh. The family doesn't exist. I should have known. I should have *seen* it. The way he behaved at el-Gala. Caine didn't want him on *Sandhog* but I insisted. I'm a bloody moron, and that bastard, whoever he is, has taken me for a ride.'

He swallowed hard and gazed at Stocker, whose expression had turned meek. 'It's *Audley,*' Stirling said, as if he still couldn't believe it. 'Your instinct was correct, Major. Audley is the Nazi stoolpigeon, and if *Sandhog* is still operational, then he must be with Caine right now.'

29

They climbed the escarpment in the milklight, hearing dry thunder and squinting at strings of lightning that drew slowly nearer, giving them glimpses of the hills above, etching their faces with veins of spectral blue. They crept up the path leadbooted, lifting their feet, planting them carefully, feeling for loose stones, crouching every few minutes to watch and listen. They wore cap comforters and had smeared their faces with fireblack, emptied their pouches of anything that rattled, bound them up with string, removed the slings from their weapons, looped strips of hessian around the stocks and swivels.

Once they heard the flat snap of a gunshot from far away: they crouched down, seeing the whites of each other's eyes, wondering what the shot meant. They continued: just before they reached the top, rain fell in sudden slashes, fat droplets sifting across stones. The rain soaked them, skewed down their necks, made them shiver: it lasted only minutes but obscured the tracks they were following. Caine decided to continue along the path anyway: he reckoned their quarry wouldn't leave it until they reached the foot of the escarpment on the other side.

They crested the scarp and saw the flicker of a fire down in the darkseamed valley. Caine took a shufti through the nightsight, made out pale shadows haunting the circle of firelight. Wallace squatted, donned the tactical ear headphones, cocked his head. Caine crouched next to him. 'You reckon it's them?' he asked.

'Yep,' the big gunner answered, pulling off the headset. 'I can make out Arab voices on this thing: I'll bet they weren't expecting a hot pursuit, not on a night like this. They're in their own place and they feel safe. That fire's less than a thousand yards off, skipper. We could hit them from up here.'

Wallace was carrying his Bren, but Caine had swapped his Tommy-gun for a Garand: the night-simulation range had convinced him of its effectiveness in the dark.

He shook his head. 'Nah. We might hit our boys. If it were daylight and we had a clear view, all right, but in this . . . No, we've got to get closer.'

It took them almost thirty minutes to reach the foot of the scarp: the fire was still glowing, and Caine reasoned that the Senussi must have decided to remain here for the rest of the night. The wadi floor was sandy, its edges thick with saltbush, knifegrass and prickly pear. They fell prone and crawled across the sand into the bush, walking on their elbows, holding their weapons clear of the ground between cupped palms. They found a place behind a nest of egg-shaped boulders amongst the trees from where they could see the fire blazing under a chalk rockface no more than fifty paces off.

Caine moved around the edge of the boulder nest, peered through the nightsight, saw the wadi brushed with steely light. To his surprise there was now only one figure by the fire: it was Bertram Audley, sitting crosslegged, gazing morosely into the flames. He didn't seem to be tied up or confined in any way. Caine panned the RG sight back and forth: he clocked no Senussi, saw no sign of Gaston Larousse. A warning klaxon trilled in his head: why would Audley's captors leave him alone? And if he *were* truly alone, why hadn't he made a break for it? The night was so dark that anyone coming after him would have lost him within thirty yards.

Caine handed the RG sight to Wallace: the gunner took a long gander then gave it back. 'It's gotta be a trap,' he grunted softly. 'They must of heard us comin' after all. They're usin' him as bait.'

Caine pondered the situation. They couldn't withdraw and leave Audley to his fate, but any action would be playing into enemy hands. He had no doubt that the Senussi were concealed in the deep shadows of the wadi, waiting for his move. He had no way of knowing how many there were. On the other hand, he and Wallace could use the darkness to their own advantage, too: they had the night-sight and the tactical ear, and the Arabs didn't. They also had superior weapons. Caine decided to spring the trap: he'd walk right in there and rely on his skill and speed to get out again.

He searched his pouches, found his Very pistol, already loaded: he crawled so close to the big gunner that their heads touched. He passed him the flaregun and the RG sight, took the tactical ear in exchange. He listened carefully through the headset, caught the crackling of the fire. 'I'm going in,' he hissed in Wallace's ear. 'You cover me through the RG: the moment you clock anyone moving, blast 'em. Once we're back in the trees, use the flare for illumination, take out any pursuers. Then we bug out the way we came.'

Wallace stuck a knoblike thumb almost in Caine's eye. Caine gave his mate's big shoulder a hard squeeze then swivelled his body round. He crawled to the edge of the cover. He was about forty-five yards from Audley at the fire. He could run it in a few seconds, and the enemy wouldn't see him in the darkness: the moment he broke the circle of the firelight, though, they would have him in their sights and would open up. Instead of running, he moved forward with the same diverlike slowness he and Wallace had used on the way here: rifle ready, ears cocked under the headphones for the slightest movement, each pace carefully measured and perfectly noiseless. Within ten paces of the fire he stopped, lay quietly down in the sand with his weapon at the shoulder: Audley was still staring gloomily into the flames, evidently unaware of Caine's presence.

Caine took a deep breath, knowing that the moment he spoke the contact was initiated. '*Bertie*,' he yelled. '*Run. Over here*.'

Audley stiffened, leapt to his feet, stared wildly about him, giving Caine a glimpse of seedcorn teeth and faded filmstar features. '*Caine*?' he shouted. '*Caine*, it's a setup.'

'*Run*,' Caine bawled. '*Run on my voice*.'

Audley hesitated for a fraction of a second, and in that moment a whiteclad Arab leapt into the firelight, a lean, agile, darkbearded figure with a rifle in one hand and a curved dagger raised in the other. Caine had sighted up and was about to drag iron when a double tap of tracer from Wallace's Bren sousaphoned, jackscrewed over him in a twin groove of blinding orange, paired shooting stars that cooked the night air with the odour of fried sulphur: Caine saw the Senussi's head burst like a split melon, rip apart in stipples of dark flesh and bright bone. Audley was already hurtling towards Caine when the sootblack dark was chivved by spontoons of fire: Caine heard slow rounds drone like the notes of a cello in the headset, heard the wheeze and thwack as bullets bombed around him. He'd pinpointed four or five muzzleflashes: he traversed his rifle, pulled iron, skeaned .30-calibre rounds at the flashes, scatterdrumming *chomp*, *chomp*, *chomp*, *chomp*, *chomp*, making the whole drywash *whoof* and boom with fire. He heard the *jing* of steel as his clip selfejected, heard the thrash of Senussi rifles, heard more shots skysweep, heard the *whazz* of ricochets. He found a new clip, fed it into the top breech: he hopped to his feet, collided with Audley, almost knocked him down. '*Make for the bushes*,' he yelled. 'We've got your back.'

He heard Audley's receding footsteps in the headset, followed almost at once by bare Senussi feet whispering over sand. Caine dropped on one knee, fired two rounds in the direction of the invisible target, heard a pigsqueal out of the darkness, smelled charred flesh, scorched cotton, sautéed blood. Feet squeaked dirt to his left: he swivelled the Garand, claymored the shadows with twin lances of fire, heard a grunt like air rushing from a punctured tyre, heard the muffled thud of a body thumping earth, heard the metallic ring of a rifle hitting stone. He stood up, poised, Garand at the shoulder, ranging the muzzle, weaving his head this way and that, straining for sound. There was a sudden chamfering of earth behind him: a greasy arm snagged him round the neck: Caine smelled goatlard and rancid butter, felt a knifethrust turned against the backbuckles of his belt: rotated his head to the crook of the elbow, yanked the arm down with his left hand, clubbing backwards onehanded with the butt of his Garand. He had a momentary sense of another ghost in front of him, a dekko of blue light glinting along a steel blade: then Wallace's Bren deadbolted a second time, crepitating through the headset as loud as thunder. Caine heard the ripfire of ballrounds tearing open the night: the dark figure was blown away. He let go his rifle, hauled down on the arm around him with both hands, exerted all his weight. He felt the Senussi flip over his back, crash into the sand in front of him. Caine's bayonet was in his hand in an instant: he threw himself on the prostrate Arab doublekneed, punching the breath out of his lungs. He felt his way across the enemy's chest lefthanded, skewbladed the bayonet through the rib-box into the heart, felt the blade jar, forced it in up to the hilt with both hands. The man twitched and went rigid: warm gore spurted in Caine's face, up his sleeve, across his shirt. He pulled the blade, wiped blood out of his eyes, groped for his fallen rifle, picked it up, dashed after Audley.

He had barely registered the deeper shadows of the trees around him when he heard the *shoooosh* of the Very gun: he heard the flare tromba above him, saw the night excoriated like a dark flap of skin, saw the drywash lit up by unearthly turquoise light. Traileyed, he clocked the prickled branches of the thornscrub come in focus around him, took in the maggotforms of dead Senussi in the wadi bed, clocked two live Arabs frozen in midwadi: barechested, spikeheaded men with narrow jaws and eyeballs glittering like beryls. They brought up their rifles: Wallace yanked iron: the Bren tuckered, chundered crimson blunderbursts. The two Senussi carommed forward in gazelle-like leaps, cavorted, twisted, spasmed, jerked: grenade-sized craters slubbered from their backs in gouts of greensick gore. They pitched over, rolled on the sandy earth as the eery flarelight sputtered out.

Caine heard heavy breathing through the headset, knew Audley was only feet away. '*Bertie*,' he hissed.

'*Here*,' Audley's voice came back. There was a scuffling in the bush: Caine felt a hand grasping his shoulder, gripped it tight, yanked Audley with him as he sprinted through the bush towards the escarpment. He heard Wallace rear up like a leviathan and tromp after them. Caine didn't let go of Audley's wrist until they reached the bottom of the slope, where he stopped for breath, made sure Wallace was still with them. The three of them crouched under the scree, licking parched lips, longing for water none of them had. 'We downed seven,' Caine panted thickly. 'Are there any more?'

Audley swallowed aridly in the darkness. 'I don't know,' he gasped. 'I don't think so. There were five: they made camp here just after the rain. Then two rearguard scouts came in. They must have reported you following, because they all melted into the shadows and left me by the fire. I knew it was a trap but I couldn't move: they'd have potted me the moment I tried it. You saw what happened when I stood up? I almost got scragged.'

Caine gave a hollow laugh. 'You can thank the "great booby" for that: I told you he doesn't miss unless he means to. Maybe you should drop the idea of putting him on a charge.'

Audley grunted in what Caine took to be embarrassment, but the sound was covered by a bass growl from Wallace. 'Where's Larousse?'

Audley's eyes were caverns in the ocean of dark. 'Dead,' he said. 'He put up a fight while they were dragging us down the slope: one of the swine shot him. I saw it happen. I don't know what they did with the body – maybe carried it off to show the Jerries.'

'Trust Gaston to go down fighting,' Wallace said. 'That must have been the gunshot we heard.'

Caine was quiet for a moment. 'You sure he's dead?' he asked Audley.

'I saw it happen,' Audley repeated. 'They put a bullet through his head at close contact range. Larousse was a hard bugger, I know, but nobody could have survived that.'

'How did they get you, anyway?' Caine asked.

'One of the bastards must have crept up on me when I was on stag, hit me over the head. Next thing I knew I was being dragged up a mountain with Larousse, both of us gagged and bound . . .'

Caine wondered if Audley had been asleep when they'd jumped him but didn't say anything. He put out a hand, felt the lieutenant's head: Audley flinched as the probing fingers touched a lump in the back of his skull. 'You must have been hit with a club,' Caine said. 'One of those throwingsticks.'

He paused, remembering how Larousse had saved their skins at el-Gala, wondering why the best men were always the first to die.

'If you was bound and gagged, sir,' Wallace asked Audley, 'why did they leave you untied by the fire?'

'Must have been part of the trap,' Audley said. 'Who knows how these Senussi think?'

Caine made no comment. He sniffed, spat dry saliva into the sand. 'Come on,' he said. 'I want to make Adud's camp by first light.'

The night was hatblack, the going hard. First light found them descending a slope of lava plates that clanked underfoot like pigiron into a watercourse full of the savoury scent of wild sage, where spinneys of cork oak, lentisk and juniper swelled in tufts among basalt slabs. Crows and ravens chittered and flew away as they approached. They rested in the trees, unable to speak for the paste clogging their tongues, their swollen, inflamed eyeballs half blind with thirst. The pewter sky was perforated by long strips of magenta, the serried ranks of the hills coming slowly into view, successive toothsawn ridges, each series a little higher than the one before.

There was no trace of water in the wadi. Caine dragged himself along the sandy bed to the nearest bend, wafting away Parthian hordes of flies that had homed in on them with the light. The sand was dotted with the abscesses of ants' nests, crisscrossed with tiny highways. As Caine knelt down, his hand dislodged a flat stone: a black scorpion scuttled away. Caine mashed it to yellow pus with his foot.

He started digging with his bayonet: Wallace and Audley joined him. They found damp sand elbow-deep: Caine took off his cap comforter, pressed it into the pit, brought it up heavy with moisture. He offered it to Audley, who took it and lapped a mouthful greedily before handing it back. Caine dipped it in again, offered it to Wallace. The big man waved it away, crouched over the hole on all fours like a great, sprawling lion, stuck his shaggy head inside, imbibed liquid that had gathered at the bottom of the seep. They stayed there for thirty minutes, downed about a cupful of water each: when they moved off again the sun was ballooning up beyond the edges of the hills to the east, a beetroot-coloured globe exploding into a blinding gold fireball as it heaved itself beyond the rim of rock.

They followed the wadi up into the hills, Caine navigating with map and prismatic compass. An hour after sunrise they came across a Senussi village of mud and thatch hovels in a tight grid on the shore of the drywash. Caine was so relieved to find the place it took him a minute to understand it was deserted. Some of the hovels had been smashed, others burnt to heaps of charred mudbrick and blackened wood. They searched the village for water, found only shattered terracotta waterpots, hanging goatskin waterbags as shrivelled as old prunes. Dust devils spun between the cabins: the men found goat and sheep carcases in convoluted shapes: fleshless skulls with vacant eyepits, packets of tangled bone in yellow skins rockhard from the heat. They found a dead camel, its serpentine neck drawn back so far that the skull lay upon its hump, its intestines and windpipe torn out by vultures. The narrow streets were littered with broken pottery, fractured buttergourds, milking pans, fragments of clothing, battered tin trays: bits of basketry and skeins of tentcloth hung from doorposts in heat-perished shreds.

A hundred paces out of the village lay a row of leafless thorntrees where a colony of yellowhead vultures flapped at them dismissively. Beyond the trees they found a deep well without bucket or rope. Caine peered over the rim, dropped in a pebble, heard the *plunk* as it struck water. He estimated that it lay at about sixty feet. 'We could climb down,' croaked Wallace. 'You've done it before, ain't you, skipper?'

Caine shuddered, recalling his life-or-death struggle to climb out of a well like this on the *Runefish* mission back in June. 'There's no way you're going to get me in there,' he rasped.

The giant wasn't listening: his huge body had tensed. He was gazing across the lavablack scarp to the north where a dim figure was making its way down a track. The man was a half-mile away, a silvery comma, insubstantial as a wisp in the hazy meltlight. He appeared to be pulling something. The three of them went to ground. They lay there for minutes watching the figure suspended in lattices of gauze shimmering in and out of focus. It had drifted within a hundred yards before Caine realized they were looking at a Senussi Arab leading a donkey, a spindleshanked old man with a Father Christmas beard and skin like sundried leather. He was clad in an offwhite turban that framed his face, sepia robes that fluttered in the breeze, and carried a Mannlicher rifle slung across his back. It wasn't until he halted the donkey five yards away, though, that Caine recognized the network of wrinkles, the anchor nose, the steady black eyes of Sheikh Adud, Layla's father, his old friend from the *Runefish* op.

30

Caine awoke to find Harry Copeland shaking him, his face drawn with fatigue, his prominent Adam's apple bobbing. 'Sorry, skipper. I know you're knackered. We all are. But we've got plans to make.'

Caine saw the eagerness on his mate's face, remembered the reason he was here: to rescue Angela Brunetto, the Italian girl he had fallen for. In the months before *Sandhog*, Copeland had never talked much about her: even when Caine had dropped hints, he'd pretended not to know what he was talking about. Yet Caine knew he was desperate to find her: this time, he guessed, Cope had no intention of letting her go.

He brushed away flies, sat up, recalled that he was in Adud's camp – a score of goatshair tents pitched in the shade of tamarix and arbutus trees on a wadi side. It was late afternoon, cool, the sky full of banked-up drumheads like floating foam mountains, veiling the sun. He glanced at his watch and saw he'd slept seven hours. 'Are we secure?' he enquired.

Copeland ran a hand through his dirtpasted thatch. 'Adud's got scouts out,' he said. 'Static and prowler. His lot haven't forgotten Umm 'Aijil: they're dead wary of the Jerries jumping them.'

Caine nodded, looked round, scrabbled dust from his eyes. Audley and Wallace were still asleep: Pickney, Gibson,

Rossi, Trubman and Netanya were sitting or moving around in the treeshade, sorting kit, stripping and cleaning weapons. He looked for Dumper and Larousse, then recalled suddenly that they were dead: two more steady men, lost due to his own foolishness, his own inadequacy.

A wave of despair broke over him: Betty Nolan must be dead too, by now: the *Sandhog* mission had been dogged by bad luck and worse decisions. The LRDG escort had been wiped out; the enemy had been waiting for them before the Shakir cliffs; the wireless had been smashed; a party of traitorous Senussi had bumped them by night: Caine recalled with horror how Gibson and Rossi had sawn off the heads of two dying Arabs, like savages. He watched the cowboy and his mate, sitting crosslegged together knee to knee, polishing M2 rounds. They looked peaceful, contented to be in each other's company: it seemed impossible that they were capable of such barbarity. Then, with a shudder, Caine recalled how, only four months back, he himself had rammed a gunbarrel down a German's throat until his gullet burst. Despite all the horrors he'd seen, he still clung to one basic conviction: human beings weren't barbaric by nature: it was the nature of war to bring out barbarity in them. He spat dry saliva, remembering something else: it was 24 October. Monty's *Lightfoot* push was due to start on the night of October 25/26. That meant the Olzon-13 had to be taken out before tomorrow night.

He got to his feet, scanned the wadi. There were goats corralled in pens of piled stone, slatribbed donkeys nosing doubtfully among the swordgrass, fat-tailed sheep penned up behind fences of Sodom's Apple stalks. There were brownskinned women with tattooed chins wearing ragged cotton shifts that clung to their slender bodies: he saw a woman shaking a goatskin slung from a wooden tripod making buttermilk, another on hands and knees milling grain on a stone quern, another feeding a snotnosed infant at her breast. There were men with treebark faces and lizard eyes in parchment-thin shirts, hooded cloaks, baggy trousers, smoking small brass pipes, cleaning antique weapons, building cookfires, brewing tea. Boys with coxcomb tufts of hair and girls with oiled plaits moved along the wadi sides chanting and hurling pebbles at flocks of sheep and goats. These tribespeople had mobbed him as he'd slouched into the camp behind Adud that morning, the women ululating, the men clamouring to shake his hand, crying '*Caine*, *Caine*,' as if he were some kind of saviour. Those people were relying on him too.

Copeland brought him tea, gave him a cigarette, sat down beside him, his SMLE across his knees. He described how, the previous night, they'd lugged the heavy manpacks of demolitions gear, working in relays, three men humping, two men covering, making only a hundred yards a time, changing over, going back for the other packs, working like galleyslaves, until Layla had arrived with Adud and the donkeys: how the old man had been horrified to hear about Sidi Mohammad and his renegade Senussi, how he'd helped them rope their burdens on donkeyback, guided them here in the pitchdark of the early hours. Caine listened until his mate had finished, then told him how they'd snatched Audley, how Larousse had been killed. 'That chap was a real scrapper,' Cope said gravely. 'He's going to be sorely missed.'

They were interrupted by two Senussi who arrived carrying between them a tin tray laden with rice and roasted goatsmeat. Copeland woke up Wallace and Audley: Pickney warned them not to pig out on the rich food. 'Take it steady,' he said. 'Our guts are as shrivelled as paper bags. Overdo it and you'll drop dead, I promise you.'

They ate sparingly from the tray, Arab style. When they'd finished, Layla came over with a spouted jug of water and a huge kettle of tea. As she poured water over their hands in turn, Caine couldn't help looking at her. The previous night he'd seen her only by moonlight, and he'd forgotten how ravishing she was: liquid brown eyes, haughty, arched nose, heartshaped lips, waistlength tumble of glossy hair, the sandglass swell of her breasts and hips. She splashed water over his hands, showing teeth like polished nacre, commiserated with him for the loss of Larousse. Caine thanked her again: he remembered the touch of her hand, the warmth of her body close to his on the wadi floor, the hint of sandalwood, the supple strength of the arm he had gripped. Then he recalled with a start how this same beautiful woman had leapt on the back of one of her fellow tribesmen and slit his throat with a knife. He thought of Betty Nolan: he watched Layla undulating away with a quiver of disquiet, disgusted, not with her, but with the terrible sleeping demons that war could awaken in men and women alike.

As they were finishing the tea, Adud came over at the head of a dozen or so armed men: Caine knew they must be the entire fighting strength of the clan. There was a spring to their step that he'd noticed before among the Senussi, as if they were bursting with an energy they could scarcely control. Yet they carried themselves with dignity, too, despite their parchment rags: they wore bandoliers of bullets and carried their rifles clasped muzzle forward over their shoulders. Caine had his men stand up to shake hands with them. Working down the row of Arabs, he saw Fred Wallace freeze suddenly, step back, glare ferociously at two Senussi in front of him. 'I ain't shakin' hands with these buggers,' the giant said.

The ceremony broke down: the Senussi stared at Wallace, astonished at this unheard-of breach of protocol. Caine hurried over to him and realized with a shock that he knew the Arabs the giant was refusing to greet. They were Salim and Sa'id, two brothers, who, during the *Runefish* mission, had been responsible for the deaths of three of his commandos. Wallace's pinprick eyes smouldered at them. '*Never*,' he spat. 'We're not takin' them with us, skipper. These sods killed O'Brian, MacDonald and Jackson. Have you forgotten that?'

Caine hadn't forgotten: neither could he forget how Wallace had itched to put bullets through the boys' heads, and how he, Caine, had forbidden it. They were teenagers, slimbuilt and wiry, alike as peas, except that Salim's face was edged with a slim whisker of beard while Sa'id's was cleanshaven. They hung back, watching Wallace's movements, cateyed. Caine was perplexed: he was aware that refusal to greet a man was an unforgivable insult to the Senussi. He needed these Arabs as allies on *Sandhog*, and unless he could get over this hiccup, the entire mission might founder. 'Fred,' he said softly. 'It was an accident, remember? They took us for Jerries.'

'Accident? Yeah, maybe: but them lads is still dead, ain't they?'

Wallace was going to say something else, when Sheikh

Adud and Manny Netanya poled up together. They had evidently struck up a relationship: both Adud and Layla had admired Netanya's half-brother, Moshe Naiman, who'd died on the previous mission. The sheikh spoke to the youths: they answered respectfully. He added a short explanation to Netanya, who turned his cadaver's face on Caine. 'These boys have never forgiven themselves for the deaths of your men, which they truly regret,' he explained. 'They offer themselves to you because they wish to make amends. They pledge themselves to fight to the death on your behalf.'

Caine glanced at Wallace: the giant was still glowering. 'How do we know they're tellin' the truth?' he demanded. 'They might've been workin' for the Boche all along, like them A-rabs last night.'

'We'll just have to take their word for it, mate,' Caine said. 'We need these blokes: if you don't shake hands with them, we'll lose the lot, and the whole scheme will be up the spout. We've come too far to let that happen.' He paused, shaking his head at Netanya, who was about to translate his words to Adud. He turned back to Wallace. 'I believe them,' he said.

The big gunner swallowed hard, spat into the sand: for a long moment, Caine thought he might stump away. Instead, Wallace raised his enormous chest, took a gargantuan breath, stepped towards the youths with his pansize hand out: Caine could sense the effort it took his friend to do it. Wallace shook hands with both boys. There was a palpable relaxation of tension: the greeting ceremony resumed. Minutes later, all of them, Senussi and SAS men, were seated in a big circle in the shade of the tallest tree.

Adud spoke first, pausing for Netanya to translate. 'You remember the village where I met you this morning?' he asked. Caine nodded. 'That was inhabited by our relatives. Then the *Tedesci* devils of the Angel of Death came: they took everyone, old, young, men, women off to the *Citadello*. Not a single one of them has returned. In other places, where the Senussi resisted, terrible things have happened: men slaughtered like animals, women violated, children kidnapped . . .'

'We found a small village in a wadi near the foot of the Shakir cliffs,' Caine told him. 'A Senussi man hanged: two women . . . murdered.'

Adud shook his tarpaper head. 'There is no end to it,' he said. 'Many of those who have come back from the *Citadello* are changed, possessed by jinns – some of them kill themselves, others kill their own families. In all my years, I have never seen anything like it, not even when the *Italiani* persecuted us, when they executed Omar Mukhtar . . .' He took a rattling breath, his old eyes bright. 'That is why we thank God you have returned – why we are ready to help you, to go into the *Citadello*, to release our relatives held there, to kill the Angel of Death. May God assist us in our plan.'

The old man drew a sketch of the crater in the sand with a bony finger: SAS and Senussi drew near to study it. Caine took out his map and pieces of an aerial photograph he'd brought with him, compared them with Adud's drawing. The Citadel's main entrance was on the western side: Caine had used it on his last visit. The spur line now passed through it, connecting with an airstrip and a Nissen-hut warehouse that Adud said had recently been completed.

While this area was heavily guarded, though, the eastern rimwall wasn't, probably because there was no way in, except over the wall itself. There were AA guns and radar beacons inside the crater on that side, but only a single lookout sangar. Caine had decided days ago that this would be the best way in: if they went for the main entrance, it would have to be taken by force: *stealth if possible, force if necessary* was the SAS way. He pointed to the eastern wall on Adud's sketch. 'We'll climb up there,' he said. 'We'll approach the target through the thornforest on the crater floor.'

It took almost two hours to agree on the plan. Caine hadn't bargained for the Chinese parliament style of Senussi discussion: every man, old or young, was entitled to have his say and had a right to be listened to. Finally, though, it was decided that the whole party would set off together: the donkeys would carry the heavy SAS kit. At the eastern wall, they would split up: the SAS would go in over the top, while the Senussi would make their way round to the main entrance, wait nearby for Caine's signal. Caine's team would go into the Olzon-13 bunkers, lay the charges, then come out and fire a green Very light. On that signal, Adud's men would blow the spur line, start a diversionary attack, distract the Jerries while the SAS liberated the prisoners, located and took out the Angel of Death, and withdrew.

The more Caine visualized it, though, the more variables he saw: too much would depend on luck. But that was always the case in raids like this: the two big problems were going to be securing the main entrance long enough to get the prisoners out, and finding the Angel of Death.

Copeland commented that there was also a problem with the diversionary attack: the Senussi didn't do demolitions. 'We'll have to send someone with them,' he said.

Caine nodded. He considered his team, wondering who he could spare. His top demo men were Gibson and Rossi, but he needed them for the climb, and for the main task: he was about to suggest Netanya or Trubman when Audley piped up. 'I'll go with them, old boy.' His winning smile was in place again, Caine noted. 'I'm trained in demolitions.'

'Anything to get out of humping a manpack, eh?' Wallace guttered.

Audley's guttapercha grin wavered but didn't die. 'I was thinking of volunteering myself as liaison anyway,' he went on. 'I mean, the Senussi don't use watches, do they? You're going to need someone to coordinate the timing.'

It made sense, Caine realized. Audley was officially second-in-command: he spoke a little Arabic, could set a charge and, as he'd said, could synchronize the timing. The bottom line, though, was that he was the member of Caine's team whom he felt he could most do without. 'All right, Bertie,' he said. 'You'll go with the Senussi.'

He shuftied his watch: the old man had told him that the eastern wall could be reached from here in two hours. 'Right,' he said. 'The only problem left is that guard sangar. Gibbo, Rossi – I want you to go ahead for a recce as soon as it gets dark; you'll need one of these Senussi chaps as a guide. Take your climbing gear: get as near to the sangar as you can. I want to know how many Jerries are on stag, and how long the stags are, and what sort of comms they have. It'll be your job to take out the guard at the right time: I don't want them giving the alarm before we even get inside . . .'

The cowboy beamed. 'Tell you what, skipper,' he drawled. 'We can fix a line to make the climb easier and quicker as well.'

Caine nodded again, pleased. 'We want to have the job done by 0700 hours. The rest of the party leaves here at midnight, on the dot. Now, I suggest that everyone gets some kip.'

A puce-coloured porridge of cloud filled the sky in whorls, and the sun was a red wedge quartered by the black ratchets of the hills. Caine made sure there was a permanent watch over the explosives, took his kit a little further into the trees, away from the bustle. He spread the fleabitten blanket he'd borrowed from Adud, lay down, and using his webbing as a pillow, crooked his Tommy-gun under his arm and went to sleep.

He dreamed once more of Betty Nolan, dancing a dark ballet on the stage of a Cairo nightclub, where he had never seen her. Someone shook him gently, and he opened his eyes to find the trees in twilight, and Layla leaning over him with the last beams of the dying sun hanging in her eyes. Caine was mildly surprised: it was the second time she'd woken him in twenty-four hours. 'This is getting to be a habit,' he told her.

He made to get up. She pushed him back, squatted down next to him in a whisper of robes. She wore no headscarf: she had brushed her hair out to its full lushness, and its silken ends touched the ground as she crouched. She looked at him, ran a hand down his stubbled cheek. 'Ever since you went, I have thought of you, Caine,' she said. 'I have thought of you a lot.'

Caine opened his eyes wide. He'd had the feeling

something like this was on the cards ever since he'd met her the previous evening. Yet he was still taken by surprise: Senussi girls weren't supposed to behave like this.

He opened his mouth to say something, but she lodged a finger across his lips. It was a familiar gesture, and it took Caine a moment to remember that it was the same one that Betty Nolan sometimes used.

'I want to be with you,' she said. 'Like man and woman. After this, I will go away with you . . . yes . . . I will go where you go. I will stay with you, be your woman . . .' Her face shone: she leaned forward and kissed him. He felt the softness of her lips, felt her soft hair fall over him, caught a whiff of sandalwood. A powerful throb of desire pulsed through him: riding on the struggle of the past few days, the fear of the ordeal yet to come, it reared up like a seasurge, threatened to take him completely. It took all of his willpower to resist it.

When he withdrew his face, she sat back. Caine looked at her. Her expression was so ardent, so compliant, that his resolve almost gave way. That passive expression, he thought, was the most potent weapon in a woman's armoury: it could move mountains, start wars. He took her hand in his: she put her other hand on his shoulder. 'Do you want me?' she said.

Caine swallowed. 'Want you?' he said. 'Of course I want you. You're a beautiful woman. You're beautiful and clever and brave. Last night you saved my life, and maybe the lives of all my men. I'm grateful, very grateful. I would do anything for you. But I can't do this. I'm really sorry.'

She raised her chin, peered down on him, eyes glittering behind the arched nose. 'Why not?' she whispered. 'I know you desire me. I have seen it in your face.' She paused, watched him closely. 'It's another woman,' she said. 'You have another woman. It is the girl with the golden hair: the one you saved from the Boche at Biska . . .' Whether she'd read some silent concurrence in Caine's face, he didn't know, but she withdrew her hand from his shoulder, and when she spoke again her voice was full of cold certainty. 'It *is* her, isn't it? That girl, that . . . Maddy. She is your woman now.'

She spoke the last sentence with such unexpected venom that Caine let her other hand go in surprise. It hit him suddenly that he was walking on a knife edge: Layla had only to claim that he'd made improper advances to her and Adud's support would be gone in the wink of an eye. Not only would *Sandhog* be down the sink, but his SAS team might even find themselves fighting these Senussi as well as the Axis.

He took her hand again gently. 'Look,' he said. 'It's true that I like you, and that I want you. What man wouldn't want you? It's also true that that girl, Betty . . . the one you knew as Maddy . . . it's true that she was my . . . my woman. But she was taken by the enemy. I'm almost sure she's dead . . .'

His voice caught suddenly: it was only when he'd said it that the truth of it snapped shut on him like a trap. His heart lubbed leadweighted: he had to wrestle back tears. Layla caught his expression, lowered her head. 'That is very sad,' she said. 'She was brave, that girl. I am sorry, very sorry. But if she is gone, I could take her place. It is terrible to lose someone close to you, I know, but I could help you forget her . . . forget your loss . . .'

She twisted her slender hands: Caine saw that all her pride and anger had drained away. 'Layla,' he said softly. 'You know I think a lot of you. This is nothing to do with Betty, it's your father, your people. I am your father's guest. If I was to do this, it would be to betray his trust. It wouldn't be honourable.'

She smiled bitterly. 'You are an honourable man, Caine,' she said. 'But for me, I don't care about such things any more. Why should I care? I have seen Senussi men kill other Senussi. I myself have killed a Senussi man, with my own hands. This war . . . it has changed everything. I want to go away with you . . .'

Caine shook his head. 'I'm sorry, Layla,' he said. 'I can't.'

She stood up, tossed her cascade of ebony hair, her eyes on fire. 'I don't believe you,' she said. 'Yes, you are my father's guest *now*, I understand that. But after that, when you are no longer his guest, you can take me with you. Why not? . . . It is that goldenhair, that . . . *Betty*. It's *her*. You say she is dead, but in your heart you can't let her go. You love her: you hope she is still alive.'

She turned and swept off into the trees, her black hair billowing behind her like a dark bridal train. Caine watched her go, feeling a mixture of sadness and guilt. He really did admire Layla: the last thing he had wanted to do was to hurt her. Deep down, though, he knew that she'd read him perfectly: that what she'd said about his feelings for Betty was exactly right.

31

When the Bombay shucked cloud cover over the Libyan coast, the Italian air defences clawhammered: onionflares burst, flak guns lobbed eddies of tracer, long-fingered searchbeams speared the night. In the cockpit, the warrant officer pilot wrestled with the controls, trying desperately to keep the thirty-ton bird stable. At the cabin door, hanging on her strop behind Hooker and the RAF dispatcher, Betty Nolan snorted gasoline fumes, watched the firework display, heard the *riprap* of the triple-A, tried to keep her nerve as the plane yawed and shimmied. She watched roundeyed as a shell as big as a drawerknob came up through the floor and plunked out through the cabin roof, just missing the extended fuel tanks. She blinked, sucked in breath, checked for the hundredth time that her static line was hooked up, reminded herself that the Bombay should clear the ackack batteries in seconds.

'*Six minutes to target*,' the dispatcher snapped.

The six minutes lasted an eternity. When the dispatcher called, 'Action stations,' though, Nolan went rigid. Her senses focused on the open door and the starry night beyond: all that mattered now was getting out. The green light flashed: Hooker vanished into the darkness. The dispatcher hustled Nolan out hard on his heels to prevent their separation on the landing zone. Nolan jumped, felt the slipstream wrench, felt the tug as her canopy inflated.

Then all fast motion ceased: she was drifting like thistle-down towards a phosphorescent blue landfall, absorbed into the quiet of the desert night.

The jump could have come off earlier if they hadn't wasted precious hours bickering. Her chief, John Airey, had agreed that Caine must be warned about Audley, but didn't want Hooker or Nolan for the mission. Hooker had just undergone surgery: Nolan was a woman, and therefore officially a non-com. Stirling said they needed an Arabic speaker who knew the area: Hooker had volunteered, and since he was Adud's G(R) contact, he was the perfect man for the job. As for Nolan, Airey hadn't had any qualms about her being used as bait in a Field Security op, so why get official now? In any case, this wouldn't be the first time she'd parachuted in behind Axis lines. By the time Avery had finally seen sense they'd been set back hours.

One major challenge was that no one actually *knew* where Caine was, or even if his crew was operational. The remains of Roland's missing LRDG patrol had been found: a clutch of burnt-out Axis wagons had been located a few kilometres away. There'd obviously been one hell of a shindy. That Caine's crew had survived they knew from Maskelyne, but the fact that they'd been intercepted so early didn't bode well. The only thing they knew for certain was that Caine was heading for Adud's camp. Hooker was familiar with its location: the Brylcreem Boys said they could put parachutists down on the plateau nearby.

Now, Nolan watched the earth's luminous crust rising to meet her, peered up to check that her periphery was unblown. She groped for the quick-release hooks on either side of her harness, snapped them down. The pack on her legs dropped: the fifteen-foot ropecoil unravelled. She felt the jerk as the pack reached the end of its tether and swung beneath her, stabilizing her flight. It was impossible to assess her drift in the darkness, but the ground rushed up on her almost at once: she pulled hard on the lift webs, braced her legs for a roll. She felt the pack hit the deck, struck the ground with her knees and ankles together. She hardly felt the impact. She rolled, came up into a sitting position. She'd seen no sign of Hooker during the forty-five-second jump, but now she could see his canopy lying lank and deflated no more than twenty yards away.

She scanned the night. The air here was clear, the moon a pale-blue float in a starblown sky. She was on a naked cinder table framed in swordgrass, sedge, and prickly pear: beyond its rim, a forested watercourse lay darkshawled in the night. Nolan couldn't see any lights down there, but the odours of humanity were strong in her nostrils: dung, urine, sour milk, goat-fat, the ash of doused cookfires. At least, she thought, the Brylcreem Boys had dropped them in the right place: Adud's camp had to be in those trees.

She twisted her quick-release catch, pressed it, felt the harness straps spring away. She wriggled out of them, turned over on her belly, grabbed the liftwebs, hauled in the canopy. When she had the silk beneath her fingers, she felt for the stuffbag under her hooded SAS smock. She untied the rope, bundled up the canopy, forced it into the bag. Then she followed the rope to her container, untied the covers, opened the rucksack, took out her web equipment. She put on the webbing, hoisted the rucksack to her shoulders. She coiled up the rope and left it on top of the stuffbag. Then she drew her Colt .45 and went to look for Hooker.

He was lying on the cinders with his head at an impossible angle, a trickle of blood issuing from one nostril, his face frosty in the creamblue light. Nolan shuddered. She holstered her pistol, dropped her pack, started to draw in Hooker's canopy: come daylight, the white silk of the parachutes would stand out like beacons to Axis spotter planes.

It was difficult work, because Hooker's leg was caught up in the liftwebs: Nolan thought he'd probably hit the ground upside down, struggling to disentangle his leg. She guessed he'd done what they called a 'rivet inspection': he hadn't cleared the aircraft properly, had hit the fuselage, had been sent spinning: the liftwebs had probably snagged his leg as they uncoiled.

In the end, she gave up, dragged Hooker's broken body into a copse of acacia thorn, covered it with the folded canopy. Then she went back for her stuffbag and dumped it next to his body. Everything would need to be moved before first light, but she couldn't do it now. She had to inform Caine about Audley while there was still time.

She followed a goatpath down the side of the plateau and into the bushes: the human scents were powerful here. A dog barked: almost at once a female voice cried out. Nolan was about to answer when she heard the snap of a twig behind her: she swirled round just as a club swished air, thwamped across her shoulders. She yelped, staggered, grabbed the club, tugged hard. The stick came free, but a lithe, blackrobed figure came with it, hurtling out of the bush, leaping on her, screeching in a wild, shrill voice, punching, tearing, clawing at her face. Nolan dropped the club, caught the girl's wrists, flipped her backwards in a ju-jitsu throw. The girl crashed into the dust: Nolan sprang on her, straddled her, pinned her down, fought to suppress the flailing claws, saw goateyes glittering in dim eye sockets, a highbridged nose, sensual lips rimpled over ivory teeth. '*Stop*,' she screeched. '*Stop*: I *know* you. You're Layla bint Adud. Don't you recognize me? I'm Maddy Rose – Betty Nolan, that is.'

The girl stopped struggling: Nolan let go her hands. For a moment they stared at each other. Nolan let her up, and they stood breathing hard, slapping dust from their clothes. Nolan relaxed; a tired smile broadened her mouth. 'You remember me?' she asked in English. 'You helped rescue me from the Germans at Biska, four months ago.'

She held out her hand: Layla shook her head, raised her chin, pouted her lips. 'I know who you are,' she said icily. 'You're too late. Caine's gone.'

Nolan let her hand go limp. 'Gone? You mean they've already started?'

'He told me you were dead,' Layla said sullenly. 'Now you have come to take him back.'

Nolan shook her head, mystified. She was about to say something when she heard dogs bark, heard women's voices lash out like whipcracks, heard the dogs whimper as they were kicked or beaten off. A bevy of Senussi ladies pushed through the trees towards her: sablehaired women with oiled plaits and tattooed faces, copperskinned and hawkfaced, like a squad of Red Indian squaws from a storybook. They were lean and sinuous in rags of blue or patterned cotton, and they glided barefoot with the grace of catwalk models. Some carried homemade rifles, others curved throwingsticks, but they didn't look hostile. They gathered around her chirruping like birds, touched her golden hair, poked at her breasts as if to make sure she were really female. Close up, they smelled of baby milk, goatgrease and smoke.

They hustled her out of the undergrowth to where the tents were pitched under the trees on the wadi bank like yawning goatshair caverns. Naked children peeped out of the shadows, pointing and chattering. Nolan didn't see any adult men: the entire male population of the camp must have gone off with Caine, she thought. Someone lit a woodfire. The women squatted near Nolan: one of them brought a wooden bowl of cold mashed potato and sour goatsmilk, pressed her to eat. Nolan couldn't resist the women's hospitality without seeming churlish: their menfolk were as much part of *Sandhog* as the SAS team, and if she was going to get to Caine in time, she would need their help.

The women crouched close together around the bowl. Nolan copied them as they dug out balls of mash with their fingers, rolled the balls deftly into their mouths without touching their lips. When they'd eaten their fill they sat back on their haunches, licked potato off their fingers, wiped them on the sleeves of their rags, passed a bowl of water from hand to hand. A wedge of half-savage watchdogs sallied in scavenging: the women tossed them leftovers, sent them away with sticks and stones. They took out calfskin pouches of tobacco, passed them round, filled little pipes made of brass cartridge cases, lit them with spills from the fire. The tobacco smelled like burnt vinegar, pungent against the background odours of smoke and uncured hide.

The women didn't ask where Nolan had come from,

why she'd come, or even how she'd managed to appear from nowhere in the night like an evil spirit. In any case, only Layla spoke English, and she had been silent throughout the meal, glowering at Nolan with suppressed passion, occasionally sweeping her hair across her face as if resenting her own attractiveness.

Nolan sat down on the sand, licked her fingers, cast puzzled glances Layla's way. This wasn't the kind of reception she'd counted on from the Senussi girl. She remembered her as cheerful and bright: Caine had extolled her tracking skills, had described with admiration how she'd suggested the use of a Senussi poison on the *Runefish* stunt. The other women had received her with grace and hospitality: only Layla had hung back. And it was Layla she really needed: the girl was the only one with whom she could communicate.

'How long since they left?' she asked.

The girl tossed her cape of black hair, puffed bitter smoke from her brass pipe. 'You are too late.'

'How long?'

Layla shrugged insolently. Nolan saw she was stalling, felt suddenly furious. Caine's life hung in the balance: so did the fate of the *Lightfoot* offensive. She was tempted to grab the little hussy by the scruff of the neck, give her a hard kick, yell in her ear that she was a filthy, ignorant little nigger who ought to be swinging in the trees with the monkeys. She opened her mouth to say something cutting, but checked herself: there was nothing to be gained by alienating allies. Instead, she stood up, hefted her manpack with one hand, fixed her eyes on Layla. 'I'm going after Caine,' she said quietly. 'I'm going to warn him. Are you coming with me or shall I go alone?'

Layla flicked back her shroud of hair, put aside her brass pipe: her eyes were leopard-like in the firelight. 'Alone you will not succeed,' she said. She stood up with a gymnast's grace, swept back her hair with both hands, displayed an oval face that was, Nolan thought, alarmingly beautiful. Layla surveyed her disparagingly from head to foot. 'You are dressed like an English soldier,' she snorted. 'As soon as the *Tedesci* see you, they kill you. Anyway, you are too late now. Caine's men, they go over the wall of the *Citadello* by ropes. You cannot follow them, even if you could find the way they go.'

Nolan wasn't surprised: she'd guessed Caine would go in across the eastern wall, especially since he had a couple of cliff-climbing specialists with him. She was certain, though, that Adud's Senussi wouldn't have gone in that way: she'd never heard of a Bedouin cliff-climber. 'Your father and his men?' she asked, twisting her face at the girl. 'They didn't go in with ropes, did they?'

Layla scowled. The other women looked on, sensing conflict, tilting their heads as if trying to make sense of the body language, the expressions, the tone of voice.

'They go to the main gate on the western side,' Layla said at last. 'They wait for the *Ingleezi* there.'

Nolan smiled, showing her charmingly overlapping front teeth. 'Then that is the way I'll go,' she said. She dumped the pack and took a step over to the Senussi girl, put a hand on her arm. 'You have to go with me,' she said. 'You have to show me the way.'

Layla shook off her hand angrily, glaring at her. '*Have to?*' she hissed. 'I don't *have to* do anything. By God, the *Tedesci* can shoot you, for all I care.'

Nolan was shocked at the vitriol in her voice. She rubbed the bruise on her shoulder where Layla had hit her with the club: she was starting to think the attack had been personal. 'Why do you hate me?' she asked.

The girl turned away. 'Because you will try to take Caine away,' she muttered. She swivelled round abruptly, her eyes glittering. 'Caine wants *me*: he told me so.'

Nolan froze, hardly able to believe what she'd just heard. Layla and Caine? It was impossible, surely? But it would explain Layla's behaviour. The girl had certainly developed a crush on Caine after he'd saved her life on the *Runefish* mission: Nolan had told him so herself. She hadn't taken it seriously, though: Caine and Layla belonged to different worlds.

For an instant, she was completely at a loss: the last thing she'd ever expected to find here was a rival for Caine's affections. Her throat felt suddenly parched. She realized that she'd underestimated the girl: Layla was clever, brave and beautiful enough for any man, no matter what world he belonged to.

She swallowed hard. 'So . . . Caine told you he wanted you . . .'

Layla clenched her fists: Nolan saw that she was shaking. 'He thought you were dead,' she blared. 'He would have taken me, I know he would.'

Nolan gasped. She hadn't understood the first time Layla had said it: now it all clicked neatly into place. Caine had believed Nolan dead. He'd turned to Layla for consolation, believing that she wasn't coming back. What horrified her was the thought that he might have committed himself, might have made promises: they might even have made love. She hesitated, trapped between jealousy and compassion for the young girl. Whatever Caine's feelings now, she still had to warn him about the traitor, Audley, and there was *Lightfoot* to think of. Monty's advance was due to begin tomorrow night: the Olzon-13 had to be out of the way by then.

She retreated back to her pack and picked it up again, took a breath to steady her racing emotions. The Senussi women were watching her with big eyes. She looked at Layla, who seemed to be making an equally large effort to control herself. 'What Caine decides to do . . . I mean, after this,' Nolan stammered. She broke down, realizing that there was no point beating about the bush: 'Look,' she said. 'Whether he wants you or he wants me, or he wants neither of us, that's Caine's business. Now, his life is in danger. If you love him, then you'll help me save him.'

Layla cupped her face with her hands, shook her head violently as if trying to shake off a horde of jinns. 'Don't ask me,' she said. 'I can't.'

Nolan slammed her manpack down in the sand, making the other women jump. She waved her hand towards the plateau. 'If you search up there,' she said harshly, 'you'll find Eric Hooker . . .'

'Hooker?' Layla gasped. 'The *Ingleezi* who speaks Arabic like an Egyptian? The one who comes dressed as a Senussi?'

'That's him. Well, Hooker won't be coming any more. Because he's dead. He died trying to help me get to Caine. He didn't have to come, but he risked his life for Caine's sake, and he died for it. You say Caine . . . wants you . . . but you aren't ready to do anything to save his life, even though he saved yours. And what about your father? He and – judging by what I see here – most of your men, have gone with Caine. They're in danger too, but you won't lift a finger to help them? What kind of Senussiyya *are* you?'

Layla watched Nolan with scorching eyes. For a moment it seemed as though she would either attack her again, or walk away. Then Nolan saw a silver-filigree pattern of tears streaking her ebony face. 'He told me you were dead,' she smouldered, 'and now you are here.'

Nolan felt a disturbing pang of sympathy. Layla was in love with Caine: her hopes had been raised, and Caine hadn't done anything to dampen them. It was Nolan's sudden arrival that had put the whole thing in doubt. She almost felt moved to comfort Layla, but stopped herself. How sure could she be that Caine hadn't transferred his affections to this lovely and exotic girl? In any case, the feeling was soon swamped by a deeper desire – to find Caine, to take him in her arms, to reassure him that she, Nolan, was still there for him, still alive: a real, breathing, living person, not a corpse.

Layla wiped her eyes, raised her chin. 'There are *Tedesci* soldiers on the western side,' she said broodingly. 'I tell you, when the *Tedesci* see you, they will shoot you at once . . .' She paused, snagged air through her highbridged nose. 'Why not you dress like a Senussi girl? We give you clothes, we black your face. You go dressed like me, and when you arrive, you tell the Boche you have come to search for lost husband or brothers in the Citadello . . .'

Nolan noted Layla's sudden shift of ground: she wondered if the girl were just trying to get rid of her. 'I'm ready to go alone,' she said, 'but we would stand more chance of saving Caine if there were two of us. Of course,

I know it will be very dangerous: perhaps you aren't willing to risk it . . .'

She tapered off, observing the hesitation on Layla's face: the girl was fighting a desperate battle between guilt, love and pride. To let Nolan go alone might be construed as cowardice, especially if she succeeded. Caine had saved Layla's life and the lives of many of her people: what would he think of her if she refused to help save his? Any chance she had of replacing Nolan would be finished.

The girl swept back her silken hair, sniffed, straightened her back. 'I am Senussi,' she said stiffly. 'I am not afraid . . . I will go with you.'

'Thank you.' Nolan said, striving to clear her voice of all smugness. With Layla by her side, her chances of saving *Sandhog* were doubled: what happened afterwards was in God's hands.

'Don't thank me,' Layla pouted. 'The thanks is to Allah. And Allah knows I do it for Caine and for my father, not for you.'

Nolan nodded, not trusting herself to comment. She was already thinking about tactics. Layla's suggestion of her going in disguised as a Senussiyya was sound: that Nolan would be shot as a spy if caught seemed the least of her worries. A practical problem occurred to her, though. 'Even if we are both dressed as Senussi,' she said, 'why should the Germans let us in? I mean, they aren't noted for their charity.'

She looked up to see Layla smiling bloodlessly. 'They are men without women. It is not for charity that they will let us pass.'

32

They parted with Audley and the Senussi in the wadi below the skirts of the rockwall, hiked up the sandslope doubled under the weight of their manpacks: even through their shirts the straps chafed their shoulders like sawgrass. The moon was a luminous orb in a limegreen splotch: the rise was steep, wooded in cork oaks and junipers with trunks like plaited hawsers, bowed from the waist by the prevailing winds as if in mockery of the team's effort. The men slunk with sombre strides through the bobs of treeshadow, weapons at the ready, taking an eternity over every step, senses sharp as icepicks. Once they heard owl wings whisper through the foliage, and once a hare snuffling. Both times they froze, scanning the shadows with sootblacked faces until lead scout Gibson waved them on.

The cowboy led them up to the base of the cliff – fifty feet of scalloped, fluted rock rearing clear out of the sandswell. The Arab guide had gone to join Adud, but Rossi was waiting for them, guarding the line he and Gibson had already fixed in place. The two of them had scaled the cliff earlier, secured the rope, lain motionless on the stone shelf, scanned the Axis sangar with their binos. The guardpost was a hundred yards off, but the light had been clear enough for them to clock the German sentry, the field-telephone cable, the unlit searchlight, the MG30 machine-gun mounted on the sandbagged parapet: they'd seen the sentry relieved at 0200 hours sharp, seen him descend a series of stone steps to the valley floor.

Now, lurking in greenbanded shadows under the cliff, the SAS men helped each other lower their manpacks, lay them carefully against the cliffwall. They had only twenty minutes before the next change of guard. Taking out the sentry was going to be the riskiest action of the mission: if the Jerry managed to talk on the phone, work the searchlight, open fire before they got to him, *Sandhog* would be shot.

The SAS team was poised ready at the rope: Rossi and the cowboy shinned up with the sureness of geckos, sprawled in the camelthorn on the granite shelf. The cowboy took a pebble from his pocket, weighed it in his beef-jerky fingers, met Rossi's glance. His mate nodded. Gibson lobbed the stone overarm as hard as he could towards the sangar: stone struck rock with a clunk that sounded as loud as a bell to their sensitized ears. There was no way the sentry could have missed it. The Reapers knew he would have three choices: report it to the guardroom, work the searchlight and punch bullets blindly into the dark, or come out and investigate. It was a gamble they'd taken often before: it almost always paid off. For a few long seconds, nothing happened: they lay spraddled in the scrub, damming up their breath, fingers tickling iron, knowing that, if the gambit failed, *Sandhog* could easily end here. Then they saw the sentry emerge from the sangar – a mallet-headed, ratfaced Jerry in peaked cap and greatcoat edging in their direction with his rifle set.

He came straight towards them, high-laced boots creaking on stones. He spotted the rope belayed to a stone pillar, stopped, crouched, peered down into the night. The instant his attention was drawn, they moved in. The Jerry felt both arms seized in a tourniquet grip, felt a calloused palm clamp his mouth. He capered frantically, snaffled nose-breath, tried to wrench his arms free, gnashed at the hand stifling him, tried to bring up his rifle. He felt a crushing smack in the chest, staggered, felt the guncotton night skeeter away from him, felt the slateblue light drain slowly from his senses until sheer blackness reigned. The cowboy felt him limp out, whipped the rifle from his hands; Rossi withdrew the gore-smeared blade from his ribcradle, continued to cover his mouth until his body lay twitching on the rock floor. He took a step back, watched blood blurge from the punctured aorta. Gibson knelt over the corpse, scrimshawed throatflesh with his Bowie knife until steel shuddered on bone. He hoiked the rope twice, wiped bloody hands on the sentry's greatcoat: Rossi cleaned his blade on the dead man's cap.

The team below irrupted into motion: they scaled the rope, they let down a second for the manpacks, they hoisted manpacks up. On top, Caine and Copeland moved forward to clear the sangar, catwalked into the position with weapons abutted at the shoulder. Cope cut the phone cable, severed the searchlight's connecting wire, stripped down the MG30, threw away the firing pin. Caine hunkered at the narrow doorgap at the head of the steps, surveyed the forest below – a dark weft of thorntangle pierced by steel colossi of radar towers, stretching away from the base of the cliff for over a mile. Caine could make out beyond it the Citadel's core, the vast, cave-ridden buttress where he'd once attended a drunken feast: it was under this great rock plug that the Olzon-13 bunker lay.

He shuftied his watch: only ten minutes until the relief sentry arrived. Cope tapped his shoulder: they moved out of the sangar, cleared the steps down to the forest edge. When they were in position, Copeland gave an owlhoot. Wallace and Trubman sloped down towards them, panting under the weight of two manpacks each. They set them down in the bush, sat on their heels with their weapons ready: Caine and Copeland made for the stairs to help with the other packs. Caine had only taken two steps when Trubman squawked. He wheeled round: a big bear of a Jerry with Pancho Sanza whiskers had stepped out of the forest, had run into Trubman, slicked his bayonet into the signaller's belly as he jumped up. Trubman was frozen against the Hun, broad head bowed, dewlaps convulsing, a dumpy hand round the Jerry's rifle stock: the Jerry wasn't making any noise, though, because Fred Wallace had his great basket of a hand around the man's mouth and nose. Caine watched the big gunner drive his bayonet into the Jerry's kidneys with all the strength of his giant arms and chest. It wasn't as expertly done as the Reapers' job: the Jerry groped and scrabbled onehanded, spat, bit, snorted snot from his nostrils, tried to scream. Wallace plunged the bayonet into his gut again and again until he slumped. His rifle came away with him. The bayonet slipped out of Trubman's gut with a gush of blood: the signaller tried to shore up his slit stomach with his hand, gave a low sigh, sank shalefaced to his knees. Wallace made sure the Jerry was dead then hunkered down over Trubman, pulled out the shell dressing from his top pocket, tried to staunch the bleeding. 'I've got him, skipper,' he mouthed.

The rest of the crew brought down the manpacks and

stood to in the trees in all-round defence. Maurice Pickney opened his medical haversack, peeled off Trubman's dressing, examined the wound, wiped away blood, changed the dressing, gave him a morphia shot. Caine squatted beside him. 'Sorry skipper,' the signaller wheezed. 'Didn't see the bugger coming, did I?'

Pickney shushed him, turned to Caine, spoke with his mouth up against his ear. 'It's touch and go, boss,' he said. 'With a gut wound like that, you can't tell. We'll have to leave him here.'

'Not on your life,' Caine hissed in the orderly's earlobe. 'I'm not leaving him for the Hun. We're taking him with us.'

Pickney looked at Caine, cobwebbed eyes standing out against the corkblack face. Caine thought he was going to argue, but instead he pursed his lips and shrugged. It took twenty minutes to cut poles from the bush, to rig up a makeshift stretcher out of spare rope. While they were doing it, Copeland crept up to Caine, spoke in his ear. 'We're not going to make it, skipper,' he said. 'We've lost too much time. We've got less than two hours till the next sentry change, till they find the dead 'uns. If we haven't hit the target by then, we're all lucked out.'

Caine shook his head. 'I'm not leaving him,' he mouthed in the sergeant's ear. 'We've only got to cover a mile.'

Caine knew what Cope was thinking: covering a mile tactically through thornforest carrying heavy manpacks and a wounded man would be like trekking to the moon. When they pulled out, Pickney, Netanya, Wallace and Gibson carried the stretcher between them, stagged by Caine and Rossi, changing a man every ten minutes: Copeland humped his manpack and ranged ahead as lead scout.

The thornwood smelled of pitch and gumsap: the branches snagged their packs like sticky fingers. Cope avoided the path used by the sentries, tried to steer them through the less dense undergrowth, but it was hard going, made painfully slow by their heavy burdens. Trubman bore the buffeting noiselessly, his hands clutched over his stomach, but often they were forced to draw him through the scrub at a crouch, covering their eyes against the brambles. Copeland signalled frequent halts: the men froze, strained their ears for reaction. They heard the hoot of owls, the chafing of insects, the chittlings of mice: several times they heard the low murmuring of enemy prowlers, the soft tramp of their boots on the earth.

Once, Cope steered them around a radar tower, its steel feet clamped in sandbag emplacements, the great scanner yawing above them. Further on, he stopped the patrol and went to investigate an anti-aircraft sangar: he found there only spent shells and an empty ammo box. The SAS team squatted by the sangar wall to sip water from their canteens, and Caine angled a peek at his watch. It was almost 0415 hours. It had taken them nearly an hour to get this far, and he judged they were only halfway. They had to put in the attack before sunup, and it was less than an hour till first light. Caine sucked his teeth, decided they would leave Trubman inside the sangar: he would be safe here, and this position would be their emergency RV.

They left him lying on a blanket with his rifle clutched in his arms, a full canteen of water and a couple of morphia syrettes. 'We aren't dumping you, mate,' Caine said in his ear. 'We'll come back, don't fret.' As they moved off again, a dry wind rose, scraping like cello strings in the treeheads.

Caine welcomed it because the sound covered their movements: Copeland increased the pace, pausing only when he heard voices or sensed movement. By the time they came to the western edge of the forest, though, the morning star was lying above the eaves of the great abutment and winedark filaments were trickling across the mountains to the east.

33

They set their packs among sandmounds caught among the roots of white-thorn and bladegrass, fanned out in the bush, primed detonators, set timepencils, saw to their shooting irons. Caine didn't want a repetition of el-Gala: he sent scouts through the bush north and south to make sure no enemy was lying in wait. He surveyed the vista, noting that it was slightly different from what he remembered: the vast windcarved reef of the buttress wall reared over them, tilting up out of the plain seventy paces away, its surface scored and grainy in the predawn haze. The acacia forest had previously extended to the foot of the butt: the Boche had evidently cut it back when they'd built the spur line. He could see the narrow gauge rails running on a low embankment across the pebbleshot earth, curving gracefully into the jaws of a cave on his right. His heart jolted. This was the entrance to the Olzon-13 bunker: all roads had led him here.

Caine panned the lenses left into the dun and grey-washed dark: the sky was still benighted, but Venus was sinking, the seep of red ochre on the hills growing rich. He observed the sagebrush around the cleft where the warm springs lay, recalled how his crew had bathed there on his previous trip. He eyetracked the rails south for a quarter of a mile to where they rounded the edge of a long stone slab – the same slab on which scores of Itie deserters and ex-colons had once gathered to greet him by lamplight. In his mind's eye he pictured the entrance to the main cave, the vaulted cavern where he and his commandos had once feasted, where he had danced and smooched with Lina, the girl later raped and murdered by the Hun. He recalled how the tents of the Ities had been pitched in the trees near the slab, remembered how Copeland had been caught there in bed with Angela Brunetto by her husband Michele.

He knew from aerial shots how the view would look from the slab now: to the right, the Jerry M/T park standing at the end of the narrow defile that formed the Citadel's 'main gate', and to the left, the prefabricated admin block and the compound where the prisoners were held. Beyond the slab, on the other side of the massif, lay the 999 Division bivouac lines. He thought of Audley, hoped that he and the Senussi would by now be in position outside the defile, awaiting the signal to launch their attack.

He studied the whole sweep of the spur line, taking in every detail, fitting in the details with the images on the maps and aerial photos he'd memorized. He glassed out the rock wall, his gaze coming to rest once again on the bunker mouth. There was no sentry post and no sign of prowler guards: the Germans were obviously relying on their perimeter defences, confident that the Citadel could be attacked only by air.

Caine let the glasses down, rubbed suetclogged eyes. All that remained was to get the Lewes bombs across those seventy yards of open ground and into the bunker before it grew light. The chemical weapon that threatened to crush the greatest Allied offensive of the war so far, the poison that had brought so much death and suffering to the Green Mountains, would be destroyed in the next half-hour.

Copeland tapped him on the arm, passed him blue pills. Caine swallowed the Bennies with a gulp of water. Almost at once he felt the amphetamine rush, felt his fatigue melt away, felt relief from the accumulated strain of the past few days. The team had survived against all odds, but he'd lost three good men in the process: he regretted it acutely. All the more reason, though, why they should bring off *Sandhog*: failure wasn't an option. As for Betty Nolan, it was too late to save her, perhaps, but he would mourn her loss in good time.

The scouts returned, reported all quiet. Caine hacked a deep breath. 'Are you ready for this?' he asked Copeland.

Cope nodded. 'Let's go for it,' he said.

Caine was about to rise when Wallace cupped his elbow. Three German troopers were strutting along the spur line, sub-machine-guns slung from their shoulders: they looked smart, alert, competent: the SAS men pressed deeper into the swordgrass, but the sentries didn't even glance their way. They lay still until the guards had rounded the end of the butt: Caine was about to move again when he heard the peanut-box rattle of a motor: a motorcycle and sidecar combo sputtered along the railway track, knobby tyres spooning up saffron dust – two Boche in khaki drills, a thirty-cal Schmeisser mounted on the sidecar bonnet. Caine lay still, itched for them to pass. He watched the combo shrink into the distance through one slitted eye: the moment it was out of sight he rose, listened, beckoned his team forward. 'Here we go, lads,' he said.

They hammered across the open ground in an untactical bunch, scrambled over the spur line, lurched on, stooped in the shadows by the cave mouth, their backs to the rock wall. There was some scrub here – not good cover, but good enough until it came full light. Caine detailed Netanya and Pickney to keep watch, had Wallace and Cope take their manpacks, led his five-man demolition squad into the tunnel's maw. It was matt-black inside, but they used their torches, sniffing firedamp and nitrate, tracking the rails around the twists and turns. A bevy of bats divebombed them, flittered out towards the soapy light.

They rounded a bend and found themselves against railway buffers in a huge cavern: the roof arched high above them, and the thin wires of their torchlight fell on a huddle of vats perched on low iron legs, a couple of horizontal tanks like ships' turbines, banks of brass pressure gauges, tangles of pipes, pumps and rubber hose, racks of rusted cylinders. There were block-and-tackle cables hanging from cross girders like strands of giant cobweb, piles of glass demijohns in fitted baskets, clusters of oil drums, a silent generator radiating a lattice of wires attached to bare lightbulbs affixed to the walls. The stone floor was covered with debris: screws of newspaper, fag butts, beer-bottle shards, enamel mugs holed and shapeless: half a dozen broken down garage trolleys with T-shaped handles stood in a ragged dogsleg by the buffers. The cavern smelled of sulphur, grease and industrial lye.

Caine blinked, took in the air of abandonment with a sick feeling in his gut. Gibson and Rossi dumped their manpacks, slouched across to the vats, ran their hands over peeling paint, fingered stopcocks and standpipes.

Copeland left his two packs on the floor, shuffled over to examine the pressure gauges. He looked round for Caine, caught in his torchbeam Caine's dark overhang of a frown, the glint of quartzite eyes. 'The needles are all at zero,' he said. Caine heard cold dismay in his voice.

'An' these here stopcocks are open,' the cowboy drawled indignantly. 'All of 'em.'

'Fucking empty,' Rossi chimed in.

'Not a fucking *dickybird*,' the cowboy echoed. 'There ain't nothin' here, boss.'

Caine dryswallowed, licked skinned lips, knuckles tight on the stock of his Thompson. He didn't want to accept it: not after all they'd endured. There was dead silence as the full horror of it hit them. Fred Wallace picked up two cylinders from the racks, held them out sideways like dumb-bells – an unconscious gesture of crucifixion. The canisters were obviously empty: they seemed featherlight in his boxing-glove hands. He hurled them down with a thunderous clang that made everyone jump: he spat viciously, tossed his jungled hair, his mandrill face a web of furrows in the torchlight. 'Jerry seen us comin', skipper,' he ranted. 'We've been fuckin' *had*.'

Shaking his head incredulously, Caine stomped to the nearest vat, hammered it with the side of his fist. It gave up a hollow ring. It was true, then: the vats were empty. If the Olzon-13 had ever been here, it wasn't any longer. He thought of el-Gala. 'Jesus, not *again*,' he spat.

At the same moment the muted snarl of motors drifted down the gallery from the outside. 'Oh my Christ,' Copeland said.

They jogged up the tunnel in a cluster, dropped their

manpacks, threw themselves down by Netanya and Pickney at the bunker mouth. They clocked half a dozen Hun wagons drawing towards them out of the slategrey halflight – motorcycle combos, roofless halftracks, three-ton trucks. They stared into the yellow flush of headlamps, looked up the black nostrils of machine-guns, saw Hun faces – opaque eyes behind dust goggles, mouths like fusewire twists. Further back, dozens of Jerries in battlekit were debussing from the open backs of lorries left and right, and more of them were coming up from the rear.

The SAS team lay squeezed together either side of the rails, spreadlegged in the full blaze of the headlights with a battery of MG30s zeroed in on them. Caine knew that a single burst from one of those weapons could blow them all to Valhalla: the Hun had them cold. They might withdraw into the bunker, but there was no escape that way: the enemy would flush them out with gas or flame-guns, or simply wait till they died of thirst.

The Hun wagons leaguered up in a broken crescent around the bunker entrance: Hun soldiers with rifles and sub-machine-guns muscled into the gaps. Caine saw gun muzzles pointed at him, felt the heat of the headlights, saw the Jerries jostle back to let through a tall officer in a glossy trenchcoat, polished jackboots and a high-crowned cap. He halted at ten paces. '*Lay down your weapons*,' he gasped. His voice was breathless, high-pitched, mezzo-contralto: it made the hairs on Caine's neck bristle, set his teeth on edge. He knew that voice. He peered at the officer, clocked a robust torso, long legs, an oddly feminine flare of the hips, eyes like pitshafts in a bone-coloured face. His gaze came to rest on the man's fingers – abnormally long, like the legs of a tarantula. Caine would have recognized those hands anywhere: this was Major Heinrich Rohde of the Abwehr – the man who'd tortured Betty Nolan, who'd caused the death of Moshe Naiman. Caine had last seen him four months earlier through the sights of a Bren gun, and had tried his best to kill him. He'd often hoped he'd succeeded: now he knew he had not.

Rohde took another step forward. '*Lieutenant Caine*,' he breathed. 'Tell your men to put aside all their weapons, and stand up slowly with their hands on their heads.'

For a moment, Caine couldn't believe he'd heard Rohde call him by his name and rank. When he'd encountered the Black Widow last, he'd been a sergeant: how could Rohde know he was now a lieutenant? How could he know Caine was there at all? None of the men had turned a hair, and Caine felt a surge of pride at their steadiness. He knew they would fight if he ordered it, but as things were they wouldn't stand a chance. There was no option but to surrender: what worried him most was the fate of Manny Netanya – if Rohde discovered he was a Jew, there was no telling what he might do.

Rohde's blackballed eyes beaded the cavemouth. '*Lieutenant Caine*,' he repeated. 'I shall have your men shot down like dogs if you do not order them to surrender in the next thirty seconds.'

Your men, Caine thought: *your* men, *your* choice. He recalled the Black Widow's uncanny ability to probe human weakness: how he'd grasped from the start that Caine was the type who'd rather sacrifice himself than let his comrades die. Caine laid down his Tommy-gun and his Browning, rose cautiously to his feet: Rohde recognized him and gave him a wolflike smile. Caine had to force the words out through rage-glued teeth. 'Do what he says, lads. Put your weapons aside. Stand up. Slowly.'

The men wove up in a teetering bunch, leaving rifles, Bren-guns, pistols, on the ground. '*Is that him*?' Netanya hissed from the side of his mouth. 'Is that the bastard who killed Moshe?'

'Yes, but . . .'

Rohde raised an inquisitive eyebrow, and in that second Netanya rushed straight at him, his lank, sinewed body jerking, jawhasps going like traps, eyes feral, mouth locked in a silent scream of revenge. It took Caine a tick to see that he was carrying a primed Lewes bomb. He felt his lips forming round a '*Noooo*' that never came out: he'd already slipped into the sort of trance he'd experienced just before the contact with the Jerry column: time went pussyfoot, objects loomed limpid, garfished up larger than life. He saw Netanya galloping like a hurdler in slow motion, saw Jerry faces blanch, saw Huns reel back, knocking each other down like dominoes, heard the Lewes bomb detonate in a rip-roaring *barrooomm*. The air mulekicked: Netanya's body melted in a blowback of flesh and smoke, Rohde vanished: a motorcycle combo keetered perpendicular, turned a breakback somersault, landed with a crunch atop its team. Caine scooped his Thompson, loosed the safety, spittlebugged rounds: the gunner on the second combo flipped, the driver's tunic scalloped out in crimson burrs.

'*Run!*' Caine bawled.

The SAS lads had their weapons: they were already moving. Wallace welted grenades; Copeland hurled smoke canisters. The bombs bunked dirt, keedled off in a frayed salvo: air flumped, grit and shrapnel blew, shellbrown smoke *whoofed* across the Hun wagons in wads. Caine saw a truck bonnet flame up like a gasjet, saw steel skew and rumple, saw glass shards fly, saw blazing bodies lollygag out of the cab, heard Hun voices wail. Before the Jerries were on their feet, the SAS men were hurtling out through the blazing leaguer, running like a whirlwind, leaping over Hun heads, vaulting the railway bank, ballclacking bullets in long spleens of fire.

Caine hit bush, heard his men crash through it like spooked beasts, heard the *clitterclat* of machine-guns behind him, saw tracer rounds fingerpoke the leaden air. He swivelled, dropped into a crouch, glimpsed blazing wagons through swills of smog and black pyres like hearse-plumes. He clocked Jerry heads bob behind the railway bank: he smelled sourgas, clocked white commas of gunsmoke, arrowheads of fire. Squads of Jerries were pepper-potting across the open ground on his flanks: fire and movement with bayonets fixed.

Caine couldn't see his men in the forest but he could hear the pump of their Garands, could hear their Brens *tockatick*. He slotted his Tommy-gun to the shoulder, sighted up, squeezed steel, felt the gun jump, sprayed enemy skirmishers, saw two of them bowl over and snaffle dirt. The cowboy moved in spirit-like, squatted beside him, bevelled teeth gritted, eyes bugging, rifle at the armpit. 'The *Very*, skipper,' he hissed. 'We need a . . .' A Jerry slug thumped between his shoulderblades, stove in his neck: his face ballooned, his jaw uncottered from behind in a mesh of teeth, bone splinters, rent ligament. His lean body tippled into the dust. Caine ducked, lurched in shock, heard a spine-curdling howl of anguish that could only have come from Rossi.

A tub-framed Jerry yomped out of the gauze, screaming, waving his rifle: Caine fired from the waist, saw red pustules volcano up across the Hun's chest and neck, saw him sledge out. Incoming rounds peeled air from all directions: he sensed enemy movement left and right. He groped in his pouch for the Very pistol, eyeballed another Jerry skittering in from his front, a lanky, stoatfaced trooper with a Schmeisser SMG muzzle-spitting at the hip: slugs sawed treebark, spiffled leaves. Caine fired his Tommy one-handed, clocked a fist-sized hole open up in the Jerry's thigh. The man screeched, timbered almost on top of him: blood whooshed from his limb in long scarfs. Caine cocked the Very left-handed, pulled steel. Air rushed and popped, green light girandoled. A lead weight clumped his head, crushed it sideways: a vice gripped his skull, a whirling cyclone sent him spinning down a red-vaulted slide into a serenity of dark.

34

A broad fan of sunlight streaked out into rococo skies: blades of flame opal trimmed away the ragends of night. Galleries of purple cloud unreeled, tendrils of brickdust hung in the hollows, light spindled along hill terraces, spun across the pates of downs covered in evergreen oak and spiny scrub as thick as fur. She lay among tufts of esparto grass like straw mopheads on the saddle of a wadi side, watching the sun weave patterns across the screes, glisten on knucklebone peaks. The Jerry airfield lay on the flats below her, a cool spill of tarmac adorned with ackack posts, a fuel dump, a windsock flapping idly on its post like a giant's condom. There were no aircraft on the runway: the only movement was at the south end of the 'drome where a chain gang of Krauts in overalls was unloading gas cylinders from rolling stock coupled to a small locomotive. They worked methodically, swinging cylinders from hand to hand, stacking them in pyramids under the corrugated-iron curve of a wall-less Nissen hut.

There were hundreds of cylinders: Nolan zoomed in her field glasses, knowing that the tubes could only contain Olzon-13. That meant Caine's mission had failed. At first light they'd heard the gnash of small arms from beyond the crater wall, clocked the crabhand sprawl of a green Very light. The firefight had stopped abruptly, but minutes later another had irrupted from the western end of the Citadel. They'd heard the low crump of ordnance: Layla had claimed to recognize the sound of old Senussi rifles and was certain that her father's men were battling for their lives. The second firefight had soon petered out, leaving a gaping silence. Layla had stared at her ashenfaced: Nolan had felt a gut-thump of despair, partly for Layla, partly for *Sandhog*, mostly for Caine, for the fact that she'd arrived too late to help him. Now, she fingered the .45 Colt hidden under the Senussi rags she'd borrowed. The pistol and a couple of No. 36 grenades were all she had: Layla carried a dagger. The notion of two women taking on the Jerry platoon and the guardposts armed only with these trifles was too futile even to consider. She stashed her glasses, shimmied backwards out of her hiding place, retraced her steps to where Layla crouched among feather-leaved terfa trees on the wadi side guarding the bony she-donkey that carried the rest of Nolan's kit in her panniers. She told Layla what she'd seen. 'There's nothing we can do here,' she said. 'Either we go back or we go on and find out what's happened.'

Layla's coaltar eyes glimmered. 'We go on,' she said.

They continued along the wadi with the donkey's hooves clicking behind them on the gravel and the water-marbled stones. The black crater wall loomed over them to the left: the thorntrees on the sides of the arroyo rustled in the wind. They rounded the Citadel's north-western face an hour and a half later in full daylight, climbing a sheeptrack up the wadi bank to where brakes of mangled myrtle and tamarix grew out of grassy dunes. Nolan glimpsed a dark figure hovering in the shadows of the trees, gripped Layla's shoulder, wrenched her down just as a shot clapped out hollow in the silence, whazzing high over their heads. She was fumbling for her pistol when Layla gasped. '*Father*. It's my *father*.'

Adud didn't seem surprised to see them, only angry at himself for opening fire and relieved that his hasty shot hadn't done them any harm. His eyes were leached out with pain: he had a graze on the shoulder and a bullet in the calf. He'd bound both wounds in strips of dirty cotton torn from his headcloth. He slung his rifle, took the she-donkey's headrope, hobbled to a tree, tethered her to it. He led the women haltingly through the forested dunes to a place overlooking a shallow canyon on the other side where a group of tribesmen huddled.

Of the dozen who'd set off with Adud, only five were left, all of them wounded, some badly. Nolan saw arms mauled and lampblacked, legs hanked in soiled bandages, seeping blood. One young Senussi whose fingers had been blown off stared catatonically into midspace, his face white as alabaster: another had the side of his skull split open in a long, livid gash. The Arabs stared at the two girls, their eyes bulbous and white against filth-pitted faces: they grunted greetings through clenched teeth. Adud pointed to the wadi floor: Nolan saw down there a crescent of cadavers, Senussi and German, starch-faced, blood-darkened slugs spreadeagled in darker-stained blots of gravel. A motorcycle combo lay smoking on its broken back, its spoked front wheel reaving slowly back and forth like a pit-winch. Next to it stood an armoured half-track vehicle in Afrika Korps livery with a machine-gun and a light artillery piece mounted on her rear. A dead Jerry was draped over her open side, his KD uniform ripped and burnt, blood trickling from his outstretched arms: the driver lay curled up below the open cab door with a black cavity in his chest and a Senussi dagger stuck through his face.

Nolan's first instinct was to rush back to the donkey for her medical kit: if some of the Senussi's wounds weren't treated with sulphenamide, they'd turn gangrenous, she thought. She paused for a moment, though, crouching down against a sandbank to survey the battlefield: the canyon below was a side-wadi opening off the main watercourse along which the spur line had been laid. She caught a glimpse of warped and upended railtracks beyond the wadi mouth and realized that the Senussi must have blown the line. Her mouth creased: the Arabs had done their job, had fought off the Hun doggedly, but their efforts had been wasted. 'I saw the Olzon-13 cylinders,' she told Adud. 'I saw them being discharged from the train at the airstrip. They must have moved them before you even got here.'

Layla translated: the old sheikh batted bloodcricked eyes. Nolan reflected that the Hun had probably waited till first light to unload the train: they'd been in no hurry. It was almost as if they'd known when Caine's party would strike, had sidestepped neatly like a matador dodging a bull: the firefight she and Layla had heard at first light must mean that the SAS team had been ambushed. She felt the gorge rising in her throat. *Audley*. That traitorous pig must have got word to the Krauts.

Adud was nodding, his eyes turning watery as it dawned on him that his men had died for nothing. Nolan almost regretted mentioning it: she had opened her mouth to say that she was going for her first-aid kit when a question occurred to her. 'How did your men blow the line?' she asked. 'You aren't trained in sabotage . . .'

'It was the *Ingleezi*,' Layla cut in. 'The one who came with them . . .'

Nolan started. 'What *Ingleezi*? You didn't say . . .'

She saw that Layla's eyes were focused over her shoulder, glanced back to see an SAS soldier with a rakish green silk scarf tied around his neck, in KDs and grimy battlekit, slouching in from among the trees only a couple of yards away. He was a lean, lampjawed man with dark hair, gleaming beryl eyes and a fixed smile: his lips were drawn back from even white teeth, like a caricature of a B-film cowboy hero. He was carrying a manpack on his back, a Garand rifle slung over his shoulder and a Browning automatic in his hand. 'I say, miss' – he winked at Nolan – 'if I'm being talked about, I should at least be introduced.'

It was Audley: Nolan recognized him at once from the dossier she'd seen in Stocker's office. She took a step backwards, groped for the pistol under her robe, her pulse racing. It was a mistake: Audley clocked the give-away movement and halted mid-step. Before Nolan's hand had even closed on her weapon, he had seized Layla's slender arm, jerked her towards him, stuck the muzzle of his Browning under her wealth of hair, into the fissure beneath her ear. The Senussi girl yelped but didn't struggle. 'Don't do anything silly, now,' Audley said hoarsely. 'I don't want to hurt this young lady, but I will if I have to. Put your hands up where I can see them.'

His face had turned waxy, his breath was coming in nasal scoops. There was something apologetic and forlorn about his expression, Nolan thought, that didn't quite mesh with the image of a Nazi masterspy. She raised her hands slowly. 'I know what you are,' she told him. 'At least, I know you aren't the Honourable Bertram Audley, that you've never won the MC. You're a liar and a traitor. You're not an officer: your supposed family doesn't even exist.'

Audley's eyes bulged: his taut cheek twitched. His mouth worked, but no sound emerged. Adud stared at him, his chapped lips forming a round 'O' of confusion: those among the other Senussi who were able to stand rose to their feet. Audley wrenched Layla's arm upwards until she squeaked, drew her back several paces. 'I'm warning you, boys,' he said.

Adud muttered an order: the Senussi laid down their weapons. Nolan glared at Audley: his features seemed to have lost their squarejawed shape: he looked feeble and guilty, like a schoolboy caught cheating. His eyes no longer glowed with confidence, his pupils were peridots, his brows glowered with resentment. 'The game's up, eh?' he wheezed. He was making an obvious attempt to appear nonchalant, but Nolan could recognize an act when she saw one: she caught an edge of hysteria in his voice, as if he were about to burst into tears. 'I guessed it somehow,' he rambled, 'as soon as I heard you talking. I was listening over there. I could have slipped away, but like a fool I thought I could brass it out. I suppose it was always on the cards that somebody would find out.'

Rage boiled in Nolan's chest: she was so furious that she considered going for her weapon and risking everything. This dirty, double-crossing rat had sold Tom Caine to the Hun: through the perfidy of this one man, Monty's whole campaign was in jeopardy. It would be worth sacrificing her life just to finish him. She let her hands drop slightly, but Audley clocked the action, drew Layla further away.

'You would, wouldn't you?' he whined. 'I know you upper-class bitches. You have no idea what it's like . . . a hoity-toity bint like you, born with a silver spoon, always had everything your own way. I know your type all right.'

Nolan blinked at the irony of it: Audley, or whatever his name was, evidently had no idea that until only months previously she'd been a cabaret girl. She studied him curiously: he was a pathetic excuse for a Jerry stoolpigeon and that somehow made it worse. 'At least, thanks to you,' he went on, almost to himself, 'I know where the stuff is. There's always a chance I can . . .'

He gave Layla a hefty push, spatted off a single shot into the air. The report rocked air: Nolan and Adud ducked, Layla tripped and fell. Audley whipped round, hared off into the trees, his booted feet going *whamp*, *whamp* in the sand. Nolan skipped out of Layla's way, wrestled her weapon from under her rags, brought it up, squeezed iron. Nothing happened: the safety was still on. Swearing, she released the catch, gripped the pistol in both hands, fired off two rounds. The shots slamped up sandspurts: sour cordite pinched her nostrils. She'd fired too late and she knew it: Audley had already vanished into the trees. She started after him, but Adud seized her arm with a clawed hand. Several of the Arabs were already staggering in Audley's wake, too dazed and jumbofooted even to bring their rifles to bear. Layla was on her feet with her knife in her hand, cobalt eyes aflame: Nolan pulled away from Adud's grip, but Layla stopped her. 'Is not worth it,' she hissed. 'Let him go.'

'He's going to the airstrip. He'll warn the Hun we're here . . .'

'Warn them of what? That we are two girls and a few Arabs too bad hurt to shoot their old guns? I think the *Tedesci* laugh at him.'

Nolan cast about, desperately trying to control her fury, to clear her mind. It hit her that Layla was talking sense: the Jerries who'd sallied out from the Citadel to engage the Senussi had withdrawn, leaving their dead on the field. They knew the Arabs were here, and if they thought they posed any real threat, they'd have been back by now. The Krauts had outmanoeuvred them, and – Layla was right again – this little bunch of benighted Bedouin wasn't going to stop them.

She clenched a fist, swore, spat in the sand. She *had* to prevent the Olzon-13 cylinders from being loaded on Axis aircraft: once the stuff was airborne, it would be too late. *Lightfoot* would be kiboshed. There might still be time to stop it, but the means didn't exist. Not unless Caine's men, or some of them, were still standing. She grimaced. The chances were the SAS men were all goners but it wasn't impossible that at least some had been bagged alive – maybe some had even evaded capture. To know for certain, she'd have to get into the Citadel, and attempting that now the Jerries were alert would be fatal. Layla's original idea of going in disguised wouldn't work, and there was no way this handful of ragtag walking scarecrows with their museum-piece smallarms was going to run the gauntlet of that narrow entrance defile. To do that they'd need armoured wagons, artillery . . .

She spun round, glancing at the Jerry half-track down in the canyon. She studied the vehicle: it was armoured, certainly, and it appeared intact. And there was a cannon mounted on its back – it looked like a 40mm. In G(R), Nolan had done training on field guns: she felt sure she could handle the piece, but there was no way she could do that and drive the machine at the same time. She caught Layla's wrist. 'Can you drive?' she demanded.

Layla's eyes opened wide. 'What?'

'A motor vehicle. Can you drive one?'

'Yes, but . . .'

'Can you or can't you?'

'I . . . they taught me to drive a car at the Italian mission school, yes. But is long time, I don't know if I . . .' She broke off, her eyes bugging as she stared from Nolan's excited face to the halftrack in the corrie below. Understanding dawned on her. 'No,' she gasped. 'You don't mean . . . that . . . *thing*?'

Nolan let go her wrist. 'Is it still working? Ask your father. Did they wreck it or just kill the crew? *Ask* him.'

Layla flashed her a last wild look and began gabbling to Adud. When she turned back, Nolan was already ripping off the rags of her Arab dress, revealing her KD uniform beneath. 'My father say they never touch the vehicle, but –'

'Then get ready,' Nolan cut her off fiercely. 'You're going to drive that rattletrap into the Citadel while I work the gun: if Tom Caine's alive we're going to get him out of there.'

35

They branded his thighs with hot spoons, snickered at him as he cringed and puked: they drew burning rags across the back of his neck. They slammed him in the kidneys from behind with a club, guffawed as he went down bawling. They kicked him in the ribs and guts: they kicked him so hard up the arse that he thought his rectum had burst. He couldn't see how many there were because his head was covered in a hessian sack: he could make out only slivers ghosting across the checkpattern light. They booted him in the solar plexus and in the scrotum. He screamed, he coughed, he brayed: he snorted snot, drooled bile, gurgled out bloody phlegm inside the sack. They hauled him up: they battered his back and shoulders with slats of plank until the wood shattered. They knucklepunched his head through the sack: they belaboured his legs with sticks, punted his shins with boot-caps, kneed him in the groin, sent him fishtailing on to a hardpacked floor to grovel in his own piss. They plucked him up and rammed him into an iron chair.

Caine's arms were tied behind him: he was naked but for his shorts, which were minging with shit and blood and urine. His head was still bleeding where Jerry shrapnel had grazed him: or had they stobbed him with a riflebutt? He didn't know. He felt like he was wearing a lead hat, his neck and thighs burned, his gut was caving in: his senses gyrowheeled, his hands and legs quaked as he waited to be hit or burned again, not knowing from which direction the next attack would come. The 999 Div. boys had been catmousing with him like this for ever: beasting him and standing back to catch their breath, and beasting him again. They were evidently enjoying it. Caine could hear their rattlebreath, could hear them titter and dog-growl in Kraut: no one addressed him, no one demanded information. This beasting had to be strictly for pleasure, because they didn't even want to know why he was here.

He waited, his body shaking, trying to muster his thoughts: while he was being beasted it was impossible to think of anything but the pain, so he had to make use of these pauses. Gibson was dead, that was certain: Manny Netanya had blown himself to bits with a Lewes bomb, killing Rohde in the process. Caine was certain now that Rohde was behind the atrocities that had taken place here: a self-confessed war criminal, a former *Einsatzkommando* complicit in the shocking massacre of Russian Jews, he was the obvious candidate for the post of Angel of Death. Caine should have clicked long ago. The one small satisfaction to be salvaged from this cocked-up mission was that, thanks to Netanya, Rohde had been taken out.

Before they'd hooded him, Caine had seen enough to know that he was in the prefab admin-block building he'd seen on the aerial shots. When they'd dragged him out of the cell where he'd come round, he'd caught, through an open door, a nauseating glimpse of Fred Wallace getting beasted. Plastered with grime and blood, the giant was bellowing in pain: he'd been made to crawl on his hands and knees while a Kraut rode him like a horse, and half a dozen others booted him, thrashed his buttocks with palmstalks, beat his limbs with sticks. Caine had almost thrown up at the sight, but he'd kept his eyes open: he'd clocked his team's kit and weapons being stashed in a storeroom, had caught a shufti of Harry Copeland's bleached face and cupshot eyes, his mouth skewed in a permanent yodel of agony, as a squad of Jerries hustled him along the corridor, thrashing him with leather belts and whips.

Gibson and Netanya were down: Wallace and Cope had survived. Trubman was wounded, perhaps dead. Pickney, Rossi and Audley were unaccounted for but had most likely been killed in action. Caine wondered how the Senussi party had fared: he didn't hold out any big hope for them. He recalled firing the green flare just before going down – yet another error of judgement on his part. The plan had been for Adud's crew to cover the SAS team's withdrawal, but there had *been* no withdrawal, which meant that, if the Arabs had come into action, they would have needlessly exposed themselves. The Olzon-13 gas had been moved already, so even if they'd blown the line, it could serve no purpose. The Hun outnumbered and outgunned them: he was sure they would by now have been ruthlessly hunted down. He sieved a thin breath through the hessian. *Sandhog* had been a fiasco: somehow Caine had felt it was doomed from the start.

He heard the scuffle of boots, ducked defensively as a rubber baton whacked him across the shoulders, spud-sacked him off the chair. Caine hit the floor yelling, rolled in filth. A Kraut kicked him in the stomach: yellow sun-spots blazed behind his eyes. They lifted him up, they stomped on his feet, they sideswiped him through the blindfold, they plonked him down in the chair. He felt his heart thud, braced himself for more, but this time it didn't come. Instead, he heard an order snapped. He heard booted feet scuttering back: a moment later the hood was whipped off and Caine found himself staring into the bonewhite face of Major Heinrich Rohde.

Caine gagged in shock: his brassweight skull wobbled. This couldn't be: only hours earlier he'd seen Rohde vaporized by Netanya's bomb. He blinked, tried to focus, took in the Nazi's muscular frame, his immaculate drill tunic, his jodhpurs, his polished jackboots, his peaked service cap with the Abwehr insignia. '*No*,' he lisped through pumped lips. '*No*. You're dead.'

'I am very much alive, I assure you, my friend,' Rohde scraped.

Caine's vision was blurred, but there was no mistaking the highpitched, effeminate voice – the voice that had haunted him all these months. He screwed up his face in denial, but couldn't tear his eyes away. The Black Widow was posed in the disturbing bathing-beauty stance that Caine recalled so vividly, all his weight on one leg, his over-wide pelvis cocked provocatively, his spiderfingered hands on his hips. His face was smooth, hairless and bonechina white, his eyes blank and machine-like.

'Your Jewboy very nearly did for me,' Rohde rasped. 'Of course, I was expecting something like that. I saw him coming and put the side of an armoured car between us. I am gratified that I did so. Can you imagine the ignominy of being killed by a *Jew*? That's two in a family, I believe: your Corporal Yid back in June, and now his brother, Corporal Yid number two. Little by little we rid the world of its pestilence. Surely there can't be many more of them out there?'

Caine's world lurched, his heartbeat gallumphed, his breath jangled. He fought to stop himself spewing his guts. The burns on his neck and thighs stung sickeningly, but the rest of his body felt numb, encased in rubber. Gore dripped down his face: his puffed-up eyelids flapped, his swollen lips shook. How the hell could Rohde have known that Naiman and Netanya were brothers? How could he even have clicked that the suicide bomber was a Jew?

Caine shivered, tasted bile on his tongue, felt his senses spindrift, struggled to stay conscious: his nostrils bubbled mucus, drool slicked his chin. He glared at Rohde, deliberately summoning up a surge of the blackest hatred, purposely dredging up memories of the Black Widow torturing him with hot irons, of Rohde chopping off Moshe Naiman's thumb with a cleaver, turning Naiman loose in a minefield, of Naiman dying in agony with his foot blown off, of Caine's hellish grapple to climb out of the hundred-foot well where Rohde had intended him to die a painful death from starvation. The deep core of revulsion focused his senses, brought him back to earth with a slap.

The Black Widow seemed to know what he was thinking, and Caine recalled the Nazi's weird ability to get inside people's minds. He didn't avert his gaze, though: he knew there was no escape this time – he had really known it all along. Rohde had outfoxed them. *Sandhog* had failed: *Lightfoot* was about to get scuppered; Betty Nolan was dead; most of the ten picked SAS soldiers he'd brought from Kabrit had been killed. He didn't *want* to live to see Eighth Army slaughtered through his own incompetence. Whatever happened, though, if there were the slightest shadow of a chance, he would take out Rohde before he died.

Caine watched with fascination as the major snapped the tentacle fingers of his right hand. '*Wasser*,' he said.

One of the guards hurried forward with a chipped enamel mug, held it to Caine's broken lips. He gulped water greedily, aware that it could easily be snatched away. Rohde watched him with apparent interest, a tight grin on his stringwire mouth. 'Good,' he said. 'Very good.'

The soldier scurried back to the squad. Rohde gave another order: the men filed away through the door, leaving only two guards. The major removed his cap, revealing a billiard-ball head-dome, edged by wedges of corngold hair.

He shifted position. 'So,' he said. 'It is *Lieutenant* Caine now, is it? It seems that you profited from your little escapade at Biska, my friend . . . profited at my expense, I might add.' Caine said nothing. Rohde took a breath, raised a golden eyebrow. 'Do you know why you are here, *Lieutenant* Caine?' he demanded.

Caine coughed, blinked fast: they could beast him all they liked, but he wasn't going to be drawn into Rohde's headgames.

Rohde snorted. 'Of course, I'm sure you *think* you are here to destroy the Olzon-13 gas supplies,' he scoffed. 'As you have discovered, though, there is no longer any Olzon-13 here. That alone should be enough to convince you that the mission was a red herring. No, *Lieutenant*, you are here because I wanted you here: I have been pulling your strings from the beginning. You are here because I brought you, because I lured you into a trap.'

For an instant, Caine's temper got the better of him. 'That's bullshit,' he choked. 'I'm not here because of you.'

'You *see*,' Rohde cackled smugly, as if talking to a third person. 'They said you were too clever – that you'd never fall for it. I knew that was rubbish, of course – that in the end you were just another English clodhopper with a bloated sense of his own superiority, like all the rest. I think I have been proved right.'

He stood up straight, arched his body, sighed, clicked his heels. 'I confess I was irritated by your *Runefish* scheme,' he went on. 'Not that I give a bungler like you any credit for it, of course: you weren't even aware that your mission was a decoy. You were merely a dumb instrument: you brought it off by sheer luck. The Brandenburger captain whose men you managed to kill when you liberated your little friend at Biska was full of admiration for you. He believed you had outwitted me: "a one-man killing machine", he called you. Garbage, of course. There is nothing special about you, Caine: it was all a fluke, nothing more. They said that to have escaped from that well you must be some sort of superman. I still don't know how you did it, but I am sure you had help. You know, I had every male Senussi in that town tortured and shot, but no one admitted to being your accomplice.'

'*Shot* . . .' Caine knew he should keep his mouth shut, but he couldn't keep down the rage he felt: the thought that innocent men had been murdered for his sake was something he couldn't stomach.

The major's face glowed savagely: Caine realized that Rohde had been playing him. He bit into the redblubbed flesh of his lips until it hurt.

'Thanks to you, however,' Rohde went on, 'I fell foul of General Rommel; thanks to you and that Rose bitch, what was her real name . . . *Nolan* . . . the Panzer Army invaded Egypt and was held back at Alamein. A temporary setback, of course, but the fact is that you caused us – caused *me* – a great deal of trouble. I am not in the habit of letting such affronts go unpunished. I left your friend Nolan to the capable hands of my agent in Cairo, *Hellfinger*: I decided to deal with you myself . . .'

Caine ground his teeth at the mention of Nolan: his redpricked eyes swam. The Nazi didn't deserve even to speak her name: Caine had to stop himself spitting in Rohde's face.

'My first plan was to have you killed in training,' Rohde drawled on. 'In fact, I arranged for a little accident on your parachute course. One of your comrades was killed, but you survived by random chance. Then I realized that my idea was flawed – yes, I admit it. I saw that your death in an accident would be a sad waste of your potential. Your command had great confidence in you, you see – that was your value. As a result of *Runefish*, you'd been decorated, commissioned – they were calling you the "best desert fighter in Egypt". It was all hogwash, of course: I knew that you'd simply been fortunate. Remarkable, isn't it, how even the most intelligent people will do almost anything to deny the idea that our lives are governed by the fall of the dice? A man succeeds by luck and becomes swollen with the idea of his own cleverness: he and others will ascribe his good fortune to his skill, his charisma, his intelligence. When he fails, as he inevitably will, they will say that he is not performing up to his usual standard rather than admit that it was all random in the first place. We are addicted to success stories, Caine, addicted to the myth of cause and effect. We do not even want to see that there is no order in the universe . . .' Rohde sighed theatrically. 'The important thing was that your superiors *believed* that you were special: I knew you were very ordinary, but also that I could make use of their faith. By setting you up with the job of sabotaging the Olzon-13, I could guarantee that no other operation would be launched against us. After all, why waste time with a backup when they were so certain you would succeed? What they didn't know was that you stood *no* chance of success: you might as well have tried to piss on the fires of hell.'

Despite his shattered condition, Caine felt pricked. 'No chance?' he repeated feebly, lifting his chin. 'What do you mean, no chance?'

Rohde snorted. 'But surely you must have guessed? You must be even more of a *Dummkopf* than I thought.' He bowed his head slightly, his eyes slitted with pleasure. 'I had a man in your team, Caine. I controlled *Sandhog* right from the start.'

Caine's vision whirled: tomtoms pounded his ears. Rohde was messing with him, feeding him a line: the Nazi bastard sensed that his deepest conviction was his loyalty to his men and was deliberately undermining it.

Caine had often felt intuitively that *Sandhog* had been compromised – an intuition confirmed by the dying Roland and the deceased POW – but he had never entertained the possibility that one of his own men was a traitor. It was true that no one outside his team was supposed to know his route in, or the location of his target but, in the real world, the accidental leakage of information was frequent. There might be a rat out there somewhere who was feeding intelligence to the Hun but, among his own men, never.

He tried to ignore the red torment of his body, the agonizing smart of his burns. He licked his lips, dryretched, raised his bloody chin. 'You're barking,' he mumbled. 'There's no stooge among my lads. And you didn't set me up for anything. You couldn't have known I'd get the mission. I nearly turned it down.'

Rohde snickered at him contemptuously, shouted something at the guards. A moment later the door clumped open and two figures came in – a longnecked woman in tattered khaki drills with a slender face and a cap of golden hair and a blackbearded man in mufti whose greasy shoulder-length mane shrouded his face like curtains. The girl's hands were tied behind her back: the bearded man stumped behind her awkwardly on a prosthetic steel limb, prodding her between the shoulderblades with the muzzle of a hunting rifle. This brutal action raised Caine's hackles long before he recognized the couple: the blonde was Angela Brunetto, the Italian woman who'd once helped him and his mates escape the Hun, whose letter to Harry Copeland had brought on *Sandhog.* The peglegged man was her husband, Michele. Only months ago they'd been the kingpins of the Italian deserter and ex-colon community here in the Citadel. Now they were pale shadows of their former selves.

Angela didn't look at Caine. She tried to hang back, her chin lolling on her chest, her eyes fixed on the floor. Michele jabbed her with the rifle. 'Come on,' he spat. 'Aren't you happy to see him? You're the one who bring him here.'

As Angela stumbled towards Caine he saw that she was thinner than he remembered – almost emaciated; her face was bruised and streaked with tears, her eyes puffy and dark-bagged, her blond hair full of dirt. She'd evidently endured beating and humiliation, yet Caine was proud to see that there was still defiance in the way she held her lean body, a hint of challenge in her eyes: the pouting sulkiness of her lips looked even more pronounced than it had been.

She stood trembling in front of Caine, shoulders drooping, head bowed. Michele cracked her behind the knee-joints with the riflebutt: she cried out and collapsed on to her knees, swearing in Italian, her eyes sparking. Michele batted her twice around the head with his open hand. Rohde chortled. Caine bristled, his muscles straining against his ropes. '*Don't touch her*,' he croaked.

'*Shut up*,' Michele snapped, sweeping back his drape of oily hair: Caine glimpsed a parched yellow face framed by the matted beard, red-edged eyes that no longer held any trace of human feeling, that seethed with the ferocious intensity of a wild beast. It struck Caine suddenly that Michele was mad. The Italian jutted his chin, gestured at his prosthetic leg. 'See what she did, Caine,' he bawled. 'The filthy *puta* shoot me in the foot. Over your bitch girlfriend. You were there, Caine. She shoot me in the foot and it turn gangrene and I have my leg cut off. This fucking little Jezebel turn her own husband into a cripple . . .'

'You were crippled from the start,' Caine grated, unable to stop himself.

Michele gripped his rifle so hard that his knuckles turned ashen: he took two stomping paces over to Caine, bent over him, spat full in his face. Caine didn't react: he stared back unflinching into Michele's tortured features. 'So you became one of the bullies you used to rail against,' he panted. 'Funny how everything becomes everything else.'

Breathing hard, Michele took a halting step back. 'It was you who change everything here, Caine, not me,' he spluttered. 'We do fine till you come. The Boche know we are here, but they never bother us. Not till you come. It was you who bring them on us, Caine: is you, not me, who is responsible for the horrors – the massacres, the murders, the madness . . .' He clenched a knotted fist and stared at it. 'I am the hand of God, that's all. I bring the divine wrath down on these people, the ones that betrayed me, the filthy Arab pigs who helped them.' He stared back at Caine, his eyes smouldering insanely. 'They call me the Angel of Death,' he chuckled, 'and that's what I am. But is you who make it happen, Caine, is you who will rot in hell.'

Caine's eyes were suddenly wild. '*You . . . ?*' he whispered. 'You're the *Angel of Death*? You –'

'With a little help from me, of course,' Rohde cut him off smugly. 'Michele has been . . . how does one say . . . the *front man*. He has displayed a certain genius for organizing retribution, I admit, but of course, I have always been there to give advice, to help him out . . .'

Caine felt Michele's saliva running down his face. His stomach churned: he felt ready to explode. Instead, he clamped his bruised jaws shut. His eyes bulged. He watched dumbly as Michele grabbed Angela by the hair, yanked her head back, whacked her with his riflebutt. '*Tell him*,' he screamed.

Angela whimpered. Michele let go of her and, when she

raised her head again, Caine saw that fresh tears were streaming silently down her face. Her eyes locked his. 'I'm sorry, Thomas,' she sobbed. 'Is true. They make me write that letter. They say they kill me, kill my friends . . . Now I wish I die. Now I know they kill you, they kill Harry . . .'

Michele was making manic faces at her. '*Harry*,' he mimicked, 'that cocksucking pig. Yes, he is here. Now I go to him, and you go with me, and I cut his fucking balls off right in front of you, you watch *caro* Harry bleed to death, you whore, bitch . . .'

He whipped round towards the door so fast that he almost overbalanced. '*Stop*,' Rohde snapped. The Nazi's features were twisted with amusement. 'We will handle Copeland in good time. First we will deal with Caine.' He glanced at Angela, who had fallen into a sobbing heap. 'Take her away, my friend, but don't touch Copeland until I give the order. You'll have your revenge in due course.'

Caine watched them go: the numbness in his body was wearing off, and he tried to steel himself mentally against the new surge of pain. There was something else there, too: a deep, harrowing sense of fear, of abject dread, was beginning to seep through his veins. Its presence surprised and irritated him: he'd faced death many times before and he'd always been able to resign himself to it. Now he was starting to quake internally: there was something unnatural in this new sense of terror he felt, as if some evil spirit had suddenly invaded his body. He tried to ignore it, to sift through the data he'd absorbed: Michele Brunetto, an Italian army deserter, had helped the Nazis use his own people as guineapigs in trials of a chemical weapon, had organized massacres and atrocities against the Senussi;

Angela Brunetto had written the letter that had cemented the *Sandhog* mission, on Rohde's orders. He felt no rancour towards her, although he knew that without the letter he probably wouldn't be here: he just wished this unexpected rush of horror would go away.

Rohde was standing in front of him again, a leer of triumph on his face. 'So you see, Mr Caine,' he said, shaking his head with mock pity, 'this has been what you English call a *setup* – a small payback for your *Runefish* mission . . .' He wiggled his tendril fingers. 'Ach, who were they going to send, Caine? You were the only Allied officer who'd ever been in the Citadel. It *had* to be you. You nearly turned it down, you say? Of course, I knew there was that possibility, but not after Signora Brunetto's letter reached you. You could not turn down a plea for help from a woman, could you, my friend? Not since you failed to stop your own mother committing suicide . . .'

It was so unexpected that Caine lurched up, forgetting his terror, forgetting that he was confined, that his body was covered in weals. He groaned as pain engulfed him: his whole body shook. How could Rohde possibly be aware that his mother had killed herself, and that he, Caine, had arrived home too late to help her? It had been the most traumatic experience of his life, and one he'd kept strictly private. Not even his closest friends knew about it, and now this Nazi slimeball was holding it up to ridicule: Caine felt that his innermost sanctum had been violated. He'd never believed in clairvoyance or crystal balls but he was beginning to think that, despite all his talk of chaos, Rohde was really capable of reading minds.

'Of course,' Rohde went on, 'I didn't know exactly what

approach you would take, but my man in your camp was able to keep me informed. You managed to evade the 90th Light Division columns I dispatched, managed to survive the Stuka attack, even to resist the Senussi I sent to meet you . . .' His stringlips narrowed into a sour travesty of a smile. Caine watched him, still not wanting to believe that there was a rat among his men. Who could it be? Rossi? With his combat record? Pickney? No way. Audley? With his establisment credentials? Even if one of them *was* a rat, how had he kept in touch with Rohde? Caine hadn't even revealed the target until the day after the sandstorm, let alone the plan. It couldn't have been wireless chatter because they hadn't had comms with base since that first contact, and the wireless hadn't even made it up the cliff.

'Not that it matters,' Rohde went on. 'Those obstacles served their purpose – they pulled you deeper in, made you more determined to succeed. No doubt it is better this way: I can watch you die myself.'

He drew himself up: Caine sensed that they were near the end. The beasting had been pure sadism: Rohde had wanted him to suffer. He had also wanted him to know why *Sandhog* had failed: that he'd been cleverly manipulating it from the start. Caine gulped at the thought: the Olzon-13 might even now be on its way to the Alamein front on Axis aircraft, ready to make a mockery of Monty's push. That must mean the Axis knew *Lightfoot* was due to kick off tonight.

'If I had told you a few days ago,' Rohde was saying placidly, 'that you would kill one of your closest comrades – that big ape named Wallace, for instance – in cold blood, before your death, you would have savagely denied it, would you not?'

The interior trembling was even more powerful now. Caine caught his breath, wondering what new horrors this was leading to. 'I wouldn't . . .'

'Oh but you would. You would if I informed you that, should you fail to kill him, your orangutan friend would be slowly tortured to death in the most painful way imaginable. You are that kind of person, Caine.' He scooped a breath, evidently pleased with himself. 'Did you know that the Senussi have a rather exquisite way of ensuring a man dies in agony? It is reserved for the most heinous crimes – child-murder or child-rape, for example. What they do is, they collect about a hundred smooth boulders of different sizes, which they proceed to heat in a fire. They stake out the condemned man naked and, lifting the redhot stones with special sticks, they place them one by one on the man's body, starting with his hands and feet and ending with his stomach and genitals. They begin with the smallest stones and gradually increase the size until the victim is not only being burned, but also steadily crushed to death under the accumulating weight of the stones. I am told it can take hours.'

Caine's chest and throat were congested: nightmare images were starting to claw at his head. He had a vision of himself as a child curled up in a dark cellar snivelling pathetically. Was that all he really was? Was that the real Thomas Caine beneath the peeled-off onion layers? Was this how he was going to face his end? He shook his head, tried to rid himself of the image. Rohde saw the movement and grinned: his blackball eyes hardened. 'That will be the fate of your friend Wallace, unless you kill him first. Conversely, it will become your fate if you *do* kill him. If

Wallace manages to finish you, *you* will have avoided a long-drawn-out death, but *he* will be obliged to suffer it in your place.' He chuckled. 'Rather an interesting dilemma, isn't it? If you allow your friend to kill you, you will be condemning him to hell: if you kill him, *you* will be faced with the same torment yourself. It will be instructive to see how altruistic you really are when the chips are down.'

Caine couldn't believe what he was hearing: the Afrika Korps was generally noted for its sense of military honour; only the most demented and sadistic of minds could have come up with such a plan, a scheme intended to reduce soldiers to animals. He faced Rohde, his face twitching, his heart jerking, trying desperately not to betray his dread. 'We are soldiers captured in uniform,' he stuttered. His voice sounded fragile in his ears, and he fought to keep it steady, to throw off the icy hand that seemed to clutch at his throat. 'We are prisoners of war.'

Rohde guffawed. 'You are *long* out of date, my friend. You are special service troops – *commandos* – are you not? Since our dear Führer signed the *Kommandobefehl*, Allied special service troops are no longer accorded prisoner-of-war status, not even if they surrender. The order was in place months ago but has never been enforced here in North Africa because Rommel didn't approve of it. Alas, Rommel is no longer with us, at least not for the time being. In short, I can do what I like with you.'

Despite the chill inside, Caine experienced a wave of anger, uncontrollably ferocious – he felt like a terminally frightened child lashing out in blind terror. 'You'll just have to fucking well shoot us, you bloody bastard. I'll never kill one of my own mates: Fred Wallace neither. You can torture us all you want, but you'll never force us to lay a finger on each other, whatever you do.'

'*Possibly* true under normal circumstances,' Rohde sneered, 'but in this case you'll have a little extra . . . *encouragement* . . . shall we say? You see, the water you drank so greedily a short while ago was laced with Olzon-13. You can already feel it, can't you? I think you will find it may alter your resolution. You know, Senussi tribesmen are almost fanatically loyal to their clan, yet small traces of Olzon-13 have induced them to butcher their own wives and children. I'm sure you have studied enough reports to be aware of what it can do.'

36

By the time they dragged him out the drug was stirring powerfully inside him. His heart malleted, his body was raddled with panic, his breath came in stabs. It was cold: the sky above the crater was a marble slab teetering with vast rotting excrescences of leprous grey. He shivered as the Jerries hustled him on: his ears pounded, a beaver gnawed at his guts. The light didn't seem right and the shadows were sinister: every staggering step took him deeper into a nightmare land. The ground itself wouldn't stay still, the air soughed with an asthmatic wheeze: Caine heard spectral whisperings, demonic voices, savage animals padding behind him. His feet sank into a squelching mush of excrement and decayed body parts: he glimpsed great centipedes writhing in the rock walls, bulges where giant termites moved under the surface, the silver slime-trails of enormous slugs: the cliffs towered over him like the ribs of monstrous dead animals strung with flags of putrid meat. The faces of his Jerry guards held traces of jackal and werewolf: their voices were growls in strange descants, their eyes full of dark hauntings, their gaping mouths reeked with butcher smells.

Rohde swept in front of him, his sleek black trenchcoat draped about his shoulders: with his broad hips rolling under the garment and his mincing jackboot gait, he looked like a haughty, imperious queen. When they halted at the pit, though, and Rohde turned on him, Caine got a glimpse of the viper-scalped gorgon Medusa staring out from behind the venomous eyes. He gasped and staggered backwards: the guards crowed at him. Rohde's gorgon eyes gave out a vulturine gleam.

A mob of spectators in khaki uniform jostled at the Nazi's elbow: Caine saw rodent faces, jackal faces, toad faces: Dobermann-pinschers in Afrika Korps caps. The creatures rolled bulging eyes at him: pink tongues slavered, leper mouths gobbled, rutwarp snouts dribbled snot. Caine heard feral whines and guttural snarls: he heard batwings rustle, heard cloven hooves and clawfeet clack. One of his guards had the head of a cockroach: another sported a gecko's flicking tongue. Caine heard alligator jaws champ, raven voices croak, saw the filthy half-human beasts paw and snap and slobber as they jockeyed for position. He smelled pigsty smells: dung and hogsweat and sour piss. He knew he was losing touch with reality: it was the most chilling sensation of his life.

The pit below him looked like a derelict, empty bathing pool: gangrenous tiles, six-foot walls of concrete smeared with claretcoloured blobs. A part of him knew it was where Rohde conducted his disgusting 'experiments', his unspeakable carnage of helpless souls. Caine felt his mind being tugged into the ocean of horror, struggled to hold on to a lifeline of rational thought. He asked himself how many 'subjects' had been killed or maimed here, how many had survived? Some had recovered completely: others had gone berserk after they'd been released, committed appalling atrocities on their own families. It popped into his head that the results of Olzon-13 exposure must depend on the individual: Rohde could not know for certain what the outcome would be.

Rohde gargled an order: Caine saw snapping-turtle jaws where the Nazi's mouth belonged, saw the mesh-eyes of a praying mantis bulging from his head. They hustled him to where an iron ladder descended: someone cut his bindings. A new wave of fear broke over him, more intense than anything he'd experienced so far. He held on desperately to the edge: he had wanted to die with dignity, to let the Hun see him meet his end like a man. Yet the drug had sapped his determination: he couldn't help himself. He sobbed in terror, sank his teeth into monkey paws, lashed out onehanded at stinking yellow fangs. They stamped on his fingers, they pushed him down. He let go, slithered the rest of the way, landed on all fours. He pulled himself up, his massive chest heaving.

The tiles under his feet were undulating as if worms were writhing below them: the walls of the pit were lubdubbing, respiring rhythmically in and out. Caine smelled an abattoir smell: fat flies and bloated flesh and putrefaction. He had only just taken stock of his surroundings when there was a heartstopping roar that almost paralysed him: in that moment a giant creature came hurtling at him out of the hazy background. The thing was of no fixed species – ogre, dragon, Cyclops, minotaur – it was *the beast* from out of his racial memory: only in his most demented fevers had Caine dreamed of such a thing. He almost fainted with terror. The drug in his bloodstream urged him to flee but he couldn't move. The beast sprang: the spring of every monster every man had ever known since the dawn of time. Caine had a vision of a monstrous frame hanging in the air, steam-shovel arms raised, iron fists bunched, long calf and thigh muscles distended, every ligament in the titanic physique tensed to strike. It was only in the instant before he moved that he realized the monster was Fred Wallace.

Wallace was naked but for fouled shorts and chapplies, his darkfurred skin a network of bloodstreaks, a map of wounds like red clawmarks across his chest. Caine saw the goliath face framed in the shag of flying gypsy hair, the deep-jowled chin glistening with saliva, the slab-like overhang of the Neanderthal brows furrowed, the swollen lips stretched back from a set of bloody teeth like broken ninepins, pinball eyes blazing with murderous fire: if ever Wallace had looked like a hellion from the darkest depths of a child's nightmare, it was now.

In that moment, though, all Caine's terror melted: his fear double-helixed, switchbladed into fighting fury. He clocked an opening: he stepped forward, he batter-rammed a salvo of deadly whacks to his friend's jawbone, *cramp cramp cramp cramp.* Caine saw the dark, glittering eyes lose focus, saw the fire in them go out. The gunner's own ramlike punch missed Caine's head, glanced off his shoulder, sent Wallace sprawling: his huge form humped into the tiles like a downed aircraft spraddling sand. The big man rolled sideways; his palmtrunk arms thrashed. Before he could heave himself up, though, Caine dropkicked him below the left ear. He heard the smack as his foot connected: Wallace's alligator skull snapped sideways, blood trickled from his ear. He howled, shook his shockbush head like a great buffalo, stunned.

For an instant, Caine's drughazed senses cleared: the

howling minotaur creature on the floor was not a creature: it was Fred Wallace. How was it possible that he, Tom Caine, had become so brutalized that he could see his most faithful friend as a beast? What kind of inhuman fiend did that make him? He checked an impulse to kick Wallace again: more waves of ferocity coursed through him, but now it was fury at Rohde, whose demonic mind had devised such a way of reducing a soldier's most noble qualities to their opposite. He wasn't going to do this. The Olzon-13 drug had already drawn him into Rohde's maze, reduced him to experimental rat. No more. He was going to fight the drug by sheer willpower: he and his mate were going to die, but they'd do it with dignity. Caine drew a rattling breath, moved towards his mate through the pulsating channel of the pit. '*Fred*,' he whispered. '*Fred*.'

Wallace had raised his body on his elbows: Caine put out a trembling hand to help him up. The gunner grasped it with his frypan mitt: Caine felt the warmth of his friend's body flowing into his, and for a moment he sensed that they were no longer enemies, no longer fighting each other to the death. Wallace staggered to his feet: Caine let go his hand. '*It'll be all right, mate*,' he said hoarsely, his voice hardly recognizable. '*Don't play that bastard's game. Don't fight*.'

Wallace's shaggy head turned towards him, and Caine saw with a shock that he was looking at a stranger. It was Wallace all right, but a Wallace who did not know him, who was not aware, even, of his own identity: the shell of Fred Wallace with a Martian staring out from behind the scarred and ravaged face. The big man's alien eyes blinked: he backed away, shaking his basket head, gasping for air.

Suddenly, he bounded forward bullbellowing: Caine

stepped back, snapped out a defensive kick. Wallace's sausage-fingered hand closed on Caine's ankle like an iron pincer, jerked him off centre, swung him round with all his force at the nearest wall. Caine smashed into the concrete, flipped forwards, his vision dimmed, his consciousness teetered on the brim of darkness. He had the hazy impression of the giant looming over him: before he could dodge, Wallace lamped him in the jaw with his right fist, smashed him again with his left. Caine's jaw cracked: toothshards flew, gore gushed from his nose and mouth. He hit the wall again, slithered down with his head buzzing, with a million cicadas chafing in his ears. He didn't even register the excited grunting and yapping from the beasts above.

As Caine sprawled on the tiles, Wallace kicked him savagely in the side. Caine's whole body jumped with the force of it. It felt as if something had ruptured inside him, but there was no pain, only numbness. Caine heard his own voice in his ears telling him that he had to get up: if he didn't, he was finished. Wallace didn't know him: it was too late to salvage his dignity. He'd lost Betty Nolan, he'd failed to bring off *Sandhog*, to save *Lightfoot*. He'd failed even to save his friend from a lingering death.

Caine heard the animals grunt and jibber, heard sauerkraut voices, heard something metallic hit the tiles. Wallace knelt with one giant knee on Caine's chest, crushing the air from his lungs. Caine's eyes dickered open and he saw that the giant was grasping a length of lead piping in his hand. So that was it, he thought, the death instrument. Rohde was making it easier for him. Wallace roared again: Caine felt an ironglove hand snake round his throat. The big man held him down with his knee and his left hand, raised the pipe in his right, his blunt primeval features strained, teeth rictusing, eyes blank. Caine fought for breath, clutched at the throttling hand. '*All right, Fred*,' he gurgled. '*Go on. I forgive you, mate: I'm just sorry I let you down.*'

This was it then: there was no point in struggling. His body had stopped shaking: no longer felt afraid. At least he could face death with whatever grace was left to him. He saw the lead pipe raised for the deathblow, felt Wallace's fingers squeezing his neck, felt the darkness calling. His senses guttered: from the deep inner dark there came a familiar beat of steel on steel, the rhythmic clash of hammers, the smell of scorched metal and charcoal from his father's smithy. He was twelve years old again and matching blow for blow with his father, watching the steel magically taking its shape on the anvil. Caine had often wished that he could have remained there for ever, in the world as it was before his father's death, before his stepfather, before the army, before the war, before his mother's suicide: he had never dreamed then of becoming a soldier. Even when he'd joined up as a youth, he'd never dreamed of the hardship, the suffering, the loss, the guilt, it would entail. He would have been happy working with metal till the end of his days.

His father stopped work, laid down his hammer, wiped the sweat off his brow with a ragged sleeve. 'What's wrong, boy?' he asked.

Caine thought for a moment. 'It's just that I didn't succeed in the end,' he said. 'I lost Betty, I lost a lot of good mates, I shot one of our own officers, and I didn't even bring it off. I didn't save Monty's push.'

His father smiled. 'You know, son,' he said. 'Life isn't a

competition: they'll tell you it is, but it isn't. It isn't a balance sheet of profit and loss. Who's to say that one fine morning in spring smelling the trees and the flowers isn't worth all the hardship you've been through? Who's to say that one day with a good woman who loves you isn't worth years of messing about?'

Caine mulled over his father's words. 'So is it time, Dad?'

His father chuckled, picked up his hammer, weighed it in his calloused hand. 'You know, you're a grown man, Tom. That's up to you to decide . . .'

Caine heard metal clang, thought for a moment that his father must have dropped his hammer. Then Wallace's fingers released his throat, the colossal weight left his chest. Caine opened his eyes, rasped air. Wallace was kneeling beside him: the lead piping was lying in the dust. Wallace's troll face was creased up like a baby's, and tears were flowing down his grizzled cheeks. He eyed Caine as if he'd just come out of a dream. '*I can't do it, Tom,*' he sobbed. 'I didn't even know what I was doing: the fucking bastard nearly got me to kill my best mate.'

Wallace's face changed as if a new thought had come abruptly into his head: he grabbed the metal bar, sprang up. In two striding paces he was at the ladder, climbing it. Caine lunged to his feet, ignoring the pain that hit him like a ballhammer. The menagerie above them was reeling and yelling: any second now gunfire would rain down. Caine dived for Wallace's legs: just as he felt the giant fall on top of him he heard a machine-gun sprattle, heard its shells fall *thumpa thumpa thump*. It took him a moment to realize that the sound had come from far off. As he and the giant rolled on the tiles, he glanced up, saw that the insects had lost interest in them. The swarm was scattering: Rohde's praying-mantis eyes were focused on some object that Caine couldn't see.

He heard the *tocka tocka tock* of a Schmeisser MG then the distinct clatter of a Bren-gun, much nearer – a steady, familar *ba-bamm*, *ba-bamm* of disciplined double taps. Caine heard rasps and croaks from far beyond the pit: the *whomp* and singed breath of a charge going off. The creepy-crawlies above them had gone haywire, jumping, stridulating, keening: Caine saw creatures stagger and collapse. He heard the pattercake *karooooomfff* of a shell exploding, a crescendo of smallarms fire. Then a second shell detonated among the Huns right next to the pit: a hiss of scorched air, a blinding white starburst, an ear-grinding rent paper rip.

Caine couldn't remember later how long they'd lain there with debris falling on them. It wasn't until he climbed the ladder that he realized his body was a mass of cuts and lacerations: he was bleeding from the nose and mouth and his side was purple where Wallace had delivered his final kick. The big gunner hauled him over the rim with the same titan's hand that had almost throttled him: up there, smoke and dust spiralled, machine-guns yammered, gunshots railtracked air. The earth was littered with German soldiers, dead, thrashing, mutilated, some with missing limbs. The dead and wounded still had a hint of jackal or pig in their faces, Caine thought: some of the severed limbs looked like the appendages of giant bugs. He saw one Jerry screaming for his mother: the man was no more than a head and a goreslathered torso: his legs and arms had been plucked out by the blast. There were kidney-coloured patches in the sand. There was a shallow crater where the shell had burst, but Caine guessed it must have detonated a haversackful of anti-tank grenades, because he didn't believe one round had done all this.

Caine shakily picked up a Jerry rifle, stared at it, hunkered down, looked around wide-eyed: 999 Div. men in bloodcaked KD were staggering about in the foreground, others were running towards the admin barracks fifty yards off to Caine's front. Scores of ragged and emaciated prisoners – Arab, Itie, men and women – were milling about. The gates of the prisoner compound seventy paces to Caine's rear hung open. They'd been wrecked by a charge. The huts inside were on fire. A Jerry halftrack was parked far to Caine's left, between him and the entrance defile: her 40mm cannon was trained on the tents tucked around the side of the central buttress where the last of the 999 company had set up a perimeter defence. It hit Caine that the wagon must be manned by friendlies: it could only have been her gun that had fired the fatal shot.

He clocked a smoke-crease, heard the deadhand clap as the halftrack's gun *perdunk*ed: a heavy Schmeisser MG truckled out tracer in its wake. He saw the shell splat apart among the Jerry tents: saw smoke fungus, dust and gravel slew. He could see two figures crewing the guns on the back of the halftrack: who were they, he wondered? One appeared to be dark-haired, the other blond: there was a suggestion of the feminine about them, but he supposed it was a trick of the light.

Some of the liberated prisoners were executing wounded Krauts with weapons they'd taken off them: others had moved behind low ridges and rocks and were ruckling fire at the Hun defensive lines. On the far side of the wagon, men in desertstained Senussi robes and turbans were lumbering about in the MT park at the end of the defile: Caine saw Senussi figures in the observation hatches on the cabs of Hun three-ton lorries bracing the machine-guns mounted there.

Caine clacked the working parts of the Jerry rifle, crouched among the dead and mutilated Boche, the dismembered insectlegs, the iodine-coloured stains in the sand. The earth had stopped lurching but his head was still buzzing from the effects of the drug. He had no idea how long he crouched there, no idea of the sequence of things. The 40mm cannon on the halftrack stonked, but Caine couldn't say if this was the first or second time.

To Caine's right, a scabfaced Italian woman with knotted hair, pendulant breasts showing through the rags of her dress, shot a wounded German in the back of the head. Some of the released Senussi were bashing in the skulls of their former guards with sharp stones. The two wounded Krauts were still staggering about in the foreground. Wallace picked up a Gewehr-41. Caine saw him squat with the rifle at his shoulder: he saw the gunner's hunched hairy back, tawny skin a crude theatre of cuts and lesions. Wallace lined up the sights, squeezed steel. Caine saw the rifle jump, saw the muzzleflame, watched the bodies marionette. Wallace stood up, walked over to the shrieking, limbless Jerry: he pressed the bore of his weapon into the man's forehead and shot him twice.

Some of the ex-prisoners were slitting the throats of wounded Germans with bayonets: some Jerries were still running towards the admin block. Caine looked for Rohde but couldn't see him: instead he glimpsed Michele Brunetto, hopping along jerkily on his pegleg, forcing Angela ahead of him at gunpoint. Caine stood up abruptly: two words burned into his shellshocked and lacerated mind. '*Harry Copeland*,' he thought.

37

A stringy German lieutenant and a squat sergeant had set up a Schmeisser on a tripod at the door of the admin block. From ten yards away, Caine heard the gun's breechblock chaw on a vacant chamber, knew they were out of juice. 'Come out with your hands up,' he bawled at them. The Jerries hobbled into the light, hands held shoulder-high: they were wearing kaiser tinlids and open trenchcoats over their shorts, and both had open shrapnel wounds in their bare legs. Caine and Wallace moved in on them: Caine saw drained, doghaunted faces, wondered blearily why they had on their coats. He saw the sergeant's weasel eyes flicker, clocked a hand worming under the folds. The officer saw the movement too, his face stretched in warning. '*Dummkopf*,' he hissed. Even before Caine had clocked the Walther pistol in the sergeant's hand, he'd pulled metal: his weapon whipsawed, gouted smoke. He saw a smiley face open in the sergeant's gut, saw viscera grope out of the mouthslit like squidlegs. The Hun dropped the pistol, spreadeagled forward, arms arcing wide. A shot from Wallace popped the lieutenant's eyeball, hit skullbone, emerged from the side of his head in a scarlet and greybanded flush. The big man leaned over him, pumping shot after shot into his chest, his mandrill features expressionless: he would have kept on firing until the mag was empty, oblivious to anything else, if Caine hadn't gripped his bare forearm and hissed, 'Steady on, mate. He's dead.'

Caine kicked open the door into the passage where he'd last seen Harry Copeland being dragged away: the entire building was graveyard-still. The interrogation rooms where he and Wallace had been tortured were closed: the only open door lay at the far end of the passage on the right. Caine had taken two steps towards it when a gunshot stopped him in his tracks. He and Wallace exchanged a glance, moved cautiously down to the door. Caine heard commotion: wolfhowls and ape-jibbers: a string of horrendous expletives in Italian. He peered around the doorjamb, clocked a surreal, almost comical sight. Michele Brunetto was sprawled on the floor, his arms flailing as he tried to grasp the prosthetic leg that had been placed just out of his reach. His hunting rifle lay on his other side, equally tantalizing, equally inaccessible: Michele's eyes were wild black scallops: his rancid hairdrapes flopped, his arms spasmed, his inkvine mouth frothed and cursed: he flipped his scarecrow body from side to side as if trying to decide which object was the more crucial, unable to get up, unable to reach either. A few yards away, Harry Copeland and Angela Brunetto were standing, bodies entwined, fitting together like complementary bits of a Chinese puzzle, their arms around each other, eyes closed, lips bonded in an endless and eternal kiss.

The vision seemed to awaken Wallace from a kind of walking trance. 'For Chrissake,' he grunted. 'Don't you know there's a flippin' war on?'

Copeland and Angela broke up: Angela kept her eyes riveted on Cope as if afraid he'd vanish. Copeland blinked at them as if he'd just returned from a voyage to a faroff land: his face was stonegrey, his body bore the livid alphabet of torture, his hair was greased with gore, yet his eyes shone like storm lanterns. 'What the hell kept you?' he grinned.

Caine nodded at the writhing Michele. 'What happened here?' he enquired. 'This bloke was gunning for you.'

Cope smiled at Angela. 'She saved my life. That arsehole was going to slit my throat and God knows what else, but she got her hands free, banjoed him from behind. Went down like a skittle.'

Caine heard the sound of a wagon scalding to a halt outside: all four of them tensed. Michele heard it too and began to squeal for help. Wallace gave the sprawling Itie a kick in the stomach. 'Just give me a reason,' he growled.

Michele's jaws snapped, his eyes smouldered. 'I'll kill you,' he spat, drooling saliva. 'I am the Hand of God. I'll kill you all.'

Wallace's face went poker-red, he pointed his rifle at Michele. 'You slimy piece of shit,' he said. 'You sold your own people down the river . . . why I ought to . . .'

'No,' Caine snapped. 'Leave him, Fred. He's not going anywhere. Once the ex-prisoners find out where he is, he won't last long.'

There were footsteps in the passage. Caine and Wallace wheeled round, weapons at the ready: in that moment Michele made a superhuman, angerfuelled effort to grasp his rifle. His hand closed around the stock: he brought the weapon to bear on Caine's back. There was an almost imperceptible swish of air: Michele's jaws snapped, his eyes beaded, his head cricked backwards with the force of the knife that had just blossomed out of his throat. The rifle clattered on the floor. Caine and Wallace gaped at Angela, who had broken away from Copeland's arms and was still poised elegantly like a ballet-dancer, her hand raised in the act of throwing. Cope was staring at her stun-faced. Michele lay motionless: gore curded from his mouth and nostrils. Angela took two lithe-legged strides towards him, crouched down, drew the knifeblade out of his flesh. When she stood up there were tears in her eyes: she examined the blood on the blade as if wondering if it was real. 'It was his knife,' she said without looking at anyone. 'I take it from him to cut my ropes, to free Harry. I cannot let him do what he want to do.'

She flung the knife down in disgust and it skittered across the floor. 'I'm sorry, Michele,' she said, her eyes fixed on the bloodless face. 'But you deserve this. You betray us all.'

Wallace picked up the hunting rifle, broke the stock over his bare knee. 'So much for the Angel of Death,' he rasped.

Caine heard English voices in the passage, tore his gaze away from Michele's corpse. He squinted outside, clocked Maurice Pickney and Ricardo Rossi shambling towards him carrying their Garands and clad in full battlekit.

Caine's face lit up with pleasure. 'You're *alive*,' he croaked.

Rossi watched Caine quietly, his stud eyes standing out like poolballs on his sallow gravedigger's face. Pickney's features crinkled along a thousand perforations. '*Alive*, 'course we're bloody alive, skipper. Who'd you think blew up the gates of the prisoner compound, then? We hid in the forest after you lot got bagged, picked up Taff Trubman. He's all right – you must have heard him on the Bren-gun. He covered us while we took out the guards and set the charges up. We laid a Lewes bomb with a timepencil on the gate and then put an incendiary inside.'

Caine nodded, delighted. 'You should both have a medal for this . . .

'Already got one thank you very much.' Pickney winked. 'Maybe if we'd bagged the Olzon-13 –'

'Was that your vehicle outside?' Caine interjected.

Pickney nodded. 'Yep – Jerry signals van we nicked from the MT park. Trubman's in there now trying to rig up the wireless . . .' Pickney cut himself short, his rawshag granny's face beaming. 'You don't know yet, do you?'

'Know what, for Jesus' sake?'

'Who was firing shells from that Jerry halftrack. The one that saved our bacon . . .' He broke off again, a maddening secret smile playing around his brownpaper lips. 'You better get out there now, skipper. There's someone there you're going to want to see . . .'

Betty Nolan was standing by the wagon's cab, staring over her shoulder nervously, when Caine lurched out of the admin block. She saw him and froze, rooted to the spot, her face drained of colour. Caine halted, stared at her: his head swam dizzily, his body swayed. This wasn't fair, he thought: the Olzon-13 was still deluding him, and this was the worst trick of all. He blinked, shook his head, trying to make the vision go away, but it didn't. Betty Nolan was still there in front of him, her face gaunt and gunblack, her uniform in tatters, her blond hair wild as sawgrass, but the same Betty Nolan, the same oceangreen eyes, the same ripe lips, the same melting look on her face.

Caine swallowed, feeling an overwhelming desire to touch her, to prove to himself that the vision wasn't real. He took three steps towards her and it seemed that he was crossing a yawning, endless chasm of space and time: then they were locked in each other's arms. Caine could feel her soft breath against his cheek, feel the warm flesh of her body yielding to his, feel her hands in his hair, stroking his face. It was only then that he allowed himself to believe that this wasn't a dream brewed up by the drug in his bloodstream, wasn't a ghost conjured by his exhausted and tortured mind. This really was Betty Nolan, the woman he loved and would always love, alive, in the flesh, and impossibly . . . *here*. He kissed her, felt her responding, felt himself drawn into her as if by the irresistible power of an ebb-tide carrying him out to sea. Time skewed to a stop, the battlesounds dimmed: a million questions coursed through his head like a torrent, but he ignored them: it didn't matter how she'd survived, how she'd got here. All that counted was this moment.

It was Nolan who pulled away first. She saw the questions in Caine's eyes, saw the words forming on his broken lips, laid a finger across them. '*Tom*,' she gasped. 'Audley's a traitor. That's why they sent me. He's probably kept the Krauts informed about your movements the whole way . . .'

It took Caine a moment to grasp what she was saying. '*Audley?* He can't be: Stirling himself recommended him for the mission.'

'Stirling made a bad mistake: Audley's not even his name. He's the rat, Tom. I got here too late to warn you, but there's still time . . .'

'Time? What do you mean? *Sandhog* has failed.'

'*Listen*, Tom. The Olzon-13 is at the airstrip. I saw it. There's still a chance to take it out: I don't reckon it'll be airloaded till sunset. But Audley's gone down there, maybe to warn the Hun that we're around . . .'

Caine was still staring at her, trying to think clearly, trying to loosen his mind from the last remnants of the Olzon-13, struggling to assimilate the new information, trying to deal with her resurrection from the dead. *Audley* . . . he couldn't believe it. He hadn't believed Rohde when he'd said there was a mole in his camp. Audley had been a pain, yes, but he was so . . . so *English*. And yet . . . and yet, when he thought about the way the officer had behaved . . . the way he'd 'lost' the wireless . . . a hundred small details: oddities that went unnoticed at the time, or had been interpreted as incompetence.

He forced himself to release her, became aware of the shooting from the 999 Div. bivouac lines – the clattershot of rifles, automatics tickertacking, the *pershomp* of grenades, the airscrape and percussion of mortar bombs.

Nolan hit him lightly on a pectoral with her fist. '*Focus*, Tom,' she pleaded. 'I last saw Audley ninety minutes ago. He was heading for the airstrip on foot. It's a long walk from where I saw him, so if we're quick we can still catch him up before he warns the Jerries . . .'

'*Warns* them?' Caine said slowly, as if the idea had hit him for the first time. 'But wait a sec. I mean, the Huns here must have a wireless – Rohde's disappeared, too. Surely they'll already know what's happening . . .'

Nolan shook her head: her phosphorescent eyes gleamed. 'Whatever they know or don't know, we've got to try and take out the Olzon-13 while it's still on the ground. Monty's push starts tonight. The whole Eighth Army is depending on us. We can still bring off *Sandhog*, Tom, but we have to hurry.'

A boom of shellfire made Caine jump: he felt the air warp, saw a dome of smoke rise over the Jerry tents. He hefted an eyebrow at Nolan. 'What about the Krauts?' he asked. 'Those Senussi and Itie civvies can't hold them for ever.'

'We've got the upper hand for now,' she told him breathlessly. 'The Senussi are manning the 40mm, and they've set up a two-inch mortar they found. They've got the machine-guns from the Jerry trucks cranked up. I've got all the ex-prisoners stood to with captured weapons. Adud's taken charge . . . and Layla . . . I've asked them to contain the Huns here for another hour so we can get away . . .'

She was interrupted by the arrival of the others, all but Angela laden down with the SAS equipment they'd retrieved from the store – manpacks, Lewes bombs, rifles, pistols, beltkit, tinned rations. Big Wallace lugged a hessian sack full of German small arms on his back; he looked like a wild and savage Santa Claus. Angela recognized Nolan and embraced her. Wallace dumped the sack in the wagon, strode round to Caine grinning through bloodscabbed lips, holding up his Purdey sawnoff in one hand and Caine's oversize Tommy-gun in another. 'Congratulations, skipper,' he grunted, nodding at Nolan. He pressed the Thompson into Caine's hands: 'Come on,' he said. 'Now it's time to get reacquainted with another old mate.'

38

Caine took his leave of Layla crouching behind a low ridge near the halftrack with Hun rounds squiffing air above them. She had tucked her lush hair under a black headscarf and, with her ankle-length dark robes, she reminded Caine of an untidy but rather beautiful nun. 'You only need to hold them till we've had a chance to get out,' he told her. 'After that, scatter in small groups across the hills.'

Layla nodded. She shook hands with him, her eyes glossy, glancing over her shoulder to where Nolan was squatting, helping to distribute arms and ammunition they'd brought with them from the store. 'She is a good woman,' Layla said softly. 'She loves you. You must take care of her, Caine . . .' She hesitated. 'I know I was wrong to think I could go away with you . . . but if you ever need . . .' She stopped herself, bit her lip: her almond-shaped eyes spoke wordlessly. Caine kissed her cheek. 'I know what you did for me,' he said, 'and I'll never forget it. Thank you.'

'The thanks is to Allah.'

They roared out of the entrance defile, past the place where the Senussi had blown the line, followed the silver rails as they twisted and turned through the maze of wadis. Caine drove, Nolan sat in the co-driver's seat scanning the skies for shuftikites while the others crouched in the rear.

Rossi checked the salvaged kit: Pickney did what he could to treat their wounds. Copeland squatted with one arm around Angela and his sniper's rifle crooked in the other: Taff Trubman, his molehead blanched and bloodless, swore every time the wagon bumped, his deft fingers groping to tune in the Jerry wireless set.

As he drove, Nolan told them all she knew about Audley, how she'd parachuted in, how she'd persuaded Layla to guide her to the Citadel, how she'd met Adud and had the idea of using the Jerry halftrack, how Audley had escaped by threatening Layla's life. 'Poor girl,' she said, shaking her head, not looking at Caine. 'She seemed to think that you'd be taking her away after all this.'

Caine made no comment. He was grateful for the risks Layla had taken on his behalf but he couldn't help wondering exactly how much she'd told Nolan. He hadn't exactly done anything to be ashamed of, but he had almost given up hope of seeing Nolan again, which she might be justified in interpreting as a loss of faith. Nolan said nothing about Hekmeth, Beeston or her escape from Eisner, and his mind still simmered with questions. He bit them back, though, knowing she was right: they had to focus on the Olzon-13 . Once it was loaded on Axis aircraft, the fate of *Lightfoot* was out of their hands: his fight with Wallace already seemed a dream, but he forced himself to remember how close they'd come to killing each other, shuddered at the thought of Monty's armoured divisions being reduced to the same state.

The van bounced on her balloon tyres, ramped along valley floors of barren gravel and cracked clay, trawled between junklots of boulders, along the foot of wild hills clothed in juniper and pine. The massed grey cloudbanks of morning were still tethered in the sky like zeppelins, coating the hills with cool, dark meres, occasionally allowing sunlight through to flare across the downs in longribbed slats. Once, Nolan sighted a spotter plane up there, surfing through the cloudbreaks, turning white and silver as the sunbeams touched its fuselage: they tensed, but the plane didn't drop altitude to investigate them: Caine remembered that the wagon sported Axis markings anyway. The vehicle laboured up a steep pass to a vast arena of undulating land between spurs of eroded mountains like the boles of vast stone trees: there were groves of tamarix and wild olive, and interlocking shelves of shattered slate sprang from the ground in ridgeback bluffs.

They saw the windsock on its pole long before they clocked the airfield: Caine stopped the vehicle in a tamarix grove a half-mile away from the Nissen hut where the Olzon-13 had been stored. They piled out of the van: for the first ten minutes they lay motionless in the esparto grass, watching for reaction. Even though the signals van had Afrika Korps insignia, if Audley had already warned the Hun that the Olzon-13 had been spotted, they might be on the lookout for vehicles of any kind. Caine scanned the warehouse carefully, his eyes lingering on the locomotive and the rolling-stock standing nearby. He couldn't tell for certain if the Olzon-13 cylinders were in the hut, but he spotted no guards. He shifted his lenses, examined the airfield – the sangars were visible: he saw no aircraft on the runway. Unless the gas had been loaded and carried away since Nolan had been here, that had to be a good sign.

Nolan glanced at her watch and found that it was already

after midday. They squatted in the trees, drank water, guzzled compo rations looted from the Jerry store straight out of the tins. 'We need to wait till last light, skipper,' Copeland told Caine through mouthfuls of tinned bacon. 'It'd be crazy to try it in daylight. They've only got to see us coming and our goose is charbroiled.'

Nolan's seaborn eyes widened. 'That's four hours away, Harry,' she said. 'One thing's for certain, the situation will have changed by then – reinforcements, air support, you name it. I reckon those Krauts at the Citadel might already have broken out . . .'

'It's too risky,' Cope insisted. 'We're trained to do this sort of operation at night . . .'

Everyone's eyes turned to Caine: he swallowed hard, stared back unflinchingly. 'We have to go in now,' he said. 'I know it's going to be dicey, but we don't have any choice.' He turned to Trubman. 'Any luck with comms, Taff?'

He saw the frustration in the Welshman's pudgy face. 'I don't get it, skipper,' he said. 'The set's working fine. I've checked the frequencies. The antenna's OK. So why isn't the damn' piece of junk *working*?'

'Just keep bashing away at it,' Caine said. 'Stay with the wagon till we get back. Angela, Betty, you stay here and cover him. The rest of us will take . . .'

'I go with Harry,' Angela interrupted, pouting. 'You can't stop me, Thomas. If it go bad, then we die together, but I don't leave him again.'

Copeland looked embarassed: his big Adam's apple worked. He was about to speak when Nolan cut in. 'I'm not staying behind either, Tom,' she said, a coy smile flickering around her alluring front teeth. 'And since I'm the ranking officer here, *Lieutenant*, you don't have the authority to make me.'

Caine looked from Angela's set face to Nolan's, saw that it would be pointless to argue.

'We're gonna need 'em, anyway, skipper,' Wallace said. 'There's only five of us to lay them charges: we'll need someone on lookout.'

Caine nodded. 'All right, then, but the ladies will be tail-end Charlies: stay outside the hut while we go in, keep watch. If it goes pearshaped, you bug out like the wind and take the wagon.'

Angela was already shaking her head. '*Non e possibile*,' she said. 'I don't go anywhere without Harry. I fight, I kill *Tedesci* maybe, and maybe they kill me, but I don't run while he is alive . . .'

'That makes two of us,' Nolan said.

Caine frowned, started to mouth something that might have been, 'Women', but stopped himself. Today *women* had saved his life.

They tooled up, taking the weapons they'd retrieved from the Jerry store: the men saddled the manpacks of Lewes bombs, the women carried Schmeisser sub-machine-guns and pistols. They moved off fast with Wallace and Caine leading, Copeland bringing up the rear, threading a zigzag path through the treebrakes, hugging the shadows of the slate ridges, using dead ground. In broad daylight like this, the kind of painstaking approach they used on night raids was pointless: the quicker they closed with the target, the less chance they had of being spotted. They moved in fits and starts, lurking in cover, ramping from point to point at a slow run. Thirty yards from the Nissen hut, they lay up in the lee of a pudding-shaped butt, priming themselves for the final effort: Caine and Wallace crawled into a thornthicket to survey the open ground.

Now, Caine could see the Olzon-13 cylinders clearly through the open sides of the Nissen hut: his heart leapt. The gas was still on the ground, and there was no sign of Jerry aircraft coming in. *Sandhog* wasn't finished – they were going to bring it off after all. The train that had shifted the cylinders from the Citadel still stood unattended against its buffers: the only slight misgiving Caine felt was the apparent lack of security. El-Gala was still fresh in his mind: after all they'd been through, after being reunited with Nolan, the last thing he wanted was to lead them into an ambush.

He was about to beckon the others out of cover when the giant poked him urgently. Caine looked back to see a lone figure working his way towards them, a tall, lean soldier in khaki drills hefting an SAS manpack, carrying a Garand rifle at the ready. He was moving fast, glancing around furtively, jogging from boulder to boulder, from tree to tree, pausing, then dashing forward again. He was coming directly towards them, giving no indication that he knew they were there. Within a minute he was close enough for them to recognize him, to clock the excited, almost exultant look on his face. '*Audley*,' Caine hissed. 'What the hell is he doing?'

Wallace opened his mouth, closed it again fast. Audley was only yards away, and his trajectory would take him straight past the thicket, past the end of the butt behind which the rest of their crew was concealed. Caine and

Wallace exchanged a silent glance: once Audley came abreast of the butt-end he would spot the others. Caine was acutely aware that this could be a setup: maybe they'd already been spotted and Audley had been sent to flush them out. They had two choices: let him pass and hope he wouldn't see them, or jump him and risk exposing themselves. Caine thought of Audley's treachery, thought of the brave men whose lives had been lost due to him, and knew he couldn't let him pass. He nodded to Wallace. As Audley stalked by the thicket, his boots tromping dust only a yard from where they lay, the big gunner moved with the speed and sureness of a python, slid forward, grabbed the legs in a bearhug, brought Audley crashing into the shade. Caine snatched the rifle out of his hands, slapped a palm across his mouth, stuck his pistol into his ear. 'One word, *old boy*,' he whispered. 'One move, and you're gone.'

They dragged him out of the thicket and into the shadow of the butt: the rest of the crew gathered around wide-eyed. The moment he recognized Audley, Rossi drew his dagger. 'You got Gibbo killed, you fucking *cazzo*,' he bawled. It took all Wallace's strength to hold him back.

Audley had turned deathly pale: his washed-out eyes bulged over Caine's clamped hand. 'I'm going to take my hand away,' Caine told him. 'You make any attempt to shout, I let Rossi carve your tonsils to hamburger. Got it?'

Audley nodded frantically, making small noises of protest. Caine removed his hand: Audley sucked breath, stared around at the others. His face twitched, his lips trembled, his attempt at an ingratiating smile came off as a death-mask scowl. '*Caine*,' he stammered. 'I'm so glad you're here, old man. I've done it, don't you see? I've laid charges on the Olzon-13 cylinders . . . they're all set to blow –'

'*Shut up*,' Caine snapped: he jabbed the pistol into Audley's chest. 'I ought to finish you right now, you filthy tub of shit. I should have known what you were when you deserted us at el-Gala. You were responsible for the death of three good men there, and now you've got the blood of Dumper, Larousse, Gibson and Netanya on your hands. They're all dead because of you. Your name isn't Bertram Audley. You aren't the son of the Marquis of Leigh, because there is no such fucking animal. You never won the MC, you never served in the Guards. You're a filthy Nazi stoolpigeon, a damn' traitor, that's what you are . . .'

'*No*,' Audley yelled, shaking his head like an injured dog, his jawblades spasming. 'It's not true. Never. I'm not a traitor. '

'*Liar*,' Nolan cut in, shifting closer. 'I discovered there was a stoolie in the *Sandhog* crew when I was kidnapped by Eisner's lot. Stocker, Stirling and I worked out it was you: everything you told Stirling about yourself was a farrago of lies. I don't know who you are or where you come from, and I don't need to: you've sold this whole operation to the Axis, and you deserve to be shot.'

'*No*,' Audley sobbed. 'It's not true. Believe me, it's not. All right, I might be a liar, and I might be a cheat, but I would never sell out my mates. Never.'

Caine prodded him again with the pistol. 'We haven't got time to waste on you,' he spat. 'Tell us who you are, quick, or I'll let Rossi have you.'

Audley stared into Caine's redspatted sclera, his jaws working silently, face pasty, eyes the size of pumpkins. 'All right,' he shivered. 'All right, I'll tell you . . .' He flashed a petrified sideglance at Rossi. 'But you promise not to let this nutter anywhere near me.'

Caine noted with a shiver that Audley's voice had changed: the officer-class accent had suddenly vanished. He grasped the man's neck, shook him like a doll. 'Traitors don't make conditions,' he spat. 'Come on, out with it.'

'All *right*,' Audley choked. 'All *right*, I'll tell you. It started when I was involved in a motorcycle accident in Cairo, see. I'd . . .'

'What's this bullshit?' Wallace boomed. 'We don't wanna know the story of yer life. Who the hell *are* you?'

Audley swallowed hard. 'My name is Reggie Higginbotham,' he whispered. 'I'm a private in the Pioneer Corps, Latrine Detachment . . .'

Despite himself, Caine almost burst out laughing. He wondered if he were still under the effects of Olzon-13: the situation was growing odder by the second.

'No, it's true,' Audley stammered. 'One day I borrowed a Guards officer's uniform: it was just a lark to impress the bints, really: nothing more. But then I crashed the motorbike and was out cold, and thinking I was an officer, they took me to a hospital for commissioned ranks only. I liked the way they treated me: it beat building shithouses, anyway. I mean, everyone treated me like an *officer*, and I thought, why not? Why shouldn't I *be* one? After all, the only difference was a bit of cloth on a uniform. I mean, it was only their good luck that they were born with a silver spoon, and my bad luck that I wasn't. Why not even it out a bit? So I decided to become Lieutenant the Honourable Bertram Audley MC, Coldstream Guards, heir of the

Marquis of Leigh – got the name Audley from an old detective novel I read in hospital, you know, *Lady Audley's Secret*? Making myself the heir of a marquis was a crafty move, because the British love an aristocrat. Terrific snobs, the British. Look at Stirling: you reckon he would've got the SAS off the ground if he hadn't been one of the aristocracy? If anyone else – even Paddy Mayne – had come up with the idea, they'd have told 'em to stuff it. So, Private Higginbotham was quietly reported AWOL, and Lieutenant Audley was born. I was amazed how easy it was: put on a toff accent, act a bit uppity, drop a few names – Lord this and the Earl of that – and even the generals are grovelling at your feet. People *want* to think they're friends with the son of a marquis, you see: they write home to the folks . . . *my pal, the Hon. Bertie Audley, son of the Marquis* . . . I reckon that's why nobody ever checked up on me: they were desperate to believe it. Of course, the fact that I'm such a handsome chap might have helped: folks always imagine toffs are handsome. As my old mum used to say, if you're good-lookin', people will swallow anything you tell 'em: it's not what you *are* that matters in life, it's what you *appear* to be . . .'

His voice trailed off: Caine, Nolan and the others were gawking at him in disbelief. 'You lying turd,' Wallace rumbled. 'You expect us to swallow that . . .'

'I'll do him now,' Rossi snarled, leaning over, his blade glittering.

'I'm not a spy, I *swear*,' Audley squealed. 'I've made mistakes, but I've done my best, honest I have. I'm not a stoolie. I'm Private Reggie Higginbotham of the Pioneer Corps. All right, yes, I'm an impostor, but that doesn't make me a traitor. I'm a patriot is what I am. When I met Miss Nolan this morning I knew I was up the creek, but I'd never have hurt that Senussi girl – I was only bluffing. I thought I could make it up, see. I thought if I really stuck my neck out, proved myself, saved the operation single-handed, you know, you might be able to overlook what I'd done . . .'

He grabbed Caine's wrist, his eyes searching the lieutenant's beseechingly. 'And I *did* it, Tom, believe me . . . I know it sounds impossible, but I *did* it . . .'

The screams and the gunshots came at the same instant: Caine heard rounds yammer, heard air shatterglass, whiffed cordite, heard slugs flump flesh. The whole team dead-logged, hit dirt: somehow Caine knew it was Pickney who'd been shot. He rolled away from Audley, brought up his pistol, found himself staring down the muzzle of a sub-machine-gun hefted by a Kraut in full desert rig. The whole area was full of them: they were in platoon strength, and they had the number 999 stencilled on their collars. They looked hard and competent, iceberg faces beneath kaiser helmets. In their midst stood Heinrich Rohde, still in Abwehr uniform, and another officer: Caine couldn't place him but was certain he'd seen him before.

'Drop your weapons, gentlemen – ladies,' the officer said smugly, in faultless English. 'Drop the manpacks, too.' Caine placed his Browning and his Tommy-gun at his feet, took off his manpack, laid it down. 'I want *all* of your weapons,' the officer snapped. 'Bayonets, grenades, little knives, gewgaws – the lot.'

Caine set down his two grenades, then stood up, eye-balled the area. He saw Maurice Pickney's body slumped head down in a stand of esparto grass, his legs twisted at obscene angles, smothered in blood.

The rest of the SAS group was on its feet now, surrendering weapons and kit: Jerries hurried forward to pick them up. Caine glanced at Audley, who was still ghostfaced. He'd expected the impostor to dust himself off and stride, preening, over to the Jerries, but he stood his ground, looking as apprehensive as the rest. It must be an act, Caine thought: Audley had been sent to them as a decoy, just as he'd first suspected. Like a fool, he'd fallen for it. If the Krauts were to shoot him right now, he deserved it a dozen times over: he'd been so intent on Audley that he hadn't even heard them coming. Not only was Pickney dead but *Sandhog* was scotched: Nolan had given him a second chance, and he'd muffed it. His fury with the traitor had drawn him right into their trap, just as they must have guessed it would. Rohde had used his weakness against him brilliantly: and this time it wasn't only his own life and the lives of his team that were at stake but those of Angela and Betty too. He dreaded to think what the future might hold for them.

Rohde's inert eyes were fixed on Nolan: only a slight tick around his mouth betrayed his astonishment. 'The *Runefish* girl, in person,' he commented squeakily. 'I thought *Hellfinger* had dealt with you long ago: his incompetence is sometimes staggering.' He minced up to her, studied her for a moment, then slapped her face so viciously that her head snapped sideways. 'You ruined my reputation with General Rommel. I'm glad to have the chance to pay you back in person.'

Caine balled his fists. Nolan had uttered no sound and

made no attempt to touch the livid red handmark on her cheek. She surveyed Rohde scornfully. '*Reputation?*' she scoffed. 'Rommel wouldn't be seen dead with a butcher like you.'

Rohde slapped her again: Nolan rolled with the blow, eyes flashing. Caine took an involuntary step towards Rohde, heard the clack of a sub-machine-gun being cocked. He stopped in his tracks: Rohde was moving towards him with the other officer at his elbow. The stranger's Afrika Korps uniform was immaculate, but its clean lines could not disguise the man's Quasimodo shoulders and shambling, simian gait. As they came nearer, Caine's mouth gaped in shock: the officer was Gaston Larousse.

Caine's senses reeled. But Larousse was dead: for a second Caine wondered if this was all some elaborate trick the Canadian was playing to get them out of here. Then the truth hit him like a straplash. '*You*,' he stammered. '*You're* the Nazi stoolpigeon. It's been you all along . . .'

The two Jerry officers halted in front of him. Rohde assumed the familiar beauty-queen stance: his paperthin lips smiled but his eyes retained their bleak, adding-machine stare. Larousse chortled gruffly. 'So sorry, *skipper*,' he said, tilting the boulder head sideways. 'I bet you thought you'd seen the last of me.'

'You stinking *pig*,' Rossi screamed: he darted forward, his face gleaming murderously, looking ready to tear Larousse apart with his bare hands. Caine clocked Schmeissers raised. '*Stop*,' he hissed. He glared at the traitor, his scoured and poisoned insides heaving with pure hatred. 'The piece of shit isn't worth it.'

Rossi stopped, shot razors at Larousse. 'It was *him*,' he drawled, scarcely able to get the words out. 'It was *him* who betrayed us. It was thanks to him they scragged my mate.' He hoiked up phlegm, spat volubly in the sand, his eyes locked on Larousse's ape-like features.

The 'Canuck' was cleanshaven now but his lynx eyes lay in the same packets of darkness. 'I'm neither a traitor nor a stoolpigeon,' he said coolly, raising his chin at Rossi. 'My loyalty to the Fatherland has remained undiminished.'

'Yeah, right,' Copeland cut in. 'I was *there*, remember, chum? I saw how many Krauts you wiped out.'

Larousse shrugged. 'There are always casualties. If I hadn't done it, someone else would have: I had to play my part.'

'My bloated *dick*,' big Wallace thundered fearlessly from five yards away. 'I seen you too, mate. I seen you slice up that AFV crew with a dagger. You ate it up like custard tart. You ain't in it for no Fatherland: you don't give two flicks of a donkey's dangler whose side you're on . . .'

Larousse waggled his boulder head at the gunner in mock sadness. 'You know, Fred,' he said. 'You were the only one of this lot I really had time for.'

'Stick it up yer arse, then,' Wallace spat. 'Nazi swine. My whole family died because of the likes of you.' A big Kraut trooper muscled in on the giant, his riflebutt raised: Rohde waved him away. 'Let the fools bicker,' he lisped. 'It's amusing to hear their pathetic bleatings.'

He tipped his feminine hips jauntily, nodded towards Larousse. 'Allow me to introduce Captain Reinhardt Kieffer,' he said. 'Brandenburger special operations division. Native of South Africa.'

Caine fought down the urge to vomit: Copeland, Wallace, Rossi and even Audley stared at Larousse-Kieffer with pure loathing in their eyes.

'I trusted you,' Caine said quietly.

'Of course you did,' Larousse said softly. 'You were meant to. I had to impress you at el-Gala or you might not have chosen me for the *Sandhog* stunt.' He winked mischievously at Audley, turned back to Caine. 'I guessed quite early that there were two things about dear old Bertie here that I could rely on: his incompetence and his desire to distinguish himself. I knew the Italians were waiting for us at el-Gala. All I had to do was tell Bertie I'd seen Axis troops coming up from the rear, and he was off like a shot, thinking he'd be the hero of the hour. That left the field open for me to "save" the section: my action made *me* the hero. Who was going to question my loyalty after that?'

Caine watched Audley out of the corner of his eyes: the impostor's face was contorted with rage. If what Larousse had just said about el-Gala were true, it sounded as though Audley was entirely innocent of anything other than the imposture he'd already admitted. Yet who knew what was truth or lies any more? It might be that Rohde was keeping 'Audley' in play for some further devilry. On the other hand, *two* stoolies in a small SAS team seemed like overkill. What if Audley wasn't a rat? What if he was telling the truth and his only crime was impersonating an officer? Did that mean he really *had* set charges on the Olzon-13? No, that was impossible: Rohde's lot would have spotted him long ago.

It occurred to Caine belatedly that Larousse's thick French-Canadian accent had gone. 'So all that stuff about your wife,' he murmured, 'about your two kids getting snuffed by the Gestapo . . . That was all lies . . .'

'The Jewish family was real,' Larousse snickered, 'only it wasn't mine. In fact, I was the one who shopped them to the Nazis, together with the real Gaston Larousse. I kept his papers in case I ever needed a false identity. As it turned out, they served me well.'

'And the prisoner,' Caine gasped, recalling the 90th Div. soldier whom Larousse had shot down. '*You* gave him Rossi's knife, didn't you?'

Larousse's dark eyes glimmered. 'That was interesting,' he said, winking at the Swiss's furious face. 'Yes, I pick-pocketed your little blade, Ricardo, and gave it to the 90th Div. boy with the suggestion that he should use it to kill you, Caine. My idea was to kill two birds with one stone: to get you out of the way and make sure the lad didn't spill the beans. If I'd just scragged him, it would have raised eyebrows. He was too slow, of course, and I had to whack him with a full mag. Best of it was, you actually suspected *Ricardo*.' He sighed theatrically. 'Ricardo Rossi, of the notorious Reapers – one of the most dedicated killers of Axis soldiers in the business – but you, Caine, for all your much-vaunted loyalty to your men, couldn't get past the idea that he was an Italian speaker. Fascinating what prejudice will do.'

Caine swallowed, remembering guiltily how he'd given the Swiss the third degree.

'Of course,' Larousse went on, 'that wasn't my first attempt at taking you out. I tried to do it on our parachute course, when I sawed through your ringclip. Lucky for you, you swapped gear with Sutherland at the last minute. He piled in, you walked. That blimp Stocker came poncing round, but he never suspected me. I could easily have had another bash, but by that time Major Rohde had decided you were more valuable alive, at least for the time being . . .'

Caine gulped, tried to stifle his fury. Larousse winked at him. 'They needed you to lead your SAS boys to the Citadel, because you were a known quantity, and it would preclude any other attack being launched. With me tagging along, Major Rohde could control *Sandhog*, whereas an air attack, say, would have been much more unpredictable . . .'

'*Bullcrap*,' Copeland yelled at him. 'Then why send a 90th Div. column to intercept us? Why deploy Stukas and a ground unit on the piedmont, or your renegade Senussi on the cliffs, to take us out?'

Larousse swivelled round on him. 'They weren't meant to take you out, Harry, their orders were to capture you and bring you here. Of course, a few casualties were inevitable. Even if Caine himself had been killed, it wouldn't have been the end of the world: the main thing was not to let your GHQ know that *Sandhog* had failed – not until it was too late to launch another mission –'

'And that time is gone,' Rohde cut in, his reedy, effeminate voice an octave higher than Larousse's gruff tones. 'We knew the route you would use into the Citadel: I even sacrificed some 999 Division men to make it more credible. We knew that you must attack on the eve of Montgomery's big push – around 25 October – tonight, in fact. While he was with you, Kieffer kept in touch with me through a clever little transmitter the Abwehr built specially for this purpose . . .'

Larousse guffawed. 'That's where you came in useful again, Bertie. I made sure I was assigned to your jeep, knowing that I could use your ineptitude to my advantage – every time you got lost or strayed from the column, I had a chance to get comms. Remember the time we went off to pot game? When the crew downed the C42? I told you I'd spotted gazelle in the dunes, said the boys would appreciate fresh meat? Remember, I left the jeep and went off to "track them down". Once I was out of sight, I used the opportunity to get comms . . . Of course, the *enemy* almost caught us on the way back . . .'

He chuckled, glanced at Caine. 'Once I'd got you up the cliffs I'd pretty much served my purpose, and I was free to do a bunk. We didn't want you getting in touch with GHQ, of course, so I made sure the No. 11 set got wrecked going up.' He winked at Audley once more. 'You *did* tie Trubman's manpack soundly enough, my friend,' he said. 'While you were off having a piss, though, I loosened the ties. I knew you'd get the blame. Caine was so miffed with you that he made you stand first stag. That was a bonus. It meant that I could get you out of the way easily when the Arabs came along, and use you as a witness of my own death. Knowing Caine's proverbial loyalty to his men, I was sure he'd come after us, and he did. He found you waiting, full of the sad details of my demise. He had to butcher a few more Senussi in the process, of course, but they were just some lice-ridden vermin we'd already written off. By then, I was on my way to the Citadel. It only remained for me to fill in my chief on your team's plans and personal details. He wanted to know everything – about Wallace's time in jail, about Netanya's little vendetta, about Pickney's queer habits, even about Caine's mother committing suicide . . .'

Caine's lips curled. 'How could you *know* that?'

'Our man in Cairo – *Hellfinger*: He had an informant at GHQ with access to SAS personnel files: same officer who blew the el-Gala operation, and all the rest . . .'

'*Beeston*,' Nolan hissed.

'Yes, Clive Beeston was ideal material for us.' Rohde chortled maliciously. 'A spineless maggot ready to barter his soul for the chance of sex with an Egyptian whore. He also happened to be the liaison between your intelligence director and your raiding-forces planning cell, so he had access to the details of every special operation.'

The Black Widow sighed with satisfaction. 'All's well that ends well, don't you British say? I admit, I hadn't expected things to go wrong at the Citadel: I had no idea that Miss Golden Girl had escaped from *Hellfinger*, or that, with the help of those Senussi swine, she would manage to break you out. Yes, it was an unexpected development, exacerbated by the fact that our wireless net was jammed. Some 999 Division men were killed, of course, but they're mostly expendable: the escapees will soon be rounded up. I have my own secret exit, naturally: I guessed your next stop would be the airfield, and I was able to collect Kieffer and my reserve platoon and head you off.'

He peered at his watch. 'The aircraft will be here shortly. By the time Eighth Army is on the move tonight, the Olzon-13 will already be in position at the front line. You've experienced what the Olzon-13 can do, eh, Caine? It was only the purest luck that stopped your giant friend from crushing your skull to a pulp this morning. Just imagine, then: in a few hours, the whole Allied army will be in the same condition . . . only they will have artillery, tanks and aircraft to use on each other . . .'

Rohde was distracted by the oboe chirr of aircraft engines: he glanced up, and for a split second Caine prayed that it might be an RAF flight that had somehow traced them. Instead, he recognized a trio of Heinkel III bombers tipple-winging down the razorblue skies like plump silverfish. His heart thunked: these planes were obviously the advance guard of the Luftwaffe squadron tasked to ship the Olzon-13 canisters to the front. The final act was approaching, and he was powerless to prevent it.

'Here they are, at last,' Rohde said, his face inscrutable. 'Move these vermin down to the airstrip, would you, Captain Kieffer?'

Kieffer-Larousse ordered them to put their hands on their heads: the Germans herded them in a bunch towards the airfield. Caine plodded in front of his men, with Audley at his left elbow: he couldn't see the boys' faces, nor the face of Nolan, the woman who'd risked everything to save him and whom he'd led into captivity, probably worse. Now he thought about it, he was almost certain they wouldn't reach a prison camp alive. No, Rohde would have them mowed down right there on the runway, where the Heinkels were now taxiing, ready to pick up the poison gas he'd been sent to destroy, the secret weapon that would turn the tide of the war in the Axis's favour.

Caine's head was still hazy: his world retained an aura of unreality that he guessed was due to the lingering effects of the Olzon-13. He wondered if Wallace felt the same: all the fear he'd experienced earlier seemed to have faded though, leaving a white-hot core of anger curdling inside him. As they neared the Nissen hut, he clocked the cylinders piled up there; saw the Heinkels coming to a standstill on the runway, heard their engines drone down, clocked a platoon of Jerries in overalls being marched towards the hut, ready to load the gas.

He sucked in a breath, skewed an eyecorner glance at the guard on his right. By chance, the Jerry was carrying his captured Tommy-gun slung over his shoulder, the pot-bellied magazine still attached. He felt a sudden breathless surge of bloodlust, an overwhelming desire to get his weapon back, to pulp that Jerry's skull to paste: to seize Rohde by the neck and throttle him. What was he doing being led like a lamb to the slaughter? He might not be able to save himself nor Nolan, nor Angela, nor his mates, but he still had a chance of destroying the Olzon-13, if only by grabbing his Thompson, making a run for it, spraying the cylinders with rounds. He would certainly be killed, but it might work.

The guard was a yard from his elbow, looking to his front. It would need only a small effort to snatch the weapon: he knew there'd been a round in the breech, and was certain the Kraut hadn't cleared it. He took a quick glance around him: Rossi was directly behind, Nolan and Brunetto following, Wallace and Copeland bringing up the rear. The Krauts encircled them, but his team seemed alert: he would have to hope that they were expecting something, that they'd act on his command. He turned his attention back to the guard, felt adrenalin stream in his gut, poised his whole body for a last, suicidal effort.

At that moment Audley's head snapped towards him.

Caine took in a blanched face, wild eyes, sweat standing out on the forehead, mouth turned down in alarm: Audley nodded frantically at the hut, now only ten yards away. 'It's *time*,' he mouthed. 'We're in *range* . . .' In that instant, Caine saw the truth in his face, knew with absolute certainty that the man who'd masqueraded as Audley, impostor or not, had done the impossible: he really *had* set Lewes bombs on the cylinders, and they were about to blow.

'*Get down*,' he bullroared with all the force his lungs could muster. He barged into Audley, threw all his weight on him, knocked him off his feet, felt him fall clear. Just as he rolled on his face, the Nissen hut peeshacked up like a suppressed volcanic plug, squidged shapeless, went lava, balled into a giant seedcore of seething orange and black, geysered out in long witch-tongues of acid flame, spumed wefts of shockfire, spouted a morass of flotsam; the sky scranched, the air bombilated, the thornbush heaved, blackgrey smoke peeshooshed, gaspockets flambéed, twists of miscreant sheetiron and foetal cinders skittered down like rain.

Caine felt the earth move, felt the shocksquall crepitate, felt the oxygen snatched from his lungs, saw Jerry bodies blowball past like uprooted treetrunks. He saw the guard with his Tommy-gun hit dirt, dryslither a yard away. He leopard-crawled, ripped the weapon from the enemy's shoulder, felt the slingswivel snap, felt the comforting shape of the pistolgrip, slipped the safety, saw the Kraut raise his head, ringbolted one round right through his left eye at hard-contact range.

Caine came up on his feet: his ears had gone numb, his senses played the chaos soundlessly, each action vivid and acute like a silent, slowed-down movie. The whole field was obscured by smoke cloud, scattered with little nests of burning waste. He clocked Krauts gouging in the dust, getting up, burning, wounded; he saw big Wallace crouched, sawnoff Purdey miraculously in his great gauntlet hand, saw him squelch a Jerry's face shapeless in a single mighty hammerblow. He saw the blond mops of Brunetto and Nolan wavering in dust spews, saw Copeland come up beside them with a sharp rock in each hand, saw him chin a Jerry, grind his face to mush. He saw Brunetto heist the falling Kraut's Schmeisser, saw her drub rounds into the back of another about to stick Copeland with a bayonet. He saw Nolan snatch a Gewehr from the fallen, potshot a third 999-man through the chest.

A round deep-fried air over his head: Caine wheeled, clocked Larousse, wide face fireblacked, lurching in on him out of the greymeld smoke that hid the runway from view. The stoolie's jaw tightened: Caine squeezed steel, felt the working parts clump and stick. He took a step forward: Audley streaked past him, screaming, ranting. Larousse's pistol chumped: Audley took the sting right in the teeth. Caine saw the back of his head detonate in clags of hair and crimson foam, saw his body ripsoar. His hands fumbled to clear the stoppage: he clocked the bowsprung shape of Larousse looming over him, drove the barrel of his Thompson as hard as he could into the Nazi's eye. Larousse squealed but didn't drop his pistol: he hurled his whole lopsided shank of a body on Caine, whalloping him off his feet, scrabbling half blind to bring his weapon to bear on him. Just as they fell, Caine jammed the Thompson's muzzle into the gorilla's mouth, yanked iron: the working parts chumped, gas *kashoowed*, the rear of Larousse's pot-shaped head spoofed out in a reef of crimson gore.

Caine rolled free, still clutching his Tommy-gun, felt his body soaked in a new layer of warm liquor: he came up unsteadily on to his feet, clocked Larousse's bagsack corpse beneath him, spun around to see Heinrich Rohde mooching out of the smog, blatting automatic rounds. He fired at him on the swing: rounds brattled, firegas spikehorned: his shots went wide. He clocked the grin on Rohde's face, clocked the leer in the cashregister eyes, saw the Nazi raise his pistol carefully, clocked the lithe shape of Ricardo Rossi close with him out of nowhere, shrieking, '*This is for Gibbo, you fucking rat.*'

He saw the vicious little Swiss blade flash, saw it almost sever the Nazi's thick wrist, saw Rohde's weapon drop, saw the knife snicker across his throat in an elegant cut. He saw his jaw oystershell, saw blood squall, saw the body slump. Rossi stepped back, pulled his knife: a Hun soldier stepped out of the smoke, shot him pointblank in the back of the neck with an SMG. Caine saw Rossi go stiff, saw a fist-sized clot of charred flesh fork out of his throat. A grenade spiffed up, hurling Caine off his feet. He staggered up: Rossi was gone, Rohde was gone, vanished into the draperies of smoke. A hand gripped his bicep, he swirled, saw Betty Nolan's wild, sootchased face. '*Get out*,' she screeched. 'It's *done*.'

Then they were off, leaping like fauns through the smoke and fire: the movie speeded up, the soundtrack rewired: a feral chorus of bawls and gunshots sleared around them. Caine took Nolan's hand, saw Cope haring away ahead of him through the smoke and dust billows, one arm round

Angela's waist, half carrying, half dragging her, heard big Wallace panting behind him like a bull.

They ran like demons, splitting up, leapfrogging, zigzagging, using knolls and ridges and tree cover, dodging, ducking, weaving: gunfire yipped around them, over them. Caine heard slugs tango past his ear, saw Nolan, two yards away, stumble and fall. He checked himself, swore, teetered over to her, saw the milkmaid face bloodstroked, the eyes closed, a thin red groove running right along the centre of her straw-wired skull.

He stooped over her, his mind blank: he clocked two Krauts moving towards him, running at a crouch, Schmeissers starspitting balefire. Caine heard the gunshots clitterclack, felt his body shutting down, felt his shoulders droop in resignation. There was no time – the enemy had him. And without Nolan it was all pointless, anyway. *Sandhog* was done: they'd brought it off against all odds. Now it was enough to wait with Betty Nolan and die.

Bren fire craunched out of a bush five yards away. Caine's face dropped in surprise: he clocked the two Jerries take off like kites, khaki torsos ploughed up into wine-coloured rings and craters. '*Get moving, you bloody fool*,' a voice creaked. Caine firemanlifted Nolan's inert body, tucked the Tommy-gun under his arm, saw Maurice Pickney's ghost face grin at him out of the thornbush. He staggered over, saw that the medical orderly was sprawled over a bipodded Bren-gun lying in a pool of his own gore, his legs a stew of purple mush and raw white bone. 'Get moving, you silly sod,' Pickney gasped. 'I'll hold 'em.'

Caine spat. 'Don't be a nutter, Maurice. You're coming with us.'

Pickney's attempt to laugh came out as a rhonchoid splutter. 'Unless you can carry me as well, forget it. My legs are in more bits'n a Meccano set: I've just pumped half a pound of morphia into 'em – can't even feel 'em any more. Get out, now, Tom, or we're all batshit.'

Caine swayed under Nolan's weight. 'I'll be back, Maurice,' he stuttered.

'For the corpse of an old *pervert*? Not worth the time o' day, mate.'

Caine champed a broken lip, choked back tears. 'Maurice, I . . .'

'No speeches, Tom. You did the job, didn't you?'

'No, Audley did it . . .'

Pickney snickered: blood seeped from his ears. 'Jesus, what about *that* for a turnup, then? Still, it's done.'

Caine was about to say something else, but Pickney was no longer listening: his goreshod eyes were focused into the background. 'Our Hun friends cometh,' he grated. 'Get thee gone, Tom. See you on the ledge.'

As Caine scrambled away through the scrub carrying Nolan, he heard the staccato clash of rimfire sprattling out from behind.

Big Wallace helped him lay her in the back of the signals truck. Copeland was already gunning the engine, Angela's arms wrapped tight around him. Taffy Trubman was slouched over the wireless ops table, but Caine and Wallace didn't even remember he was there until they'd jumped in and slammed the door.

'*Hit it*,' Wallace bellowed.

Copeland accelerated, wrestling with the steering

wheel: the motor churned and steamhammered, the gears dopplered, the balloon tyres creaked and flounced over stones. '*Skipper*,' the signaller trilled above the noise, his waxy face lighting up like a bulb, 'I got comms, didn't I? Don't know how I did it, but I did. Wasn't a dicky bird for yonks, then all of a sudden I get a signal as clear as a flippin' bell . . .'

'What's the news?' Caine bawled back.

'GHQ warns you to be careful about Audley.'

'Talk about old hat.' Caine guffawed. 'Audley just saved the mission. Is that all?'

'Nope, it's not all. Bomber Command has dispatched a Wellington squadron to blow the airstrip to kingdom come, and a Lysander's already set off to pick us up. Our orders are to head due south out of the Jebel: RV is scheduled for two hours from now, at a disused airstrip in the desert piedmont.'

He held up a neatly folded Jerry map, wheezing with pain. 'I've got the grid ref,' he groaned, 'and I've plotted a route. I reckon we'll just make it, as long as we don't run into any Axis patrols. Assuming the petrol holds out, mind.'

Caine let out a long sigh, felt a stream of relief gusting through his body like a cool breeze. 'We'll make it,' he murmured. 'Thanks, Taffy. You all right?'

'Apart from feeling like a sack of wet shit tied in the middle, you mean?'

Caine sighed again, felt his head spindle, felt his senses going like the clappers of hell, zipping through the night skies at a thousand miles an hour. He had to grip a wall bar hard to stop himself from passing out: his body ached, head to foot, inside and out, like a single, continuous, festering sore. He blinked at big Wallace, at the bearish torso, the rags weighted with bloodcake and grime, the tangled boars' hair, the pindot eyes, the troll face streaked with a dozen varieties of dirt and body fluid. He laid a hand on his own bruised chest where the big man had kicked him, wondering if the ribs were broken. Wallace, sprawled against the steel skin of the bucking wagon, followed his movement, his face raddled with embarrassment. 'I'm sorry, Tom,' he said. 'I was so out of it, I didn't even recognize you. What I saw was someone else . . . some *thing* else . . .'

Caine shivered. 'Don't go there, Fred,' he warned, forcing himself to shrug, forcing into his tone a casualness he didn't feel. 'We were both told that we could save each other a lot of pain. We weren't ourselves: we were pumped full of that junk. Don't let's go there, mate – ever again. The important thing is that we're here, now, together. The buggers can't change that . . .'

'Where's Maurice?' Trubman cut in.

'Dead,' Caine said. 'At least I reckon he must be. He held off the Krauts so I could get Nolan away. He wasn't killed in the first contact, but his legs were crippled . . .' His voice broke down: he felt tears starting in his eyes like iron studs. 'I couldn't carry him *and* Nolan . . . I just *couldn't* . . .'

Wallace was staring at Nolan: Caine followed his gaze, saw her eyelids flutter. He bent over her, stroked her forehead with his grimy hand: she moaned softly. Her head-wound had stopped bleeding: Caine was desperately aware that he had no drugs to give her, not even a clean dressing. Everything they'd brought with them had been lifted when they'd been bagged: the main medical kit had gone with

Pickney. He told himself that the wound wasn't deep: it had been a jammy one – just a graze, really. She'd be concussed, but she was going to be all right. He saw her eyes flicker open, green crystal glinting like dawnstars against the bloodgreased, dirtstreaked face. 'Did we do it, Tom?' she whispered. 'Or did I just dream it?'

Caine took her hand in his, kissed it, felt tears of gratitude flow down his cheeks. 'We did it,' he gasped. 'Audley did it. Private Reggie bloody Higginbotham of the Pioneer Corps, Latrine Detachment, did it. We *all* did it. Now let's get the hell out of here.'

They came down the escarpment just before sundown, halted the van for a few minutes on the piedmont to scan the way ahead. They'd made good time: the RV lay only twenty klicks to the south and they still had forty-five minutes to get there. Nolan had recovered enough to stand up: Caine helped Trubman out to stretch his legs. The signaller produced his last halfpacket of 'V' cigarettes, handed them round in celebration. The Green Mountains lay behind them, cloaked in shadows: above the peaks and ridges an eggyolk sun lay frying in diesel clouds, raw colours scalpelling cordillera faces into gateaux layers, bloodbrown, and chocolate cream.

Copeland puffed smoke, one arm still around Angela: since they'd been reunited earlier that day, Caine thought, they'd hardly let go of each other for a minute. 'Well, we did our bit,' Cope said. 'In a few hours *Lightfoot* will be rolling: at least it'll be Olzon-free.'

Trubman looked troubled. 'There's something else, mind,' he said suddenly. 'Something I haven't told you, I mean. Today is October the twenty-fifth, isn't it, boys?'

Caine had to think. 'Yep,' he said. 'It's the day *Lightfoot* kicks off: 25/26 October 1942.' He took in Trubman's doleful countenance. 'Cheer up, mate, for Chrissake. I know you copped a bad one, but you're going to be all right. We've all been through the mill, you know. Jeez, I came within a whisker of getting clobbered by one of my best mates.'

'It's not that,' Trubman said dismissively. 'No, it's something they told me on the net. I haven't quite got my head round it yet: in fact, for a while there I thought I might be hallucinating.'

'Yeah, well join the club,' Caine said.

'What is it, Taffy?' Nolan asked, sensing something serious in the wind.

Trubman's eyes narrowed: he blinked at the others warily, as if he was about to reveal something disturbing. He took in a deep breath. 'They told me *Lightfoot* has already started,' he said.

Caine stared at him: his stonegrey eyes gleamed in the twilight. 'What do you mean, *already started*?'

The signaller sucked air into his plump cheeks nervously, looking as if he expected to be assaulted. '*Lightfoot* wasn't set for tonight,' he said. 'It was set for two days back, October the twenty-third. We were told it was tonight, the twenty-fifth, but Eighth Army's already been on the move now for forty-eight hours. They must have given us the wrong date in case we got bagged and the Hun made us talk. When you think of it, it would have been mad to trust us with the real date, anyway . . .'

Copeland let go of Angela suddenly, crushed out his cigarette stub with a chapplie. 'Nice one, Taffy,' he chuckled. 'Good joke – *ha ha ha*.'

'It's no joke, boy,' Trubman said, his voice shaking. 'I'm tellin' you, *Lightfoot* kicked off two days ago. They announced it over the net . . .'

'Ah, that's it,' Copeland said, relieved. 'Axis propaganda.'

'Yeah, that's what I thought at first: only there's a code they use to show it's authentic, and this had the right code. The report said that Monty's deception plan worked like a dream. The Axis thought he was going to push south, but he pushed north instead. Took Rommel completely by surprise: he wasn't even in North Africa. The Kraut GOC was General Sturm, and the first thing Monty did was send a unit to take him out . . .'

He stopped: there was a yawning silence. All eyes were on him now. 'It started with a huge artillery barrage,' he went on timorously, 'The Sappers cleared out a lot of Axis minefields and the armoured divs. moved straight through. There's been a lot of fierce fighting, but so far it's been a major success.'

Caine stared at the signaller's mole-like features. Copeland watched him, fascinated, as though he'd been confronted with some impossibly complex problem at chess. 'But wait a sec,' he said at last, 'that means we took out the Olzon-13 two days *after* the battle started . . . Is that right?'

'Yeah,' Wallace chimed in, 'and that just don't make sense.'

'Yes, it does,' Nolan said grimly, sitting up. 'If *Sandhog* was a decoy.'

There was pindrop stillness as her words registered.

'You mean a *hoax*?' Wallace roared. 'I don't believe it: it *can't* have been.'

'Fred's right, it's impossible,' Caine nodded. 'Stirling would have told us.'

'It'll have been much higher up than Stirling,' Nolan said. 'Higher than G(RF), higher even than the DMO or the DMI – so high-level that only Monty and a handful of brass could have been in on it.'

'Wait a minute, wait a minute,' Wallace said, flapping a huge, scabbed hand. 'What exactly are we sayin' here?'

'I'm *saying* that you were sent on *Sandhog* not to take out a deadly secret weapon, as you were told, but to convince the Axis that the push was coming forty-eight hours later than it really was.'

There was another silence while their exhausted minds ticked over.

'It ain't possible,' Wallace gasped.

'Look,' Nolan said. 'The Axis took it for granted that you'd hit the Olzon-13 on the eve of *Lightfoot*. The fact that you were scheduled to hit it on 25 October would be, for them, confirmation that the push was coming on that date, not before. What they didn't know was that you were sent in late deliberately, to deceive them. By the time you got there, *Lightfoot* would already have kicked off.'

'But even if *Sandhog* did involve a decoy element,' Copeland objected, 'taking out the Olzon-13 must still have been an important part of it, surely? I mean, it still had to be taken out, right?'

Nolan shook her head sadly. 'Wrong,' she said. 'War's fluid, Harry. The Olzon-13 weapon would only have been an effective threat on the *first day* of the offensive. Two days later, it's already become a side issue: the situation's changed, the train's left the station, the window's closed. Think of it. We only saw three Heinkels at the airstrip – nowhere near enough to carry the whole stock.'

'Yes, but that was only the advance guard, wasn't it?'

'Maybe, but for all we know the Axis might have lost most of their transport aircraft by now and couldn't even ship it to the front if they wanted to. That's just one example: there are dozens of other variables that will have changed in the past two days.'

'It still don't make sense,' Wallace insisted. 'I mean, Rohde musta known *Lightfoot*'s real date – at least, he wudda known if it'd started two days back.'

'He didn't though, did he?' Nolan said. 'You heard him as well as I did. He said, "We knew that you must attack on the eve of Montgomery's big push – around 25 October – tonight, in fact." The only thing he'd forgotten, or didn't want us to know, was that at least one of the reasons they reckoned *Lightfoot* would start tonight was because that was the date *Sandhog* was scheduled.'

'But how could he have got it so wrong?' Trubman demanded.

'Hold on,' Wallace said slowly. 'Didn't the bugger say sommat about the wireless net bein' jammed?'

A look of profound understanding crossed Trubman's broad features. '*Of course*,' he croaked, slapping his thigh. 'That's *it*. That's why I couldn't get comms all that time. I knew there was nothing wrong with the transmitter. The whole net was jammed.'

'It must have been jammed by our "Y" Service boys,' Nolan said. '*Lightfoot* is already underway but, until an hour ago, the Germans here didn't know about it, because the Allies were blocking their comms. Two days on, and they were still waiting for it to happen.'

'*The great shadow-play*,' Caine murmured.

'What?'

'Something Maskelyne said. "All missions are part of the great shadow-play," he said. "The war that you believe is being fought out on the plains of the Sahara is actually being fought out inside your own head." I hadn't got a clue what he was talking about at the time, but now I'm starting to see.'

'Now hold on a minute,' Wallace spluttered, as if the penny had only just dropped. 'Are you saying that we went through all that shit for nothing? The dead, the wounded, the beasting, gettin' pumped with that drug, me and Tom trying to snuff each other out, Audley, Pickney – all *that* was just wasted . . .'

'Even if the Olzon-13 hadn't been destroyed today, it wouldn't have changed anything,' Nolan whispered. 'We were just part of the shadow-play, don't you see? Just passing shadows. Whatever we'd done, whatever happened to us, it wouldn't have made any difference at all.'

39

'Monty said *Lightfoot* would take eleven days,' Stirling declared, 'and he was right. Say what you like, the little ferret knows what he's doing.'

Caine thought about the men he'd lost on *Sandhog*: the anguish that he and the other few survivors had gone through, just to help deceive the enemy: he'd almost ended up getting his brainbox aired by one of his best mates. 'Perhaps so, sir,' he said, stubbing out his Player's Navy Cut in a cutglass ashtray, 'but maybe he shouldn't play his cards so close to his chest. That way, I might have come back out of the Blue with more than three of the ten men I took in with me.'

They were sitting at a table in the Shepheard's Hotel dining-room: the place was full, buzzing with talk, electric with the clink of cutlery, alive with the sway of waiters in tarbooshes, scarlet cummerbunds and pure white gallabiyas. As Caine knew to his cost, the restaurant was meant to be 'officers only', but Stirling had made Copeland, Wallace and Trubman 'honorary officers' for the evening. The three enlisted men were perfectly at their ease: they were currently leaning back in their chairs, scarred and battered but smart in freshly starched KDS, toking luxuriantly on cigars, glasses of brandy in their scabbed, disfigured hands. Betty Nolan and Angela Brunetto sat together, both clad in the identical khaki-drill uniforms of honorary captains.

Blond-haired and bright-eyed, they might almost have been twins, Caine thought, except for the fact that, while Angela's expression was smouldering and sultry, Nolan's was misty and almost child-like.

They'd been back from Libya a fortnight: they'd largely recovered from their ordeal, though none of them could be classed A1 fit. The worst, for Caine, had been the flashbacks: times when the familiar world had come apart at the seams, when he sensed monstrous creatures lurking in dark portals beyond his ordinary, everyday life – if you could call life in wartime Cairo ordinary. Even more terrifying, he sometimes sensed a fugitive half-human beast padding the lost labyrinths of his own mind, as if there was something inside him that wasn't himself. The quack said these symptoms were the last vestiges of his exposure to Olzon-13: it was some comfort to know that Fred Wallace was experiencing them too, though there were also occasions when Caine looked at the big gunner and broke out in a cold sweat, seeing the ghost of that great minotaur demon in his blackbead eyes. At these times, his only comfort lay in Nolan.

The table was littered with 'dead soldiers' – empty wine and beer bottles – cheek by jowl with discarded glasses, coffee cups, quarts of whisky and cognac. At one end, Paddy Mayne and John Stocker sat hunched over their elbows, deep in conversation. Mayne puffed a cigarette, Stocker pumped out smoke signals of Dark Empire Shag from his pipe.

Stirling sat back, his continuous dark eyebrow furrowed. He picked up his empty pipe and stuck it upside down in his mouth, then removed it again. 'Don't feel bad about being part of a decoy plan, Tom,' he said. 'We all were. The whole build-up to *Lightfoot* was one vast deception – Op *Bertram*, they called it. Only two or three people knew the entire picture. Obviously, when two armies face each other across open desert, you've got to use some pretty sly sort of trick or the result will be stalemate.' He paused, chewed his pipestem. 'First, the GOC was going north but had to make the Axis think he was going south: hence the dummy divisions deployed down there, like the one you . . . er . . . ran into.'

Caine swallowed hard, remembering Maskelyne and Roger Glenn.

'Second,' Stirling went on, 'he had to deceive them as to *when* he would move, or the entire shebang would have been a waste of time. Do you know he even built a dummy water pipeline going south, constructing it at a measured daily rate, so that the enemy could calculate at what date it would be completed, and conclude that the push would begin on that date? Same sort of idea as *Sandhog*, really.'

Caine raised an eyebrow. 'How many men were killed building the pipeline?'

Stirling shook his head, irritated. 'Look, Tom. I know we lost men: they were *my* men, after all, and no one regrets it more than I do. The point is that it wasn't just us who were bamboozled. It was all part of the same scheme, to make the Hun believe the offensive was coming later than it really was. And it worked. *Lightfoot* has been a huge success, despite all the men we lost on it. The Panzer Army is no longer a threat to Egypt, or to the Middle East. Rommel's finished. This time, he won't be back.'

Stirling picked up a glass of cognac and took a hefty

swig. Caine sipped his whisky, placed the glass back on the table. He lit another Player's Navy Cut, blew smoke, thinking that it still didn't excuse the loss of good mates. He noticed that Stirling was watching him intently. 'You should be proud, lad,' his CO said. 'You and Nolan – and your men, of course – have played a major role in this campaign. You played a part in luring Rommel into Egypt with *Runefish*, and in *Sandhog*, you helped to ensure that he withdrew with his tail between his legs. You thoroughly deserve the DSO I've put you in for, and – after the stuff she went through with Eisner and Hekmeth – Miss Nolan more than deserves the bar to her George Cross . . .' He leaned over conspiratorially. 'Monty is so delighted with you that he wants to meet you in person. In fact, he's coming here tonight to congratulate you all.'

Caine stiffened, almost dropped his cigarette. 'Coming here?' he mumbled. 'The GOC?'

Stirling shrugged. 'Why not? It's time the SAS got some recognition.'

Caine smiled wanly. Montgomery coming in person to greet an SAS subaltern, a female staff officer and a trio of other ranks? No wonder his commanding officer was chuffed. Through Caine, 1st SAS Regiment had been redeemed: there would be no more talk of scrapping it, at least for the time being.

'Congratulations, Mr Caine,' a pedantic voice said, breaking into his thoughts. He looked up to see John Stocker, small, bald, beady-eyed, heavily bespectacled, holding out a hand. Caine stood up to shake it: Stocker sat down in the vacant chair next to him, stuck his pipe in his mouth, tracked smoke, took the pipe out. Unlike almost everyone else in the restaurant, he was wearing a battledress suit – a rather threadbare and dishevelled one at that. Caine remembered that the DSO had been a university professor before the war and reflected that he still looked like a boffin wearing a uniform that didn't belong to him.

'I'm sorry about the mess over Audley,' Stocker said. 'I mean, Private Higginbotham. He somehow slipped through the net. I wouldn't have believed it possible for a Pioneer Corps private to have got away with masquerading full time as a Guards officer, but you live and learn.'

Caine glanced at Stirling and saw that a faint flush had come to his cheeks.

'Yes, sir,' he nodded, 'but Audley – *Higginbotham*, that is – paid his dues in the end. He laid Lewes bombs and set timepencils on the target all on his own initiative. He proved himself a pretty brave and resourceful soldier. All right, he was a bit twitchy and unreliable in the field, but who knows? With proper training he might have made a good officer.'

'True,' Stocker agreed, 'and how many more of them might there be? I mean, enlisted men who, given the opportunity, might have turned out to be excellent leaders . . .'

Stirling snorted. 'But it's not only Audley, Major. I must say, you Field Security boys haven't exactly come out of this business with flying colours. What about Larousse? What about his attempt to sabotage Caine, which you blamed on the Gyppos? He's another one who "slipped through the net", eh?'

Caine traileyed Stirling: his cheeks were still pink, and he guessed that his CO's uncharacteristically hostile manner was an attempt to disguise his embarrassment over 'Audley'.

Ater all, Stirling had claimed him as 'a friend', had insisted on his being included on *Sandhog*, over Caine's implicit objections.

Stocker surveyed the lanky young half-colonel through intense blue eyes. 'With all due respect, sir,' he said quietly, 'you accepted him in your regiment.'

'Of course I did,' Stirling replied hotly, reddening further. 'Because Field Security approved his documents . . .' He stopped short, perhaps realizing that he was on shaky ground. 'Anyway,' he added quickly, 'what about Eisner? You allow Hekmeth to kidnap Miss Nolan, hoping to lure him into a trap: you have his house under surveillance for more than a week, then you let him get away. What about *that* for a botched job?'

Stocker slipped off his glasses and began to clean them with a white pocket handkerchief. He had gone very quiet: Caine remembered the spectacle-cleaning from their last meeting, and guessed it was Stocker's habitual means of remaining centred.

Stocker didn't look up. 'You have me there, Colonel,' he said offhandedly. 'Eisner is, of course, a dangerous man, and he's still on the loose. However, I think I can say that we have had some success with regard to his contacts. We know who he is now, for example: the stepson of Idriss Hussain, a gangster specializing in prostitution, who has the dubious honour of being the king's pimp and is connected with the royal family through the palace major domo, the Italian, Antonio Pulli Bey . . .'

'Pulli Bey? *Really?*' All of a sudden Stirling seemed genuinely interested: the subject of Audley, and the object of saving face, appeared forgotten.

'Yes. The king's Nazi sympathies are well known, and it may well be that there is an Axis conspiracy extending via Idriss right into the royal palace. I'm sure you'll agree that this is important intelligence. I have no doubt, too, that Eisner can call on the support of his stepfather's "mob" when he needs it: hence, I suspect, the twenty armed cutthroats who snatched him from custody a few months ago.'

Stocker replaced his glasses, stared at Stirling again. There was a hardness and power in his glance that belied his mild manner, Caine thought. Stirling outranked him and was a much bigger man physically, yet Caine sensed that Stocker possessed a formidable intellect and an iron will that would make him a dangerous man even for Stirling to cross. 'Then, of course, we also arrested the traitor Beeston,' he continued, smiling faintly, 'thus removing Eisner's chief source of intelligence in GHQ. I'm confident that it was Beeston who gave away your operations at Benghazi, Tobruk, el-Gala and Fuja, through his lover, the bellydancer Hekmeth Fahmi, of course. Interestingly, Hekmeth also grew up in Idriss's house, so she is a sort of sister to Eisner . . .'

'Where is she now?' Stirling enquired. 'I heard she was convicted of treason.'

Stocker regarded him expressionlessly. 'She was. She was sentenced to death, actually, but I managed to get the sentence commuted . . .'

Stirling looked puzzled, then he guffawed. 'So even you are susceptible to a pretty face and a shapely bottom, eh, Major?'

Stocker didn't look embarrassed. 'No doubt I am,' he

chuckled, 'and I have to admit that I've never met a woman who possessed such powerful sexual magnetism as Hekmeth. In a way, I pity Clive Beeston. I mean, he was a rabbit caught in a headlamp glare: he was powerless, absolutely trapped. I think he would even have committed murder if she'd demanded it. I admit, too, that she *did* try to turn her headlamps on me, although she soon gave up. I think she found me a little less . . . susceptible . . .'

A wry grin appeared on his face. 'In any case,' he went on rapidly, 'that wasn't why I got her sentence commuted. It became clear to me that she wasn't a genuine Nazi supporter – unlike Eisner, who is wholly German. No, Hekmeth helped Eisner because he was like a brother to her but underneath she is an Egyptian nationalist. By showing her that her patriotic interests did not coincide with those of a victorious Germany, I was able to convince her to talk.'

Stirling was totally enthralled now. 'Not bad,' he said. 'Not bad at all. And what happened to Beeston in the end?'

Stocker sighed. 'He was given an opportunity to play a key role in Op *Bertram*. He was asked to take a decoy map across an enemy minefield in an AFV. Naturally, the vehicle hit a mine, and the major was killed. The enemy discovered the map: it showed as "good going" an area of desert which was, in fact, extremely "bad going". They were so convinced of its accuracy that they sent an entire Panzer division that way during their attempt to hold back *Lightfoot*. They consequently got the whole unit bogged down in soft sand, thus removing one vital link from the battle. So, in death, Major Beeston became a hero, and redeemed himself for all the secrets he'd given up.'

'A rare touch of Machiavellian genius,' Stirling chortled. 'Whose idea was that?'

'Mine,' Stocker said.

Caine shivered, clocked the look of surprise, then of respect, on his CO's sharp features. Stirling nodded. 'Well,' he said, picking up his glass, 'I rather think it's time for a toast.'

Caine moaned inwardly. They'd already drunk too many toasts – to his Britannic Majesty, to Monty, to the SAS Regiment, to Caine, to Nolan, to Caine's boys – even to Angela. Stirling rose: Caine noticed that he was slightly unsteady on his feet. 'I propose a toast to *Torch*,' he announced, so loudly that many of the other customers stopped talking. Some of them staggered to their feet and raised their glasses, too. Caine grimaced and stood: the others followed suit.

'What the 'ell is *Torch*?' Wallace boomed.

Stirling lowered his glass, tipped the gunner a surprised look. 'You don't *know*?' he asked incredulously. 'Yesterday, a huge Anglo-American army landed in Morocco and Algeria – *First* Army. The Yanks have been with us since Pearl Harbour, of course, but this is their first big deployment of force . . .'

'God help us,' Cope groaned. 'Green as grassstalks.'

'Maybe, but we were all green once, Sergeant: there's an awful lot *of* them, and they've got darn good kit. A whole new phase of the war has begun. Allied strategy is now to clamp Rommel in a vice from both sides, biff him into Tunisia, finish him off there . . .' He paused, lifted his chin. 'For your information, First Army is already forming its own SAS unit – 2nd SAS Regiment – under my brother,

Bill. There might even be an SAS *Brigade* down the line. You boys had better enjoy your time in Cairo, because there'll be a new job in Tunisia very soon.'

They drank the toast. Stirling paid the bill, and they wandered out on to the terrace, looking over Ezbekiya Square. The outside tables were sparsely populated, the famous botanic gardens all but hidden in the darkness. There was the familiar swirl of movement in the street: officers on elegant walkabout, cateyed girls in khaki, jibbering street-sellers. The air was cold, the night sky bedecked in stars. Caine paused for a moment at the head of the steps, wondering if Stirling had meant it when he'd said that the GOC would be coming to meet them. Nah, it couldn't be: the old man was too busy for that. He watched Copeland, Wallace and Trubman chatting to the girls, was just about to ask Nolan if she wanted to leave, when a nasal voice rang out. 'You are under arrest, Lieutenant Caine.'

40

At first he thought it must be a joke. Then he saw Major Robin Sears-Beach glowering at him not five yards away, his two prominent front teeth hanging out like paving stones. The deputy provost wore spotless BD, knifeblade creases, black MP armband, toecaps like polished ebony. He wore a pistol in a blancoed-white holster and carried his swaggerstick under his arm. Below him, six steps down, a squad of Redcaps was drawn up at attention, as if in review order: Caine couldn't understand how he'd missed them before. There was a moment's hiatus while Stirling's little squad eyed the MP officer. Then Stirling strode over to him with Paddy Mayne at his side. Stirling was tall and powerful, but beside Mayne he looked like a telegraph pole next to a barn door. 'What do you want, Major?' he demanded.

Sears-Beech pointed at Caine. 'I intend to arrest that man,' he said. 'There is a warrant out for him. He's charged with kidnapping and abducting a superior officer, Major Jasper Maskelyne, and with the attempted murder of another, Captain Roger Glenn . . .' His eyes were dark patches in the starlight. 'Shot him in the kneecap,' he went on. 'Glenn'll be lucky if he ever gets out of his wheelchair . . .'

'I think you'll find,' Stirling said slowly, 'that Mr Caine was following orders at the time.'

Sears-Beach chuckled crudely. 'You won't get away with

that one, Colonel,' he sniggered. 'Caine's done the dirty for the last time. He's for the high jump . . .' Sears-Beach hadn't reached the end of his sentence when Paddy Mayne's iron knuckles crunched into his jaw like a pile-driver. The MP's mouth clicked shut, he dropped stonelike on to the carpet, where he lay panting, drooling blood, spitting out shards of broken teeth. Stirling looked down on him, his single mesh of eyebrow raised, as if surprised to find him there. 'I did warn you, Major,' he said.

There was a clamour among the onlookers: some sat and stared, others jumped to their feet. Sears-Beach was on his hands and knees now, coughing blood, his cap and swaggerstick beside him. The MP squad was moving cautiously up the stairs, batons at the ready: Mayne stood on the top step ready to repel them, bunching his cabbage-sized fists. Caine, Wallace, Copeland and even Trubman moved into place beside him: Stirling stood to the rear. Stocker put his arms around the shoulders of Nolan and Brunetto and led them away.

The leading MPs came to a stop on the middle step, realizing that they were in the weaker position. Studying their faces, Caine thought he recognized among them the two big lancejacks who'd helped Sears-Beach beast him in the holding cell. The Redcaps held their sticks at elbow-level, looking apprehensive. At that moment a Humber staff car screeched to a halt at the bottom of the steps. The back door opened, and out jumped a sprightly little officer with the features of a terrier, wearing battledress and an overlarge tankie beret decorated with the badges of a dozen different units. Caine recognized Lieutenant General Bernard Law Montgomery, GOC the Eighth Army.

The Redcaps stuffed their batons away hurriedly, came to attention, saluted. Monty sauntered up the steps breezily, nodded to them, hands clasped behind his back. 'Ah, there you are, Colonel Stirling,' he said. 'Thought you might have left without me. Got delayed, you know.'

Stirling snapped up a trim Guardee salute: Mayne and the others stood to attention. Monty returned the gesture with a flick of his lank fingers. 'So,' he said. 'Where's Caine?'

Caine stepped forward. Montgomery gripped his hand, shook it fiercely, stared into his eyes. 'Congratulations, Lieutenant,' he shouted. 'You've done a splendid job. Outstanding. By golly, the war would be over in weeks if I had a few more chaps of your type.'

'Thank you, sir,' Caine said. Monty seemed loath to let go of his hand. 'Now where's that little lady?'

Caine looked round, saw Stirling hustling Nolan forwards. Monty caught her hand, shook it with both his own. 'My dear,' he said. 'You are beautiful, clever and courageous. As I was saying to Mr Caine here, our army could do with more men like you.'

The audience tittered: Nolan smiled, showing her deliciously assymetrical front teeth. The GOC let go her hand. Just then, he caught sight of Sears-Beach, standing unsteadily at Stirling's elbow. The major was capless and dishevelled, his nose bleeding, his blouse stained with mucus and gore. Monty bore down on him indignantly. '*You*, Major,' he piped. 'How dare you turn out in public in that state? Look at you: drunk, and it's not even ten o'clock. An absolute disgrace.'

Sears-Beach spluttered, eyes starting, lips curled back

from coypu teeth. '*Sir*,' he slurred. '*Sir*, I'm Major Sears-Beach, deputy provost mar——'

'*Provost?*' the GOC yelled. 'Is this the way the provost behaves? Brawling? Falling over? Drunk in public by ten o'clock? Look at *me*: I neither drink nor smoke, and I am a hundred per cent fit. By Jiminy, I'm going to talk to your OC. If you're not a buckshee private on the front line by this time tomorrow, I'm a Dutchman.' He swept a thin hand expansively towards Caine and Nolan. 'You ought to take a leaf out of *their* book, Major. Those are *real* soldiers: see that girl who looks as if she couldn't punch her way out of a paper bag? Just won the bar to her GC. While you HQ wallahs are hanging around in bars, drinking till you fall over, some people are out there at the sharp end, having a crack at the Hun . . .'

'But, *sir* –'

'Don't *But sir* me, Major. Get out of it. Now. And don't let me ever see you in that state again.'

Shaking visibly, Sears-Beach picked up his cap and stick, stuck the cap on his head. He saluted the GOC with a tremulous hand and stumbled off into the night.

After Montgomery and the others had departed, Caine and Nolan lingered in the street for a few moments with Copeland and Brunetto. 'What will you do now?' Nolan asked the Italian girl.

Brunetto shrugged her lean, mobile shoulders. 'There might be place for me in your intelligence,' she pouted. 'If they can get over me being Itie, that is. Mr Stocker, he say he help.'

She hugged Nolan, then grabbed Caine and kissed him

on both cheeks. 'You save me,' she whispered, tears coursing down her cheeks. 'You and Harry and Betty and the others. I repay you some day. I never forget.'

Embarrassed, Caine glanced at Copeland: he was surprised to see that the sergeant's normally deadpan features were heavy with emotion.

'That goes for me, too, skipper,' Cope said in a choky voice. 'I owe you one.'

'You owe me nothing, Harry. Just let's thank Allah we're still alive.'

Caine and Nolan strolled arm in arm across the square to the taxi rank, where cabs and gharries came and went and a long dogsleg of officers and girls stood in line. They were about to resign themselves to the back of the queue when a battered cab pulled up beside them. The driver wound down the window: in the darkness, Caine caught a glimpse of weathered dark skin, a ragged handlebar moustache, deeparch sockets holding darker eyes. The man had a prominent belly and wore a patched coat over a pyjama-cloth gallabiya and a woollen hat pulled down across his ears. He looked like a Nile boatman or an illiterate fellah. 'Get in,' the driver said in a cracked voice. '*Quick*. You wait for queue to finish, you wait one hour.'

Caine hesitated. They were already getting disapproving glances from others stuck in the queue. '*Get* in,' the fellah repeated. 'I give you cheap. I have five children, no food.'

Caine glanced at the man's pot belly and wondered wryly when he'd last gone hungry. Then he opened the door for Nolan, got in after her. For a moment they sat there, holding hands, locked in each other's gaze.

'Where you go?' the driver snapped.

Caine couldn't tear his gaze away from Nolan's deep-melt eyes. 'To your flat?' he whispered.

She nodded, giving him the dreamy, faraway look that always sent a hot flush down his spine. He told the driver her address in Garden City. 'Do you know it?' he enquired.

Johann Eisner edged the taxi jerkily out into the stream of traffic and accelerated, weaving between horsecabs and handcarts. He changed to second, blinked at Caine's reflection in the rearview mirror. '*Know* it?' he repeated softly, running the tip of his tongue along the horsehair moustache. 'Oh yes, sir. I know it well.'